THE
LIES
WE
TELL

ALSO BY THERESA SCHWEGEL

The Good Boy

Last Known Address

Person of Interest

Probable Cause

Officer Down

THE
LIES
WE
TELL

Theresa Schwegel

Minotaur Books
New York

THE LIES WE TELL. Copyright © 2017 by Theresa Schwegel. All rights reserved. Printed in the United States of America. For information, address St. Martin's Press, 175 Fifth Avenue, New York, N.Y. 10010.

www.minotaurbooks.com

The Library of Congress Cataloging-in-Publication Data is available upon request

ISBN 978-1-250-00178-8 (hardcover)
ISBN 978-1-250-02244-8 (e-book)

Our books may be purchased in bulk for promotional, educational, or business use. Please contact your local bookseller or the Macmillan Corporate and Premium Sales Department at 1-800-221-7945, extension 5442, or by e-mail at MacmillanSpecialMarkets@macmillan.com.

First Edition: July 2017

10 9 8 7 6 5 4 3 2 1

For Julianne

If you can't remember anything,

you have nothing to be scared of.

—STIAN HOLE, *GARMANN'S SUMMER*

THE
LIES
WE
TELL

1

"Ready or not, here I come." I see Isabel's bare toes peeking out from the cracked-open closet door in the hall. Hide and seek is her favorite game. She's terrible at it. She's not quite two.

Since I already know where she is, I stay in bed and finish reading an unsettling article in the *Trib* about proposed healthcare reform that sounds great for perfectly healthy people.

"Where did she go?" I ask. The question provokes a giggle, a would-be giveaway if she ever chose a different hiding spot. I've lost count of how many times I've counted to ten this morning and still, being discovered delights her.

I decide affordable health care is an act, fold up the paper, and try to "find" her.

"Spa-ghe-tti," I sing-song her nickname as I get out of bed and collect the half-dozen board books she left between getting lost and getting found. If I'm not pretending to look for her, I'm pretending it doesn't bother me at all to pick up and put away what I already picked up and put away.

I guess it doesn't bother me, usually. I'm a little off today.

"Could she be in the . . . bathroom?" I ask, because that's where I'm going.

"No," I say, finding the Tylenol and swallowing two, "she's not in here." I'm hungover: during yesterday's trip to the beach I got too much sun and too much heat and so this morning my lower back is killing me, my left leg, too.

In the mirror I can see Isabel standing in the closet, though I pretend I can't. Silent, she watches me from under her sheepdog bangs; she refuses to wear a barrette.

"Is she in the—" I stop short when my phone rings in the kitchen.

Isabel explodes from the closet and says, "Bodies?" her attempt to say "pictures," because she thinks, pretty accurately, that the phone's primary function is to view photos. Maybe because the camera is the only app I let her play with besides Peek-a-Zoo. Or maybe it's because the pictures are the only way she sees her dad. My brother. George: who they mean when they say, *Oh, brother.*

The phone is on the kitchen counter; someone's calling from the office. I say, "No pictures. Work."

Isabel nods, repeats "work" without much of an *r.*

"Simonetti."

"Who's in charge over there this morning?" It's Steve Duppstadt, one of the detectives who assigns cases and the one who always gives me flak about Isabel. He's got three teen girls, though, so I know he gets a lot more than he gives.

"Dupe," I say, "you have something for me?" I hoist Isabel up, my good arm, and carry her back to the bedroom.

"I'm hoping you have something for me," he says. "You get anywhere on that battery handout Thursday? Victim, Rosalind Sanchez?"

"Close to nowhere. Sanchez changed her mind. She won't press charges." I put Isabel on the bed and join her under the covers, my hiding spot all morning. "Didn't you see my report?"

"I did. But the suspect's name popped up again today. Johnny Marble. Same charge, same MO. I thought you might be able to help."

"On my last day off." I pull the covers over our heads, a pretty good fort. "What about Kanellis?"

"Andy!" Isabel says. She loves my partner no matter how I feel about him.

I give her the *shh* finger and say, "It's his case, too."

Dupe says, "He's looking for Marble."

"Isn't that what you're asking me to do?"

"I want you to talk to the victim. It's Marble's mother. Her home-care worker called it in, and when the responding officer arrived, Mom refused to cooperate. She won't press charges, either—same as your case. But I'm thinking, if you give her the grit on Sanchez, maybe she'll change her mind."

"Maybe," I say. "Where's mom?"

"Transported. Sacred Heart Hospital."

"So it's you asking me to do this, or Kanellis?"

There's a telling pause. "Both of us."

"That miserable prick—" I catch myself saying it; I hope Isabel didn't. "You know what this is: Kanellis doesn't do hospitals."

"I also know you're the best person for this job."

"Pwi . . ." Isabel tries to work her mouth around the *r*, "pwi—"

"No," I say to Isabel.

"Come on," Duppstadt says, "it's your case, too."

I should say no, the way I'm feeling. But I don't want him or anybody else getting the idea I can't do it.

"Okay, Dupe, give me the details."

I get my book from my purse and take quick notes—the who, the where, the how bad. Apparently Marble, an old guy, beat the crap out of his mother, an older—and impaired—woman. The caregiver said Marble showed up asking for money and when the vic refused,

Marble decided to show her what it's like to "be broke." Did enough damage to get her an ambulance ride. I wish I could say I found the details shocking. I wish I didn't know shit like this happens all the time.

That's part of the reason I take notes: this many years in to the Job, it's hard to keep atrocities straight. The other part is that I used to keep an accurate mental file about things like this, and also things like my keys. Then Isabel came along.

Also, yes, I've got mild cognitive impairment. But come on: name me someone between the ages of zero and dead who doesn't have occasional trouble concentrating.

When I hang up I realize Isabel has, in record time, completely dismantled my purse. What was expertly packed is now all over the floor. Every Kleenex out of the pocket pack, all cards and cash out of my wallet. Change is stacked in neat piles, goldfish swims in the carpet. She's hand-sanitized, and she's got my lipstick. It's open. It's pink.

"Isabel. Give me that."

"No," she says, in two syllables.

Since taking it away will only cause tears, I find Meatball—her favorite plush bear—and offer a trade. I squeeze his foot and he says, "Hello, Isabel!"

Isabel isn't interested. She clutches the tube and twists.

There is a brief struggle that ends when I swipe the tube. "Sorry, Isabel: not for babies." Tears blur her sharp gray eyes. *Like her mother's,* strangers often tell me.

"I'm sorry," I say again. I repeat myself a lot.

Isabel, she cries a lot, but at this age she's trying on the tears more often than not, so I pretend to ignore her while I repack my purse, pull on a pair of black straightlegs, and button a sheer fitted shirt over the white tank I'm already wearing. Then I pick her up and hug her while she hugs Meatball and cries some more and I get that this is about more than the lipstick: she's getting pretty attached to me, and she knows I didn't put on this monkey suit for a trip to the zoo.

"I love you, Spaghet." I also love that she's still little enough to cling to me, a precious reflex.

I hate that my reflex is to get on with it, but time's a-wasting, so, "You know who else loves you? Almost as much as I do?"

She leans back and wipes her nose. "Mabicabi?"

"Yes, honey. I bet Maricarmen would love to play with you while I go to work." Of course, Maricarmen doesn't know this yet, but if she's home, she's game.

"Okay," she says, with just a little reluctance.

I carry her and she carries Meatball and when we get to the kitchen I offer her an apple, a real project for a kid who only has a few front teeth. She has at it while I pack the diaper bag and also the other bag with stuff I forget, like diapers.

When I'm ready to go I find the apple abandoned on the kitchen floor and Isabel under the table. She's eating Cheerios that fell from her tray the last time we had a box of Cheerios, and trying to feed them to the bear. I shouldn't scold her for finding something I forgot about, so I tell myself it's good she's sharing.

"Isabel," I say, "let's get your shoes on."

"No," she says, one syllable this time. She scoots back, away from me, Meatball her shield.

"Please, Spaghet—"

"Can you guess what I am?" Meatball says. She pushed his button. "Oink!"

I am certain he's programmed to push mine.

"Shoes," I tell her.

"No," Isabel says, this time because she thinks I'm answering the bear.

We go around like this a lot.

Meatball giggles. "I'm pretending to be a pig!"

I leave them there and go get my own shoes.

I'm by the front door forcing my own feet into my tac boots , my left foot really cramping, when I hear the postman drop mail in the box at the front door. I wonder if it's mostly addressed to Tom.

I tell myself it's a legitimate reason to wonder about him, and then I wonder a bunch of other things about him, and then I wonder when I'll finally start to wonder about someone else.

Then, from knee height, Meatball asks, "Will you give me a hug?"

I look down and Isabel is standing there, holding the bear by his paw.

"Your timing is impeccable." I gather them up in my arms.

Though it's just down the street, we drive to Maricarmen's, a bungalow painted mint green with holiday decals in the windows and gnomes on the steps and wind chimes and lawn ornaments and all sorts of other shit that's meant to be decorative. To me it looks tacky. To Isabel it's a wonderland.

We met Maricarmen one evening last October when we strollered by and Isabel was interested in the huge inflated Snoopy situated among a bunch of haunted house–grade Halloween decorations. I was interested because I'd seen Maricarmen chase some gangbangers off the block earlier that day. We got to talking, and Maricarmen kept talking. And talking. I learned her life story right there: her migration from Sinaloa, her promising career as an operations manager at El Milagro Tortillas, her husband's unexpected death, and then—surprise—the unbelievable debt from an undisclosed gambling problem. On her own she repaid his debts, raised four children, and welcomed eighteen of her children's children. She was obviously a strong woman, but not a hard one.

I didn't feel the immediate connection Isabel did—what can I say, I'm more hard than strong. But when Izz nuzzled in Maricarmen's lap, I felt relieved. I'd been doing it all myself. I'd been so lonely.

Then, I talked and talked—about almost everything. I didn't tell her about my disease; I don't tell anyone about it because there's no cure and there's nothing to tell except what a ruthless bitch it is. I did tell her I was a cop, which is something else I don't advertise except that it's pretty easy to figure out. I said so because I wanted her to know I could help her with any trouble on the block. I was referring to the gangbangers.

Turned out Maricarmen already knew I was a cop, and one of the gangbangers was her grandkid, and she was actually trying to chase him away from me.

So our story goes that I wound up helping the grandkid when he was facing time, and Maricarmen wound up Isabel's go-to babysitter. We became fast friends, fierce maternal instinct our bond.

"Mabicabi!" Isabel says, recognizing the house.

"Yes," I tell her, happy that she's happy. "When I get back, we'll go for a swim, okay?" I always promise her something before I go, if only to make myself feel better about going.

"Swim! Swim!" She repeats herself a lot, too.

I leave her in the car seat singing her abc's, most of the letters *b*, while I unpack the trunk. I take a case of Mountain Dew—Maricarmen accepts most Pepsi products as payment—and Isabel's things. It always feels weird to know my service weapon is in there, underneath the little-person stuff.

I put down the bags etcetera to get Isabel out of the car seat and then I pick up the bags etcetera and we head for the crosswalk. At the curb I say, "Hold my hand," and Isabel looks up at me, curious, because she *is* holding my hand. I squeeze hers and try not to think about what I can't feel.

On the sidewalk she says, "Mama," and reaches for me, because she wants me to carry her, so I do, along with everything else, despite myself. Her hair smells so sweet.

When we get to the gate, Maricarmen appears in the front doorway, and Isabel gets down and then literally jumps up and down.

"Mabicabi!"

"*Hola*, Isabel!"

I open the gate and Isabel runs up the steps ahead of me to wrap herself around Maricarmen's leg.

"Girls, no *zapatos*?"

"It's summertime," I say. I got about two steps in those block-heeled boots and took them off, making myself incapable of arguing with a toddler who doesn't understand the point of wearing shoes in the first place.

I put the bags etcetera inside the door. "I just need an hour or so. A work thing."

"I wish, just once, you had some other excuse."

Isabel runs around her legs and cheers, "Cicles! Cicles!" to be redundant as well as repetitive.

"I'm making tamales," Maricarmen says, so I don't have to ask about lunch. She always plays down a last-minute favor by playing up a meal.

"See you in a—" I start to say to Isabel, but she's already off and running toward the kitchen. Sometimes I wish goodbyes were harder for her.

"*Hasta pronto*," Maricarmen says.

I beat it over to Sacred Heart hospital. I get into my boots and get out of the car. I pop the trunk and immediately decide to ditch the duty belt; it's heavy. Hot. I tuck my .40 S&W in the back of my waistband. My star goes on a lanyard around my neck and my bag over one shoulder, cross body, so my hands are free, though I may as well tie my left hand behind my back—the way it's buzzing, tactility blunted, it's like I'm wearing an oven mitt. Never aspired to be ambidextrous, though; I've always attempted more of a balancing act.

Inside, I show my star at the desk and they tell me where to find Kay St. Claire.

I walk down a corridor and wonder what's up at the other end where somebody is yelling her guts out and it turns out that somebody is in Kay St. Claire's room and the only two people in Kay St. Claire's room are a nurse and presumably Kay St. Claire, the one doing the yelling.

"I need to leave!" is what she yells at me. One eye is swollen shut, one arm is in a sling.

"She is welcome to refuse treatment," the nurse tells me, "but if she wants to leave, she needs to put on her shoes."

Funny thing.

"Kay St. Claire?" I ask.

She looks at me with her good eye. "CeCe?"

"No. My name is Detective Gina Simonetti. I'm here to talk to you about your son, Johnny Marble."

"I want to talk about why they brought me here. There's nothing wrong with me. They know that. I want to go home."

"You've been hurt," I say, "that's why you're here."

"You don't know hurt." She throws her shoes across the room. Her good arm is pretty good.

"Mrs. St. Claire, your son is a suspect in a similar crime involving a young woman. Two days ago, she was treated for broken ribs and a black eye that looks a lot like yours."

"Is that so? Well, did they bring her all the goddamned way down here to talk to her like she's a noodle?"

"Excuse me," a young guy says from the doorway and I turn back to find a young kid in a lab coat. His badge reads DODD.

"Did you call Robin?" St. Claire asks him.

"We're still trying to reach her."

"She'll get me the hell out of here."

"Um, yes," he says, like it's never going to happen. Then he looks up at me—literally—though I bet we'd be the same height if not for my heels. He looks away so he can say, "May I, sort of, speak to you in the hall?"

"Sure," I say. I wonder, once out there, what sort of bullshit he's scripted to say.

"I just," Dodd says, his gaze drawn to the ceiling like there's something up there besides fluorescents, "the attending physician wants to, I don't know, maybe speak with you, and he told me to page him when you arrived."

"Did you page him?"

"Yes."

"Then you've done an excellent job."

I wonder why he's acting like all his fingers are thumbs. Then I bet he's probably wondering why I'm acting like such a bitch.

"Listen," I say, "I'm happy to talk to the doctor—really. It doesn't sound like Mrs. St. Claire is interested in cooperating with anybody. But right now, I need to know if she wants to press charges. May I do that?"

"I think you would need to talk to Dr. Kitasaki first."

"Where would I find him?"

Dodd takes me to the lunchroom and angles toward a table where a striking man in scrubs—presumably a doctor—sits across from a dude in a suit. The doctor unwraps a Saran-wrapped turkey wrap, the skin between each of his fingers raised and rough, a red, scaly rash that looks like contact dermatitis. The suit toys with thin wire-rimmed glasses, his trouble more internalized. The only hair he's got grows thin and blond in a bad spot at the top of his head, which I can see because I'm standing over him.

The doctor looks up at me as he takes a huge bite of his unwrapped wrap. I feel bad interrupting because I know how it goes: on the Job and with a toddler, I eat when I can get food and a minute in front of me, and it ain't dainty.

Dodd looks like he's lost, so I step in front of him and say, "Gentlemen. I'm Detective Gina Simonetti. I'm here about Kay St. Claire."

The suit puts on a smile, and then his glasses, the overhead lights reflecting white squares in his eyes. He stands up. "I'm James Novak."

"Are you the doctor?"

"He is the CEO," Dodd says, looking at the floor tiles.

"Please," Novak says, "M.D. is a more important title around here. I am proud to say, though, that I am responsible for bribing some brilliant minds, like Dr. Kitasaki, here, to work with us." He opens up his stance to the doctor. "I believe he's the man you're here to see."

Kitasaki nods, swallows, pulls out the chair in front of me. "Call me Kuro."

Dodd says, "Dr. Adkins is waiting, sir," and whisks Novak off. Or probably he just follows him off. I don't know; I'm just glad Dodd is off.

When I sit, Kitasaki says, "I told Dodd to keep you guys—you—away from St. Claire. She's in no shape to answer questions."

His objection isn't unexpected, but his dead-on south-side accent totally throws me. An attractive Asian doctor who sounds like an intelligent version of my cousin Vito? I'm in love.

"She's the victim of a crime," I argue, though I don't think I sound argumentative.

He takes another bite of his lunch, chews awhile and says, "St. Claire is having an episode brought on by trauma. Patients in her condition are very easily aggravated. She is confused—this is cat-astrophic for her—to be attacked, and then taken out of her famil-iar environment, and then interrogated—"

"I haven't asked her a single question yet."

He swallows. "I just think you should know it's common for patients like her to blame the people who mean to help."

"I'm told her son is to blame."

Kitasaki looks at me. "The woman's got dementia. *I* could be her son." His pager buzzes; after giving the device a cursory glance he says, "My job is to help St. Claire get better. Please, give her some time to do that." He shoves the rest of the wrap in his face, tears open a wet wipe, and cleans his hands while he gets up.

"I'll take what you said into consideration," I say, "but we aren't working at cross purposes, here. My job is to help her, too."

"I think your job is to find the bad guy," he says. "I'm not him."

"I didn't—" I start, but he walks away. So much for love.

I wait about four minutes and then I go back to St. Claire's room to do my job.

St. Claire is alone, staring out the window, eyes dull. She must be doped. Her hair is wavy and much longer than most women her age wear it but it's beautiful, really, a soft, rippled gray. Her face is mapped by wrinkles.

"Mrs. St. Claire?"

"CeCe," she says, the emotion that was caught up with the name before now tucked under a fast-thickening blanket of medication.

"Is CeCe your daughter?"

St. Claire lolls her head toward me. She doesn't look pleased. "Who are you?"

"I'm Gina." I step forward and show her Isabel's photo, the screen saver on my phone. "I have a daughter, too. Her name is Isabel. Would you like to see?"

St. Claire squints at the photo. "She looks like you."

"She's my everything. I guess all parents feel that way about their children, even in the worst circumstances—"

St. Claire starts trying to get away from me, off the bed, like I'm coming at her with a six-gauge needle. "Who are you?" Her good eye is wide now, and fixed on me.

I back off, tuck my phone away. "I am Gina Simonetti. I'm—" about to show her my lanyard but—

"Where is Robin?"

"Robin?" Suddenly I feel like I'm talking to Isabel—translating non-sequiturs—but by now, I'm pretty good at deciphering non-sense. I get it: "Robin is your caregiver."

"She doesn't know where I am. She could be waiting at the house. She'll be so worried about me."

"Well, she's the one who called the police. She knows where you are."

"No, she doesn't. Or else she'd be here."

"Okay," I say, deciding to U-turn, come at it from the other direction: "I am here, now, because you were hurt. Do you know how you got hurt?"

She looks at me, then, and things seem to come into focus for her. "Oh yes." Her eyes sharpen, and she breaks a smile. "My boy."

"Johnny Marble," I say, and I think we're getting somewhere, but then I feel someone behind me, and I realize St. Claire isn't looking at me, but over my shoulder.

I turn to see a man twice my age on his way out the door. Her *boy*.

"Johnny Marble!" I call out, like it'll stop him.

I chase him down the corridor past an elderly patient with a tracheotomy tube who's rolling an IV cart. "Call security!" I yell at her, though I don't have time to tell her what to say and I don't know if she can say anything anyway.

The man turns the corner and lopes down a long corridor; it

doesn't seem like he's running as fast as I'm trying to, but his legs are long so he puts distance between us pretty quickly. I try to get a good visual to make sure it *is* Johnny Marble. I put him over six feet and at two hundred pounds. He's wearing loose cargo pants and a purple warm-up jacket. His hair is a tamped-down Afro. I can't say for sure it's him—I only saw his booking photo—but there's a reason he's running.

And I saw Kay St. Claire's face. He's got to be Marble.

At the end of the hall he ducks into a stairwell marked FLOOR 4 WEST and by the time I get there, thanks to the fire code, the door's closed itself. I draw my gun.

I turn the handle and kick open the door and clear the landing and then I step in and check the stairs going up to five, and he isn't there, which I anticipated since he's probably trying to get the hell out of here. I get my back against the wall next to the door just as it swings shut and then I wait for my eyes to adjust. A dim rectangle of light projects from the door's small window, and there's faint ambient light from the EXIT sign; neither is a guide. A droning hum from the hospital's power systems rushes from the vents. I feel my way down a few steps, into the dark. It's like I've stepped inside the guts of a machine; I worry that he knows how it works.

"Johnny Marble!" I call out again, the sound of my voice swallowed by the noise.

I can't see, and I can't hear, but he can't be far. Somewhere below. I can smell him. Sour. A stress-sweat.

I move to the opposite wall and find the landing below, another pair of faint lights from the EXIT sign and the door a dozen steps down. The landing is empty. From there, the steps to the third floor double back, disappear to black.

I wait. I shouldn't wait. He may have already exited the third floor.

Then I think I hear him breathing. Out of breath. Or fucking panicked, adrenaline forcing him to breathe. Or is that me?

I keep my back to the wall and feel my way down a half-dozen steps, my left foot cramping like the sole has pulled apart and I'm walking on bones.

That's probably why I miss a step. I catch the rail—I catch myself—but my gun clatters to the landing.

That's probably because I let go of the gun to catch the rail.

"Johnny Marble!" I shout because I want to act like I'm coming at him, strong, even though I shouldn't have come this far. I feel around for the gun and find it and hold it in both hands and wait. That's what I should do: just wait.

Then I hear him—

"Gina Simonetti!"

How does he know my name?

I aim my gun to clear the next landing. As I start down the steps, I hear the ground-floor door blow open. "Security!" a male voice shouts.

And Marble *is* trapped, now.

He comes up the steps, back toward the third-floor exit, and I'm on my way down to meet him, but I misstep again—my brain unable to get the right messages out—and this time, since I'm not about to lose my gun, I wind up losing my feet out from under me. I lurch forward. From eight steps up it's like I'm diving, and I dive right into Marble. I knock him down and we hit the landing and my head hits him in the face and his head hits the steel and then neither one of us makes a sound. He tries to push me away but I'm afraid if there's space between us he'll take the gun so I slip my free hand, my left hand, around his torso. I pull myself to him and I try to hold him there. Right there.

It doesn't work.

He rolls on top of me and pushes my face against the landing. I try to grab for his jacket and I can't do it. I try curling up, to protect myself, my gun, when he stands and jerks me up by my bag. I'm dangling, splayed, head and arms off the floor, and I've got my gun but can't find my aim; in the two rectangle spots of light, though, I can see him. His mouth is bleeding. He doesn't seem to care. He begins to laugh.

And then he drops me.

My head hits the steel this time, and when I look up again I see three of him standing over me. I think he's got my gun and I bet he's going to kill me and I know it's my fucking fault.

But what I wonder as this man—this fucking beast—laughs at me, is if the very last thing that'll cross my mind is that Isabel's first word was mama, and when she said it, she meant me.

"Security!" the male voice shouts again, closer. Not close enough.

I close my eyes and wish I'd prayed long before now.

2

They say pregnancy changes the brain; that a mother develops a heightened sense of smell, and sometimes hearing. One study claims all the senses become more focused—that a sort of hormonal hypervigilance develops—in effect, turning a mother into a twenty-four-hour baby-security system.

I was never pregnant but I'm telling you, I have that same awareness for Isabel. I can feel her blink.

Additionally, I have marked morning puffiness under my eyes, frequent nausea due to a diet consisting mainly of leftover cheese sandwiches, and the patience of a two-year-old with everybody except the two-year old. I have become a mom.

And being a mom is the real reason I forgot what it's like to be scared. It's not my star, or my gun. It's that I'm perpetually worried about someone else.

I actually wasn't worried when Calvin the security guard found me on the landing and acted like I was near-dead. I wasn't scared when he radioed dispatch and checked my airway and took my pulse and palpated my neck and did everything except what I wanted him to do, which was to go after Marble. I tried to tell him so, but the words must've been caught up somewhere between my brain and my mouth.

He said, "Help is on the way. Don't worry, Officer. You're going to be okay."

I said, only to myself I guess, "We're in a fucking hospital. Don't you think I'll be okay?"

I wasn't scared—not even though I knew that as we waited, Marble probably walked out the front door with my gun.

What could I do, though? I was flat on my back. My head ached. Both hands were numb and a new and incredible electric pain surged up and down my entire left side. I felt like I'd been plugged in. Electro-shocked.

And that's when I finally got scared, because I was certain there'd no longer be a way to hide the fact that I have multiple sclerosis.

Listen, I'd done the math before on a cop working with an undisclosed disease like mine: it equals an early retirement and in my case, probably a lawsuit. I've still got eyes on me for cracking up a squad when I was after a thief; I had to make that accident—my fault—look like a gutsy collar. Add to that the fact that I just basically handed my gun to a suspect, and I'd estimate coming away with something like absolutely nothing. No pension, no severance, no star.

And then no income, no insurance, no Isabel.

No more being her mom.

While Calvin radioed dispatch, I shut my eyes and kept them that way. Same with my mouth.

When the doctors arrived in the stairwell and determined it was safe to move me, they put me on a stretcher and brought me back into the bright and cold and white. There, everybody sounded worried, which made me worry some more.

What if they already knew? What if they could plainly see, through their expert lenses, everything I'd been hiding?

Somewhere along the way I started to feel not so worried. I felt real dreamy. The doctors' voices trailed off and I could no longer make out the words, so I imagined them breaking apart into letters. And I imagined the letters floating, joining some swirling ether of abc's. The last thing I remember was wondering if the doctors left, or if I did.

When I come around, I find an IV in the crook of my arm that's connected to a crash cart where my vitals hold steady. A computer sits opposite the bed, a Sacred Heart logo screen saver ponging around. And on the other side of the room, Dr. Kitasaki is washing his hands in the sink.

"What the fuck?" I think I say and apparently I do because Kitasaki turns around.

"You're awake."

"You're observant."

Kitasaki dries his hands, no indication he's bothered by my attitude, or his rash. He says, "I'm glad you're awake."

The room lights are bright and the curtains are pulled and I can't tell if it's day or night. "What time is it?"

He checks his watch. "Almost four."

"Shit," I say. "I need my phone. I promised I'd be home before dinner."

"Well, you missed dinner. Breakfast comes around seven—"

"It's four in the morning?"

"Nearly."

"Why are you here?"

"Surgery ran late. Have to do rounds when I can—"

"Can you get me my phone?"

He points to a red-and-white sign by the door that reads NOTICE: CELL PHONE USE PROHIBITED. "You're in intensive care. Your partner—Andy?—he said he'd notify your family."

Isabel isn't going to understand. She needs to hear my voice. "Can I use the room phone?"

"First things first." He pulls on latex gloves, shines a light in each of my eyes. "Any headache?"

Yes. "No."

When he leans in to look through the ophthalmoscope I can smell coffee on his breath and I want to puke. "Dizziness or nausea?"

Yes and yes. "No, neither."

He tucks the light away and raises his hand. "Follow my finger."

I do. "I'm telling you, I'm fine." I think.

He snaps off a glove and he looks relieved about it. I look at the rash as he raises his bare hand beside my left ear and rubs his fingertips together, then does the same on the right. "Does this sound the same on both sides?"

"You're the one who's not hearing me. I told you: I need to make a call."

"You're almost done. Palms up."

Though I see him do it, I don't really feel it when he uses the capped end of his pen to draw a sensation down each forearm to my palms. "Same on both sides?"

"Yes," I lie. I can't feel the left one.

He goes to the end of the bed, draws the same inkless lines up the bottoms of my feet. "Same," I say and I'm not lying this time because I don't feel anything on either side.

He snaps off his other glove, turns to the computer, and begins typing. He types for quite a while.

Does he know I lied?

I wait until I can't wait anymore, my heart stuck in my throat when I ask, "What's wrong with me?" I'm ready for the guillotine.

Kitasaki finishes typing and turns to me. "As far as I can tell, it's a TBI."

"What does that mean?"

"Sorry—traumatic brain injury."

"That seems right." My heart could come out of my mouth and fly around the room. A TBI. I like it.

"But," Kitasaki says, "I haven't yet seen the CT scan results. "

Wait. "You gave me a CT scan?"

"We were worried about swelling in your brain."

"Don't you need my consent for that?"

"You gave us your consent."

"No fucking way I did."

He comes back to the end of the bed and rifles through some papers stowed in the chart holder. "Your intake forms are right here." He shows me my signature.

"How did I sign anything while I was unconscious?"

"You were actually awake for about an hour yesterday afternoon."

No. Fucking. Way. Even if I was up and dancing, I couldn't have signed anything—with my right hand useless? I know I should shut up, but, "I don't believe it."

"It's common to feel confusion," he says. "You hurt your brain."

"I would remember signing that."

"Well, you also asked to make a call, just as you are now. Do you remember that? We tried contacting . . ." As he flips through the file, he maintains an even, unbothered expression; it's infuriating. "Here it is. Next of kin: George Simonetti? But he—"

"Shut up. You called my brother?"

"He was the only Simonetti in your phone contacts."

"There's no way I asked you to call my brother."

"Actually, you asked us to call your partner. We thought that meant, you know—husband? Or, life partner? We didn't make the connection, about your—about Andy, until he arrived with Sergeant Iverson."

"Iverson was here?" This just keeps getting not any better. Carrie Iverson is a true-blue bitch.

Kitasaki fiddles with one of the monitors I'm connected to and plugs a new port into my IV.

"What's that?"

"Dexamethasone. For the swelling. If you're uncomfortable, I can add a pain reliever—"

"I'd be plenty comfortable if I could just make that call."

"Yes, of course." He puts the phone on the rolling table and positions it next to the bed. "Dial six to get out."

I pick up the phone and realize I don't know Mari's number—or anybody's, for that matter—by memory. But god damn it, that has nothing to do with my disease and everything to do with me being reliant on technology, like everyone else.

I watch Kitasaki mark a code on the nurses' whiteboard. I don't know what it stands for and so I don't want him to go without getting at least one good answer.

"Doctor?"

"Yes?" He stops.

"What did my brother say, when you called?"

He shrugs. "We couldn't reach him."

I put down the phone and I'm disappointed, because I don't know why the hell I expected a good answer to that one. I admit, "He's not actually someone I'd call."

"I know what it's like," Kitasaki says. He looks at his hands, the rash. "Nobody expects doctors to have problems, either."

"Does it itch?"

"I was talking about my student loans." He smiles. "I'll come back after breakfast to go over the test results."

"I'll be here," I say, though I'm not at all happy about it.

I sit back, let the IV do its thing, and try to believe my world is still intact. Yes, it's necessarily built on a few false hinges, and yes, I'll lie my ass off to keep them well-oiled and working. Who can criticize? So I've got a name for what's wrong with me. I've got an idea about the expiration date for my legs. Does that make me less fit for the Job? I'm in better shape than most cops I know. I take care of myself and I'm not walking around, my heart ticking like a time bomb or my blood sugar tempting diabetic fate. I know my limits.

At least I thought I did.

Still. I will not let an off-duty favor gone to shit ruin me. I will not let a bad guy hurt me in my off hours. If I can just keep cool a little longer and reasonably demonstrate I have an acute, work-sustained injury, I'll bet I can get on my way by noon with a pre-scription, a PT referral, and permission to get back to work.

I close my eyes and try to imagine I'm at home with Isabel. We're in bed and she's still asleep, cuddled up, her hair tickling my nose. Or else she's at all angles, restless, her feet in my face.

But when she wakes, I'm there. I'm the first one to see her moon-eyed smile.

I think of Isabel at Maricarmen's this morning. Waking, wondering where I am.

I can't sit here until noon.

I swing the IV cart around the bed and use it, a crutch, out to the hall. I need it: though I've experienced this numbness before, I will never get used to feeling my legs move at the same time I can't tell where my feet land.

At least I know it will get better; thankfully, these past two years, it's never been much worse than the first bout. A relapse is what it's called, though the term makes me think of an addict who is trying not to feel anything. For me, a relapse is more like a charge: I have to fight the numb.

That means I have to prove I'm all right.

I push the cart down the corridor and turn it around and do it again and I don't see anybody. Even the nurses' station is empty.

On the third pass I decide I feel pretty good, the steroids smearing a nice thick salve over my symptoms. I'm not a fan of the stuff, though—not after trying to break up my brother's romance with painkillers. George prefers the numb; he'd rather be soothed than try to be strong.

Up ahead another patient exits one of the rooms, her own IV cart in tow. She has a pretty pronounced case of kyphosis and as she moves, she leads with the top of her white-haired head.

I take my cart the other way, toward the elevators.

On the fourth floor, the door to Kay St. Claire's room is half-open. I roll in. Opposite the bed, the Sacred Heart logo beats on the computer monitor. Along the far windows the curtains are open, and outside, dawn is starting to fill in spots the parking lot lights don't.

And in the bed, St. Claire is asleep. Her form is tiny underneath the sheets, except for where they've bolstered her legs. She is still— so still, in fact, I have to step closer to see the slight rise and fall of her chest.

Machines behind her assure me she's alive in winks and spikes, keeping hospital time. Judging by the number of ports connected to her IV line, she'll stay just this still as long as they like.

I move to the foot of the bed, and from this perspective I see two perfect arcs over her legs—over, not under. I lift the sheet. Her ankles are cuffed. They have not tried to make her comfortable; they did not give her time to calm down. They drugged her and they restrained her.

And that just pisses me off.

There's another reason I don't tell anyone I have a neurological disease: because what's inherent in the diagnosis is that you're a victim. And when you're a victim of your own body—whether you're

twenty-nine or seventy-nine, and whether your breakdown is physical or mental—you are pitied. You are pitied, and pandered to, and
exploited.

Doctors use different words. Care. Compassion. Treatment. But
softening the language doesn't change the fact that it's a fight you
aren't going to win. And right now, forget semantics. St. Claire is
fucked.

"Please," she says.

I step back like I'll disappear that way, but she doesn't see me to
begin with. Her eyes are closed.

"Please," she says again, the word drug-thick and slow.

I don't know if she's dreaming. I don't say anything.

"I need help," she says. "They're taking everything."

A doctor would diagnose paranoia. Or delusion. Dementia. Or
confusion.

Looking at her, restrained and medicated, it sounds to me like
she knows exactly what she's talking about.

"I will help you," I say. Because she is also the victim of a crime,
and I'm the one who's supposed to stop the son-of-a—her son—
from doing the victimizing.

She reaches for me—toward me, anyway—so I take her hand. It
is warm and dry. I can feel her bones. She holds on, even though
consciousness slips away.

I hold on, too. I stay there with her until the sky brightens over
the parking lot. Then I stay a few minutes more, because in the light
of day, I see myself right where she is, someday. And I won't want to
be alone.

3

When I wake up again, the sun up and glaring at me, I'd kill to wash down a couple Tylenol with a press pot of Dark Matter, my usual migraine buster. The fact that I'm able to think about coffee without wanting the pink dish is an improvement from last night. Still, my head feels like someone replaced my cerebrospinal fluid with dry-mix cement. Yes, there are the real drugs I know Kitasaki and company would love me to take to get comfortable. But I can't get comfortable.

I like the nurse even though her perfume makes my eyes hurt. Her name is Victoria and she has colored rubber bands in her braces that match the breast cancer awareness ribbons patterned on her scrubs.

At five after seven, someone in standard blue scrubs brings breakfast. I don't want it. I ask for a newspaper instead, since I figure I'd better show everyone I feel well enough for bad news.

When I get today's *Tribune*, I stare blankly at the headlines while I mentally regurgitate what I'm going to say to the doctor. Kitasaki or whoever. Then I turn to the Nation and World section, where it reads JAPAN TO WEAN ELDERLY OFF TUBES. The article is as shocking as it sounds: in the face of government cutbacks, a quarter of a million old Japanese people are about to get starved to death. I wonder what the coroner writes for cause of death. Liberal Democratic Party?

I flip to the Chicagoland section so I can feel bad about our own politics but really, I'm watching the clock tick toward eight. At eight, still nobody. I can't wait. I use the room phone to call information for Metzler's office number, and I dial him.

"Doctor Rick," I say to voicemail, "it's Regina. Sorry I haven't been in touch; I've been really busy with Isabel." An obvious and disappointing excuse, but, "We're doing well. And hey, we'd love if you'd come by, see the house? It's, well, we're making it home . . ." I pause, but I can't go on. Metzler has known me my whole life; he's known my family since he was stationed with my dad at Fort Bragg. And so he knows all my shit, and also when I'm full of shit. "I'm sorry," I say. "I hate asking for favors. But I was involved in a work-related altercation yesterday, and I'm in the hospital. Sacred Heart, on the west side. I'm sure you know it. Anyway I've had tests and I'll have more tests, and I'm fine, I just—since you know me, I'd like you to be my advocate. And obviously I'd like to keep this between us. Okay. I'm in room 210. Please call."

I hang up and imagine Metzler shaking his head, wondering once again why he ever made a single promise to my dad.

It's not about me anymore, though. This is for Isabel. Did I say that, in the message? I should have said that. Metzler knows. I hope he knows.

A minute later, the phone rings.

"Doctor Rick?" I say, and I feel a surge of relief.

"It's Andy."

My partner. "This is your fault."

"Yet you're still speaking to me. I'm stuck on the Kennedy, but I should be there before the doctor."

"I'm well enough to leave, and you're just now getting up the nerve for a visit?"

"I was there—you don't remember?—I was there until ten o'clock last night. I didn't leave your side until Iverson got a uniform outside your door. And you weren't well. At all."

"I'm fine now. And there's no uniform here."

"There'd better be. A suspect who beat up three women and one's his mom and another's a cop? Iverson said she'll make sure you don't leave that place with so much as a hurt feeling."

I want to tell Andy that there was nobody out there this morning, but I don't want another reason to be accused of being confused. I let it go, because, "I've got to get out of here. I miss my baby."

"Isabel is fine, G. I just talked to Maricarmen. They're baking *galletas*. Isabel's morning is a rainbow of sprinkles."

"That makes me feel so much better."

"Good," he says, ignoring the fact that I didn't mean it. "Listen: when you were sleeping last night, I counted sixteen people I'd never seen before waltz in and out of your room. Even with a star outside, I'll bet there's at least one young journo who'd tuck his smartphone into a borrowed lab coat for a story. Or some bowtie administrator who'll try to talk you into signing on the dotted line over a lawsuit. If they get in, you make like you're suffering from that head injury."

I hadn't added the media or the hospital into the equation. Still, "You don't have to worry. All I plan to say is that I'm ready to go home."

"Good," Andy says again.

After we say goodbye, I get curious about the supposed cop outside my door. I roll my cart out there and find a kid in uniform, nameplate SHANNON, sitting in a hall chair playing a game of Yahtzee on his phone. There's a crushed white paper bag stuffed into a foam coffee cup on the seat next to him, and he may as well have powdered sugar on his face.

"Hi," I say. He doesn't say anything, though there's no one else around I could be talking to. So he's deaf, or else an asshole who thinks a hospital detail may as well be a snipe hunt. Either way, I'm standing here, so—

"You know where the donut shop is, right? Actually I'm not really in the mood for donuts. I'll take hash browns. And a sweet tea. And what the hell, a dozen Vanilla Kremes. For when I am in the mood. Then maybe I won't say anything to Iverson about where you've been all morning."

"What?" He looks up and when he sees who I am his lips find their way to a pout. But that's because he's on his way to get some more donuts.

"You can run over there now," I say. "Obviously I'm fine all by myself."

"You look fine," a man says behind me.

I close my eyes and pray my gown is tied tight in back.

"Shannon," the man says; his tone tells me he doesn't like Shannon much.

I pivot the IV cart and turn to see Ray Weiss, a cop I don't like at all.

"Hello," I say, and then, "goodbye." I decide to forget the bit with Shannon; I just head back to bed, cart-first.

I know Weiss from when I was on the Evidence Tech Team's North Unit 377 and he was patrol in 24—we worked the same crime scenes. Mostly, though, I know him from the old days at Union Park. I used to party and I could hold my own over there, beer for beer.

I remember one night in particular, with Weiss. It was right after I was diagnosed, and the last time I went to the Union. A group of cops dwindled to us two. I was only there to finish my drink; I'd already pegged Weiss as a guy who was aware enough of his physical advantages—excellent arms, full head of hair, a real smile—to assume he had a free pass on his attitude. His attitude was crap. He was argumentative and proud of it. And he bullshitted me like I was one of the guys.

That night, I had plenty of booze in my system and enough left in my glass to decide to call him on his attitude. He was talking football—or more correctly, arguing—that players who suffered long-term cognitive issues caused by concussions shouldn't be compensated—when he leaned over and very drunkenly glanced down between the open plackets of my dress shirt. As though I had just unbuttoned it for him.

When I caught him looking, he said, "So."

Then I realized I did miss an all-important button, and that was because I couldn't feel my fingers, and that was because my brain was no healthier than a pro bowler's. No way I was going to explain that to some guy who figured me for a friendly fuck and a fist bump. I got up and left.

The sick part of it was, I liked Weiss.

I quit the Union after that. Had to. For one, I was getting a reputation as a real stumbling drunk. The stumbling was true. Two, a rumor had started about me sleeping with a witness. It wasn't entirely false.

I only saw Weiss once after that night. It was the Fourth of July party at Keegan's Pub; a cop's cousin owns the place. Tom was busy so I brought my brother along as my date and that's when my brother got introduced to Weiss's date, Soleil Devere.

And she is the real reason I don't like Ray Weiss.

I'm back in bed and I want to pull the covers over my head when Weiss comes in. Instead I say, "You don't have to stay. I'll be released just as soon as I talk to the doctor."

"I'm not here for the door," Weiss says. "I'm here about Johnny Marble."

"You're fuge app? I thought you were never leaving the beat car."

"It's not that different. Now I just look for particular shitbags." He smiles at me. "It's been awhile, Gina."

"Nineteen months."

"Nineteen—? How do you know that?"

"Because that's when Soleil came into our lives. Who could forget? She's so wonderful."

Weiss looks down at his feet. "If it matters, I have never been able to stop people from doing what they want to do."

"Is that your excuse for why you just do whatever you want to do?"

"I'm here to help you."

"You mean you need my help. Finding Marble."

"He's my shitbag." He sits on the daybed. I know the trick; he's getting on the level, literally.

Whatever. "I can't help you."

"Can't, or won't?"

I don't answer.

"I'm sorry. I was told you hit your head. If you can't remember—"

"Oh no. I remember." I've got the story down, every detail, backward and forward. I know what I've got to say to the bosses, the doctors, the medical section, the media—it's not the truth, exactly. But it's what'll get me out of here. It's what'll get me back to work, and back home to Isabel.

Still, to lie to Weiss, right now; it feels against the grain. I mean, I should be on his side.

The problem is, I don't know if he's on mine.

"You do know it's a game," Weiss says, "looking for someone who doesn't want to be found."

"Guess you're losing," I say. I gaze out the window at the same shitty parking-lot view St. Claire has upstairs.

Weiss stands up. "I'm sorry. I wish Soleil wasn't all you remembered about me." He gives up on a smile and heads for the door.

Damn him, throwing down that old card. A fold.

Before he gets out the door he has to step aside because—

"Ms. Simonetti?"

I see the gurney first, then the large black man in green scrubs who's pushing it. He wears an orderly's tag but I can't read the name. He locks the gurney wheels and checks his paperwork. "I'm here to take you to your MRI."

My voice falls down my throat. "I'm going to hold off," I try to say, "I'm waiting for my primary physician."

"Who's your primary?"

"Richard Metzler."

The orderly flips the page, creases it at the staple, and shows me: "Metzler is the ordering. He called it in."

"He can do that?"

"You just said he's your doctor, ma'am."

"I haven't even talked to him."

"He musta spoke with the hospitalist."

"What the fuck is a hospitalist?"

The orderly doesn't look bothered by the question, but Weiss does. He tries to slip out around the gurney.

"Weiss—wait," I say, because I don't want him to know I'm panicking about the MRI—a test that'll give my MS and me away— so I say, "Johnny Marble looks like his booking photo. He runs like a suspect. He smells like your locker room. He's got my gun. I don't think that's much of a map, but his mother is upstairs. Kay St. Claire. Room 406. Maybe she can help."

Color Weiss surprised.

"Also," I say, unable to stop any of this from coming out of my mouth, "you should talk to the security guard who found me. His name is Calvin. He was there in the stairwell with me. He might have seen something I didn't."

"Calvin," Weiss says, as the orderly helps me out of bed.

"Or Curtis," I say, because what the fuck, I do have a brain injury.

"Thanks," Weiss says, "I'll come by later—let you know what I learn."

"Don't bother," I say, "I'll be home by then."

He waves over his shoulder without looking back and I think that means he'll see me later, no matter what.

I know the drill when they prep me for the MRI. I have had three in two years.

"No," I'm not claustrophobic. Nor do I have a pacemaker, tattoos, or any history as a metal worker. I have no bullet wounds. I am not allergic to gadolinium. I am not pregnant.

The radiology tech has a lazy eye.

It is freezing in the scan room.

The tech gets me on the flat bed and gives me earplugs. He secures my head in a coil. He puts a pillow under my knees. He offers me a blanket.

I know he does this twenty times a day and I appreciate the gesture but there's no getting cozy, here. I decline.

He tells me the test will take forty-five minutes, and that there's an intercom in the tube so he can tell me what to expect and when to hold still.

I wish he could tell me what to expect and when to hold still after this.

He's already out of the room when the bed moves into the tube. I close my eyes and I won't open them again until it's finished; I know there's a mirror I can look into to see my feet, but I can't feel my feet.

The tech's voice sounds like it's coming through a tin can when he asks, "Are you comfortable?"

A ridiculous question.

I say I am.

"This first test will run about two minutes."

I know. I wait for the knocking.

I try to be still. As the machine works its way around me, I wonder if it captures images of the tears that slip from the corners of my eyes.

4

When they take me back to my room it's a different room and an old cop with a thick white mustache is now on the door. I can't read his nameplate but he stands up when I roll by; unlike Shannon, he's probably attended enough cop funerals to respect the fact that I'm still with us. And he probably appreciates an easy afternoon.

I'm on the fourth floor now, just around the corner from Kay St. Claire's room. Apparently I no longer need intensive care, though I wouldn't be able to tell the difference since the minute I get off the gurney, I'm cared for pretty intensively. In the first hour, at least a dozen people come and go. Only one of them isn't some kind of medical professional and she's delivering a bouquet sent by someone in the department who doesn't know I hate to watch flowers die. And all of them ask some version of the same innocuous question: How are you feeling?

I remember Andy's warning, and tell them all I'm fine.

When Kitasaki asks, I say I'm great.

In between people I take a few minutes to enjoy the Coke and fries Andy brought from Greek Corner—I was in the tube when he came by and though he didn't stick around, he was astute enough to know I'd be starving. And he knows the two things I can stomach no matter the circumstance—Coke and fries, after a murder or the morgue. Also, Shannon left food—bravo—but the hash browns went cold and the sweet tea got warm, so I pitched them. The point was made anyhow, and the donuts will keep for Maricarmen.

When a nurse comes in and asks how I'm doing, I tell her I'm going to sleep. I'm not tired, but I don't want to have to say I'm fine again. Not until Metzler arrives.

It's just after three o'clock when he does.

"Regina," he says and pulls me into his arms. I hold on; it's been a long time since I got a hug from a grown-up.

He says, in my ear, "Your brain looks like Swiss cheese."

"My brain looked that way before. I feel fine."

"You're having an exacerbation. When did it start?"

"When I woke up." I don't say which day. "What happens now? Now that the other doctors know? They know, don't they?"

"I'm sure. I'm also sure they don't care. They're in the life-and-death business, and you're going to make it."

"But don't they have to intervene? Or disclose findings?"

"HIPAA laws prevent your diagnosis from being disclosed to anyone other than you or your power of attorney. And your insurance company."

"Pretty sure I just met my deductible."

"I'm glad you still have your sense of humor." He sets me back, holds my shoulders, sizes me up. He looks just as good as the last time I saw him, and not a day older. He'll be a hundred years old and look just like this: pleasant and kind eyed. Well-fed and well-rested. And always like he knows just a little bit more than he lets on, but wouldn't get any satisfaction from saying so.

"Tell me, Regina," he says in a stern voice that sounds like a bad impression of my dad.

"It's a relapse. It's nothing new. I'll be fine."

"An injury signals a body's immune system to fight. You know your immune system is already fighting your nervous system. You need to start treatment for your disease."

"I'll be okay."

"You'll run yourself into the ground."

"I know my body."

"I know *you*."

He stops arguing—if that's what I can call it—to give me his routine exam: finger to my nose, tuning fork to the toes, all that. I think I do okay.

When he's through, he takes my hands and looks them over. He asks, "How can you hold a gun?"

"Not very well, obviously."

"How can you hold Isabel?"

"That's totally different."

"Yes," he says. "A child's life is a steady trickle of hysterical strength." Then, while he's holding my hands, he looks into my eyes: the real exam. "What about your own life?"

"Before this, I had almost all the pieces in place."

"Tom?"

"I said *almost* all."

"It doesn't sound to me like he fits."

"He doesn't. But he continues to pay his half of the mortgage, so I can't write him off completely."

"And George?"

"He hasn't come around. Still giving it up to God, I guess."

"He isn't as willful as you are."

"I'm not willful. I'm rational."

"I want you on medication."

"I can't be sick all the time."

"There are new options. An oral dose—"

"I read about that one. Side effects may include a heart attack? Forget it."

"Think about the future, Regina. Think about what is happening in your brain that you can't feel or know."

"I could walk out of here and get hit by a bus. I can't feel or know that, either."

"You claim you're nothing like your brother, but you both got your father's contentious disposition. You sound exactly like him— "

"And, same as my dad, I'm asking you to help me. Even if you don't agree."

"What is it you want me to do, Regina?"

"I want you to write this up to the medical section as an acute brain injury and let me go back to work. And to Isabel."

"Without regard for what I know as your physician."

"With complete regard for knowing everything about me, as my friend."

He looks down at his own hands. Thinks about it. Probably thinks about my dad. Says, "Okay."

He takes out his prescription pad and starts writing. "I agree with Dr. Kitasaki—he wants to get you started on a five-day corticosteroid treatment for the TBI. You'll get the first IV now and then a nurse will come to your home for four more days."

"I can go home today?"

"After the treatment."

"That's great," I say. "I miss Isabel more than my feet." I make light of it so I won't cry.

He tears off the scrip and hands it to me. "I'll write up the report for the medical section just as soon as you fill this."

It's for Avonex, the interferon I took when I was first diagnosed. It's awful. No way. "What if I refuse?"

He tucks his pad away. "As your friend, I don't want to screw up your life, but as your physician, I can't let you screw it up. Fill it and face this. If only for Isabel."

He hugs me again and I feel so, so weak.

But. Isabel. Of course I will.

I wipe the tears that came anyway. I say, "Okay."

Metzler gets up. "Be willful now, Regina. It will make you well."

When he leaves I fold the scrip in two, and two, and two again. My ticket out of here. It's going to be a shitty trip.

I get my first dose of steroids and then they spring me—or rather, they stick me in a wheelchair so they can get the bed ready for someone else while I wait for my discharge papers. After a little small talk I ask Flagherty to leave—he's the old cop—and he's pleased since it's a half hour from the end of the shift and he can waste the time he's got left on the clock in the can and head straight to choir practice.

Yet another someone in scrubs gives me a printout of the steroids protocol—who to call and what to expect—along with a hospital-stay satisfaction survey. If these people were smart, they would have given me some M&Ms and some fucking Fritos. I'd have checked five stars all the way.

Sitting in the wheelchair makes me insane. I keep replaying and deconstructing this sentence, as stated by Tom: *I don't know if I can handle a baby and a wife in a wheelchair.* The first thing that's fucked up about it is that Isabel isn't his kid and nobody asked him to handle her. Second, we never talked about me being Mrs. Sheridan number Two. Third, this came out of the mouth of a forty-year-old guy who takes heart medication and anxiety medication and sleep medication. I was twenty-eight when he said this. I never took so much as Pepto-Bismol till I was diagnosed, and until he said it, I hadn't allowed myself to entertain the wheelchair idea. So the only part of the sentence I can figure to be accurate is *I don't know.*

I hate sitting here.

There's a shift change, so all the old doctors and nurses split and the fresh crew busily ignores me. I sit, like an invalid, as the clock ticks past Isabel's dinnertime. I didn't order dinner. I was hoping I'd be home. I was hoping we'd have those donuts, a special dessert.

I'm thinking donuts might be my dinner when someone says, "Miss Simonetti?" and I hope to God it's the guy who's going to roll me out the door.

His tag tells me he's Calvin.

My face probably tells him I think he's finer than frog hair.

He's dark-skinned, mixed race, tall, and tight as a rail. His arms look like they could carry me a mile and his smile makes me glad I'm already sitting down. I obviously didn't get a look at him in the stairwell, because I would have known his name for certain, and I wouldn't have minded his help at all.

Yes, clearly, I just mainlined pharmaceutical hormones.

"Are you ready to go?" he asks, rounding the back of the chair.

"Can I walk?" I don't want him to see me like this.

"Sorry. Policy says you have to be escorted."

"Then please, steer me to where I can override it."

He wheels me to the elevator. I try not to find the silence awkward.

On the way down he asks, "Is there someone waiting for you?"

"Yes," I say. "A friend is picking me up." I lied to the nurses about this, too—even faked a phone conversation—so I wouldn't have to call in favors to get my car home. I'm parked in the lot. I can drive.

I watch the elevator's floor indicator like strangers always do and I want to strike up a conversation, I don't want Calvin to be a stranger, but everything I think to say seems stupid. So when we descend from three to two I err on the side of the law and ask, "Is Kay St. Claire still here?"

"I think so. But, like I told your partner, the only time I hear anything about patients is when the nurses are sweating."

"Andy was here?"

"If that's the cop who came by and asked about you again."

"About me?" *Again?* That wasn't Andy.

"He wanted to know if I knew anything, since I'm the one who found you in the stairwell. I guess he thought I could tell him, since I'm not a doctor."

It had to have been Ray Weiss. Why the fuck was he asking about me?

Calvin must peg me as panicked because he says, "I didn't tell the guy anything. It's hospital policy—I don't say what I see."

The elevator stops on Two and a woman gets on, phone to her ear. While she has the *I'm in the elevator, I might lose you* conversation with whoever's on the other end, I decide we both need to shut the fuck up.

Once we're off the elevator and approaching the front doors, I ask Calvin, "May I borrow your pen?"

I detach the HIPAA disclosure from my discharge papers and write my number on the back. Then I hand his pen back clipped to the HIPAA and I say, "I don't know what hospital policy is regarding you helping a patient."

"So . . ." he starts, obviously wondering about the number.

"So," I say, slipping off my ridiculous no-slip socks, the red-rubber-hearted soles keeping me from winding up on my ass. "I was here to talk to St. Claire. I'm very concerned for her well-being. Because as you know, Mr. Marble was able to get to her here, and that's pretty brazen. He is, obviously, a danger." I get up from the chair and pull on my boots and turn to face him. I still have to look up, but from here he's perfect. Per-fect-shun. And I swear I feel just fine.

"So . . ." he says again, since I still haven't mentioned the phone number.

"So, I need you."

Calvin looks about as interested as he does unsure, which is better than I expected.

"I need someone—you—to keep an eye on St. Claire," I explain, pressing my fingertips to the HIPAA disclosure he stowed in his shirt pocket. His chest is solid. "Would you call me?" I ask. "If anything seems screwy? You don't even need to tell me what it is. Just call."

"Okay," he says, though he's definitely unsure, now. He hands me the plastic bag one of the nurses packed with all my stuff.

"Okay, then." I turn and leave and I try to be smooth about it.

When I get to the parking lot, I stand there like an idiot while I try to remember where I parked. Then I hear—

"Miss Simonetti?"

And Calvin jogs up next to me with the box of Vanilla Kremes he rescued from underneath the wheelchair. "Are these yours?"

"Oh, I forgot." I take the box. "Probably seems cliché."

"No. I'd say this is all pretty unusual."

"I don't know if that's better or worse." I'm embarrassed, so I turn and wave, pretending I see my ride waiting just as far away from him as I can get. I hope I'll find my car nearby.

"Bye," I say, over my shoulder—over my shoulder enough to see he's watching me walk. I wonder how my ass looks. I wonder how he thinks it looks.

I wonder if it's Calvin or the exacerbation that makes it so I can barely feel my feet beneath me.

Isabel is waiting for me in Maricarmen's doorway. I swear she's taller. I put down the donuts and grab her up in my arms and I have never been so happy.

"Mama," she squeals. I don't correct her.

"Mama," Maricarmen says, different meaning, "Are you okay?"

"I'm better, now." Maybe not physically. But, I'm barefoot again, and, "I'm here." I press my lips against Isabel's head.

"Okay," Maricarmen says, gathering Isabel's stuff, "You gotta get her home. But you want to know there was a man outside your place this morning."

"What do you mean?" I try to keep the fear out of my voice, but I can't keep it from making the rest of me tense, so I hug Isabel some more.

"I don't know," Maricarmen says. "I put the baby pool in the front and I was watching Isabel swim. But then I see this man, down by your house, and I figure it's a delivery or something, because he had the hat. I thought he was lost, so I yelled down there. That's when he took off. I called to Geraldo—my cousin? He was here for lunch—and told him to stay with Isabel. I went down there, and that's when I saw there was no box or nothing. He wasn't there to deliver nothing but trouble."

I put Isabel down and she goes straight for the donuts. It's after eight, and she shouldn't have any more sugar, but I don't stop her. She takes two.

I ask, "What did the guy look like?"

"He had dark clothes, like the hat, black, or brown—"

"What about the man, what color was he?"

"I don't know, Mama, on this block, everybody looks Mexican to me."

"Was he younger than me? Older than you?"

"Everybody is younger than me."

"Was he taller than me? Shorter than you?"

"He was tall."

But. Maricarmen is 4'11". Tall is also everybody.

"How about facial hair?"

"I don't think so? He had a lot of hair on his head, though."

"I thought he wore a hat." My own hair stands on end.

"Under the hat. It just, it stuck out to me, I wanna say."

"I'm sure it was nobody." I say this because eyewitnesses always confabulate evidence. And my questions were leading. And, I don't want her to worry. No sense in both of us doing it.

She takes Isabel's other donut. "You want my boys to come past, make sure it's nobody?"

"I've got a whole police force for that." Johnny Marble knows my name, but he'd be a fool to find me. Wouldn't he?

"I just worry," Mari says. "You girls home alone—"

"Home?" Isabel asks, looking up at me and smiling, her face vanilla-frosted.

"We'll be fine." I hope I sound believable. I grab Isabel's bags. "Come on, baby."

"*Buenas noches,*" Mari says, watching us go. I'm sure she'll send her boys past, once we're home. I'm glad for that.

There's still a little daylight, so I leave the car where it is and we walk. Well, I walk, and I carry Isabel. And I feel strong. There's something about having her in my arms that steadies my nerves.

Except that one nerve Mari hit, the man outside my place.

I feel like I'm on patrol as I watch the street at the same time I ask Isabel all kinds of innocuous things, like, "Did you have a good time?" and "Did you make cookies?" and "Did you learn any new words?" She answers "*Si*" to everything.

As we approach the house, I feel both anxious and fierce, police training and mama-bear instinct intensified by steroids making my attitude, if nothing else, lethal. At the door I step over a pile of mail and disable the alarm, which I had installed after Tom left. Yes, I have a personal gun tucked away. A Ruger LCP. No, I don't ever want to untuck it. Not with Isabel here.

"Heyo?" she asks the house, her little helium voice rising so high that I imagine a question mark.

I lock the front door and reset the alarm and sit on the floor to rub my knees, another two reasons I shouldn't wear heeled boots. I work my numb fingers along the sides of each of my legs and it feels like someone else is doing the massaging.

Yes, this is a strange MS-plus, but since human touch is scientifically proven to be physically and emotionally beneficial for health, at least I've got me. As much as I hate being alone, I'm not such bad company.

"Nest?" Isabel asks when she comes back, with Meatball, to find me right where we started. She rubs her eyes.

"Absolutely," I say, because the dove's nest, as we call it, is our bedtime ritual, and my favorite part of every day. "Let's get dry pants first."

In her room, I change her diaper and we make funny faces and we laugh. I like feeling silly. I like making dumb noises that would be embarrassing in any other circumstance.

Then she gets serious because she needs to rearrange her stuffed animals. She likes things in order. She doesn't get that from her dad.

While she's organizing, I search the house for a pacifier—she has at least four, though I can never find one right off. I finally dig one out from between couch cushions. Then I disable the alarm for the back balcony, round up Isabel and Meatball, and take them out back.

"Aypane?" she asks, as though I make them appear.

"I'm sure we'll see one." I lift her into the dove's nest—actually a bunch of lawn-chair cushions and pillows I stripped from Tom's outdoor furniture and put inside an upended round table. "You two get comfortable," I say while I check the fenced-in yard below where the rest of the furniture sits bare. I've got sensors down there; nobody's set them off.

I climb in beside Meatball, and we lie on our backs and look up at the sky. Tonight there are snips of sunset colors, wisps of clouds and, most importantly—

"There's one!" I exclaim when I see a plane headed to O'Hare— and I really do exclaim—"Where's it going?"

"Antanta," Isabel says, because she either chooses there, where Tom is, or California, where I wish I were. Or sometimes she says Lombard. Where George is. Sad that they all seem equally impossible to visit.

"You want me to tell you a story about Atlanta?"

"Antanta." That's her *yes*.

I've never been to Atlanta; it's where Tom went to open up another Cloverleaf, his gimmick bar. He would never call it a gimmick, but finding a new cop-populated neighborhood to open another "public house" that sells Irish beer on the cheap seems like a pretty good scheme to me. In Edison Park it works like gangbusters. I certainly bought my share of rounds there, before Tom started comping them.

"Antanta!" Isabel demands, because I didn't actually say any of that.

"Okay: Jezebel Pickle goes to Atlanta." Jezebel is our main character. She helps people out of pickles, or she eats them, depending on my mood.

"Once upon a time," I start, "Jezebel is asked to help an old lady named Kay who lives in Atlanta. So she flies down there—"

"Aypane!"

"That's right. On an airplane. And when she gets there she finds Kay and she sees that the old lady is sad. Because her dog—what's her dog's name?"

"Juan." Juan is Maricarmen's grandson. The one I helped out. Isabel must've seen him, and probably a kid or two of his, when she stayed this time. I'm thankful she didn't come home throwing signs.

"Juan snapped at Kay and ran away," I say. "And so Jezebel takes the job. And she finds Juan, of course. But he's mean and ferocious and he barks and he bites."

Isabel pops in her pacifier and snuggles against me and pulls the bear to her face, all precursors to la-la land.

I tell her some more of the story, the Jezebel version of my incident with Johnny Marble, and I'm trying to find a way toward a satisfying conclusion but before I get there, I look down at Isabel, and she is passed out. Dead weight, dreamland.

Good thing, because I wasn't sure I could sell a happy ending.

Since she's asleep, I'm content to stay awhile and snuggle. It's amazing, how a little kid who just wants familiar comfort provides it, tenfold.

When the sky's blue goes black and clouds come in, orange against the city lights, I take Isabel into her room and hold her in my arms for a few minutes more, swaying just so. Seeing her sleep so peacefully always puts me at ease; I figure I must be doing something right.

Then I hear my phone, the real world intruding. Nerves raveled, I'm as gentle as I can be as I put her in her crib and get the call just in time.

"Hello?"

"Hello," a robot says, "this is CVS pharmacy calling for, Gina, Simonetti. Your prescription is ready for pickup—"

I hang up, go back into Isabel's room, and get another look at her. I'll do it for her.

For her, I'll do whatever it takes.

5

"Mabicabi?" Isabel mumbles through her pacifier. When she wakes up, she's in the car seat and we're on our way to daycare.

I turn to show her the smile on my face. "No, baby. Today is Miss Gabby."

"Miss Gabby!"

I'm glad she loves daycare. That makes it suck just a little less for me.

The pharmacy is out of the way but it has a drive-through, and keeping Isabel strapped in saves time. I don't know why I'm in a hurry to get to the station; nobody's expecting me.

When I get the scrip I call Metzler. "Your turn," I say to his voice-mail.

"Your turn," Isabel repeats.

"That's right," I say, because her *r*'s are starting to sound like *r*'s.

We park outside Diana's, a Puerto Rican place on Augusta, for *empanadillas* and *platanos maduros* to go. We stuff our faces while we walk to West Town Day Care, a converted house on Sacramento across from the park. I like that they take the kids outside when it's nice. And that Isabel gets to run in the grass. Feel the sun on her face. Chase around a wide-open space.

I try not to think about the sickos who troll the park for kicks, the gangs who supposedly put their differences aside to play basketball on the court across the street, or the fact that I'm leaving a baby in a place where gunshots ring out as often as summertime fireworks.

"Good morning, Isabel," Gabby says when she opens the front door and buzzes the gate. She looks like she rolled into work straight from last night's club.

Some parents might object to leaving their kid with a twenty-something who parties, but I think twentysomething girls should party, so long as they can hack a hangover well enough to show up the next day. I wouldn't be able to handle a throng of toddlers for eight hours on my best day. It's not rocket science; it takes more patience.

Anyway, there was only one time I thought about offering Gabby a couple Tylenol.

I help Isabel climb the steps. I wipe her hands and face and hug her before I hand her off along with the week's payment.

"Bye," Isabel says, her confident little bird-peep voice.

"I love you," I say, and I have to get out of there before I snatch her back and take her with me. I feel that impulse every time, and every time I have to remind myself that daycare is the only way I can get another day with her.

My commute to the station is quick and I'm in the parking lot at Area Central before I finish the *empanadillas*. I did buy six. I try to actually chew the last two.

Just before eight o'clock I check my makeup in the rearview and change into heels. I've got to stand tall today. I've got to walk the walk.

When I get upstairs on the floor, I find Majette holding court with a couple patrollers. I walk up behind him as he's saying—

". . . the suspect gets the big idea he's going to rape her. He fuckin' tells her so. What's she going to do? No gun. No backup. And she knows this psycho already beat on his own mother, so it's not like he's gonna go soft for anybody. He's not going to listen to reason. So he's got her pinned there in the stairwell, and he's taking off his belt. But Simonetti? She's not going down that way. So she goes for his ballsack—"

"I did the four-ball, actually," I interrupt; may as well do some street-fight damage to Marble's eyes while I'm recounting my supposed heroics. Majette's version obviously isn't accurate, either, but in this room, a good story can't be entirely true.

Parrillo, one of the uniforms, says, "I don't know how Marble walked away after that, girl."

"He ran." It's not a lie.

The guys circle around me, waiting for the rest of it. Good thing I've got it rehearsed.

"It was pretty intense," I say. "Majette's right, the guy was psycho . . ."

Then everybody gets quiet, faces straight, like what I said was preposterous. "What?"

I turn around. The answer is Iverson. She's come up the steps behind me.

"Simonetti." She doesn't look surprised. Or pleased. Then again, she's got the reputation for being about as personal as a backhoe.

She says, "My office."

When I follow her in there she shuts the door and directs me to the folding chair in front of her desk. She asks, "How are you?" just like she would ask anybody else, if she had to.

"I'm great," I say, and as soon as I sit down I want to get up; I feel like a speed train, unstoppable, and I don't want to pull the brake. "I'm ready to work."

Iverson sits down. "I don't get it. Any normal cop in your situation milks the Medical. Goes to the fucking Bahamas with paid leave and a clear conscience and only comes back when the physical therapist won't let him skate anymore. This is not that. What is this?"

Part of me thinks she knows what this is, and that she's hoping I'll tell her so I'll prove we share a trust.

The other part of me thinks she suspects what this is, and that if I tell her I'll prove to be an idiot asking to get fired.

So now, for my next performance: "I think you know enough about my situation with my brother's child to know I've got to provide a stable home."

"Your personal life is not my problem. Unless this thing with Johnny Marble is personal?"

"Only in that he assaulted me."

"He didn't do anything to you until you went looking for him."

"I wasn't looking for him. Duppstadt called and asked me about a case I caught last week. Marble's the suspect. After Dupe told me what happened to Kay St. Claire, I offered to go talk to her."

"On your day off."

"I had time."

"Bullshit. Why didn't Kanellis go?"

Now she's angling—trying to get me to bust Dupe or Andy to save myself. But if I didn't do anything wrong, "I take full responsibility."

"Including whatever damage was incurred by chasing the alleged suspect?"

"What, he's going to sue me? He saw me, he ran. I ran after him."

"And then?"

Here goes. "Marble exited the stairwell and ran down the stairs. I followed. As I was pursuing him, hospital security entered below— from the first floor—and Marble must've assumed he was trapped. I was descending the stairs when he came back up at me. I thought

I had enough momentum. I threw myself at him. I thought I could keep him off his feet until security reached us."

"What about your service weapon?"

"Marble stripped it. He stripped my gun from my hands." There. I said it: I told the lie. I look at my hands.

Iverson doesn't say anything. Does she know I'm lying?

I look at her; I know I've got to be firm on this point: "I knew there were civilians present—in the stairwell below, and in the halls and behind the walls all around us. I was not going to use my gun unless I had to. So I fought him. He overpowered me—"

"—And took your gun."

"Yes."

I look up at her. She is smiling.

"What?"

"How do you feel?"

"Fine." She can't see my hands tingling.

"You're sweating."

"It's hot in here."

"You're shaking."

Fuck. She knows. "I'm nervous. I didn't know I'd have to defend myself—"

"What did you think was going to happen? Coming here?"

"I thought I'd be getting back to work. My doctor said I'd be cleared with the medical section—"

"And you wanted to make a show of it."

"A show?" She's calling me on it. I'm too rehearsed. But, "No show. I want to help Kay St. Claire. And Rosalind Sanchez—they're the real victims."

Iverson sits back. "I'm sorry, but that's just fucking stupid. You aren't a social worker. You don't sympathize with victims. And you don't get credit for a fight you lose any sooner than you do for winning one without following the rules. Like I told you the last time you sat in that chair: this job is not about you. It's about safely and systematically getting the bad guys." She looks at me and waits until I make eye contact again and then she says, "I don't think you can do it."

"Are you firing me?" I can't believe it. I feel stuck to the seat.

"No. I do that now, and I'm the one admitting your mistakes." She leans forward, over her desk. "Twice now you've shown me you think the chase is more important than the charge. That's not being police. It can't happen again."

"I understand."

"I want to be on your side. I want to believe you respect the rules. But if you want to keep the Job, you've got to get smart. You want to keep the Job, you stick with this plan: you take the Medical and a day or two at home while I find you a desk. You play nice with whichever dick I send over to follow up with you about your gun. And you let us get Marble."

"You're telling me if I want to work, I can't work?"

"That's right."

I try to look like I'm okay with the plan. I don't think I pull it off. "Are there any leads? On Marble?"

"I've got the best people I know on the case."

"Weiss," I say, because he's the only one I know, but I immediately feel like I gave away a secret.

"Weiss is one of them, yes." She says his name like he's a square of sod.

"He came to the hospital," I explain, as if he isn't a threat, investigating me instead of Marble.

"Do you have a problem with Weiss?"

"No."

"I don't know if I do or not." She sits back again. "No matter. I only need him to find Marble. You: you're the one who's going to put him away."

"You want me to testify? As a victim?"

"A victim, yes, and a hero. Unless there's some truth you don't think you should tell." She isn't saying I should perjure myself. She's saying if I'm going to come clean, I should do it now.

I can't. "I'll testify. Of course."

"Good. Just make sure you sit on your hands, or something. The shaking is questionable." Iverson waves at the door. "Now please, get out of here." She finds paperwork in front of her and begins to read, her goodbye.

"Okay," I say, dumbstruck.

I get up and go out and close the door behind me and I try for a game face but really, I must look like I just got my star taken away, so I make like I'm in a rush and head for the elevator. Nobody bugs me. Maybe they think I just got my star taken away.

When I get in the elevator, I'm alone, and I see myself in the mirrored security camera. It distorts my face so my eyes sit on the sides of my head and my nose is a flattened hook.

I'm as stupid as I look, if I believe Iverson is on my side. She acts like she's giving me a chance, but if she wants me to testify, what she really wants is for this Marble case to go away, me first.

The thing is? I can't testify. Because it will be a case against Marble for what he did to me—not his mother, not Sanchez—just me. And it will come down to my version of the fight versus his. And Marble will be the one telling the truth.

That means I've got to get somebody else to take the stand.

I call Metzler on my way to Rosalind Sanchez's apartment.

I get his voice mail. "Hi Rick, it's Regina. There must have been a mix-up with the Medical Section—they put me on limited release. I can't do the job from a desk. Will you please call me back?"

I get stuck in traffic on the Dan Ryan, so I get my book and use the time to go over what I know about Sanchez.

By the time I spoke to her last Thursday, she'd changed her mind about pressing charges, so most of what I've got comes secondhand from Mike Day, the responding officer, and he didn't give me much either. I know Sanchez is a student at UIC. She lives on campus and works part-time at Fatso's, a hamburger joint in Ukrainian Village. The night of the assault she'd been at work, and just after midnight set out to grab a beer with a friend. That's when Marble attacked her.

Sanchez knew Marble—he was a regular customer at Fatso's. She told Day that Marble was a weirdo, and that he would often sit and watch her.

At one point she complained to her boss, but he told her if she wanted to be choosy about her clientele, she should get a job selling something nicer than hamburgers.

Sanchez said Marble didn't visit Fatso's the night of the attack. She saw him later, on her way down Rice Street. As he approached, she recognized him and started for the other side of the street. She hadn't stepped off the curb before he headed her off and hit her twice: a one-two, chest and face. Broken rib, black eye.

The motive is unclear because he didn't filch her bag or feel her up—no robbery, no sexual contact. He just stood over her on the sidewalk. Sanchez said he studied her "like a bug." And then he left her there.

Just like he did with me.

When I talked to Sanchez, she acted like I was the one who assaulted her. She was defensive, almost defiant. I guessed she'd been over the incident so many times that her own story made her too afraid to fight him. I did get her to admit she didn't do anything to deserve the attack, and that she didn't want to go to court and face "that monster." I told her if she didn't take him to court, it might happen to someone else. She declined.

I hope she'll change her mind when she finds out it happened to me.

I park outside her apartment on West Fourteenth Street just before ten. I thought about calling, but I don't want the safe separation between us to make *no* easy for her. I leave my star and my book in the glove box and change into runners. I want her to see me, not an authority.

The girl who answers the door is on her way out, and she is not Rosalind Sanchez. She wears black skinny jeans and a black tank and her dyed-black hair is a precise frame for her catlike face.

"Hi, I'm looking for Rosalind."

"She's not here."

"Do you know when she might be back?"

"I'm Rosie's roommate. Not her mom. I don't keep tabs." The girl locks the door, both of us outside of it. "I'm late for class." She fakes a smile and departs in long strides down the sidewalk. Catwalk.

"Nice attitude," I say.

She glances back, cuts me a look.

I let it go. I don't know why pretty young girls get so mean.

I go back to the car and call Sanchez. She doesn't answer. I don't leave a message.

I hang up and call Andy.

"Gina: I was just about to come visit."

"Just in time. They let me out last night."

"No kidding? How do you feel?"

"Starved. Can I buy you lunch?"

"I'm off lunch."

"What, you're on the no-food diet now?" The last one was no-carb. Which meant no beer. It didn't last.

"Protein shakes, baby." Andy uses *baby* like an exclamation point, and he says it to everyone, so I don't take it as a slight.

"What are we talking?" I ask. "Steak through a straw? I might be hungry enough."

"Why don't you come by the house and I'll fix you one? I'm sticking around today. I got carpet cleaners coming."

"Okay. Tell Loni I'm on the way."

Loni is a six-pound fluffball dog. A Bolognese. She was Donna's. Donna was Andy's wife. Cancer got her, quick and unsentimental, about a year ago. I tried to be there for Andy, but he said I'd just be one more person who'd say they don't know what to say. He was right.

Loni's got what's left of Andy's heart. That's why the carpet cleaners. The day Donna died, the dog started peeing in the bedroom. At first, Andy thought she'd become incontinent. Tests turned up nothing. The vet theorized that Loni was depressed and gave her antidepressants. Those improved the dog's demeanor, but made her preference for the bedroom even stronger. Andy tried enzymatic cleaner and tin foil. Then chemical deterrents. Then reward training. Then he put her food there; she peed on that. Next, he tried locking her out; she spent the night scratching at the door. When he tried locking her up, she spent that night scratching herself. He's ripped out the carpet. Twice.

And, Loni's got no competition. I know this because his hot young girlfriend sleeps in the spare room when she stays the night.

On my way up to Andy's I try Metzler again. I don't leave a message. After that I call headquarters and get put through to the Medical Section. I tell the operator who I am and ask to speak to my case manager.

I get voice mail. "Hello, this is Elaine Brille at extension 15539. I'm out of the office today. Please leave a message and I will return your—" I'm not going to bitch on record, so I hang up.

I turn off the main drag early and cut through the neighborhoods. Andy lives in Edison Park, home of the Cloverleaf. I won't drive by the bar. Of course that doesn't stop me from wondering about Tom.

When he left the first time, in January, it was a trip to Atlanta to scout a lease. He'd wanted to open another Cloverleaf for a while, and the deal seemed like a sure thing. He said he'd split time, here and there. I didn't like the idea because I didn't want a part-time boyfriend, but I didn't say no because he never signed up to be a full-time dad. Funny, how I thought we could make it work.

During his second trip in February, I discovered that the broker he hired in Atlanta was an old girlfriend, and that Tom's plan was to split time between us, too. Funny, how he thought we could make *that* work.

I spent Valentine's Day putting all his shit in the basement, and celebrated with Isabel and a two-pound bag of M&Ms.

In March, Tom left me a voice mail—the deal in Atlanta, and likely the deal with the old girlfriend—went bad. It wasn't a call to apologize, though. He just wanted to tell me he thought we should sell the house.

I called him back, said, *sure thing.*

We haven't yet come to terms.

Andy is outside his place smoking a cigarette when I pull up.

"They let you drive?" He always has to say something stupid like that when he gives me a hug.

And I always have to say something like, "Try not to slobber on my shoulder."

"I'm glad you're okay, G."

I smile; I want him to think I am. "How about that shake?"

He responds by rocking his hips in a move that is one-hundred-percent white guy and should be even more embarrassing, but he plays it through, well past the joke, and he takes such joy in it that I actually find the whole thing kind of sexy. I say this with nothing but platonic love. And also a head injury.

He stomps out his cigarette and I follow him up to the house.

Inside, Loni gives me the stink eye from her perch on the back of the couch. I'm not a threat, but I'm not Donna, either.

"Hi, Bologna," I say. "You know, you remind me: I have to pee."

Andy says, "Make sure you put the seat back up."

I duck into the bathroom.

I sit on the toilet and look around. The tub is filthy, but must be functional, since a damp towel hangs from the shower curtain rod. Andy still hasn't painted, or replaced the mirror. He started the renovation when he went on furlough, a few months after Donna died. It's been at least six months since furlough. This is the only bathroom in the house. When I'm through, I try to wash my hands, but the faucet doesn't work. I look at a blank wall. I don't know how he can stand it. He can't see himself.

In the kitchen, Andy's filling a fancy blender with soy milk, almonds, sugar-free maple syrup, and protein powder. He smokes while he does this.

I get in the way to wash my hands. "You're a real advertisement. I don't know for what."

"The Vitamix sells itself. I can make avocados into ice cream with this thing."

"And here I didn't think you could fuck up fudge marble."

"It's healthy."

"So is an apple."

"If cynicism is the key to longevity, you're going to be one hell of an old lady."

"Cynicism is no match for secondhand smoke."

He runs the blender.

When he's done I tell him, "I went to work today."

"To prove that you sustained significant head trauma?" He coaxes the goopy brown mix into a tall glass.

"I thought you would be impressed."

"Nope."

"Iverson wasn't, either."

"C'mon. She's trying to protect you. The press gets this? You know how they love to string us up. You'll be the bad guy. The loose cannon. The white cop who went after the unarmed black. Iverson can't risk the attention. She needs this filed and forgotten."

"Then how come she wants me to testify?"

Andy takes a strong drag from his smoke. After he blows it out he says, "Well, either she wants to do you a solid, or she wants you gone."

"She says she's on my side."

"Then you're fine." He puts a straw in the glass, hands it over. "Try the shake."

I do. It's awful. "Listen," I say, after I manage to swallow, "I'm walking a real fine line between being tolerated and being terminated. I need to show Iverson I'm real police."

Andy stubs out his smoke. "I get it, Gina. I've chased plenty of bad guys during bad times. That's why I get it. Because I used to be like you. I used to think it was my job to fix other people's problems. But now I know that was just a real good way to ignore my own shit."

Andy's phone buzzes and when he checks the display, his expression falls somewhere between curious and resigned. It's probably a text from the girlfriend.

"Whose problems are you fixing now?"

He puts down the phone without responding. "Mine. All mine."

I think about his bathroom. I hold the thought. "Marble is my problem. I need to find him." I think about another sip of the smoothie. The thought is as far as I take it.

"You can't do anything, Gina. If Iverson wants you to testify, there's no room to fuck up between now and then."

My phone's the one that buzzes this time. It's a call from a number I don't recognize. Maybe Metzler from some hospital. Maybe Elaine Brille from an extension. Maybe, just maybe, Rosalind Sanchez.

"I have to take this."

When I step into the front room, Loni gives me a dismissive look and titters into the kitchen.

"Simonetti," I answer.

"Hello, Gina? This is Calvin. From Sacred Heart?"

Holy shit. "Hi." I hear my voice and it doesn't sound like me so I don't know what else to say.

"You told me to call, about Kay St. Claire? This is left field, but she needs a ride."

If I can't get Sanchez to talk, St. Claire is my only hope. "I'm on my way."

I hang up and go back into the kitchen and find Andy slicing avocados.

"You'll love the ice cream," he says.

"Kanellis. I don't need ice cream. I need help."

Loni scratches at his ankles and he picks her up and hand-feeds her a chunk of avocado. "I'm sorry, Gina. I can't."

"Says the one who got me into this."

"Now I'm saying you should get out." Loni licks his face and I want to knock them both over like one of Isabel's paper-block towers.

"I'll get out of *here*," I say, and I make for the door. When I get there I say, "I hope that bitch pees on your pillow."

6

Having been through Sacred Heart's disorganized discharge process yesterday I figure I have plenty of time to stop for a taco and guacamole at L'Patron on my way back through the city. I try not to think about Andy as I sit in my car and stuff my face. Avocados, I'd like to tell him, were meant for this.

I'm parked in the hospital rotunda when a dozen hospital staff members exit the building carrying matching cardboard file boxes packed with personal items, the telltale sign of a layoff. Three gentlemen in suits, who must be either private hires or Feds, herd them away from the entrance. I see James Novak, the CEO, just inside. He looks displeased. Though I can't imagine anyone actually wants to choose a hospital, the situation can't be good for business.

Most of the staff wander a similar path to the parking lot; some stop to commiserate. I recognize my nurse Victoria. She turns to another woman in scrubs and they hold hands and whisper and wipe tears until one of the suits tries to urge them along.

Victoria gives the woman a hug and gives the suit the finger.

Behind the suit, Novak is there, stifling a grin.

Mine's not stifled.

Amidst all the sad so-longing, Calvin wheels Kay St. Claire outside. I jump out of the car and hope he doesn't see me check my teeth for shredded beef.

When they roll up, St. Claire sees me and asks, "Is this the car service?"

"As you requested," Calvin says.

"I'm Gina," I say, to see if my name rings any bells.

"Gina," she says, and she seems pleased. She obviously doesn't remember me and she doesn't mistake me for anybody, either.

I help Calvin help her into the passenger seat. He smells nice. She doesn't. I buckle her belt.

"Here are your walking papers," Calvin says to her. "You're probably the only one happy to be getting these today."

Kay tucks her discharge forms squarely into her giant purse and when I close the door and step onto the curb to have a quiet word with Calvin, she gazes out the passenger window, like there's something scenic about Sacred Heart's apparent lack of heart.

I say, "I forgot my chauffeur hat."

"It was the only thing I could think of," Calvin says. "Her caregiver doesn't drive. She refused to let her daughter come. I knew she wouldn't agree to a police escort. And as you can see, we don't have the resources for a hospital chaperone at the moment."

"Budget cuts?"

"No budget to cut. The state stepped in this morning. They say this place has millions in unpaid bills on account of the low-income patients. The state offered some money to stay up and running in exchange for some restructuring. It's looking more like a demolition to me."

"What about you? It's pretty brave to run outside hospital policy right now, isn't it? What if St. Claire finds out you lied?"

"Paperwork right there in her purse says this *is* a police escort."

"That means I'm the one who has to lie."

"You're a detective, right? Isn't lying what you do? To get people to talk?"

"I see the department's reputation precedes me."

"Well, you don't *have* to lie—"

"One six five—" Calvin's radio cuts in, "security to Northeast Four, station fourth floor northeast, a former employee is attempting to leave the premises with hospital property—"

"One six five, responding," Calvin says. "You got her?" he asks me; it's clear he's got to go.

"Okay." But wait: "The number you called from earlier—was it a hospital line?"

"My cell."

"Good. I'll be in touch. To follow up about St. Claire." I had to tack on that last bit; I got shy.

"I don't need to know about St. Claire," he says.

"Oh. Well." Shit.

Then he says, "You should call, though."

I smile and I leave it at that because that's exactly where to leave it.

When I get in the car St. Claire says, "This is a nice car."

"Thank you." She obviously hasn't noticed the car seat, the ever-lingering odor of sour milk, or the pervasive stickiness. I just hope she doesn't ask for music because the radio doesn't work and the only CD I've got is *Green Gorilla Monster & Me*.

I key the ignition. "Where to?"

"Thirty-twenty-four North Racine, please."

"Lake View?"

"No, you can't see the lake from there."

I was talking about the neighborhood—Lake View—because there are at least four hospitals in between here and there. I don't get why they'd transport her all this way. It's got to be some insurance thing.

I head north on Kedzie over some rough blocks, liquor stores and liquor drinkers on every other corner, the street as acceptable as anywhere else to congregate. Kay looks out the window; in its reflection, her face is blank.

At a stop sign, three boys hanging out on a broken bike rack are a picture of summertime boredom, the bills of their hats pulled crooked, a bag of barbecue potato chips and a palm-passed joint the only things on deck for the afternoon. They watch us stop, and go, though I'm sure we are a blur.

"Where are you taking me?" Kay asks.

"I'm taking you home."

"This isn't the way."

"Should I take a different route?"

"You should let me drive. I have a perfect driving record."

"I don't think that's within company policy."

"I would pay you."

"It's not the money."

"I don't think you know where you're going."

"I can show you," I say, pulling up a city map on my phone.

She refuses. "I don't understand those devices. I don't like this." She starts to look panicked. "Who are you?"

"I'm Gina," I say.

"Where are we going?"

"Home." I crack my window. Thanks to Isabel, I've learned to curb both endless repetition and potential meltdowns by offering seeming opportunities, so, "You know what? It's nice outside." I roll down her window. "Look. The breeze is nice. It'll help shake that hospital chill. And here"—I turn into Humboldt Park—"I'll cut through the park. We can chase the breeze."

"The breeze?" Kay asks, like it's a questionable concept. But she reaches her arm out the window, lets her fingers swim in the air, and seems to shift mental gears. She says, "I started driving when I was thirteen years old. My daddy's tractor first, and then his car."

I guess toddler logic worked. I think about using it to gently broach the Johnny Marble subject, so I don't sound like a cop. The thing is, toddlers aren't gentle about anything. They're just honest. So, what the fuck.

I say, "I'm sure you're a better driver than I am. You know, I totaled a car once." I don't tell her it was a squad, or that it was six weeks ago.

"What happened?"

"Well, it was real hot outside, and the air-conditioning wasn't working. And I have this disease where if I get overheated, I have issues. So I was driving and I got what's called transient disability glare. I was suddenly blind in one eye. It threw my depth perception off and so I wound up sideswiping the car next to me and spinning out."

Kay looks at me like I just told her exactly what I just told her.

"Don't worry," I say. "I'm fine now. Well, not *fine*. Lately, I'm having trouble with my hands. And my feet. My left foot feels like a bird claw. Or that's how I imagine it. But it's nothing new, and it'll go away. And you know, I feel a hell of a lot better now that I'm out of the hospital. What about you?"

"Are you crazy?"

"No. I'm just telling the truth. What about you? Why were you in the hospital?"

"Well," she says, and she starts to laugh, "they think I'm crazy."

"I was talking about your eye."

"What's wrong with my eye?" She touches it and flinches; a rediscovery. "I guess I must've upset Daddy again."

I've heard it's common for people with Alzheimer's to dwell on a certain point in their history. Something so deeply imprinted on the brain it remains as clear as today. No way Kay's father is still alive, but he might've left some real marks when he was.

"Robin says it was your son Johnny who did that to your eye," I say, to bring her from the bad old days to the bad nowadays.

"Robin doesn't like Johnny."

I stop on the red at Diversey and pretend to look at my map while I switch to the Smart Voice app. I should record this, if only so I can play it back for her should I have to convince her to testify.

"Do you remember, Kay, was it Johnny?"

"He was frustrated," she says. "He never had it easy. And he never would accept my help. Even when he lost his job. You know, I think he lost his self-worth right along with it."

"The same thing happened with my brother," I tell her. "He got hurt on a construction job. Had to have back surgery. But he didn't want my help. He didn't want anything, really, except painkillers."

"Oh, honey, I'm sorry to say it sounds like we have a lot in common. Johnny's on more drugs than I am."

And . . . we're getting somewhere. "What does he do for work?" I ask, to keep her talking.

"He's a musician."

"What does he play?"

"Music."

Of course. "Do you like his music?"

"He doesn't let me listen anymore. Not since he left."

"Moved out, you mean? Because he still comes around, obviously."

She doesn't answer that. Just looks off, somewhere past here.

I say, "I guess it's hard to stay mad."

"Mad isn't much, when you love someone."

I wait to turn onto Lakewood while a woman pushes a stroller across the street, the canopy pulled.

"Isn't that nice," Kay says.

"I have a little girl," I tell her, again.

"Oh, little girls are wonderful. Until they aren't yours anymore. Boys—they'll always be Mama's. There's a dependence, there."

I wonder if that's why she won't press charges. "Is Johnny dependent on you?"

She looks over at me. "Who are you?"

Here we go again. "I'm Gina. Your driver." I hear the impatience in my voice. As though she's wrong. As though I'm not leading her on. Still. "I was asking about Johnny because you'd said once that he's the one who gave you the black eye."

"My eye?" She touches it again. Realizes. Says, "It wasn't my Johnny. It was the police."

I stop the Smart Voice app because suddenly I don't feel so smart. Why did I think I could get a confession from a woman who, lucid or not, only wants to protect her son? "The police beat you up," I say, not that I need her to elaborate.

"Yes. Well. I was so angry when they said I had to pay to keep Johnny out of jail."

"I don't think that's how it works," I say.

"Now you think I'm crazy, when I'm telling the truth."

"You're claiming the police are extorting you—"

"They said I couldn't be with Johnny. Daddy agreed. They sent him away."

She's getting worked up now, and she must be drawing from that deep brain imprint.

"I'm sorry," I say. I shouldn't have pushed. I only confused us both.

I pull over and park. We're six blocks away. So long as Kay knows the gas from the brake, we can make it. And god damn, after what I just put her through, she deserves to make at least one good memory.

"What are you doing?" Kay asks.

"I'm thinking: screw company policy. You want to drive?"

Kay's hair stands on end, static, an extension of her delight. She says, "I have a perfect driving record."

Six blocks later I'm thankful there is no actual company that has any sort of policy. Kay may as well have been driving a tractor.

"There's the house," she says and turns hard, wheels bucking the curb, then climbing it. "I don't remember the street being in such bad shape," she says, like the pavement is the problem.

She unbuckles her belt and starts to get out; the front right wheel is wedged up on the curb so the car can't roll but—

"You have to put it in park—"

"Where?"

"Press the brake," I tell her and when she does I shift the gear. "There. Park."

"Park," she repeats, like it's a pleasing new concept. Then she gets out and stops on the sidewalk in front of the house, outside the gate. It's an old brown-brick duplex on a corner lot. It looks like it's been remodeled at least once: newer windows with honeycomb blinds, modern landscaping, a bright red door. And even if it hadn't been updated since it was built, the address is money. She must have some.

I grab Kay's bag and get out to wish her well. The chauffeur routine was a nice idea, but I'm no better undercover than Kay is behind the wheel. Anyway I've got to get back, pick up Isabel.

When I approach, Kay's mouth hangs open. She says, "I never wanted to leave this place."

"I'm sure you're glad to be home. I've got your bag, here. Are your keys inside?"

"Keys," she repeats, like she has a vague recollection.

"Should I check?"

"Oh, CeCe. I don't have the keys anymore."

"I'm Gina."

"Isn't it beautiful?" She curls her knobbed fingers around the wrought-iron fence.

I check the gate. It's locked. "How are you supposed to get in?"

"I didn't think about that."

I feel my temper surge. "You don't have keys? What are you supposed to do? Where is Robin?" I shake her bag. I hear keys. I go for them.

"Mrs. St. Claire," I say, and hold up her key ring, anchored by a plastic-framed photo featuring a mall-studio portrait of three of the same-looking kids no older than three.

I ask, "Will these help?"

I hand her the key ring. She looks at the photo. "Who are these people?"

"I don't know. Your grandkids?"

"I don't think so."

"Well, they're adorable."

"Of course they are," she says, "they're children."

I make that my segue. "Mrs. St. Claire, it's been a pleasure, but I have to go. My daughter is waiting for me at daycare."

"We'd better go, then."

"Thank—Sorry, what? We?"

"Well, I don't live here."

"This is thirty-twenty-four North Racine. That's what you said."

"Yes, that is what I said. And this *is* home. But I don't live here anymore. Not since Daddy moved us out to the farm."

"Which was . . . ?"

"The summer. 1959."

"Are you—" *fucking kidding me,* I'm about to say, and I'm pissed—I mean, I'm on the other side of town, I'm already late, and I had no idea we were following a sentimental map—but then I see Kay's face: the lines drawn away, hope in the hint of a smile. She is

home, that theoretical place so many of us spend our adult lives trying to re-create.

And then I think about how much time I give Isabel to get things
wrong. It's cute, when she botches an answer to a simple question,
or mixes up a name. I take pleasure in watching her think. Why am
I annoyed to see a grown woman struggle with the same things?

Tears get in Kay's eyes, another memory surfacing—1959, maybe.
When she was a girl. When she realized home wasn't here anymore.

"I'll give you a minute," I say, and I go back to the car; I'm not
going to be the one moving her out to the farm this time.

While I wait, I slip the hospital folder from her bag and check
page one, where her address is listed as 2221 West Haddon. We have
to double back to Ukrainian Village. I don't know why I didn't check
her paperwork.

And I don't know why I think I'm so great. I'm twenty-nine and
most of what I know I learned from the street or a Google search.
Kay is eighty. She has children. Grandchildren. A history. Even if her
mind is going, she's got a lot more to go on.

When she gets in the car, I ask, "Where to?"

I'm relieved when she tells me the correct address.

Afternoon traffic starts to build and I try not to bitch about it. I
can't blame Kay if I'm late. And anyway, if she remembers any of
this at all, I'd like her to remember me fondly once the noise of the
day burns off. I'd like her to remember the joy she felt, behind the
wheel.

When we get into the neighborhood, I realize Kay lives just blocks
from where Rosalind Sanchez was attacked. Makes sense; Marble
probably visits the hamburger joint and other local businesses when
he comes to visit. I should do the same, and soon.

I snake around a dead stop on Damen and take side streets and
when I pass St. Mary's of Nazareth Hospital and find Kay's street

runs right into it—literally dead-ends at the ambulance entrance—
I'm back to wondering why she was taken to Sacred Heart. Insurance is not the same as assurance, I guess.

I turn onto the street against the one way and back up to the address. Kay's is a two-story brick walk-up, one of the only original A-
frames on a street of old multi-units and gut rehabs whose structures
stand tall on property lines, the new houses' interior square footage
pushing sale prices into the millions. I'll bet there's at least one
developer who regularly checks for Kay's name in the obits.

I park in front of a hydrant and by the time Kay reaches for the
door I'm opening it, her bag and keys at the ready.

"Robin," she says.

"I'm Gina." I say it more patiently this time. I take her hand.

"Robin," she says again, and then I get that she's talking about
the rail-thin crew-cut blonde coming out her front gate.

Shit.

I slip the discharge paperwork from Kay's bag—I'm not supposed
to be the police, or a police escort, and I don't want to get caught in
a lie by somebody who won't forget.

"Mrs. Kay," Robin says, and I think she is beautiful except for her
uniform and until she smiles; nobody can wear scrubs with style, and
her equine teeth ruin her face. She greets Kay with a hug the old
woman doesn't appear to want.

"You're Robin?"

"Yes. And you—?"

"I'm late." I hand her Kay's bag and keys and make for the car.

"I didn't pay her," Kay says. "Wait—"

I don't.

7

I'm twenty minutes late to pick up Isabel, but we still have time to play before my IV treatment, so we make a pit stop at the playground north of Division.

While Isabel runs around the slides, I call Metzler for the third time. He doesn't answer. I'm starting to take it more personally.

At three-forty, the bell rings at the school across the street and a hundred grade-school kids burst out the doors. The kids are all older, faster, and more reckless than Isabel, so when they chase toward the playground I take Isabel over to the opportunistic ice-cream man who has parked his cart at the gate. I buy two coco locos and Isabel and I sit on the grass and watch the big kids.

Once the ice cream is gone and most of the school kids are, too, I say, "Spaghet, will you swing with me?"

She gets up and runs off toward the swing set.

"Wait for me!" I get up and three steps later, my left heel catches on the rubberized surface. I tumble. I roll. I recover.

Isabel comes back. "Mama?"

I find a smile and explain, "Somersault."

She giggles. She doesn't know a somersault from a degenerative disease, but she does think I'm pretty funny.

At the swings, I wedge my butt into the black rubber seat that cannot possibly be comfortable for any woman whose hipbones have given an inch. I lift Isabel up to straddle me. We take the chains, her little hands beneath mine. And then we swing.

When she leans back, mouth wide as her eyes, I see she's finally getting another tooth. She's in low percentiles for height and weight, too, but there isn't much I can do for her physical development. I can only help her heart and brain grow.

When I lean back, she lets go of the chains and wraps her arms around me. I close my eyes. I know that pretty soon, she'll want to swing by herself. Until then, I'll let her hold on, just like this.

I lean in. I whisper, "I'm with you." She knows.

When the clock turns four I promise her a treat at home and when we get there, I fix a plate of raisins and oyster crackers—still haven't made it to the grocery—and set her up in front of a Disney distraction, TV being the treat. Yes, I know, doctors say no screen time before age two. But please consider she came from a place where they never took her to the doctor and the tube was running Spike TV 24/7. This? For Isabel, this is therapy.

I eat a handful of her crackers and then I go into the front room and pace back and forth in the window as I wait for Lidia Marzalek, RN, from Complete Care LLC. It's five thirty-one; she should be here any minute ago.

At five forty-five, a woman in a curve-tailored business suit comes up the steps. She's got a briefcase. She looks sharp. I wonder if she's Iverson's. I open the door.

"Ms. Simonetti? Sorry I'm late. I'm Lidia, from Complete Care."

"Great," I say, without the enthusiasm that should accompany the word. I half hoped she was here to pry instead of poke. "Come on in."

She follows me into the kitchen. "I haven't been over this way in a while. Lots of new building going on."

"Uh-huh." I hate small talk, may as well make that clear. I move the newspaper and this morning's coffee cup off the kitchen table. "You can set up here."

"Have you lived here long?"

"Almost a year. We . . ." I hesitate because without Tom around, "we" makes it seem like Isabel is a decision maker. "I think it's a good investment. Do you want something to drink?"

"No, thank you."

I open the fridge and I'm glad she said no, because the only something I've got is a pair of light beers.

"Well, sweet thing," Lidia says. She's talking to Isabel, who's come in to investigate, and who's hiding her face with her hands. She still thinks she's invisible that way.

"Lidia works with me," I say, figuring Lidia's suit tells the same story. "We just have to do a little work."

"Help someone?" she asks, because that's what I tell her I do.

"That's right." I pick her up and kiss her face. "We are going to help someone, and I'll be done before you can count to a hundred."

"I not." She's right. She can't.

"But you can try."

"One," she starts, as I carry her back into the TV room. I plop her down on the couch and lose her to the singing princess before she gets to three.

Back in the kitchen, Lidia has everything ready to go, the needle assembled, the alcohol swabs torn open. She passes me some paperwork and a pen and asks, "You've had this treatment before?"

I know she's working from the medical order I'm about to sign and I know it includes all the information she needs, so, "Yes. Yesterday." I'm not going to offer anything extra.

"Have you experienced any side effects?"

"Nothing unmanageable."

"I have a heparin lock, will it be okay to leave the catheter in for the remaining three treatments?"

"No." I'm not prepared to have the "What is that?" conversation with Isabel. Or anybody else.

"I understand," Lidia says, "but I always ask."

I sign the order and pass it back.

She swabs the fold of my elbow and ties a rubber band around my bicep. "For most people the needle is the scary thing, no matter the sickness, or the medicine."

I don't know if she's trying to get me talking or what. I stick with or what.

"Make a fist." She gets my arm into place and says, "Just a pinch."

I watch her insert the catheter. I don't feel the pinch.

"There we go. This should take about ten minutes. Do you mind if I step out to make a call? I'm running behind, and—"

"You don't have to explain to me." Because I'm not about to explain to her.

Lidia goes out to the porch and I sit there and watch the drip. In the other room, the princess is getting betrayed by the guy she thought she loved who turns out to be a power-hungry throne thief. I don't know why princesses never anticipate these things.

Five minutes later, Maricarmen blazes through the door ahead of Lidia.

"Mama," she says, "I got tamales. You share these, okay? I'll split them up. For you and Isabel, and for your nurse here, okay?"

"You don't have to—" Lidia starts.

"Yes she does," I say. Maricarmen feeds everyone, no matter what.

"Things are good?" Maricarmen asks, about the IV.

"Things are fine," I say. "Just part of the protocol."

"And so no delivery man."

Fuck. I don't want to talk in front of Lydia, but I can't shut up when Mari's around.

"No deliveries at all," I say, hoping she'll get the hint.

"Okay, you don't want to talk right now," Mari says. "I just worry you keep the drama bottled up, you know?"

"There's no drama," I tell Lidia.

"I love drama," Lidia says. "That's why I became a nurse. You know the soap *General Hospital*? I swear I worked there."

"You could have," Mari says, "those fancy clothes."

I don't get it: why isn't she picking up my distress signals?

Lydia says, "I wasn't allowed to dress this way at the hospital. I lived in scrubs. Part of the reason I took this job was because they let me wear pants that fit. . . ."

While she's talking Mari comes to me, leans over, and whispers, "Her pants are ugly." So we're fine.

As they bullshit about where to get discount deals on designer fashions, Mari filling in what would certainly have been my silence, I think of my uniform. I rarely wear it anymore, and it fits the way wearing a size medium fits instead of a size six. But there's a comfort in it; an identity. I would miss being able to wear it.

Pretty soon all I can think about is how uncomfortable I am in the pants I'm wearing. Thanks to the steroids, I'm no six. "Are we almost done?"

Maricarmen must think the question is for her because she says, "Okay, okay, let me go kiss the baby."

When Mari goes to Isabel, Lidia begins to remove the IV, still talking as though I'd been in on the conversation—

". . . Things move so fast, there's no time to think, let alone get to know your patients. Half the time I only knew who was who by the billing code." She disconnects the catheter and starts packing up. "I do miss the drama, though."

"Wish I had some for you." If only she knew.

Lidia puts a business card on the table, her phone number handwritten on the back. "You've got the Complete Care information already, but here's my cell in case anything comes up in the next twenty-four hours. Please, call me directly. Otherwise the service will kick you to the first available nurse—"

Maricarmen comes back through and says, "I'm going," holding up a hand to God on her way to the front door.

"I'm right behind you," Lidia says, taking her briefcase and her tamales.

I get up. I say, "See you tomorrow," but I don't bother following because they're at the door and Maricarmen's already shifted gears—

"You take those tamales out of the husks and heat them in a pan with oil—" she says, right before the door latches and locks.

I set the alarm and then I convince Isabel to ditch Disney in favor of tamales and a bath. She loves the tub. She loves to kick and splash and she really loves these stupid rubber fish I bought, especially since she discovered they can squirt bathwater great distances. She always aims for me.

After tonight's bath we're both soaked so after I put Isabel in a nightgown I change into a tank and running shorts—psyching myself up for a workout later, or else setting myself up for a guilt trip— and then I disarm the back door for the dove's nest.

It's nice outside; a breeze came in with the evening, and the neighbor's wind chimes plink and ting. I sight check the yard below. I tell myself Marble is three states away by now, if he has any sense. And if he doesn't, my Ruger is in the closet.

See how I try for balance?

"Aypane!"

Isabel decides the first plane she sees tonight is going to California, and so tonight Jezebel Pickle flies to San Francisco to help a goldfish find his way home. The problem with the goldfish is that his memory only lasts a minute—yes, this one's based on today's trip with Kay St. Claire. Jezebel and the fish stop for directions at a cheap noodle shop in Chinatown, where a chocolate-covered fortune cookie tells their fate.

Isabel doesn't know what fate is and so decides its name is George. She often chooses George to be the sidekick—the funny, flighty character who makes all kinds of mistakes but still manages to save the day. It breaks my heart when Isabel brings him into the story. It's really hard for me to make George a hero, let alone a fate.

I give the lost fish a home, a nice little bowl next to a nice little girl's bed, and get Isabel into her own bed. Then, instead of a workout, I head for the kitchen. Chinatown made me hungry.

I find canned green beans, frozen peas, and fries. I wonder what Andy could whip together, the Vitamix. I cook all three separately.

While I wait, I read an article in the *Trib* about Blue Cross/Blue Shield breaching member contracts by paying executives millions in bonuses. Boy that would piss me off, paying a monthly premium to make sure I can afford to get sick and then finding out I'm actually paying some rich asshole's greens fees.

I'm thanking the CPD stars for good employee health care benefits when the phone rings. It's Metzler. Finally.

"Regina."

"Have you been hiding from me?"

"Certainly not. I was simply giving you the day to reflect, and to realize that it doesn't matter what anybody says you can or can't do; you will do what you want."

"Limited release wasn't what you promised."

"I didn't promise. We agreed: you take care of yourself, I get you back to work."

"I am taking care of myself. My boss told me to go home today."

"A witch doctor wouldn't be so dumb as to send you straight back to the street. You were injured. You need time."

"Listen: if you make me take time, I'm going to have a lot more trouble than a numb foot. Please, I've got to go back to work. I've got to set this one case straight. Then I'll take as much time as you say."

"I want you to finish the steroid treatment. Start your medication. Then come see me at my office, and I'll clear you."

"You aren't listening."

"Neither are you."

"Oh, I hear you. You're saying I'm on my own." I hang up and get one of the two beers.

When the food's ready, I can't eat. I drink the beer, though, and open the other one; I usually don't have two but I used to drink gin on the regular, the feel of it on my tongue the first indication of a smooth buzz. I miss that buzz. I'm going for it.

I take the bottle into the still-wet bathroom along with the Avonex box and the complimentary sharps container. I run my own bath and soak while rereading the injection instructions. Yes, I'm going to have a hell of a drug hangover. But tomorrow, I'll feel better doing what I'm not supposed to do if I've already done what Metzler wants me to do. Yes, again, that's balance.

The syringes are pre-filled now, which is supposed to make taking the drug less of a hassle. I'll admit I kind of liked assembling the shot, before—mixing the powder with the solution, filling the syringe and locking the needle—it was mental preparation. Now, sitting on the tub ledge with the syringe ready to go, I just can't do it. I tell myself to relax and at the very least my left leg should, it's been trouble since I fell, but my quad is locked up, resistant. I finish the beer and shut my eyes and hold my breath and I'm right about to do it. But I don't.

I take a breath. I swab my skin. I am not afraid of needles. I count to three. I think about Isabel counting all the way to seven. I start the count again.

The doorbell rings on two.

I cap the syringe and shove it into the Avonex box and shove the box in the cabinet. I put the beer bottle in there, too.

I pull on my shorts and shirt and eat some toothpaste and put my hair up and use hand sanitizer because I figure that will confuse any smell of alcohol on my breath.

The bell rings again; I hurry up so Isabel won't wake.

The bell rings again anyway, just as I'm getting to the door. I try not to sound irritated when I ask, "Who's there?"

"It's Ray Weiss."

I wish I'd disguised my voice. I wish I could tell him I'm not home. I wish I could cover my eyes and become invisible.

I disable the alarm and open the door.

"Hi," he says, and scratches his eyebrow, a reason to look away from my bare legs, my short shorts, me—braless.

"I just stopped by to see how you're feeling."

"A little awkward, at the moment."

"I brought soup." He offers me a blue box of Mrs. Grass. "Just like my mom used to make. It's—I don't know. I like it."

"Thank you," I say and then I can't believe I say, "You want to come in?"

He follows me into the kitchen where I left the beans, peas, and fries on the countertop so I explain, "My niece," though that doesn't cover the first empty beer bottle.

"You want something to drink?" As I'm asking I realize all I've got now is tap water.

"Thank you, but I can't stay."

"You're on the clock?"

"No."

"You're just here to check on me."

"Yes. I am."

And I am uneasy.

He shifts on his feet. "Also, I feel like I owe you one."

"The soup should do it."

"I'm talking about what I said before, about Soleil. I didn't know she made your life so difficult. And I'm not owning that—she's her own mess—but I certainly don't want to be part of the reason you're unhappy."

"Who says I'm unhappy?"

"I didn't mean—never mind." He looks at his shoes. "I just wanted to tell you that I went to St. Claire's this afternoon to see about Johnny Marble. And I got St. Claire to change her mind. She's decided to press charges."

There's no way. "She's got Alzheimer's, Weiss. Her mind changes with the minute hand."

"Well, better her than you. On the stand, I mean."

"You can't put her on the stand. She's a victim, but she's no witness."

"She says she wants him found. "

"Of course she does. He's her son." I am uneasy. "Anyway, isn't that your job? To find him?"

"It is. And I will. But putting him away—that's up to the court, right? I was afraid that without Sanchez's cooperation, and with St. Claire backing off, that they'd want to rope you in."

"Iverson already did rope me in."

"That's a stupid move. There isn't an ASA in this city who wouldn't want to take a shot at a cop on the stand. Especially since the state's attorney got elected taking a stand against us. I know, I've been there. Questioning will be all over the place so it looks like you are, too." He starts to pace, does a voice, "'Please tell the court, Ms. Simonetti, how you came into physical contact with the suspect? Would you say you intended to engage him? Is it possible that low lighting in the stairwell may have caused you to misjudge your distance from the suspect? How much do you weigh? Will you demonstrate for the court how, exactly, he obtained your weapon? When was the last time you took firearms training?'" He stops and looks at me. "And you, Gina, with your head injury? And your gun missing? You're a first-round knockout for any decent state's attorney."

"I have no problem taking the stand." I have to say that.

"I don't know, I guess I'd worry, too, about what Marble might say when it's his turn. Because if it's just you, your word against his, then we're talking about sympathy over substance of testimony, really—"

"Did you say you came to see how I was feeling or that you came to make me feel shitty?"

"God. I'm sorry. I only wanted—I wanted to help."

"I don't need your help."

"Well, maybe St. Claire's involvement will take the pressure off."

"I didn't know there was pressure."

"Okay . . . so maybe we just back up and pretend I showed up with soup." He hikes a thumb toward the bathroom. "Do you mind if I use the head before I go?"

"Go a-head." It's not funny, but none of this is.

When he closes the bathroom door I'm afraid I'm going to totally lose my shit so I go out front, the stoop. I've been so worried about lying on the stand, I hadn't thought about the fact that someone might *try* not to believe me. It's pretty obvious an attorney could dig up my disease, dirt for Marble's defense.

Fuck. Weiss is right: I cannot testify.

I also cannot tell him that.

I hear the toilet flush and I make a thing of putting my hair back into its knot so I'm doing something that seems normal when he comes outside. I tell myself I have nothing to hide.

"Nice night," Weiss says.

"I guess, if you aren't sweating a felon at large or your testimony against him."

"I thought you'd be happy. About St. Claire, I mean."

"I'm not happy about any of this." I stand up. "Thanks for the soup," I say, like *goodbye*.

I don't stick around to hear him say I'm welcome.

I go inside, lock the door, check on Isabel, and slip out the back to run the steps. I will run them 100 times. I won't take the drugs. I can't be sick now. I've got to focus. Get straight. Get strong.

I've got to find Marble before Weiss does.

8

By six A.M. I've cleaned the kitchen and read the paper online. I'm still not mentioned, and neither is Marble. News of Sacred Heart's financial distress is a headline, though: apparently, the state is stepping in with a half-million bucks in temporary assistance while a new board tries to get a handle on the hospital's fiscal situation. Calvin was right: it's got something to do with how insurance pays for low-income patients. Sounds like the place is bleeding money.

The article doesn't mention the layoffs directly, but James Novak, who's said to be a millionaire himself, is quoted as saying, "It seems we can no longer afford to save both lives and jobs." The black and white of it—that health care is also unaffordable to the practitioners—bothers me. So does the fact that Kay St. Claire, someone who can, based on her pricy address, pay for health care—was transported there.

I dress for work in my closet with the lights off so I won't wake Isabel, who snoozes soundlessly in my bed after a restless night. It was my fault: when I couldn't sleep, I selfishly brought her in with me. We didn't do each other any favors.

While I cobble together breakfast from what's left in the pantry, I put on a pot of Tom's decaf. It tastes okay, though without caffeine, there's really no reason for it. A sad but obvious metaphor for our relationship.

I find a packet of plain oatmeal and put water on the stove. I'm on the phone holding for Iverson when Isabel carries the sharps container into the kitchen. She looks pretty proud of herself.

"Where did you get that?" I ask, though I know: I left it on the tub ledge last night. I forgot about it when Weiss rang the bell. I wonder if he saw it. Fuck.

"Bye bye." Isabel struts past me, the bright red plastic box her newest handbag.

"Where are you going?" I ask, playing her game even though I know it.

"Work."

"Come eat breakfast." I stir oatmeal into the water.

She tries stepping into the heels I wore yesterday.

"Come eat breakfast before you go, please?"

She ignores me. Reaches for the doorknob. Is tall enough, in one heel, to turn the knob, but doesn't yet know how to manipulate the lock.

"Isabel. Breakfast? We have to go soon—"

I get kicked to Iverson's voice mail. At the beep, I try to sound pleasant when I tell her I'm hoping for a desk and to please call. In the meantime Isabel is teaching herself how to work the lock.

I tuck my phone in my bag. "Isabel. Come here, please." I say please like *now.*

She turns around and looks at me. And then she sits down with the sharps container and tries to get that open.

It could go on like this. Some days, words mean nothing.

And on those some days, bribery is the only way.

I look through the junk drawer and find a fun-size pack of M&Ms leftover from Easter. "Hey, Isabel," I say, opening the package. And then I give them to her one by one, candy-coated rewards for her compliance in all matters related to getting her dressed and ready to go.

Before we leave, I eat the oatmeal. It sucks.

I don't regret the decision to take a child who's had chocolate for breakfast to the grocery store until we are the cleanup in aisle six.

Shopping was taking a long time—of course I left the list sitting on the kitchen counter—and Isabel was upset I wouldn't buy cereal she liked because of the princesses on the box. But how that escalated into three broken jelly jars can only be the result of a strung-out toddler.

When the jars hit the floor and shattered, Isabel thought it was funny until she worked out that I didn't think so at all. Then came tears.

I told her not to cry. I said, "Don't cry."

That was all it took to get more tears.

Telling her to calm down backfired, and pretty soon she was screaming. "Mama!" she wailed, as though I'd stolen her from her real mother.

People were looking. Pretending not to look.

I tried to be reasonable. It didn't work. And then stayed reasonable but had to yell, so she could hear me over her own screaming, "Isabel. Enough!"

Then came the kicking.

The kicking always gets me, same as it did the day I took Isabel from George's apartment. It was her first birthday; George and Soleil threw a party. There was plenty of revelry but there were no other kids and no cake and, thanks to Soleil, all the apple juice was mixed with Jack Daniels. I was the only one who brought a gift.

I watched George with Isabel. He was lovable and laughable. I knew he had been through a hard time since Isabel's birth mother disappeared; I also knew he was drug numb. The prescription medication for his back injury was dulling him entirely.

I watched George after he helped Isabel unwrap my gift—Meatball—and then he put her down to play with the bear while he shook hands with an old friend. She didn't know what to do with the bear. She didn't yet know to squeeze its paws or give it a hug so that it would talk to her. She wanted her daddy. So she put Meatball aside and pulled herself up to standing using a folding chair next to her dad. At the very same time, that old friend rested his drink on the seat. George didn't notice. He didn't see Isabel.

At that moment, I knew. Nobody saw her.

I took the drink before Isabel got to it. I drank it.

And then I took Isabel. I put my arms around her and she kicked me in the legs and cried but nobody stopped me, because nobody could say she hadn't had any of Soleil's apple juice. She kicked her little legs, fighting the whole way.

Now, here in the middle of the Jewel, I put my arms around Isabel as she fights me and everything that came before me. She kicks me and I close my eyes and I could cry, too, for her. Because I'm all she's got, and I don't know what the fuck else to do.

When she starts to wear down, I stay with her. I hold her and I tell her, "I'm with you." I tell her over and over. I stay close. My face is wet with her tears. And then, finally, I feel her give in. I feel her little fingers clutch my shirt. She stops kicking. Her cries soften to tears. And eventually, her tears dry.

She's asleep by the time I get her to the car. I load the groceries and on the way home, I peek at her quiet face during every red light.

I feel bad—I say I'm the only one responsible enough to take care of her and yet somehow I manage to set her up for breakdowns.

When I pull up in front of the house, there's an unmarked waiting outside. Before I park, I get a bead on the old cop in the driver's seat. He's working a crossword. I won't pretend he isn't there, but I'm not going to go over and introduce myself. He's the one getting paid to be curious. I'm the one with melting Popsicles.

I wake Isabel and she sits on the front steps and tries to peel an orange while I move the groceries in stages—from the trunk to the bottom step. Bottom step to the top step. From the top step inside; inside to the kitchen.

When I get Isabel inside, too, I change her pants and peel her orange.

I've got noodles cooking and nearly all the groceries put away when the dick finally knocks.

I take Isabel with me, a buffer, to greet him at the door.

"Simonetti?" he asks.

He's not an old-timer but he's old enough to have worn his mustache in and out of style. He doesn't look at Isabel. Usually it's the rookies who ignore kids, either because they're too on point or because they're too young to have kids.

"I'm Pohlman," he says. "Stan Pohlman."

As a rule I hate calling cops by their first names and I don't want him to call me by mine so I say, "This is Isabel," who is transfixed, because at her age, any guy with a white mustache is a guy worth knowing.

Pohlman ignores her. Not even a glance. Says, "I'm here about Johnny Marble."

"Come in."

I get him to the kitchen table and strap Isabel into her highchair and say, "I'm making lunch. Are you a mac-and-cheese guy?"

"Coffee."

Okay. I get it: we aren't going to be friends. Fine with me.

I make coffee. I give Isabel a half a banana and she squishes it through her fingers while she watches Pohlman look over the papers he's pulled from his book. The one I can see looks like a report.

I say, "I'm ready when you are."

"Don't you have somewhere you can put her?"

"Here's fine." I pour juice for Isabel. "Iverson said to expect you. She also said she'd find me a desk—"

"I don't know anything about that."

"Macaroni!" Isabel yells, the demand setting Pohlman's teeth on edge.

"Macaroni is coming."

"Macaroni!"

". . . is coming." I've developed a tolerance for incessant noise; I also know how to put a stop to it. But I'm not sure I should. Isabel might be the trick to making this little sit-down short and sweet.

Just to make sure, I untwist the spillproof cap to the juice cup before I put it on the table, just out of her reach.

When the coffee is ready, I set a mug in front of Pohlman. I say, "Let's talk about—" and then the timer goes off.

"Macaroni!"

"Johnny Marble," I finish. And then I go back to the sink to strain the noodles.

Pohlman closes his book. "You're distracted."

"Do you have kids? Because this isn't a distraction. This is just lunch." While I mix the noodles and cheese etcetera, I decide his non-answer means I should segue, so I say, "Truthfully, I could probably juggle knives while I tell you, verbatim, what the narrative in that report you have says about Marble and me."

"I don't need the story," he says. "I just want to know one thing: how did Marble get your gun?"

"We fought," I say. "I lost."

"You were armed. You didn't fire."

"There were civilians involved."

"You put them in danger."

"I chased Marble. I tackled him. He was bigger than me. I couldn't hold him."

"Verbatim," he says, and pushes the book away. He rubs his eyes. "Something is missing."

"Nope. It's all there."

"Someone can take your gun away from you, you shouldn't have a gun."

I stand back; I don't want Isabel to see how I must look when I say, "You want to tell me you never lost a fight? Try me."

"Mama?" Isabel senses the change in my voice.

"I never lost no fight to a tomato can." Pohlman sits back. "It's my opinion—which the First Amendment says I'm entitled to—that you're either stupid, or you're lying. It's also my opinion that either way, you lose a fight *and* you lose your weapon? You should admit you're unfit to carry and do something else with your life. Save the children. How about that."

"How about that," I say. I'm seething.

"Mama?"

"Yes, baby. Do you want your juice?" I push the cup toward her and she predictably knocks it forward; apple juice splatters all over the table and on Pohlman's book, which he tries to save, which causes him to spill coffee all over himself—an unintended bonus.

"Goddamn—" he stands up.

"Sorry," I say, "I was distracted."

"Goddamn," Isabel says.

The look Pohlman gives me makes me think I'm lucky he doesn't pull his service revolver and take advantage of the Second Amendment.

"The bathroom," I say, and show him the way.

As soon as he's in there, I get his book.

I find the report and give it a quick once-over. I find Marble's address and copy it onto my forgotten grocery list. I turn to the next page and do a double take, because Iverson is the one who took my statement at the hospital. I don't remember talking to her. She must know more than she let on. She must have written less.

"Mama?"

"Partner in crime," I whisper, and kiss her face.

I close the book and get Isabel on my hip. I unspool a bunch of paper towels. I give Isabel the cardboard cylinder.

When Pohlman comes back, we're on the floor. I'm cleaning up the mess and trying not to look guilty; Isabel is beating on the hardwood with her new cardboard toy with complete abandon.

I look up at Pohlman. "I really am sorry about this." I offer him a paper towel.

He declines and reaches for his book; I think he means to leave.

"Stan." I don't think I quite make it sound like his name belongs to him. But, "Listen. I can tell you what's missing."

"I'm sure," he says. Not like he cares. He folds his arms, tucks the book. He doesn't plan on believing me.

Still: "I believe my statement says that Marble hit my head against the landing and took my gun."

"Something like that."

"Well, right before something like that, when I knew Marble had me, when I knew he was too strong? I held on to him. That's how I fought. It was all I could do. I had the gun between us, but I couldn't get a shot off. I could only hold on. When he shook me off and stood over me, I didn't know where my gun was. But it didn't matter. Marble could have killed me. With his bare hands. With one hand. And he knew it; he was laughing. And I knew it, too." I stand up. "From the moment I saw him, and from the very first step I took toward chasing him: I knew he could have killed me. I chased him anyway. That's the part that's missing."

Pohlman sizes me up. I'm smaller than him. For a second I think he's going to let up. He's going to sympathize. But the hard lines around his eyes remain, and he says, "You *are* stupid." Then he heads for the door, no goodbye.

Isabel looks up at me.

I tell her, "I'm not stupid."

I find my phone and dial Maricarmen. Turns out I need her this afternoon.

It'll take me a half hour to get to Marble's. I call Andy on the way.

"Kanellis."

"Hi." I say it like I'm sorry.

"Feeling better?" He's asking about my attitude.

"Yes. But you understand, don't you? That work, for me? It's like, well, I can't not work. It's an addiction—"

"Don't say it, G."

"I wasn't going to. I'm just saying: you understand. I can't quit."

Andy has tried everything to stop smoking: patches, gum, hypnosis, electronic cigarettes. He's at the point where he's talked about it so much quitting is always everyone's first question. Especially since the cancer angle got so sharp. Now, he just wants people to quit asking.

He says, "You are welcome to change the subject."

"Well, I hear the Marble case has taken a turn."

"Really? *That* subject?"

"I hear you're the lead."

"Yeah, and then I caught two other cases. I take back what I said about you lounging in rehab. I wish you could come share the load."

"I will—"

"I said *could*. Not would. And you can't. Anyway, I don't know if the charges will stick. St. Claire is completely animal crackers. Her caregiver backs up her story, though. That woman is a fucking guard dog."

"Good thing for St. Claire."

"I don't know about that. When I get to be that age, I'll spend my last dollar on a bottle of goodbye before I pay some rude bitch to point me toward my own toilet."

"Maybe St. Claire doesn't like to be alone."

"Who likes to be alone? There's a reason I'm dating a twenty-four-year-old. Same reason you spend your off hours with someone who's two."

He's right, of course, but I don't know how he seems so at ease with it.

"What I'm saying is, St. Claire seems like she could afford nice. I wouldn't list that among Robin Leone's qualities."

"I'm glad someone's standing up for her."

"I'm glad it's not you."

"So now what? Now that it's you?"

"I'm going to try to get Sanchez on board. I figure if I tell her about St. Claire, she might come around."

"I hope she does. I hope someone sane steps up."

"I gotta go," Andy says. "Get better."

"I'm fine."

"Then get finer, baby."

We hang up.

I do feel better knowing Andy plans to talk sense to Sanchez. If she agrees to testify, the prosecution could try building a serial case, and if they want to win, they'll steer wide around what happened between Marble and me.

Still, I'm *not* stupid, and I know Pohlman isn't the only one who thinks I should turn in my star. Only way around that is to prove I'm police.

I park on Western just south of Sixty-third in Chicago Lawn. I tuck my Ruger into the tight waist of my pants. I carry four screwdrivers, my phone, and a pair of gloves in my bag, and I head for Marble's apartment.

Weiss said it's a game, looking for someone who doesn't want to be found. From my days as an evidence tech, I'd say the likely way to win is to look at everything except who you're looking for. The incidentals are what provide clues to a person's character—who they are when they aren't committing a crime—and those things paint a bigger picture. Those things give direction to where Marble may be now.

The apartment sits above a beauty supply shop that claims to specialize in human hair and wigs. Iron fencing protects the ground-floor windows; the glass is covered with yellowing posters of products and the slick-looking people who supposedly use them. Behind the glass, the actual products and people look nothing like the ads.

The common door has no lock. I slip on my gloves and go in. The entryway holds just enough space between doors for mailboxes; I use my Phillips slotted 3/32 to let myself into Marble's. I tuck his mail under my arm and climb the stairs to 205. The lock takes a pick and a T8 star driver to get in.

When I open the door the smell is overwhelming. Thanks to the police who preceded me, the place is a mess, drawers opened and emptied, Marble's life stuff turned inside out. And, there are cages all over the room—single animal crates, standing hutches, multistory wire birdcages. What I'm smelling, then, is dried-up shit.

Mental note. Character: compulsive.

I walk the single path set by police tape. The apartment is a studio, and there isn't much room in the room. The kitchen is a fridge, a burner, a sink. The bathroom is a toilet and a mirror. Bordered by the yellow tape, the single bed is strewn with magazines; its head-board is a ledge marked by clean squares, dust left around evidence the team took.

Behind me, something moves, and I turn with my gun aimed at a cockroach skittering across the floor. Another one follows.

Mental note: negligent.

I let the bugs off the hook, tuck my gun, and pick up the mail I dropped. I get my back against the wall while I go through it. There is a circular for the local pizza place. A flyer for a cleaning ser-vice. A credit-card offer for someone named Nam Pak Cho, maybe the former occupant. And there are a couple of bills—ComEd and *OK* magazine—addressed to someone named Christina Hardy, maybe another former occupant. Or a current girlfriend, though there's none of her touch here.

Then, there are three magazines: *Twist*, *M* and *OK*. Each cover features splash-framed teenage pop stars. Not a single one of them should interest a man old enough to be my dad.

Mental note: lewd.

When the fridge fan quits I hear a different kind of buzzing, and find flies congregating at the card table in the middle of the room. There, the police tape droops, a sign it's been stretched. And at the table, over the single folding chair, is Marble's purple warm-up jacket.

He's been here.

Mental note: fucking fearless.

I move the tape. I walk around the table.

The flies are interested in the open mouth of a Dr Pepper two-liter and the rings of syrup left by an empty plastic cup. A white paper bag sits open on its side. Inside: a half-eaten sub.

I lift his coat. Smell stench. Hold my breath and check the

pockets. I don't find my .40 S&W, but I do shake out a near-empty bottle of pills—Risperdal—prescribed by a Dr. Adkins to Kay St. Claire.

I take pictures of the bottle. The jacket. The animal cages. The room.

I put everything back the way I think it was.

And then I get the fuck out of there.

I'm in a hurry to get home even though I can't tell anybody about what I found at Marble's. Hell, I can't tell anybody I went there. I can only wonder where Ray Weiss is looking. I didn't want his character to be the one in question.

It's exactly four thirty when I pull up in front of the house and park behind Lidia's car. I put my Ruger in the trunk and tell myself that just like with my disease, nothing is different here except me, and no one has to know what I know. Yet.

I let myself in and the first thing I hear is Isabel's sweet voice singing *e, f, g*. I want to dash in and hug her and be glad nothing has changed about her, not in the space of an afternoon, anyway. I pull off my boots.

"Who's with Izz?" I ask as I pass through the kitchen, where Maricarmen is at the stove and Lidia is setting up her gear at the table.

Mari says, "You can't believe it."

I hear Isabel get mixed up after *k*, and it's George who helps her through *l,m,n,o,p*.

"It's the delivery man," Mari says.

The cold panic I've been wading through since leaving Marble's shifts like a current, and I know I'm about to be dragged along a familiar course, shallow and rocky.

They're in the living room. George is sitting at Isabel's electronic activity table pushing buttons, and Isabel is sitting next to George. She is thrilled, because he is a kid like she is.

And no matter how mad I am at him, when I see him, I'm just a little less mad.

He looks clean: his bushy hair is cut to short curls. He's gained weight, so his old black Ramones T-shirt fits again. His tennis shoes look new.

"Daddy, get up," Isabel says, because she wants a turn at her own toy.

What George could do is show her he's playing the notes that make up "Three Blind Mice." Or better, he could pull his daughter onto his lap and show her how he's doing it.

Or, I don't know, he could just be a grown-up and get out of the fucking way.

"Just a minute," George says, trying to finish the verse.

He can't remember.

Have you ever seen such a sight in your life?

"Georgie," I say. I'm the only one besides Mom who ever called him that.

He looks up and smiles and he seems sober and I'm relieved. I say, "Give me a hug."

"Regina." He gets up and hugs me and I smell his sweat, boozy. *Seems* sober.

I kiss his cheek. I get in his ear. I say, "Son of a bitch."

I feel Isabel's arms around my legs. "Mama!"

I pick her up and hug her and get in her ear, too, though I don't say anything. I'm hiding. Not because it's awkward for George to hear her call me *mama*; I shouldn't have to justify that.

But Tom, gone.

And Lidia, here.

And Johnny Marble, god knows where.

What am I going to tell George?

I feel his hand on my shoulder. "It's nice to see you, G."

Of course I invite him to dinner.

In the kitchen, Lidia is telling Maricarmen, "I hated using the electronic health records. Not because I didn't understand the technology, but because the technology turned patients into problems." She pulls out a chair for me, keeps talking. "I wasn't treating the person anymore, I was doling out drugs based on a diagnostic code."

Mari looks at me like she's heard it all for the third time.

Behind me, George asks, "What's for dinner?"

Glad he can get comfortable.

"*Albondigas*," Mari says.

"What is Allbondeegas?" Lidia asks, white as her crisp-collared shirt.

"Mexican meatballs," Mari says.

"Meatball?" Isabel asks.

I put her down. "Why don't you go find him?" I sit and Isabel forces herself between my legs instead.

"Mama," she whines.

"George," I whine.

"Bell," he says, something nobody has ever called her. "You want to play outside?"

She looks at me, then goes into hiding under the table.

Part of me is glad she isn't warming up to him, but I don't want her to see me plugged in, so I drag her out from under me and say, "Your daddy wants to play," giving George the go-ahead.

"Come on," he says, "let's go outside and look for bugs." He picks her up and cradle carries her like you would an infant. She's too surprised to cry.

Maricarmen shoots me a look. "Food's ready." She puts down her spoon. "I've got to get back. My cousin." It's a bullshit excuse; she's following George.

"Thank you," I say, because of that.

"I'll call you," she says, and heads out.

Once she's gone, too, the silence is noticeable. While Lidia takes my blood pressure, I try to think of something to say, but everything I come up with feels too much like work. Eventually, I decide a question is better—and one involving her seemingly favorite subject—her work. "Were you at a city hospital? Before this?"

"I was. Northwestern. It's an exceptional place, though as I was telling Maricarmen, I couldn't get on board with the shift to cyber management. I started to feel like the bottom line was compromising my ability to care for people. I was supposed to follow an electronic protocol instead of my gut."

"I guess it's all streamlining these days."

"Saving time saves money . . ."

"Does it save lives, though?"

"Listen, you wind up in the hospital? The only guarantee is that somebody's got to pay for it."

"It shouldn't be about money."

"Oh, it's always been. Now, though, it seems like the money goes to the wrong people." Lidia removes the catheter. "All done here. You're over halfway through and you seem like you're doing well. But how you seem is not the same as how you feel. So tell me, are you experiencing side effects? Nausea, irritability, sleeplessness, increased urination, muscle weakness, pain?"

Yes to most of those things, but so what. "I've just got one pain, at the moment. He's outside with Isabel."

"Go on, then," Lidia says, and gets her briefcase. "I'll pack up, quick as I can."

I find George and Isabel on the sidewalk playing catch with a rock. It's a good thing Isabel can't catch.

I take the rock. Isabel frowns. I ask George, "How are you still alive?"

"I get by on my looks."

I'll give him that. "Are you ready for dinner?"

"Macaroni!" Isabel takes off running toes-first, trips, falls face-first, gets back up and takes off again.

"Graceful," George says.

"She gets it from you."

Lidia is on her way down the steps as Isabel starts to climb them herself so Lidia frees a hand to help. She says, "Careful, now," and what I hear is indirect criticism. I hear judgment without context. I hear her questioning my parenting, which pisses me off, because the actual parent is right behind me and somehow, he gets a pass.

Lidia says, "I've seen too many things."

"Let me worry," I say. I scoop up Isabel and climb the rest of the steps.

"She's always been a worrier," George says to Lidia. He doesn't get the context, either; he never has.

I skip the goodbye and take Isabel inside and assume he'll follow.

I dish soup and as we sit down, I realize the last time George ate with Isabel she didn't have teeth, or the ability to hold a spoon. I expect him to marvel at her, or to at least make a comment, but he just sits down and digs in.

Then I realize that for George, the last time he ate is probably an equally distant memory.

We eat just like we used to with our folks, nobody saying much.

After dinner, I get Isabel a popsicle and situate her in front of a cartoon about a girl and her talking stuffed bunny. When the cheery soundtrack kicks in, I see George's shoulders square and tense, so I say, "What. You've finally outgrown fantasies?"

"Can we talk?"

"We can try."

He follows me back into the kitchen and I get myself a beer. I don't offer him one, and he doesn't ask.

"How's Soleil?" I ask, on offense now.

"We split," George says. "She didn't want to get sober."

"And you did?"

"I am."

"Define sober."

"I didn't come here to fight, Gina."

"Why did you come?"

"I need a favor."

I twist the cap off the beer. The fact that Soleil is out of my brother's picture means she might be back in Weiss's. But that's a separate issue, and with George, I can only ride him about one thing at a time.

So. First. "You get a message that I'm injured, and in the hospital, and you don't know where your daughter is, and you come here three days later for a favor?"

"It's actually Tom I need to talk to."

"He's not here." I take a sip of beer so I don't have to expand on that fact.

George crushes a fist of black curls on top of his head. "I can see he's not here. Do you think he'd mind, though, if I borrowed one of his shirts? I have an interview tomorrow."

I nearly choke. I put down the beer. "Where?"

"I met this guy. A builder. The market is coming around, and he's got a bunch of projects on the west side. He needs another Roll-off driver. I know there are other guys in the running, so I thought if I dressed up a little, showed him I'm serious—"

"You think a nice shirt is going to cancel out the drug test?"

"I'm clean, G."

"What about your CDL?"

"Reinstated."

"What about your back?"

"My back is fine."

What can I say to that? He sounds exactly like me.

But. "Why now?"

"Procrastination isn't paying the bills."

"What bills? Aren't you staying at Soleil's?"

"I'm going to get a place. I just need to save a couple weeks' pay."

I want to ask why they split. I want to ask if he's heartbroken. I really want to ask about Weiss. But. "What does this mean for Isabel? You're about as real to her as that talking bunny. Daddy. I'm sorry. You're a story."

He looks hurt. "I know that. I know I'm not much of a dad. And you and Tom have things set."

"I'm the one who has things set."

"You always do."

He smiles at me like he's proud of me, which is one reason I'm not going to tell him about Tom just yet. The other reason is that George could take off tonight and disappear again for six months. I'm not about to open the emotional floodgates with the one person who gets the privilege of being worse than anybody and always being guaranteed another chance. Always. Family. It's fucked.

"I'd just like to see her more," he says. "You know, more often. Like, take her places."

"I'm not going to keep her from you, but I'm not going to let you take her, either. Not until you can prove you're as real about this as

you say. Real, and real clean. If you want to see her, you are welcome to be here. Here, until I'm certain you'll come back."

"I'll do whatever you want."

"Start by coming for dinner again tomorrow night."

"I'd love to." He comes over to give me a hug. I don't stop him.

He says, "You know when I got the call, about you? It shook me.
I mean, I never thought anything bad would happen—"

"I told you: I'm fine. The IV treatment is protocol so I can get
cleared to work. As for the case, there's nothing to worry about: every
cop in the city is looking for the guy who—" I stop talking because
I realize George is waiting for me to stop talking. "What?"

"Honestly, G? It was Isabel that got me here. I started thinking,
what if she needs me, someday? I can be a decent person. I want to
be a decent person."

After another sip of beer I say, "Of course you can borrow a
shirt."

I wait until I'm sure George won't return before I set the alarm.
I don't take Isabel out to the dove's nest; I don't tell her I'm worried
about our safety, either. Instead, I tell her it's a different kind of night,
a special night where she can watch one more episode. She doesn't
know the word, but she's happy when the bunny gets back on TV.

I spend the twenty-two minutes doing pushups and squats. I
shoot for alternating sets, ten of twenty-five, but I can't stay focused
on the count, so I do one exercise until I can't do any more, then
switch. And then I do them again. It's good to be responsible for the
burn. It's good to be physically exhausted for a reason.

I can't stop thinking about Weiss. Back when Soleil first got together with George, Weiss was always on standby. When she wanted
to get high, it was George. When she wanted to get sober, it was
Weiss. When she wanted attention, she knew which one would give it.

But George getting sober? George leaving? That can't be okay. She'll need someone to rescue her. She'll need Weiss to rescue her. And to ruin George.

I have to wonder if that's what Weiss was driving at when he came by with the soup. Saying he wanted to help, except really saying there was no help. Looking for Marble, but not looking very hard. Maybe what he's looking for is a way to ruin *me*. To make it so George would be stuck with Isabel, and Soleil would be inclined to stick with him.

It sounds crazy. But Soleil makes men crazy. I know it. I've seen it.

My arms are nearly as useless as my hands when I carry Isabel to my bed. It's impossible for me to put her down gently and when I do she stirs, so I stay for a minute. I'd stay all night, if I could just fucking relax.

As I lie there, I look out at the dove's nest, and I think about what kind of story I'd have told tonight. So far, all of Jezebel Pickle's adventures have been based on making myself out to be a hero.

The thing is? In real life, I'm no hero. In real life, I'm fucking terrified there's nothing I can do except watch everything fall apart.

9

I wake up thinking about Johnny Marble.

Probably because I went to bed thinking about him. Didn't help that I spent some late-night time researching what I found at his place. One of the more disturbing things was Risperdal, the prescription drug for Kay I found in Marble's coat—it's an antipsychotic that's usually used for schizophrenics; there is mixed opinion about using it for Alzheimer's patients. In all populations, it has potential side effects like aggressive behavior, agitation, and anxiety—and those are just the *a*'s.

I don't know why Marble would want the stuff—it doesn't cause a high—but he certainly wouldn't be the first person to pop a pill, just to see. Imagining various drug-induced scenarios where Johnny Marble was high anyway, and high enough to think he should come after me, I quickly developed some anxiety myself: some real middle-of-the-night bogeyman stuff. By the time I shut off my computer I was convinced he'd snuck in through the basement unit and was just sitting there on Tom's old couch, racking the slide of my service weapon real slow. Waiting for me to fall asleep.

After that I started thinking about Sanchez, and why she wouldn't press charges. How she got spooked. Same with St. Claire, who may well be haunted by him. Backing down could have been out of allegiance to her son; it also could have been because of a threat. Fear is a powerful decision maker, even if it's irrational.

The whole thing made a cohesive case for me to be the one to testify. Yes, I'd have to lie, but wouldn't that be justified by telling the truth on behalf of his other victims? Wouldn't I be doing my job—serving and protecting the people who needed me?

This morning, in the plain-white light, I'm not so sure. Marble wasn't after me. I chased him. I started the fight. And that doesn't sound like serving or protecting. That just sounds nuts.

When I get out of bed I decide to do normal things. Like laundry. Which wasn't normal, for me, before Isabel came along—I never did my own. I took it to a one-armed guy up on Granville: I'd unload six weeks' worth of dirty clothes from my trunk, and two days later he'd give it back to me folded so tight it all fit in a single kitchen trash bag. He'd hand it to me with his only hand and smile as though he was happy to do it. I'd leave him a substantial tip and walk out picturing him folding shirts with his teeth.

I guess the new normal is me, numb-fingered, folding footie pajamas. And I guess I am happy to do it.

"Mama?" I hear Isabel calling as I switch a load of whites to the dryer.

When I open her door, she's standing in her crib with one hand on the rail, Meatball clutched in the other, both of them waiting patiently.

"Good morning, Spaghetti!"

"Work?" she asks.

"I was thinking snuggle." Isabel curls against me as I carry her and the bear to my bed.

We get under the covers. I brush her hair from her face, tuck the longer strands behind her ears. She fingers Meatball's eyeball and hums a tune I don't recognize.

"What are you singing?"

She hums the notes again. I can't place it.

"It's pretty." I tell myself it's some banda song she heard at Mari-carmen's. Or some new sing-along from daycare. It could be a melody she made up, all on her own. I tell myself I'm wound up about a lot of things, but this shouldn't be one of them. I'm not a cop today. I'm taking time.

And I can't help it. "Where did you hear that song?"

"Dada."

Then I know the Aerosmith song. And then I'm annoyed. "Let's get breakfast."

In the kitchen we share blueberries while I cook waffles. I turn on the radio to get that damn song out of my head, and George, too. I stir M&Ms into my coffee, and use them to make Isabel chocolate milk. And to teach her about colors.

After breakfast, we play the laundry game: I fold, she unfolds. Disperses. Hides. She's got a good strategy; I'll find socks among her toys days from now. But I work quickly and she gets distracted, so when the basket is empty, we both win.

At seven thirty the phone rings; it's Iverson. "I got you a desk. Eleventh District, second floor. See Delgado."

I try not to sound panicked when I ask, "Frank Delgado, Internal Affairs?"

"Financial crimes, now."

I'm still in my pajamas, drawstrings hanging. I'd planned to take time. To stay home with Isabel. To hide.

But even if Delgado still worked IAD I couldn't say no.

"I'm on my way."

Between my reluctance to get dressed and Isabel's refusal to do the same, it takes us nearly an hour to get out of the house. I forget nearly everything I need and Isabel's bag, too, and I drop her off at West Town Day Care wearing a dirty diaper. I give Gabby twenty bucks and apologize for a last-minute addition to her overcrowded roster. She looks at me like I'm the one with the hangover.

I get to Eleven—a ten-minute local route that makes my office at Area Central seem as far away as Central America—and ask for Delgado. We've never met, though I heard plenty about him when he took fire after covering for an off-duty cop who beat up a bartender. I think what happened was somebody had to admit to keeping the off-duty cop out of jail so there'd be enough blame to go around to actually keep the off-duty cop out of jail, and that somebody was Delgado.

I assume Financial Crimes was a quiet lateral move, though any move out of IAD is really a demotion. Those guys might work in a vacuum, but when they're sucked back out of it, they're no more the police than the dirt they tried to sweep.

I climb the stairs and find Delgado sitting in front of a computer, elbows on the desk, eyes watering while he stifles a yawn.

"Delgado?" I ask, even though it says so on his nameplate and, as far as I can tell, he's the only one on the floor. I guess I expected him to be older.

"Yeah." As soon as he opens his mouth, he can't fight the yawn.

"Gina Simonetti. Iverson sent me."

"Right." He wipes his eyes, pushes back from his desk. "Welcome to the exciting future of police work." He grins like there's a punch line. "This way."

He leads me along a bank of empty computers. "We have a few guys in court this week. Or, you know, a lot of them, they telecommute."

"No need to show up to a cyberchase," says a kid at the last desk in the room. He doesn't look up from his monitor. He doesn't remove his earbuds and he never quits typing.

"That's Welter," Delgado tells me.

"Walter," the kid corrects.

"Welter," Delgado says again, some kind of tease. He points to the other side of the computer bank. "We also share the floor with Fugitive Apprehension. They're never here."

I stop in my tracks. Either Iverson had no idea she put me on a desk next to Weiss, or she did it on purpose, and bigger wheels are in motion.

Delgado looks back at me. "You okay?"

I feel sick. "The future of police work looks bleak."

Delgado rolls out a chair and offers it to me. When I decline, he sits and makes himself comfortable. "All anybody talks about are the murder numbers in this city. Financial exploitation never makes the paper, let alone the front page. Identity theft, loan fraud, wire fraud, forgery—that's what they should be talking about. That's what's happening. And all in a click, without leaving the comfort of the hacker's own homepage. Most people don't know they've been cleaned out until their credit card gets denied. So what we do here, basically, is wait."

"Until it's too late," Walter says.

"Isn't that what police do?" I ask. "Show up after the fact?"

"Not me," Walter says.

"He's a digital native," Delgado says, dismissive.

"There are a few crooks who still do crime the old-fashioned way, Delgado. You can catch them."

Delgado rolls his chair forward, intentionally blocking Walter from my view. "Don't listen to him. Right now, we got two guys out on a money-pit scam. They've got a line on a not-so-handyman working his way through Grand Crossing. He's got a good game."

Walter rolls his chair over, back in the conversation. "I love that guy. He's still getting referrals. How could anybody be such a sucker? Dude may as well have an infomercial." He puts on an ad man's voice to ask me, "Do you need new siding?"

"I don't," I say. "What's the game?"

"Say you're a homeowner with a small job," Delgado says. "A leaky window, maybe. You get this guy's name through a friend of a friend. He's been in the business a long time, he's got connections, he gets everything at a discount."

"Passing the savings to you," Walter chimes in.

"And the estimate is free—no skin there. So he comes over, takes a look at the job, and then he discovers some other issue. Bad roof flashing, maybe. His estimate winds up twice what you anticipated, but you're actually relieved because you weren't going to fix the window yourself and you sure as hell aren't getting up on the roof and lucky you—he's willing to take care of both problems and still save you money. So there you are, you have a deal."

"A cash deal," says Walter.

"He takes most of the money up front," Delgado says. "For the materials. Then he starts the work, and that's when your one little job turns into a giant money pit. Your gutter clogs, your roof leaks, your fence collapses. One thing after another. And you keep paying him. It goes on like that until a hundred-dollar job turns over ten times the cash and you're still thanking him because gosh, what a mess it turned out to be. You might even tip him when he's done. And then you're the friend of the friend."

"Who would fall for that?" I ask.

"Old people, mostly."

"He probably breaks most of the stuff he fixes," Walter says.

"I have to say I appreciate the word of mouth, though," Delgado says. "At least he works for it. So much of what we investigate is online or on paper. There's just no heart to hitting Delete."

Walter says, "There is, however, strategy, efficiency, concealment, artifice, and much, much more money."

"No balls, either," Delgado says. I think he's talking about Walter.

"So what's the job?" I ask.

Delgado gets up, gives me his chair, and says, "Welter will get you up to speed. Or he'll be busy gaming, or whatever the fuck. But you? You'll be answering the phone. Taking calls, logging calls, transferring calls. Or filing your nails. And I mean no disrespect. I spend a lot of time filing my nails."

"He does," Walter says.

When I look at Walter's screen I see he's writing code, and I'm afraid the learning curve is going to be steep.

"Okay," Delgado says. He takes out Walter's earbuds. "Show her the ropes?"

When Delgado splits, I sit down. "Where do I start?"

"You do know how to answer a phone, right?"

"What about the ropes?"

He stops typing and looks at me. "Come on. You were given the desk so you could sit here with your feet up, and you'll disappear just as soon as your bruises do."

"Wow: that's pretty presumptuous. I begged to come back to work. And it's no favor, me being here."

"It's no favor to me," he says. He spins his chair around to look out the window behind his desk. "I'm not trying to be a noob," he says, "I'm just saying it'll take more time trying to show you how to help me than it will for me to do the job myself. So just answer the phone. I'll handle the rest." He feels around his chest for his earbuds.

I turn my chair to look out the window, too. We're on the second floor, so there's nothing to see but the leaves on the tree that blocks the view. "I don't know what you think about me, but you're wrong."

"It shouldn't matter what I think about you. Everybody cares what everybody else thinks. It's nonsense. Like there's a right way to be a cop. You know that whole 'Welter' bit? Delgado thinks he's making fun of me. Like welterweight, you know, because I'm skinny and I don't drink cheap beer and talk about stupid shit with the rest of them. But I can guarantee he doesn't have a clue that welter, as a noun, is defined as a state of disorder. And that's what this job is: unraveling what hackers do. I'm putting the mess into some kind of order. So what? Delgado doesn't respect me and he doesn't have to. He says this job is his two-year breeze toward pension. And he doesn't believe that this really is the future of police work." He turns his chair around, finds his keyboard.

"It may be the future," I say, "but it's not the only kind of police work. Somebody has to actually catch the bad guy."

Walter shrugs. "Robots."

I try not to laugh. "I'm sorry. Robots seem a long way off."

"So does lunch."

The phone rings.

"It's for you." Walter puts the buds back in his ears and gets to work.

For the first hour, the phone rings endlessly, though there are only two calls I log for Financial Crimes. I transfer some to Property Crimes and kick most of them back to 311. I'm a switchboard operator. It's busywork and it is boring as hell.

By the second hour I can't sit still. My neck is tweaked from cradling the phone, muscles locked up top-down, spine-out. One arm aches, the other burns. I think I'm getting tennis elbow. My left hand is a mitt. The sensations are confounding: pain shoots from my sacrum down my left leg, from the charley horse to my numb-nub toes. The only thing that should feel like it's falling asleep is my ass, sitting here so long.

I stand up. I take calls that way.

Detectives come and go on the floor; most of them don't pay me any mind. The third time I see the same guy eyeball me, though, I think he must know something. I assume he's from Fugitive Apprehension. I assume he knows Weiss. I wonder what he heard. Why I'm here. Who got me this desk. What he wonders.

I sit down again.

I look over at Walter, deep in code. I wonder what he knows about me. And what it'd take someone to get him to tell it.

I don't know who answered the calls before I got here and I don't know who will if I'm gone, but I don't care. I get up again. I go.

I take my own phone with me and pretend I'm on a call. Downstairs, as I pass by processing, I recognize a sergeant and a couple uniforms who assisted me on an arrest some time ago. None of them says hello. Instead I get hooded glances. A single nod. Yes, they're in the middle of booking a suspect, but still. I shouldn't feel like one.

I say *yes* to the phone like there couldn't be a single thing wrong. My smile is full. I am confident and polite. I am fine.

I am full of shit.

In the basement, the vendeteria is empty, leaving no argument against a stop at the machines. At first I decide to be sensible: I buy grape juice instead of Coke. Then I read the fine print on the label: it's 10 percent juice; zero of that is actually grape. I crack it open anyway. It tastes like 100 percent sugar. Screw sensible. I drink half of it, one tip to my lips.

I move on to the snacks. I stand before the machine, its bright wrappers and empty calories. Another dose of sugar that would rush happy signals to my brain, if only for a moment. If only to fix one simple problem—my steroid appetite.

I'm about to select M6 for Snickers when I hear someone else come in and pull out a chair behind me. Immediately self-conscious, I press the button for chips—the baked, healthy kind—a good joke for anyone who's ever been on steroids.

I promise myself all the M&Ms at home later. I do have an image to fake.

I get the chips and I'm ready to make a proud exit when I see it's Ray Weiss sitting there, shoving a sandwich into his face. He chews, swallows. Smiles.

I get goose bumps. I kinda feel like he followed me.

I don't know what to do, so I find my phone and answer another imaginary call.

"Hello?" I ask, and I feel as genuine as my juice. "Yes, speaking." I walk toward Weiss and make sure my expression matches the exclamation, "Oh, yes!" because I should be thrilled to talk to the very nice person who called just now.

I walk by and when we make eye contact I point one numb finger toward the phone to show Weiss I'm on it. As if he couldn't tell. I mouth *sorry*. As if I should apologize.

Weiss watches me, his expression unchanged—the same smile I remember from when he brought soup.

I think of Soleil and then I ask the nice person on the phone, "Do you think he's got an ulterior motive?" On my way out the door I recycle the juice can and then I take myself straight back to my desk.

When I sit down I say, "Hey," to Walter, but his ears are budplugged. I wonder if he doesn't hear me, or doesn't care to.

It shouldn't matter what I think about you, he said.

I agree. I also just spent the past twenty minutes hoping people were listening to me say things that would make them think great things about me.

And I did a repeat performance for Weiss.

Obviously I've gone insane, all in half a day at a desk.

I sit down and plow through the chips. Then I find a stick of cinnamon gum in my bag and chew the flavor right out of it.

I use a headset when I resume answering and transferring calls to free up my hands for a little online research. Before I ran into Weiss, Walter made me wonder what a regular cop could find out about me if he sat down and logged in. I decide to try.

I go to CLEAR and click around until I find the Personnel Concierge tab. There, I can check my status with the medical section. I've never done it before—call it willful ignorance—but thankfully, only the basics are posted: my contact information, my case worker Elaine Brille's information, and my emergency contact information. George. Go figure.

I try to imagine what he looks like today, wearing Tom's shirt, his curls sticking up funny because he pulls at them when he's nervous, or when he's frustrated. I hope he's on time for his interview. And that he doesn't say anything stupid. And I hope he gets the job.

Speaking of. I click on Brille's information and send her an e-mail to let her know I'm feeling fantastic and ready for the Job. It bounces—she's still out of the office—but the auto-reply feels like she rejected my lie.

And then a thought circles back about CLEAR. I'm using a police computer. Why the hell am I looking for myself when I could be looking for Johnny Marble?

I log out of the Personnel Concierge and while I answer calls, I let myself into LEADS, AFIS, and ICLEAR.

Information is limited; I have the clearance to see whatever I want, but I'd have to identify myself in order to get to the good stuff. I don't know if Delgado monitors the use of these computers, but I'll bet whoever's supposed to be investigating Marble would see my name. I don't get very far before I quit.

Then I take a call from a woman who wants to press charges against her ex. She says he's been using her credit card to send her unnecessary, offensive gifts in the mail. Just this week she received a facial hair–removal device, a life-size Sasquatch lawn statue, and a platinum-plated dildo. I tell her to call her credit card company but she says she did, a month before—right after she received a hard-core porn DVD ten-pack called *Bushy Girls*. She cancelled the card, but says he must have opened another card in her name, with another address. She says he's ruining her credit. I log the information and assure her a detective will be in touch.

When I hang up, I get to thinking about Johnny Marble. He was getting mail for someone named Nam Pak Cho and someone else named Christina Hardy. I assumed they were former occupants, but they could be current associates.

A quick online search entering the two names together gets me to a site called Intelius that shows a connection between them. It takes a dollar and ninety-nine cents to find out how. I use my phone and pay by credit card to find out Cho is a dead lead—literally dead, at eighty-six—and Hardy, née Christina St. Claire, is Marble's thirty-five-year-old sister. She has a second address in Berwyn, a nearby suburb. I wonder if Hardy is like Tom, who still gets mail at our place because he hasn't made permanent plans, or if she's like me, who helps her brother out because he hasn't ever had a plan.

I take a few more calls, and as the clock ticks toward noon, I think Delgado is right, Financial Crime is a pretty good breeze; this could be a routine, this could make for a normal life . . . but it's temporary, just like my relapse, and I'm going to have to find my own normal again. Besides laundry.

Which is why I'm gone at noon, on my lunch hour, on my way to Christina Hardy's.

The drive to Berwyn is bullshit. The map says it'll take me about twenty minutes, but construction forces a rush-hour grade stop-and-go. I want to kill someone. I chew another piece of cinnamon gum to bits.

I finally exit the expressway and follow brake lights down Ogden Avenue until I turn off the main drag and find the address, a shabby yellow A-frame ranch that stands out for its kid stuff: plasticky push-and-scoots stand sun-warped and faded in the yard. Big Wheels and Little Tikes toys clog the walk, and the driveway is blocked by a kiddie pool. There are no children.

I park on the street and go up to the door. There are still Christmas lights strung around the front bushes. An air-conditioning unit rattles in the window.

I knock and the metal screen door bangs against the frame.

A plump brunette dressed in an extra-large BEARS T-shirt answers the door. Her hair is sweaty. I can't tell if she's wearing shorts.

"Christina Hardy?"

"Yes?"

"I'm Gina Simonetti." I flash my star. "I'm here to talk to you about your mother."

"She didn't—she called you?" Christina crosses her arms and looks down at me, both eyes, both chins heavy. I wouldn't call her real happy about seeing me.

"May I come in?"

"Yeah," she says, though she doesn't hold the door.

In the front room, two boys about five years old dance around beanbags as they shoot at each other, their virtual representations chest-clutching on TV.

"Alex, Eric, say hello to the police officer."

"Hello," they say in tandem, without looking at me. They are years older than the photo on Kay's key chain and have sprouted from toddlers into gangly, sharp-elbowed boys.

Christina leads me into the kitchen where the third boy, who is smaller, sleeps in a red wagon. She asks, "Is this about the money?"

"Should we talk here?" I try to whisper, because I don't want to wake the kid if I just hit the proverbial jackpot. "I don't want to disturb him—"

"No, he's fine. I mean, he's not fine; he spent the morning hugging the toilet." She leans over, strokes the boy's hair. "Poor little Sammy-Sam. He was born first, but he's my baby." She stands up, pulls at the neck of her T-shirt. "Anyway, whatever you want to know about my mother is no secret. We don't hide crazy around here."

"You'd mentioned money," I say. "Maybe we should start there."

"I had nothing to do with it. I try to be nice and take the boys for a visit and the next thing I know she's acting like I'm writing myself checks. It's insulting, is what it is. Especially because all her money? It was my father's. She got rich leaving him. That's how you know I'd never ask her for a dime. That and, I mean, look around: does it look like we're sitting on a fortune, here?"

Interesting that she's arguing her innocence. I nod my head like I'm sympathetic. I guess I am, a little: "It's got to be tight, three young ones."

"And this one, always sick."

"When did say you visited your mother?"

"I didn't. But it was yesterday."

"You're aware, then, that Johnny Marble—your brother?—is accused—"

"Half brother. Same fruit loop mom. And yes, mother told me about Johnny. But what did she expect? He always had it worse than me. I mean, at least I had a father. I feel bad for Johnny, really. Even if he did it. In fact, I hope he did it. Because she's goddamned mean."

"You are aware of her condition."

"Yes. But trust me. She's always been this way."

"Have you spoken to Johnny recently?"

"No." She looks sorry about it. "I quit paying for his phone, maybe he's still mad about that. You never know, with him. What sets him off. Who knows."

I offer her my card. "Will you let me know if he contacts you?"

She looks at the card. "No."

"You should know he's a suspect in more than one incident."

"He's my brother." Her brown eyes look black.

"He may be a danger to others. To you. Your boys. Or himself—"

"Do you think I'm dumb? You think that runs in the family, too?"

Sam stirs in the wagon. "Mommy?"

"Sammy," Christina says, her mom voice resetting, and helps him sit up. "You want some Seven Up?" She uses her bare hand to wipe his nose and then she looks at me. "Are we done here?"

"Mommy?" Sammy says again, head wobbling as he grabs the side of the wagon and leans over and throws up.

I step back. I take morgue breaths.

"Oh, Sammy." Christina gets a kitchen towel and wipes her legs, her son, the wagon, the floor.

I'm about to excuse myself when there's a knock at the front door.

"Alex, Eric," Christina yells, "get that!"

"I can let myself out," I say, but then Alex and Eric come into the kitchen, and they're escorting Weiss.

"Weiss," I stretch his name to three syllables: *what the fuck.*

He ignores me. "Are you Christina Hardy?"

"CeCe," she says, wiping her hands on the same towel. Her smile is coy—another reason we are nothing alike, despite the fact that apparently, Kay mistakes me for her. "And you are?"

"I'm Ray Weiss." He points to me. "I'm her partner."

"Your partner was just leaving." She sounds like she hopes that's still happening.

"Mama," Sammy groans.

Weiss asks, "Is your husband here, by chance?"

Christina picks up Sammy and holds his head against her shoulder. "Matt doesn't come home Wednesdays. He works two jobs. He's out in Elgin today, at the Lexington Inn. He does maintenance there. And at the middle school."

Seems like she has this answer thought through, too, so, to throw her off, I ask the boy, "Hey, Sam, did you get to see your grandma yesterday?" because kids don't rehearse.

Christina glares at me, whatever sweet was there going sour. "Should I be calling my lawyer? Or are you about ready to go ahead and fuck yourself?"

"She'll be outside," Weiss says, about me, to me.

I go.

On the way to the door, Alex or Eric says, "So long, sucker!"

I'd like to think he's talking to the game.

I'm getting in my car when Weiss skips out of the house.

"You want to take a ride to Elgin?"

I stand behind the car door. "I don't see Mr. Hardy being any more forthcoming."

"You think Christina's hiding something?"

"Something, yes." I look at him. Then I don't. I ask, "Why did you follow me?"

"Earlier, in the caf? I wanted to ask how you were, but you blew me off. Then I saw you again in the parking lot, and I tried to catch up. You took off. I got the idea you were avoiding me. So, yes: I was curious, and I followed you. I lost you on the Ike. At the merge. You drive— It's impressive, how fast you drive."

"If you lost me, how did you know to find me here?"

"It's my case!"

And just like that, I'm on defense. "I only came out here because St. Claire asked me to talk to Christina." The lie sounds obvious to me, but it's all I've got.

Weiss does a double take. "St. Claire knows her?"

Is he joking? "Are you joking?"

"Are you laughing?"

"Kay is her mother. You didn't know that?"

"I don't need to know that. I'm looking for Johnny Marble. It's a fairly straightforward assignment."

"Then why do you keep finding me?"

"Good question." His smile feels like an indictment. "I don't think you're being forthcoming, either. About what happened with Marble."

"Please," I say. "It was a fairly straightforward assault." I get in the car and I should close the door but I feel the need to say, "Next time you wonder if I'm avoiding you, don't."

I close the door. Start the car. Drive. But I wonder. And check the rearview.

Weiss is gone.

10

I go back to the office and spend the rest of the afternoon at my desk and I do exactly what I'm supposed to do and when there's nothing to do I try not to think about Weiss. The way he looked at me, the way he said I wasn't being forthcoming—he made me feel exactly the way I did the first time Tom took my hand: cornered in my own trap.

With Tom, it was shortly after he'd agreed to testify in the case I was investigating. We were having coffee under the guise of discussing the crime. When I said it was brave of him to come forward with information—which seemed appropriate, as the crook we hoped would get convicted was a longtime felon who'd souped up the space next to Cloverleaf for the purposes of torture, murder, and disposal of a body—Tom must've heard me say he should *move* forward. When he reached for my hand, I saw the dopey look in his eyes. I didn't stop him, though I knew I was in trouble.

With Weiss, too, the context is also confusing, and it's real clear I'm in trouble. The thing is, I don't know *how* to stop him.

I'm filing my nails when Andy sneaks up and puts his hands on my shoulders. I know it's him because he always smells like peppermint candy and hand sanitizer and, despite those, cigarettes.

"Boo," I say.

"Did they belt you into that chair?"

"It's comfortable."

"How about a cigarette?" That means he made the trip here to talk at least ten feet from anybody else.

"Let me log out."

Outside, we get ten feet from the building and twenty more from the dick who's out there smoking alone.

Andy lights up and then he says, "Sanchez is out. She won't testify."

"Okay," I say, "but you've still got St. Claire."

"And you."

"And me." I wonder if I sound reluctant.

"You know, I'm starting to think this thing boils down to nothing more than a family dispute. These people, they're—"

"These people? What's that mean?"

"It means the apple doesn't fall far from the crooked tree. No state's attorney is going to want to take this to court. St. Claire isn't going to convince a judge of anything but her insanity."

I don't say anything; I'm thinking.

"Gina, why won't you let this go? How come you want to find Marble?"

I don't say anything; I'm afraid of what he's thinking.

"Gina. Why can't you tell me?"

"I did tell you. He tried to kill me. Isn't that enough of a reason?"

This time he doesn't say anything.

So I say what I was thinking: "A lawyer would take this, if he could make a connection. Marble tried to kill me and Sanchez and St. Claire. I chased my way into the case, but how are Sanchez and St. Claire connected?"

"They aren't."

"I wonder," I say. I don't, really, and I don't think there is a connection either, but pretending does provide me the opportunity to ask, "Did St. Claire mention anything to you about stolen money?"

"What?" Andy looks at me sideways. "No."

I meet his look, sideways. "Duppstadt told me the caregiver said Johnny wanted money, and St. Claire refused, and that's why he beat her up. So maybe Johnny stole from her. It could be how this whole thing started. If you can get Kay to talk about the money—"

"You've been talking to Weiss."

I straighten up and raise my numb right hand. "No. Swear to god."

"Then how is it that he called this afternoon just to give me the exact same advice?"

"Maybe he talked to St. Claire." I'm certain I don't sound convincing.

"Gina." He steps back and points to the ground with his cigarette. "Look at your feet."

"Why?" I get scared, thinking the left one has actually become visibly deformed, but they both look like plain old feet.

"You think Weiss is going to sweep you off of them when he wants to take them out from under you."

"I don't understand."

"You don't want to admit it. I probably wouldn't, either, especially when the son of a bitch is so charming. But he's got you thinking that you both want Marble. What he wants?" Andy studies the end of his cigarette.

I feel gut sick. "What does he want?"

"I don't know, but it's more than Marble. And I'm pretty sure he's using you to get it."

I take the cigarette. I smoke the rest of it.

"Gina, what's he got on you?"

"I don't know." I realize saying so is a confession.

He lights another smoke and we stand there for a while, neither one of us enjoying ourselves. He says, "When Weiss called me today—well, I guess it was the second time he called—he wanted to know about you. I say what the hell does Gina have to do with anything, she's off the case, all that. But he says relax, he just wants to know if you're feeling okay."

That son of a bitch. "He knows I'm fine. I told him so when he showed up at my house the night before last."

"I think he was asking me to see if I'd defend you or not. Which I did. And you're welcome. But when I say, enough about Gina, what do you have on Marble? He says he went to Marble's sister's today. He said he thinks she was covering for him; that Marble had been there. And that maybe they're in it together, stealing from St. Claire."

"Marble was at Christina Hardy's?" I'm floored. Why didn't Weiss tell me?

"Jesus, Gina," Andy says, because I guess I just admitted that I was there, too. He fishes his phone out of his front pants pocket, scrolls, and hands it to me. "Read the latest text he sent."

Today 2:17 PM
Marble is on foot. Backtracking to check his apt.

"Did he go back to the apartment?"

"I don't know, Gina. What I want to know is why a guy whose specialty is supposed to be finding people hasn't got Marble by the neck already. I mean, if the suspect is on foot you call K9. If he's on a train you work with the CTA. If he's got old haunts, you get a team and stake them out. But not Weiss; he wants to go around all by himself, jerking chains to see which ones come loose."

"You think I've come loose."

"I think you're getting jerked." He puts his phone away. "Do you know where Weiss was before he transferred to Fugitives?"

"When I knew him, he was splitting time between the bar and his beat car."

"Sounds about right. Until he disappeared for a while last year. When he surfaced, so did the case that took out that west side heroin trafficker and his whole crew. Five of the local guys pinched were cops. Nobody will admit Weiss was undercover, but he was part of the crew, and he's one of only two who are still the police."

"How do you know that?"

"Because I still go to the bar, baby."

I want to throw up. I stamp out the smoke.

Andy looks at me. "Here's what I'm going to do: I'm going to talk to Iverson. I'm going explain about Sanchez. And St. Claire. I'm going to tell her it's a no-win, if it's even a case. But you, Gina? You need to get away from this. As far away as you can."

"What about Weiss? You think Iverson will call him off Marble?"

"No. Marble is a wild card she's afraid the press will pick up and play as a race card. She's actually glad he's got your gun. Evens the score—otherwise, you know, white cop, black man—that would never work out in your favor."

God damn. "I don't see how any of this is going to work out in my favor."

"Yeah, well, the way this all looks, now? I think I can convince Iverson to bury the whole thing. That'd do us all a favor."

A band of squads gather in the parking lot across the way, a signal for the pending shift change. I tell Andy, "I have to go pick up Isabel."

He tucks his cigarette and gives me a one-arm hug. "I'm going to save your ass, G. Though I don't know from what."

"Thanks for the bad news."

"Don't let it get worse."

I get Isabel from daycare and I'm so happy to see her and so anx-ious that I won't get to see her anymore that I have to hold her tight until I can get the tears back in my eyes.

"Mabicabi?" she asks once I pull myself together and strap her into the backseat. The way her voice warps the question into an ex-clamation bothers me, because it sounds like she wouldn't mind at all, being with Maricarmen instead.

I dial Mari to preemptively cancel her visit. I've got plenty of stuff to talk to her about but before that, I just want some time with my girl. While the phone rings I say, "It's you and me tonight, Spaghet."

And then I remember George.

I hang up, because if George actually does show up, I'd like a trusted ally there.

When we get home, I prop a kitchen chair at the counter so Isabel can help me start the meat sauce. I make one hell of a meat sauce. I don't measure. I use ground beef, all the mushrooms. Too much garlic. As much oregano. A little red wine. I drink more than I use. I'm nervous, I'm paranoid. I'll be better on a buzz.

Isabel gets insistent about helping me stir and when I take the slotted spoon away, we both wind up having a tantrum: she's not in the mood for my instructions, and I'm not in the mood for her help. When she gives me a pouty lip I find Meatball and put them in front of the TV. I need to think.

When George does show up, I'm going to have to tell him about Tom. The truth, yes, but only in part. I'll say he's away on business; I'll leave out the last phone call, that demeaning 'baby and a wife in a wheelchair' argument. I'll confess to George that I don't think it's working out; I will never admit I knew it from day one. I will say Tom is coming back; I won't say he isn't coming back here.

I'm also going to have to tell George about Marble. In part. I'll say I chased a suspect. I won't say I didn't catch him. I'll say we're safe; I won't say I lie awake at night hoping I'm right. And I certainly won't say I'm afraid I'll lose my job because of him.

The sauce is simmering when Lidia arrives.

"It smells delicious," she says.

"Maricarmen isn't the only one who can cook around here. I hope you'll take some with you." I made too much; I couldn't help it. George looked so hungry yesterday. And I haven't had a reason to make anything more complicated than cereal in at least a month.

When we sit down I say, "I actually have a terrible headache," so we don't have to talk. Or at least so I don't have to.

"It's common," Lidia says as she gets the IV going. "Steroids tend to make patients feel so good that they overdo it. It's typical on a day like today."

I don't know how she knows what today was like. I won't admit she's right.

"Most drugs I administer are palliative," she says, "meant to take feeling away. This one? It seems to hit every last nerve."

"I'm amped." I have to admit that. I can't sit still. I want to scream.

"Better than the alternatives, I promise. Morphine is the worst. Confidentially? Some days I have to give doses that send patients into respiratory depression. I spend the whole session watching them to make sure they're still breathing."

"Isn't that illegal? For you to give that much?"

"I've yet to meet someone dealing with terminal cancer who's worried about the law. Anybody in pain—or anybody watching someone in pain—is going to want me to do my job."

"Must be hard on you."

"I just have to believe I'm doing what's best."

"I want to throw up," I say, because that line—*doing what's best*—that was my mom's line, when she divorced my dad.

"Oh, dear," Lidia says, "can I help you to the bathroom?"

"No. It'll pass." Someday. I close my eyes.

I was a senior. George was a freshman. They sat us down one day and said they were separating. She said love was easy; marriage was not. She said she was *doing what's best.* My dad didn't say anything. He never argued.

I knew what was best, and that she was about to ruin it, but nobody wanted my opinion—these were grown-up things that had to be worked out over time. Time was a key word, and she kept buying it—just by doing what was best.

In the meantime, there was no place for us, so George and I finished out the school year at the Metzler's. Rick and Janine came through on their role as godparents, saintlike in their willingness to provide us a local address and a normal life so we could remain at our school. My dad got an apartment. He came for dinner most nights. My mom called every night, but she never had much to say.

I didn't know time was up until I met the boyfriend. Mom asked George and me to the house one summer Sunday and there he was, this totally regular guy, a totally regular smile. Jim. A regular name. No warning he'd be there, no way to talk about what he was doing there. I saw his toothbrush in the bathroom. I saw the same old bedspread on the bed. And then I knew that home, as certain an idea as I had about anything, was gone.

I knew my dad was clueless so I asked her: didn't she feel guilty? She said guilt was a useless emotion. Then she asked me if I thought Jim was cute.

I left George there. I never went back.

Six years later, she called my dad. I was there; it was Christmas. I could tell by his face that it wasn't good news. He hung up the phone, packed a bag, kissed his then-girlfriend goodbye, and moved back to the house. My mom was sick, and so he stayed with her, and he helped her die.

I couldn't understand. How could he give in, after all those years? He said he wasn't giving in. He was forgiving.

When she was dying—her last days—my dad asked me to come. She died before I got up the nerve to go.

"Are you okay?" Lidia asks.

"I'm fine."

When the IV is done, I send Lidia off with some spaghetti sauce and join Isabel to watch the rest of *Mickey Mouse Clubhouse*, a stark contrast to my mood.

At ten to seven, I take Isabel out front, so we'll greet George.

Isabel turns circles on the sidewalk to make herself dizzy. So many circles that I'm dizzy. She falls, she recovers, she does it again. She can't walk; she thinks it's hilarious. It's a high.

I wish turning circles did it for all of us.

Just after seven I carry her inside. I don't want George to think we're willing to wait. I tell Isabel we're having a special dinner. I put water on for the noodles. She plays with the plastic bottle of Caesar dressing while I make a salad.

At seven fifteen, I cook the noodles. I look out the window a dozen times.

At seven thirty, I feed Isabel. Noodles with butter. Warm bread. A glass of milk.

"Special?" she asks.

"Special?" I ask back, looking out the window once more. "No. What I said was spaghetti. Spaghetti is special, though, like you—"

She looks disappointed. She should. I shut up.

At seven forty, I eat her leftovers.

At seven forty-two, I say fuck it. I turn off the sauce. I close the front shades. Then I arm the front door and I take Isabel and a party-size bag of M&Ms out to the dove's nest.

It is still light: the sun is setting, but the sky is clear and blue and bright. We can't find a single cloud, or the moon. Planes way up leave white trails; I tell Isabel that's Jezebel up there, racing back and forth before the sun sets. I say she's searching for the truth. I say it's hard to find. Harder to tell.

She hee-haws. I tell her about donkeys. I talk about being stubborn. We hee-haw. We laugh. We chew M&Ms with long jaws, side to side.

At eight o'clock, I tuck Isabel into bed. She falls asleep before I say good night, a chocolate ring around her pacifier.

I change into shorts. I run the back stairs, my left leg dragging, until I can't lift my legs anymore. Then I climb. Then I crawl.

After that I take a shower. I consider the Avonex. I think about Marble. I reconsider.

At nine-fifteen, I fix dinner for two. I eat alone.

I won't call George. No way. I bet he has a good excuse why he didn't come tonight; I know he's as used to being disappointing as I am to being disappointed.

I can only guess what he's doing that lets the excuse seem good enough.

I pour myself a beer while I think of all the things I could be doing right now, if not for George. Eating out, that's for sure. Eating out with someone else, maybe. Someone who uses a fork. Who speaks in full sentences.

And, I'd be having a drink. A real drink, because I would actually enjoy a buzz, if I didn't have anybody to worry about but me.

Halfway through that real drink, I would *be* me. Undistracted me. Unedited me. The me people like—and want to be with, even—not by default, but because I'm kind of funny and I can be insightful and sometimes thoughtful.

Nothing against Isabel, but it'd be nice to have someone in my life I can't stop thinking about without knowing a damn thing about him. Someone I want to learn about, and from. Someone I want to wake up with who doesn't come with stuffed animals.

I go to bed, move a plush turtle out from under my pillow, and stare at the ceiling.

I wonder about Calvin. I think of Tom, and then Lew, the guy I dated before Tom, who legitimately moved out of state for work. I think about Jake, my very first boyfriend. I wonder about Weiss.

My cell rings just after two A.M. I think I was asleep.

It's George. "I'm outside."

I find clothes and put them on and stumble to the front door. I disarm the alarm and unlock the door and open it and block it. I say, "Kitchen's closed."

He says, "Soleil put all my stuff out on the alley."

"You didn't think she'd be reasonable, did you?"

"Can I stay?"

I put him on the couch in the TV room.

When I come back with blankets, he asks, "Where's Tom?"

"Atlanta." This time of night, I don't owe him any more than that.

I toss a pillow on the couch and I'm about to go back to bed when I realize George is still standing there.

"You need something else?" I ask.

"I don't know. A hug?"

I give him that, and though I know I'm being a little harsh I'm not going to pretend I'm at all sorry about Soleil, so I say, "There's spaghetti in the fridge."

"I knew you'd understand."

"I wouldn't say that." I go back to bed.

11

In the morning, I get up and get ready without waking Isabel, who's in bed with me this time because of George. I was glad he'd come, but I feared we were convenient hosts on his way to another mistake. I want Isabel to know her dad; I don't want her to suffer the emotional drag-around.

I resist looking in on George on my way to the kitchen. Though I'm sure he thinks he's been through too much to raise an eyelid at this hour, there's a part of me that thinks he'll be gone already, and I need coffee before I face disappointment either way.

I brew a pot and while I wait, I prepare for another normal workday—that is, I sit down and think of all the shit I'm going to have to say to people to make it seem normal.

When I'm sufficiently caffeinated, I decide somebody else in the house needs to be up, too. I pour coffee in a second cup and carry it into the living room. I'm fully prepared to drink it if I find nothing but blankets on the couch.

The blankets are on the floor. George is in boxers, one arm over his face, one foot on the table. He is skinny but flabby, his body deflated, an addict's.

I could wake him and ask him to help me wake Isabel. I imagine gray light in my bedroom window, my soft kisses as she tries to get her eyes open. I imagine George standing there like a moron.

I put his coffee on the table and go wake Isabel myself.

"It's a new day," I tell her. She opens her eyes and smiles, all six teeth. "Guess who's here to see you?"

"Mabicabi?" she guesses, because who else, really.

"Guess again."

Though she keeps guessing while I change her pants, her list of possibilities broad enough to include cartoon characters, she doesn't guess right; sadly, her daddy is the implausible one. "I'll show you," I say, and carry her into the TV room.

"George. It's a new day." The way I say it this time isn't meant to bring a smile to his face.

"Oh." He sits up like he was awake all the while and knows exactly where he is, and how he got here. Or, like someone smacked him in the head.

But then he sees Isabel, and his face reminds me of when we were kids. Little kids. When the people we expected to be there were there, and we were so happy about it.

Still, "We have to leave in a half hour. That means you have to leave in twenty-nine minutes."

"Wait." He rubs his eyes. "I thought maybe I could spend the day with Bell."

I put her down; she attaches herself to my leg and peeks at him. I try to sound nice as I pick up one of the blankets and fold it and say, "What a toddler needs is routine and until you are clear on that concept yourself, you don't get to play daddy. Spend this twenty-nine minutes with her, before we go." I gently knee her toward him; she's curious, and takes a tentative step in his direction.

"Okay," he says, but he reaches for the coffee instead of the kid.

I toss the blanket on the couch and take her back up in my arms. "You do know that she'll be my dependent in a little over two months."

"Isn't she, you know, already dependent?"

I look down at her, looking at him, leaning into me. I say, "I'll get breakfast ready."

In the kitchen, I put out a spread: Greek yogurt, strawberries, blueberries, cereal. Bread. Butter. Almond butter. I hear George in the bathroom. I know he's in there sloshing toothpaste around in his mouth while he wets his hair. I know he'll use the hand towel to clean his face and his ears and wipe the mirror and sink. I wish I knew what the hell he's thinking.

Isabel is in her chair happily noshing on berries when George comes in, wet-headed. He notes the breakfast offerings, opens the pantry, and asks, "Is there Peter Pan?" He finds Tom's stale Corn Pops. Yes, Corn Pops can go stale. So stale even I wouldn't eat them on a steroid jones.

"Peter Pan?" Isabel asks, a TV twinkle in her eye.

"No," I say to both of them.

George pours half the cereal from the box and uses too much of Isabel's milk, which I know he'll leave in the bowl. I don't say anything.

I cut the crust off almond-buttered toast for Isabel and say, "I've got to make a call. Would you mind helping Isabel get dressed when she's done?"

"Okay," George says, like I asked him to launch a rocket.

"Okay!" Isabel repeats, like I told her Daddy was going to launch a rocket.

I stuff the crust in my face and go into my bedroom to call Metzler. I leave another message. I call Elaine Brille and leave another message. I call Andy. I leave a message. Then I peek in Isabel's room, and she's still in her jammies, and they're playing.

"Children," I say. "*Ándale.*"

Isabel knows what I mean.

I'm in the kitchen again eating my own piece of toast that's really just an excuse for butter when Isabel appears wearing her pink-hearted pajama top, long red pants, the shrug sweater meant to accompany a dress that no longer fits, and cheetah-print socks. I don't care that George lacks fashion sense; it's the common sense that worries me.

Still, I don't say anything. Except, "Her shoes are by the door. So are yours. I'll be there in a minute." I slip into Isabel's room and tuck a summer outfit into her bag; there's no use making George feel like an asshole about every single thing.

We shoe up and say goodbye and head off in our own directions. Not that I know where George is going. Not that I'm going to ask.

"We'll be home at four o'clock," I say. "You're welcome to come back."

George says, "I'd like to."

I hear, *We'll see.*

I drop Isabel off at daycare—minus the sweater—and drive to Eleven. I pop peppermint Lifesavers the whole way, though they do nothing to get rid of the metallic taste in my mouth. I may as well be sucking on dimes. I know I should drink more water; I also know that if I do, I'll waste my bathroom breaks in the bathroom.

Not very strategic. Especially when I don't know my strategy, exactly.

I bypass the station lot and park on the street. I put on my heels and they're totally uncomfortable but at least my feet feel something. Finally. The rest of me is a steroid-hot mess, including the cluster of acne that appeared overnight on my chin. One has its own heart-beat. I feel it, too.

When I head inside, I walk the walk of someone who's got some-where to be. I don't give anybody the chance to say hello.

Upstairs, Frank Delgado is at his desk, on the phone. He waves and gives me that punch-line smile; I look back at him and nod like I already heard the joke.

Walter is in his chair, staring at his screen, eyes slits. There's an energy drink on his desk and from my desk I can smell taurine and sweat.

"Morning," I say.

"Is it?"

"Have an Adderall," I say. "I need your brain."

He sits up. "Hello wall?"

"What?"

"Please explicate."

"I want to know how to find somebody. Online. Off the record."

"Shit. I'm never on it."

I give him Marble's name and within a minute he's got access to everything it took the rest of us months to accrue. Phone records, school records, criminal record; it's all there.

He lets me scroll through it.

"Can I print this?"

"No thank you," he says. "That makes it evidence. Besides, you don't need evidence. If you want to find this guy, you just need in-formation." He toggles screens. "I'll send it to your phone."

In my bag, my phone rings. "That's you?"

"I don't work *that* fast."

Turns out it's Andy calling, so I send him to voice mail; he doesn't need to know what I'm up to.

Walter yawns, reaches for my phone. "Let me see that."

"Why?"

"You want to find the guy, right?"

Handing it over feels like sharing a secret.

He swipes and taps and eventually hands it back. "I set it up so it'll alert the next time he uses his Ventra card. Last time was yesterday, Pace route 386. That bus goes out to Tinley Park."

"You hacked Ventra?"

"That word has such a negative connotation. I'm simply redirecting information." He yawns again. "The alert will tell you when he gets on city transit. It'll be up to you to catch up with him before he gets off."

"How do I explain it, when I find him?"

"Also up to you," he says, "except the part about me."

"Who?"

"Exactly. You don't know who installed an app so you can read the files you asked for, either. You'll get the link in an e-mail from a ghost account—look in your spam. Delete it when you're done with it. Or before you get caught with it. I also put my private number in your contacts, in case you need tech support. It's under 'Dialup.' As in what you probably still use for home Internet." He sits back, pleased with himself.

"Whatever," I say. "I have a bundle."

"So cozy."

"I owe you, Walter. What do I owe you?"

He turns back to his screen. "Accepting that premise alone is the same as admitting I did something I shouldn't have."

"Never mind, then." I get my bag. "If Delgado asks, I took an early lunch."

It's early, just before eleven, when I pull into Fatso's parking lot. I'm planning on multitasking—getting the skinny on Marble at the same time I get a double Fatso with cheese.

Inside, I'm the only customer. The place smells of last night's grease, the deep fryers and burners idle. I check out the menu and the two girls behind the counter who are young and not Hispanic and not Rosalind Sanchez.

"Morning," the cook says. He is white and bald and not Fatso.

"Good morning." I pull up Johnny Marble's booking photo on my phone and show it, along with my star. "I'm looking for this guy," I say, "and a cheddar Polish with fries."

The cook leans over the high counter and squints at the photo. "Still looking for Johnny, eh? Funny, I never thought he had much sense. But apparently he's outsmarting you all."

"He freaks me out," says one girl, which makes the other girl look real skittish.

"Jumbo shrimp freaks you out," the cook says. "Rosalind is fine, girls. She didn't die. She quit. Now please, Shawna, show Jen how to ring up a Polish with the discount." He winks at me, gets the grill going, says, "Don't listen to them. They'd post selfies with Johnny if they could."

"They shouldn't," I say. "He is a suspect in two other incidents."

"Yeah? Boy. I'd like to tell that to Rosalind. You know when she quit, she said she felt unsafe here? Blamed me for the late hours. Ticked me off, and also inspired me to put a call in to my attorney. But then I thought: hey girl, maybe don't walk around by yourself in the middle of the night. Maybe be smarter than your phone. You wanna know: while she was on break one day I saw her trip over that picnic bench out there while she was texting. She skinned herself up good. I'm sorry she got hurt then, and I'm sorry about whatever happened with Johnny. But she can't blame Fatso's for being a fathead. I don't think I'm breaking news when I say she's got less sense than the so-called monster you're looking for."

I didn't call him a monster—not out loud, anyway. But, "What would you call Johnny?"

The cook thinks about it. "Johnny, I guess. Just Johnny."

Just Johnny. **Jesus fucking Christ. I can't get the same story about Marble twice: he's a monster. A tomato can. He's had it rough. He's as rough as they come.**

At least I've got more than opinions to go on now.

I sit on the picnic bench Sanchez tripped over and while I eat, I open the app Walter installed; Marble's information is all there. I scroll, and scroll, and scroll. I don't know what I'm looking for until I find a document from Tinley Park Mental Health Facility. Discharge papers dated 2012. Diagnosis code DSM 295.90. Released with medication compliance and community placement boxes checked.

You never know what sets him off, Christina said.

That bus goes out to Tinley Park, Walter said.

I'm stunned. Marble, like his mother, is officially nuts.

I copy the diagnosis code and switch to my web browser.

I find DSM 295.90 in the *Diagnostic and Statistical Manual of Mental Disorders.* It's the code for undifferentiated schizophrenia, which is schizophrenia that doesn't fit the criteria for the usual types of schizophrenia. It's all kinds of crazy: hallucinations and/or delusions and/or disorganized speech and/or extremely disorganized behavior. Or not. It affects thoughts and sometimes mood. Or mood and sometimes thoughts.

I go back to my browser and search for the Tinley Park Mental Health Facility. I find a news article from 2012, when the overcrowded hospital went bankrupt and was forced to shut down. Patients were either transferred to other sites or released.

What the fuck is with all these cash-strapped hospitals?

As if on cue, Calvin calls.

"Simonetti," I answer. I'm pretend I'm cool, and that I didn't just throw down two thousand calories.

"Gina, it's Calvin—from the hospital?"

"I remember."

"I thought you'd want to know: St. Claire was readmitted."

"What happened?"

"I don't know. A detective just showed up, though. From Sex Crimes."

"I'm coming."

"Okay, but don't, ah—"

"I didn't hear it from you." I hang up.

When I arrive at Sacred Heart I don't see Calvin and I don't look for him either, though I would like to see him because he is nice to look at.

At the desk, I show my star and ask for St. Claire. The nurse must be new because she's totally flummoxed by whatever she's looking at on her computer and none of the buttons she pushes seems to help. She says, "I'm sorry. The system is running really slow."

While I wait, I check my phone. There's no alert.

I'm scrolling through Marble's records again when I hear the distinct ca-lick ca-lick of a woman who knows how to walk in heels. I look up from my screen and see Sloane Pearson. She's a Sex Crimes cop and she's a shit disturber and she's no fan of mine, mostly because her ex-boyfriend Eddie Nowicki was.

She must be here for St. Claire.

She can't know that's why I'm here. I tuck my star.

"Pearson," I say and then I approach her, because I don't want the desk nurse's system to hit stride and jam me up.

"Simonetti." Pearson is beautiful. Sleek-jawed, almond-eyed, bitch-perfect beautiful.

"They've admitted my aunt," I say. "Pancreatitis."

"That's too bad." She looks like she wants to keep walking.

"You working?"

"Always." And then she does keep walking.

"Detective?" the nurse says.

Pearson stops. Because I'm supposed to be here for my aunt.

"Okay, you got me," I say to both of them. "I was pulling weight."

"Amateur," Pearson says and she's still shaking her head after she turns and goes.

I slide my finger across my throat at the nurse and call after Pearson: "She's my favorite aunt."

Once Pearson's gone I tell the nurse, "I'm undercover."

The nurse whispers, "Room 216."

St. Claire is asleep, the TV news blathering on above the bed. Except for the shackles I recognize underneath the sheets, she looks well enough—better than last time I saw her. Her eye is healing, and her hair has been curled. And she'd been made-up: lipstick has seeped into the wrinkles around her lips, and her eyebrows, now smudged, were drawn in brown arcs.

I step inside and close the door. "Mrs. St. Claire?"

She doesn't stir. I approach the bed, pull her chart. The diagnosis box says she's here because of a trimalleolar ankle fracture. I lift the bed sheet, untucked at the bottom. She isn't in shackles—she's in a cast.

There's a knock as someone pushes the door open so I drop the sheet. It's Dr. Kitasaki, who doesn't look at all interested in seeing me.

"Gina, is it?" he asks, coming around the bed. He offers a hand.

I'm hesitant to take it, on account of the rash, but I don't want to offend him.

I shake and say, "Gina it is."

"It's nice to see you up and around. Are you back to work already?"

The way he's still holding on to my hand makes me think he wants to escort me out of the building, so I assure him, "Detective Pearson has taken over the case. This is just a personal visit."

"That's very kind," he says.

I finally pull my hand away and look at St. Claire. I ask, "What happened to her?"

"HIPAA laws prevent me from discussing that with you. She hasn't yet given authorization to share her personal health information. In criminal situations, as you know, victims are protected—"

"I do know. But what's your opinion? You can discuss that."

He feels too close when he looks at me. Or maybe at the acne on my chin. He says, "Her wounds tell us a story, and her caregiver told the same story. That's all I can tell you."

"Will St. Claire press charges, now?"

"That's not my business. I believe I told you before that my first priority is her health. I am trying to keep her comfortable—"

"But do you know, did Robin—the caregiver—did she say who did this?"

He steps back, removes his gloves. "That sounds like an investigator's question."

"Maybe. But if you believe St. Claire is in danger, you can take measures to protect her."

"She is safe here."

"But what about when she's released? She's headed straight back to the scene of the crime."

"Hospital policy precludes my doing anything more than treating her."

"Yes, but you can help *me* help her. You can use professional discretion."

"I am."

"I see," and what I see is that he isn't going to budge. "I guess I'll send flowers."

"That's very kind," he says again.

When I look at Kay, I feel a surge of anger. Flowers don't help anything. I've never sent flowers in my life.

"What about you?" Kitasaki asks. "Are you feeling well?"

"I'm fine." That's *my* professional discretion.

"I have to say I'm amazed you're here at all, given your condition."

I can't tell if he's being honest or condescending; if he's talking about the TBI or MS. Doesn't matter; he's got me either way. I feel myself shrink. I say, "HIPAA laws prevent me from discussing that with you."

He humors me, a nice smile.

I take Kay's hand, to make it a different kind of personal. I say, "I just wanted to see her. To let her know she's not alone."

"I can assure you, she is not alone." Kitasaki pulls Kay's chart, makes a note, and says, "I've got other patients waiting."

"Thank you," I say, though I don't know why.

"Be well," he says on his way out the door.

I look at Kay. The heart monitor blinks steadily, pledging her stability. Otherwise, she's lifeless. Drug suspended. *Safe,* according to Kitasaki. *Comfortable.*

This is not my idea of safe.

This is not comfortable.

This? It's bullshit.

12

I get back to Eleven just in time for a wall of calls started by a local grocery chain's announcement of a security breach that includes customers' credit card data. The press release says potential victims should contact local law enforcement.

Walter and Delgado and me: we are local law enforcement.

As I fumble my way through my first call, Walter graciously writes me an identity-theft cheat sheet. It says to tell callers it's best to file a report in person. It also says to offer local police station addresses and the FTC's Web address and the grocery's customer service number. As the afternoon rolls on, I give out that information, though callers become increasingly dissatisfied. They want breach specifics. Dates and locations and details. I tell them I don't know. I get yelled at. A lot.

When I realize I'm being used like a search engine, I get impatient. I actually tell a few callers they've got the wrong number. A couple times, I hang up.

I also decline a call on my own phone from Elaine Brille and another from Andy. And I decide the real reason I'm impatient is because I'm waiting on a Ventra alert. For that, I'd blow this joint. It doesn't come.

I quit at quitting time, and my ears ring on my way to pick up Isabel.

"Mama!"

Today when I get her, she wipes her runny nose and then gently touches my face with the same hand—clues she's picked up some other kid's bug and I'm probably next in line for it.

"Oh, Spaghet," I say, because she feels heavier; either she grew, or I lost strength, or both. I wish I could stop time.

Before we get in the car I ask, "Do you have to go potty?"

"No."

I get her in the car seat and on the way home, I think about how I never thought I would say the word *potty*. It's a ridiculous word. I say it all the time.

Predictably, by the time we arrive home, she's filled her pants. At her last doctor's appointment the pediatrician said Isabel was old enough to potty-train. She suggested a three-day crash course. I said we would; we haven't. Truth be told, I'm not ready. I don't want her to need me less.

When we're home we've got a half hour before Lidia arrives, so I pick up the mail, carry Isabel into the bathroom, strip her down, and throw her in the tub.

I sit on the toilet lid and look through the mail while Isabel plays, bath crayons tonight's toys of choice. When I'm through I use the blue crayon to draw some clouds because I'm bummed the mail is all mine, now, and I have made the marketing lists for lower insurance, a new MS drug, and a chairlift. It's depressing; even the postman probably feels sorry for me.

I check my phone for the 800th time—no alert—and I'm

annoyed when Isabel splashes me. I'm about to scold her, but then I remember me there, in the tub, five years old, my grandma where I am, reading a Catholic missal, smoking a True 100.

She was ignoring me. I splashed her. Ruined her cigarette.

She threw the butt in the tub and left me there.

My grandma was a grown-up with grown-up things to do.

I may be, too, but I put the phone aside, get my feet in the tub, and splash Isabel right back.

Once we're both drenched, we leave the tub looking like a crime scene, the red crayon—her favorite—drawn in heavy, jagged lines over my clouds.

I dry myself off and wrap her up like a burrito and carry her to her bedroom. She is silly and delighted as she sings almost half the alphabet. I let her choose an outfit—the same silky nightgown she picks out every time—and I've got her jammied and ready for prime-cartoon-time.

We're watching yet another Disney mom bite the dust—this one killed by a barracuda—when Lidia rings the bell.

I hug Isabel—yep, the cartoon got me—and say, "I love you."

Isabel looks up—actually looks away from the screen—and says, "I yayou." Yes, she's parroting, but she's never parroted this before.

I stay where I am and hug her some more.

The third time the bell rings, I get up and dash to the front door. Except my claw foot catches the mat in the hall. I faceplant.

"Are you all right?" Lidia asks, when I open the door.

I'm stupid, but, "I'm fine."

I sit and rub my foot while she prepares the IV.

She says, "I know what you're dealing with, and I know you'd like to deny it. But your symptoms—the balance issues, the stiff leg, the discomfort—they're no secret."

"Not feeling like talking to you about them doesn't make them secrets."

"It's hard, isn't it? The disease is unpredictable. The symptoms make you feel terrible and the drugs make you feel worse. Doctor says you should take them to delay the disease, so you don't feel even worse tomorrow. Or next year. Or in ten years. But the doctor doesn't know. And you don't know. All you know is that you're afraid. What if this is as good as you'll ever feel? Can you even remember what good feels like? You're fear-tricked, so you go on faith. Or you go to the pharmacy." She takes my arm. "Or, you fight. You know what I'm talking about."

"Don't know what you're getting at, though."

She inserts the needle. "I had one patient, I'll tell you— confidentially? She was about your age. She had multiple sclerosis, and she believed her walking was compromised when she ate. Her fight was the food. Wasn't long before she became so weak and so thin she broke both her legs, and then she surely couldn't walk."

"I don't have a problem with food." Obviously.

"What I'm saying is: don't fight the wrong thing."

I sit back. "How do you know what I'm fighting?"

"I don't. But I'm a mom, too, so I know how directly your well-being impacts your child's."

"I want Isabel to be happy," I say, despite the fact that every single parenting book I've read trumpets empowerment over expectation, action rather than emotion. "I can't control everything," I admit.

As if on cue, the doorbell rings. "For instance."

I get up and take the IV bag with me to let George in.

"Hey, Georgie." He's carrying a duffel bag and a brown bag and he's got Tom's shirts on a hanger over his shoulder. The bags make me nervous, but I don't say anything.

"Is it okay?" he asks, about his stuff. "I didn't have, I mean, I just need somewhere to put this—"

"You can leave it all right there for now." I mean next to the door. That's as close to *yes* as I'll get.

He hangs Tom's clothes on the coatrack, leaves the duffel, and gives me a hug. I know by his breath that there's a sixer minus-one giving weight to the brown bag. And I know that means he didn't get the job. Still, I don't say anything.

As he follows me into the kitchen he says, "Gina, I was wondering—"

I hold up my good hand. I know what he's wondering. "You can sleep in the living room." The basement unit isn't finished, otherwise I'd make him a better deal—so long as his end came sans Soleil.

"Thank you, it will just be—"

"It's temporary." I turn away. "George, say hello to Lidia."

"Hey, Lidia."

"How you doing, George."

I sit down again and look up at him. "You know Tom will kill me if he finds out I gave you anything more than an opportunity."

"I know. And listen, you don't have to worry, I'm taking you up on that—"

"I'm not worried. You can use that shirt and tie as many times as you like. You can be here when we are here. You can enjoy our company. And you can thank me when you're on your way."

He looks ashamed, but he's the kind of guy who needs to be told what's what, and I seem to be the only person who'll tell him.

"Take the opportunity," I say.

"I *am*," he says, like I offered to kick him in the knee.

"I'm ordering pizza," I say, to stop being a bitch. "You want anything?"

"I don't have any cash."

"Then I'm also giving you the opportunity to eat. Pepperoni okay?"

"Sausage is better."

"Don't press your luck. Go say hello to your daughter."

George saunters off. I guess I was still being a bitch. I can't help it; he sets me up for it.

And, he's been drinking. I'm about to get up, take the IV in there, supervise them—but then my phone buzzes. It's the alert:

> *Ventra Card activity notification*
> *ID number M 7091442414*
> *(RI) Tinley Park-80th Ave Metra northbound*
> *5:36pm*

Tinley Park. Marble never left Tinley Park.

What the fuck.

"I have to go."

Lidia looks at the IV bag. "You've just got another three minutes or so."

"I have to go now." I reach for the catheter; I can remove it myself.

She reaches, to stop me—"Please—"

"Get this out of my arm. I have to go." I call to the other room, "George!"

Lidia removes the catheter. She looks displeased; so what.

I dial Maricarmen.

"Buenas?" It's Geraldo. I'm starting to wonder if he's really her cousin; he's there a lot lately and she doesn't complain about it like she does with the rest of the family.

"Geraldo. It's Gina—"

"Maricarmen comes from the mercado."

"When she does, will you tell her I need her to come over? It's a work emergency, and Isabel is here with George. You can come, too—"

"You can bring Isabel here?" he says, the broken question a solid offer.

But I can't waste time getting everybody organized and out of here. Johnny Marble will be off the bus before I get Isabel to put her shoes on.

"Thank you," I say, "but I've got to go right now."

"Okay," Geraldo says. "We will come."

Lidia applies gauze and folds my arm and I get up and yell, "George!" as I head into the living room, where I find him wearing a blanket like a cowl. I don't see Isabel; I guess they're in the middle of some game. And while I appreciate that, "George, I need you to be a grown-up now. I have a work emergency. Lidia is on her way out and Maricarmen is on her way over—"

"Mabicabi!" Isabel jumps out from underneath the blanket.

"—and she'll stay until I get back."

George pulls the blanket off his head. "When are you coming back?" There's a distinct hint of possibility in his voice. It worries me. I shouldn't go.

But then I see what was in the brown bag. Not beer. A bus. A plastic bus once full of little plastic people who are now lined up in a row on the coffee table, smiling, looking at me. They're saying, *Come on, Gina. He really is trying.*

"I won't be long." I grab Isabel into a hug and she squirms; she wants to go back and play. "I love you," I tell her. I tell George, "I'll leave cash on the counter for the pizza."

"No problem."

"I would hope not." See? He sets me up for it.

I go into the bedroom to change my shirt. The Metra station where Marble boarded is an hour from here, but my guess—my hope—is that he's coming back to the city. I'll head for a station closer in and if there's no new alert, I'll be waiting for him when he gets off the train.

When I get back to the kitchen, Lidia isn't packed up. She's got papers all over the place. "I've got the medication you take from here on out, and some forms for you to sign."

I open my bag, get my pen.

She says, "You take these for five days to wean yourself from the intra—"

"I know how it works."

"Okay, but if you don't have time to listen, I still need to ask you to sign the form that says you understand the weaning process, and the doses, and the potential side effects—"

"Just tell me where to sign."

She does. I do.

"These are your discharge—"

"Again," I say. "Dotted line."

Lidia looks offended as she quietly points to the Xs on three other pages.

I sign Xs. "Is that it?"

"That's it." She begins to carefully tear off carbon copies.

"Thanks," I say. "You can leave the copies there and let yourself out." I put forty bucks on the counter and start to bail when Lidia says—

"I'm sorry if I upset you. I'm sure you know what's worth fighting for."

"Yeah, I've got a pretty good handle on that." I pull on my boots and I'm out the door.

Once I'm on the road I decide to take the expressway and meet the Rock Island line eight miles south at Thirty-fifth Street.

On the way I call in the pizza, and then I dial Andy.

"I just talked to Sloane Pearson," he says, foregoing hello.

"Can you meet me?" I ask, hoping to dodge the lecture.

"Where?"

"The Metra at Thirty-fifth Street. I got a tip on Marble, he'll be there."

"No way in hell, Gina. If Pearson gets legs on this case, Iverson will have your ass—and mine, too—if you so much as send St. Claire a get-well card."

"Pearson can't make this a case. Marble's been in Tinley Park since yesterday. That means he couldn't have assaulted St. Claire."

"Then why are you still after him?"

"Because I'm feeling helpful. What did Pearson say? When she called?"

"Gina, I can't."

"Damn it," I say, to the brake lights just past the circle. Lots of them. When a blue-and-white passes on the shoulder, I find my way toward the exit; I'll snake the side streets.

"I know you're frustrated," Andy says.

"Then why won't you just tell me what she said?" I cut over to Canal and head south and it seems like a fine idea until I come upon another jam—this one, White Sox fans; I'm probably the only person who isn't trying to get to the ballpark.

"Gina—" Andy starts, right as I lay on the horn; I wish I had my own blue light to convince these people I've got somewhere to be. Fuck it: I drive in the oncoming lane, turn left at Twenty-third Street, drive around a DO NOT ENTER sign onto what's not a road, shoot under the expressway and over some gravel and up on a curb.

"What was that?" Andy asks. "Did you just hit something? Or someone?"

"I took a shortcut." I'm headed south again, on State Street, the other side of baseball traffic. "It's not like I'm asking you to do something illegal. I just want to know what Pearson told you."

"Jesus. Will you slow down?"

I do. "I did. So tell me."

"Okay, G. Apparently, St. Claire took a near-fatal dose of medication. Either the wrong meds, or the wrong combination of meds. She passed out and fell and broke her ankle. Somehow she regained consciousness and managed to call 911."

"That's not a sex crime. Why'd Pearson get the call?"

"The doctors saw evidence of sexual abuse, and said Robin Leone showed up with a pretty detailed ear perker about finding Marble forcing himself on St. Claire. Apparently Leone intervened and kicked Marble out of the house."

"It's bullshit. Marble wasn't there."

"How do you know that?"

"I can't tell you."

"Okay, well, I gotta tell *you* that calling bullshit isn't quite as strong an argument as the eyewitness account from the woman who stopped the attack."

"It wasn't Marble."

"Pearson is waiting on the doctors to let her talk St. Claire into a rape kit. That will prove it was or wasn't."

"What about Robin? If she can call the cops on Kay's behalf, why can't she step in and make decisions?"

"Yeah, there's a problem there. St. Claire has Marble listed as her proxy."

"The hospital can't override that apparent mistake?"

"Nope."

"Well. You tell Pearson I'll find Marble. Then *he* can agree to the tests."

"I think I'm not going to answer my phone anymore. I think I'm going to open a beer and get in the hot tub and soak until I'm stupid."

"At least I'll know where to find you," I say and then I say, "Shit!"

and hang up, because when I turn at Thirty-fifth I see the train parked over the viaduct. I park in a tow zone and I should get my Ruger out of the trunk but I need every second, so I run up the steps and I yell "Police!" wielding my phone like a weapon at the army of baseball fans deboarding the train. I fight the crowd but when I get within reach of the train doors they press together and seal shut and the conductor isn't waiting another moment. He must not see my star held up over my head, little and lost amidst the swarm of black and white.

And just like that, I missed the fucking train.

I skip down the steps and back to the car and I head for the next stop.

It's no *French Connection*, okay? It's me cutting over to LaSalle and getting caught at Thirty-first Street and watching the fucking caboose bump around on its way to the next stop. It's me waving goodbye from the wrong side of the tracks. It's me kicking myself for picking the Thirty-fifth Street station, and for not following baseball.

And then it's me realizing the next stop is the end of the Rock Island line.

I get on 94 and there's no traffic. I can beat the train. I peel around the curve at Twenty-sixth and take the ramp to Congress and I'm there—I'm *here*, and by my clock, I've got three minutes before the train arrives.

I make an illegal U-turn and park against the one way at LaSalle by the old post office, half on the sidewalk. I turn on my hazards, and this time I get my gun.

The station sits under the Chicago Stock Exchange. This time of day, the markets are closed, so the street is mostly empty, though a thin crowd of smokers stands outside the Option Room, an after-work tavern with inflated cocktail prices that seem reasonable against the cost of a couple bumps of coke. I know this because Tom has a pair of trader friends who always made me glad Tom wasn't one. They spent plenty of cash on all kinds of options.

I duck into the station and head toward the arriving train; I hear the engine huff and chug on its slowed approach.

And then I'm detoured by a BUILDING A NEW CHICAGO sign that blocks the usual pedestrian route to the platform. Orange arrows direct me down the only path anybody can take and it spans the length of what seems like two trains. Unfortunately, it lets out on the temporary "in-service" elevated portion of the platform. A line of passengers waits here—waits, yes, because the train doors are closed. Arriving passengers are currently exiting the other side. Where all the conductors must be. Where Johnny Marble must be.

Sonofa.

I look for a way around the train: on the construction platform below I see barricades, electrical equipment, hazard signs, and no good or safe or quick way around.

The only way to the other side is outside. Back the way I came.

Or forward, and through.

"Police," I announce, showing my star. Most people step aside. One, a blue-shirt trader-type, doesn't budge; instead he makes a booze-brave comment to his friend about my nice tail. I think they're both surprised when I say, "You should see my smile." I don't. They move.

At the front of the line I reach up and bang on the train door's window.

"Police!" I yell this time, though my voice is swallowed up by the big engine's idle. I may as well be trying to get the train's attention.

It takes a minute before a conductor appears, and I'm certain he'd have appeared at that very minute anyway, by his watch, time to board. When he sees my star his expression doesn't change a bit and I don't think he tries to move any faster as he puts the big archaic-looking key in the door release and then the door sighs and opens, a slow yawn, and I'm sure Johnny Marble is already street side.

And then, just before I step up to board, my phone alerts:

> Ventra Card activity notification
> ID number M 7091442414
> LaSalle Blue Line station
> 6:49 pm

Streetside, he was. And now he's gone underground.

I tuck my star and look down as I backtrack through the crowd I just pushed aside. I feel like a jerk, especially when I reach the boozed trader face-to-face and I do offer a kind-of smile and he looks down at me and says, "Sorry, honey, your smile doesn't make up for your mouth."

His friend laughs. I move on, nice tail between my legs.

On my way to the street, I re-read the alert. I don't know where I'll go; the L doesn't work like the Metra or the CTA. Once through the turnstile, there's no way to determine a traveler's direction, let alone the destination. There's no sense in going to the Blue Line stop; by the time I get there, Marble could be anywhere. He could switch lines, change trains, change his mind, or sit on his butt and ride all the way to O'Hare.

I won't know where he is until he uses his card again.

I double back to where I parked and find a squad blocking both my car and the outside outbound lane on Congress. A uniform with a young face stands between the vehicles. He's handsome. And he's writing me a ticket, just to ice the cake.

His nameplate says ANZALONE. He sees me and he says, "You can't park here."

"I'm about to be not parked here anymore." I show him my keys and my star.

"You still can't park here."

"I know that," I say, and I don't care how good-looking he is because, "you're going to be sorry when you have to tell your boss you disrupted traffic and wrote me for a parking violation while the suspect I'm trailing walked right past you and hopped the blue line. A suspect who assaulted his own mother. And a young girl. And me."

He stops writing. "Serious? Are you okay?"

"Do I look okay?"

"You look pissed."

"That's because the suspect is still at large. On the blue line. Headed away from here."

"You aren't going to find him on the L by yourself."

I must look more pissed, because he says—

"I don't mean you-you. I mean the theoretical you."

"Neither one of us will, now."

"Where's your backup?"

"Standing here writing me a ticket."

"Me?"

"Listen. I have an informant. I just have to wait for it. For *him*. For him to tell me the suspect's getting off the train." I call up Marble's booking photo on my phone and show it to him. "He came up from Tinley Park so I think he's headed north, or maybe west. His mother lives in Ukrainian Village."

"Johnny Marble," Anzalone says, off the photo.

"I want him off the street," I say. "I don't care who takes the collar."

A light clicks on somewhere above Anzalone's head. He puts his ticket book away and takes out his own phone. "What's your number?"

I tell him, he calls, we're connected. "I'm Dario," he says.

I put ANZALONE in my phone. "I'm Simonetti."

"Should I follow you, Simonetti?"

"I don't know where we're going yet."

"I do," he says. "Come on."

Anzalone uses his cherry lights as an excuse to ride the Kennedy's shoulder during rush hour. I trail him. He gets off at Lake Street and soon we're parked at the six-way outside the Grand L stop, where the Blue Line makes its escape from the Loop.

It's a smart idea: just outside the rush, and we can shoot north or west or northwest easily.

Anzalone gets out of the squad and lights a smoke.

I park behind him and we take up watch together, monitoring the stairs to the trains underground. After a bunch of passengers come up and disperse, none of them Marble, Anzalone asks, "How are you tracking this guy again? You have an informant where?"

I don't want to tell him anything that could have repercussions, so I say, "I don't want to tell you anything that could have repercussions."

"Like your last case."

So Anzalone did some detective work on the ride over. The 'last case' he's talking about is the last one everyone talked about—the one where I was supposedly forced to leave the evidence tech team because I was "sleeping with a witness." Like most rumors, it's 10 percent true: I did leave evidence tech, and I did eventually sleep with Tom, the witness. The rest of the truth was that I had been diagnosed with MS, I thought everybody on my team was catching on, and I put in for a transfer. My last case with the team was the one next door to the Cloverleaf. Tom didn't know me and so had no reason to think there was anything wrong with me. And then when he did get to know me, and there was something wrong with me . . . well, that's where we are now.

I'm actually not sure which version of the story is worse.

"Listen," I say to Anzalone. "It doesn't matter how I find Marble. This can be your collar. Your story."

He looks off, down the street. "I don't usually tell a story. I usually tell the truth."

"That's probably why you're still writing parking tickets in the Loop."

"There's no harm in trying to be a good guy."

"No passing the sergeant's test, either."

He takes the last drag of his smoke. "I guess you have to be tough."

"You mean the theoretical you?"

"No," he says, flicking the butt to the curb. "Just you."

I don't want to answer so I take out my phone, the way the theoretical we avoid small talk these days, and scroll through Marble's information again.

Then, "Hello. How ya doing. Hi."

I look up and Anzalone's turned around, elbows on the rail, being officer friendly to another procession of passengers who come up the steps and head for cabs and buses and Richard's and Emmit's, the pubs across the six-way. Most of the women return the hello. None of the men are Marble.

Which makes sense when my phone buzzes again.

The alert:

> *Ventra Card activity notification*
> *ID number M 7091442414*
> *CTA #2059 Division & Ashland Westbound*
> *7:12 pm*

I show Anzalone my phone. "He's on the bus."

"Let's go out to Western, come back on Division. We'll meet him head-on."

"That bus won't take more than ten minutes. I don't know if we'll make it."

"We will." Anazalone makes for the squad and I follow him west, lights and sirens, the late sun glaring at me.

We're on approach just as the bus rolls to a stop at Leavitt. Anzalone doesn't hesitate—he pulls into the oncoming lane and parks in front of the bus, ass-out, so there's no way around. I pull in next to him and park against the one-way; I assume he won't write me a ticket this time.

I jump out of my car and meet Anzalone at his trunk. We don't talk about who'll do what, we just do. He gets the visibility vests; I take the traffic cones. I set the cones out to make a lane for westbound traffic while Anzalone clears the doors and boards the bus to talk to the driver.

I walk around the bus. It's about half full and mostly Hispanic— exactly the demographic in another six stops or so—six stops, my neighborhood.

If Johnny Marble is still on this bus, I have to wonder if he's on his way to visit Mom. He could be on his way to me.

Around the back of the bus, I realize my hands are shaking. I don't feel them. I don't feel my feet, either. But this is not MS. This is adrenaline.

I edge around the rear doors and pull my Ruger. I shouldn't, but I do. There's a Hispanic woman standing inside holding a child's hand—I can see the top of the little girl's head, her ponytail. The woman looks irritated, and pulls on the stop request cord; she must not understand what's happening.

Then she sees me. Then she sees my gun. Then she backs up, shields the girl. Turns. Falls. Scrambles.

There's a domino effect: passengers around her who have focused their attention on the officer at the front of the bus are now startled, and follow her lead—a bum rush toward the front.

I hear the driver on the bus speakers: "Remain seated, people. We got a situation up here."

The announcement doesn't inspire confidence. Other people get up. Most people get up.

Johnny Marble does not.

He's sitting in the middle handicapped seat opposite the rear doors; there's nobody sitting on either side of him, and there probably never was. Save for the beard that's grown in clumps, he looks the same: he's even wearing his purple jacket—so he's been home again—and he's looking down at the black plastic bag clutched in his hands. It's almost as though he's deaf: he doesn't move at all, and his detached expression doesn't change.

He looks like a psychopath.

I step back. I yell to Anzalone: "I've got a visual!"

Marble doesn't react. Just keeps looking at his bag. I feel like it could blow up.

I run to the front of the bus. I tell Anzalone, "He's there. He's just sitting there. Acting like there's no problem."

"Okay, okay," Anzalone says to me and to everybody, and from this angle he looks taller, and older, and official. He takes the driver's microphone and says, "I need everybody to sit down. There's been a mistake. So please just sit down, and I'm going to come through and make sure everybody's okay, and then I'm going to leave, and then you can all be on your way." Anzalone hands back the mic and comes down the steps to ask me, confidentially, "Can you do this?"

"Hell, yes," I say. This is it.

"Where is he?"

"Handicapped seat opposite the rear doors. Purple jacket. He's holding a bag. A black plastic bag. I can't—I can't tell what's inside." Panic makes me stutter. "I think it could be my service weapon."

Anzalone's eyes skip from mine to the Ruger, fear striking. "He's got your gun?"

"But we've got him. We can seal up the bus, call backup."

"No way. If he's armed, we have to get him now. You stay with the driver. I'll walk Marble off at the rear. Once I do, tell the driver to close the doors and hold tight."

I almost say *thank you,* but that'd be like admitting I'm scared. So instead I say, "I'm with you."

Anzalone climbs back on board. I follow him and take position at the front, Ruger ready. I nod to the driver and watch the passengers watch Anzalone, who sidesteps his way back, hand poised at his holster.

The driver warily observes the scene from her oversize rearview mirror. When I look through it I can see Anzalone, but I can't see Marble, because most passengers have stood up to get a look at who Anzalone's after.

I turn around and feel eyes on me, but the only person looking is the little girl, now first in line to exit. She holds on to her mother's purse straps as her mother holds the overhead strap. The girl's eyes are big and brown and knowing—as in, she knows something isn't right.

At the back, I hear Anzalone say, "Johnny Marble?"

Then, someone back there says, "This doesn't look like a mistake to me."

"No," someone else says, "this looks like stop us all and frisk the old black man."

"What'd the guy do, huh?" a woman with purple streaks in her hair asks me; I don't answer because I'm focused on what Marble might do now that Anzalone's in front of him.

Anzalone's face is a mixture of distress and resentment as he stands Marble up, looks over the crowd, finds me, and gives the signal.

"Will you open the rear doors, please?" I ask the driver.

As she complies, Anzalone moves behind Marble and steers him to the exit.

Another passenger in back protests: "A man's got a right to ride the bus."

Another says, "This is the mistake, officer. Treating the poor man this way—"

Anzalone turns on the top step. "If any of you knew what he did, you'd be thanking me." Then he helps Marble down the steps and off the bus.

I lean over, tell the driver, "We'll get you back on route in just a minute."

"Be quick, or I'm gonna need you for crowd control."

I grip the handrail on my way down the steps, nerves like blown fuses. I hit the sidewalk and turn and stop because Anzalone is whirling and thrashing around like someone set him on fire. Marble stands behind him, stone. The black plastic bag is on the sidewalk, caught by the neck of the twenty-ounce soda that had been inside.

I draw my gun.

"Anzalone?" I try to sound firm as I angle toward them—but not directly, because now they're both dangerous.

"Jesus fucking fuck!" he yells. "They're all over!"

I get close enough to see a cockroach fall from Marble's coat and land on its back, immobilized, legs running the last race.

I move around the men and find my cuffs and when I get behind Marble I say, "I'm here behind you, Johnny, and I'm going to ask you to put your hands up, on your head."

Marble doesn't move.

"Do you hear me, Johnny?"

He still doesn't move. I curl a cuff around his wrist, lock it, and raise his hand, deadweight, behind his head. When I do, another cockroach falls from his coat. I jump back, a stupid move, but Marble's hand remains where I left it, cuffs swinging.

"Fucking roaches," Anzalone says.

"Fucking roaches," Marble says. And then he starts to laugh.

I remember the roaches. And I remember the laugh. Not methodical; mechanical. Not meaningful. Unaffected.

"He's infested," Anzalone tells me.

I lower my gun and walk around to face Marble. He doesn't see me; he doesn't look. He just stands there, arm still held behind his head. There is drool on his lips and his beard is caked with spit. His laughter is unemotional, warped and flattened.

I say, "Johnny Marble."

I don't think he even registers my voice, though the roach who peeks out from his shirtsleeve seems to look at me, its antennae twitching.

I ask, "Do you know why we pulled you off the bus?" He sets his eyes on me, empty as his laughter, and then I realize questions are pointless, because his ability to tell me the truth, however intentioned, will be no better than his mother's.

I cuff his other hand and then Anzalone finally approaches. He says, "Johnny Marble. You have the right to remain silent. Anything you say can and will be used against you."

Marble stops laughing. Says, flat, "Fucking roaches."

13

I follow Anzalone to Area Central. Even though he works out of the First District and we arrested Marble in Fourteen, I convinced him we should process Marble where they know the case. And where they know me.

It didn't take much to convince him—I think what did it, actually, was the cockroach that leapt from Marble's hair to Anzalone's shirt after the arrest. When I offered to transport Marble along with his bugs in my car, Anzalone was quick to agree.

I only want to accompany them so I can tell the part about how we came to find Marble and I only want to tell that part so Walter doesn't get involved. I told Anzalone I'd give them the story up until I asked for his help. I said he could tell the rest. I imagine he'll skip our rocky beginning, and stop short of telling anybody how scared shitless he is of cockroaches.

Anyway. Now. Driving. Marble in the backseat: my chance.

"Johnny."

I look in the rearview: he stares at the headrest in front of him.

"Were you on your way to your mom's, just now?"

He looks out the window and the light finds his eyes; I wonder if some part of his brain thinks we've arrived at her place. He wipes his mouth, his dirty shirtsleeve.

"I'm afraid no one told you," I say, "she's in the hospital."

He closes his eyes.

"I'm sure you know she's sick—" I start, but my phone rings and sends Marble into a fit: he tries to cover his ears but he can't in the cuffs so he screams over the ringing, rocking back and forth so violently I swear I have to right the steering wheel.

I silence the phone. I don't care who it is. I've got the man who can make this case sitting in the backseat—the guy I made out to be an animal who turns out to be more like a vegetable—and I'm not going to lose him now.

"Johnny," I say, soft as any mother, "shhh."

I shush him for a while, same as I do with Isabel when she's upset; with her, too, what started the fit might not be clear to me, but I do what I can with the hope we'll both be equally relieved after.

Pretty soon Johnny's screaming turns to a monotone moan and his rocking becomes rhythmic, self soothing.

"I'm here with you," I say. "It's okay."

He stops rocking. He looks in my direction. I think he hears me. I think the kid gloves are working.

"I'm sorry, Johnny. I didn't mean to upset you. I don't like it when the phone rings, either—seems like it's always someone with bad news. The phone won't ring again." I show him that I put the phone down on the passenger seat.

He stops humming. He is listening.

"Johnny: no more ringing, okay? And listen: I've got good news. Do you want to hear it?"

He doesn't say yes, but I tell him anyway: "What I was saying, before the phone rang? I was saying that your mom is sick. You know that. What you don't know is that this time? This is different. Because she can get better. But Johnny? She needs your help."

He takes a deep breath. He tries again to cover his ears. He either doesn't believe me, or he knows something.

"We're headed to the police station right now, and that might be scary for you but I promise, Johnny, no one is blaming you. And you aren't in any trouble. In fact, I know you were in Tinley Park when your mom got hurt. I know you didn't hurt her. I think, though, that you know who did."

He looks at me. Straight at me. His voice sounds programmed when he says, "Gina Simonetti."

"Yes, that's me. You recognize me. I saw you at the hospital a few days ago. You were afraid, and you ran away. I ran after you—you know why I did that? Because I needed your help. And I still do. Could you tell me—yes or no, even?—if you know who hurt your mom?"

Johnny's eyes are empty. Black.

I think of Isabel again: if soft questions don't work, there's nothing more efficient than a good lie.

I take my foot off the gas. "You know what? I'll make you a deal. I'll let you off right here, right now, if you'll just tell me—"

"You broke the deal."

"I haven't made it yet."

"You broke the deal."

"What deal?"

"Stay away and mama is okay. Stay away, and mama is okay. Stay, away, and mama, is okay—"

I step on the brakes, middle of the street. "Who made you that deal?"

A driver behind me honks; I wave the car around. A stream of traffic follows. Ahead of me, Anzalone pulls over to wait.

"Did someone make you a deal, Johnny?"

"You broke it."

"I'm trying to help you. I just need a name."

"Gina Simonetti," he says again, and I know that's all I'm going to get.

I fall in behind Anzalone and drive another few blocks to the arranged spot where we'll park, out of the way of the station, so nobody with a star gets wise to our cockroach caravan. Anzalone parks and jumps out of the squad and as he comes toward us I say, "We're here now, Johnny, and you're going to have to go inside. Unless you can tell me who hurt your mom?"

Anzalone opens the back door and reaches for Johnny, who catches my eye in the rearview just before he's yanked outside, and I immediately feel fucking horrible. He didn't have to say anything to tell me he had no part in what happened to Kay. And if he knows who did—if it's the same person who made him that deal—he wouldn't say so, as powerless as he is already.

"I'm sorry," I say, though he can't hear me now.

As I follow them into the station I wonder if it's the right move, showing up to take credit for another mistake.

I follow them, though, because I have to show my face. Let everyone see that I did the job no one else could, and I did it despite the fact that Marble is innocent. I follow them because the story doesn't really end here, and I'm going to have to finish it.

When we get inside, Anzalone takes Marble to processing and I head up to the sergeant's office. I don't know if Iverson's there, but it shouldn't matter. If I'm doing the Job I'm not looking for favors; I'm looking to get it done.

Upstairs, the energy is fresh as the night shift prepares for the street.

I cross the floor and see guys I haven't seen since it all went down and guys who probably have no idea what went down but I walk by, tall, a direction, a finish line.

I know they're watching, and it's okay; I'm steady as I go.

Until I get to the sergeant's office, and Iverson is at the door. Waiting for me.

"Simonetti," she says, and goes inside, like I should follow.

I do.

"Close the door."

I do. I stand just inside of it. I say, "I can explain."

"I don't want you to say a word."

I don't. She comes toward me and stands in front of me.

"I—"

"Shh." She puts her finger to my lips. "Please. Don't. Because, Simonetti? This. Is. Fucking. Brilliant."

Then she gives me a hug.

I'm dumbfounded, and I feel about as receptive to her as Anzalone was to the bugs, but I fake it. I hug her back. I smell her perfume, and her sweat. I say, "I just wanted Marble off the street."

She steps back, picks up a legal pad from her desk. Her smile is loose, like she came back to the office from the bar. The Job can do that, too; it can buzz you up. But I don't get it, because—

"I thought you'd be pissed."

"I am. Yes. At the team, and at your partner, and at Weiss especially. But you know what? The vine is already flowering, just for you. It's beautiful, really. 'An injured female officer goes rogue to catch the psycho who attacked her—'"

"Marble isn't psycho. He's just sick."

"Thank god the story is out of your hands." She makes herself a note. "The commander's got a CompStat meeting in the morning. He's waiting on a statement. How do you feel about dangerous? May I call Marble dangerous?"

"More like special."

Iverson's smile thins. "I can't say that."

"Why didn't anybody know he was mentally ill? Didn't Mike Day look at Marble's priors when he caught the case?"

"I don't know." She makes another note.

"What about Duppstadt? Doesn't a second offense warrant a look at Marble's file before the case is assigned?"

"I suppose."

"Didn't anybody do their homework along the way? Why am I the only one who picked up on his condition?"

She stops writing, looks at me. "When, exactly, did you pick up on it? When he attacked you? Because I don't remember you saying anything about 'special' in *that* very compelling narrative."

I don't know what to say to that. I'm certainly not going to re-hash the other details I accidentally left out or intentionally altered.

Iverson puts the legal pad aside. "Simonetti, our job is not to determine the mental capacity of a felon, or a fugitive. Our job is to find the guy. To get him off the street, as you said. And as you did."

"I know that." I mean, that's what I was thinking when I walked in here.

"You also know that the best thing you can do now is the very thing you were supposed to do in the first place: leave it alone. Go home and get better. Let me make it sound good to the bosses. Let Marble be the bad guy. Let Anzalone have his big moment. And let your silence be proof that whatever happened is over."

"What about testifying?"

"If this new sex-assault charge is accepted and the case hits court, we won't need you or the other vic, either. We'll have physical evidence. DNA. And we'll have Pearson."

"What happens to Marble?"

"We'll keep him for forty-eight, see if Pearson can make the charge stick. If she can't, we'll find him a new facility. Either way, I promise he's going to be locked up somewhere." Iverson goes around the desk again, finds the flask she'd been nipping from, and toasts me: "Congratulations, Simonetti. Now if you'll excuse me, I have a statement to write."

"Thank you," I say, though I'm not sure what I'm thanking her for. I think I just agreed to lie some more.

I let myself out. When I see Weiss, I think about letting myself back in. He's sitting in a folding chair against the wall like he's waiting to get up.

Iverson must have called him in; he knows what for. Part of me wants to say *ha, ha!* but the rest of me isn't so childish; the rest of me can surely come up with something more caustic.

He looks up. "How are you feeling?"

"Much better, now that Marble is locked up." *Ha, ha.*

"I'm glad," he says, and though he sounds like he means it, he may as well have told me he's dying, the way he looks. Like somebody sucked the hot blood right out of him.

I don't care. Weiss wanted the arrest? I got it. He was on to something bigger? Something he was going to use me to get? I squashed it. I saved myself.

I say, "See ya," and get out of there without another word. Iverson told me to be quiet; I'll take that cue.

When I get outside, the western sky is a brilliant orange, caught between day and night. I clear the steps and then I root through my bag for my phone to check the time. I'm hoping I'll make it home before Isabel goes to bed. If I'm a little late, I'll let her stay up awhile, tell her the Jezebel version of this story in the dove's nest; I'll bring M&Ms *and* chocolate milk. If I'm way too late, maybe Mari will stick around and let me tell stories.

I don't find my phone until I get to my car—I guess I left it on the passenger seat when I followed Anzalone and Marble into the station.

I have four messages; I play them as I head for home.

One: "Regina Simonetti, this is Elaine Brille, from the Medical Section. After reviewing your file, I'm calling to inform you, that I am only able to clear you for active duty, once your physician sends an updated report, issuing clearance." She sounds automated, her weird phrasing. I think of Walter; I'll have to tell him the department is a step ahead on his idea to hire robots. Brille says, "If you have medical questions, please contact your physician. For insurance questions, visit the Personnel Concierge at the department website. If I can be of further assistance, you can reach me at the following extension—"

I delete the message; she didn't tell me anything I didn't know. Anyway, there'll be no calling Elaine Brille again. The only way I plan to get through to her now is to take Metzler's report straight to her office and demand she ink her stamp.

Message two: "Regina." It's Metzler. "I'm calling because my answering service received a call from George, and I haven't been able to reach him—"

I stop the message. Something's happened. Something bad has happened.

I pull over. The last two messages are from the same random number. I panic. I back out of my voice mail to see Isabel smiling at me from the screensaver. I wonder if this moment is going to be my before, and if pressing PLAY again will lead to an unfathomable after.

I wonder if I am way too late.

I press PLAY.

"Gina: George. It's Isabel—it was an accident. She fell. I think she's okay? She threw up, and then she seemed better, but now she won't stop crying—"

"Where's Maricarmen?" I ask over the message.

"I gave her some medicine I found—"

"Jesus fucking Christ." I put the car in DRIVE. "What medicine? What happened?"

"I want to call her doctor, but I can't find a phone number. Will you call back? I don't know what else I should do."

"Call a fucking ambulance!" I yell. I drive like I'm driving an ambulance.

I skip to the next message, recorded thirty minutes later. "Gina, George. I've been trying to get ahold of you. Isabel fell, and she hit her head. Maricarmen is here now and—"

"Where was she before?"

"—she thinks I should take her to the hospital. I just—I don't have her insurance information. Or her birth certificate. I don't know if I'm even allowed to drive her, I don't have a car seat? Anyway, call back at this number, okay? It's Geraldo's phone. My battery died. And Isabel—well, maybe if she heard your voice—"

I hang up. I drive. The road is a blur, but I just fucking drive.

I double-park in front of the house. I blow through the door and stop when I find Maricarmen, Geraldo, and George at the table. Maricarmen looks relieved to see me and starts to get up; Geraldo looks guilty, like I caught him doing something more insensitive than eating a slice of pizza. George just sits there chewing, one of my beers in hand.

"Where is she?"

"She's asleep," George says, like it's some kind of accomplishment.

I want to take the bottle from him and break it over his head.

Maricarmen steps between us. "Mama. This is not the time for anger—"

"You're right. There will be plenty more time for that." I turn for Isabel's room.

I step over a gang of stuffed animals to open the blinds. The moon puts a blue square of light on the wall above the crib.

I peek in. The sight of her breaks me.

She is asleep, clutching her bear. She's got a knot on her little forehead the size of a golf ball. There's dried blood around her pacifier, and on the bear's face. I smell her wet diaper and her unwashed hair.

I want to pick her up, I want her in my arms, but I'm afraid; I don't know what kind of fall she took.

I do know that head injuries are the leading cause of disability and death in children under four.

I also know that children either bounce back quickly from concussions, or they never do.

I use the lightest touch to move the hair sweat-pasted to her cheek. "Isabel," I whisper.

She doesn't stir.

"Come on, baby. Wake up. I'm here." I take the bear; Isabel's arms tense and she moans an objection.

"Hi, Meatball," I say. "I'm so happy to see you. Have you been taking care of my Spaghetti? I hear she took a tumble." Talking to the bear puts a shiny cover over my shaky voice.

Isabel stretches her legs and reaches for the bear: all limbs in operation. I give him a kiss and put him back in her waiting arms and she rolls on her side to snuggle up with him.

"Isabel. I need you and Meatball to wake up now."

Because she moved easily, I decide it's safe to pick her up. I reach in and wrap an arm around the backs of her legs, the other around her shoulders. I lift her carefully, though my voice isn't all that's shaking. "Isabel. It's Mama."

She opens her heavy eyes.

"Hi, baby."

When she realizes it's me, she spits the pacifier out of her mouth to say, "Mama." The way she says it sounds like both a complaint and a comfort.

"Spaghetti," I say.

She shows me a sleepy smile. And also that she's missing a tooth.

"Oh, Isabel!" I turn her around to put her face in the moonlight, and to confirm that one of her six-and-a-half baby teeth—top front—is gone.

"What happened?" I ask, though I know she can't tell me. I pull her close and hold her and I stand there teetering back and forth in my stupid, heavy boots. She whimpers; she's picking up on my anger. I try softening my stance and my voice when I say, "I wish you could tell me what happened."

"You left the door open," George says, from behind me.

"What?" I'm as shocked to hear him speak up as I am by his answer.

"When you left. You rushed out. Isabel was upset. She tried to follow you. The door wasn't closed all the way."

"Where the hell were you?"

He tugs at his hair. "I was right behind her. I didn't know the door was open. She slipped through and by the time I got out she was an inch out of my reach, and she went down."

I try to picture the scene. The timing. The truth.

"I didn't leave the door open," I say and I'm not defensive, I'm certain.

"Well, it was open." George comes in and steps all over the stuffed animals, his beer bottle held loose, by the neck. "Thank god Lidia was still here. Because at first I thought Isabel got through it with maybe only a scratch, you know? Like she did a tuck and roll?"

He examines Isabel's forehead like he knows what the fuck he's talking about. "I thought you were fine, right, Bell?"

It's ridiculous, the way he talks to her. Like a buddy he helped in a bar fight.

"You weren't crying at all," he says. "You sat up and looked around. And I came down the steps and I said *Are you okay?* And you—what did you do?"

Isabel looks up at him, then at me, and she's confused—not by the question so much as her dad thinking she has the words to answer.

"You puked!" he says. "There was puke and blood everywhere. God, it was so gross! And I picked you up and carried you upstairs and man, I thought we were both gonna die. Your mouth was gushing. I was so freaked out. But then there was Lidia, how about that for luck? She helped me get you cleaned up, and we—well, Lidia—she's the one who figured it out—that the blood was all from your gums. I didn't know gums bled like that! But once we got you cleaned up, and gave you some ice cream, it was no big deal, right?"

"Not a big deal at all," I say, "if you didn't know she had a tooth there before."

"What?"

"It's broken. At the root. Probably why she couldn't stop crying." I start for the door. "She needs to see a doctor. Not a lucky nurse."

Isabel says, "Mama?"

I say, so nicely, "Hold on, baby. I've got you."

Isabel holds on tight.

George follows me into the kitchen, where Maricarmen has put the pizza away; now she and Geraldo sit at the table, both of them silent, Mari obviously trying to get a bead on the situation, Geraldo probably wishing he hadn't come along. They get up when I come in.

"I'm sorry," Maricarmen says.

"Don't be sorry," I tell her, "it's my fault for leaving her here with him."

"Hey—" George protests.

"Lidia said she will be okay," Mari says, sticking up for him.

"You're some kind of team, now?" The sudden solidarity pisses me right off. I free up my good hand, get a grocery bag from the cabinet, and fill it with whatever I think Isabel might want in the next twenty-four hours. Snacks, toys, socks.

George tries to help—he tries to take the grocery bag and help—but I turn away.

Maricarmen says, "My youngest broke his arm when he was three. Children, they heal very quickly—"

"No offense, but I'm going to get a professional opinion."

"Should I come with you?" George asks, following me to the door.

"No. I think you should go."

"Gina—"

I don't argue. I don't look back.

I call Lurie Children's Hospital on the way.

14

The day Metzler told me I had multiple sclerosis, I went numb.

I went to see him because I couldn't feel my left hand. I'd been overtraining at the gym, and I thought I'd pinched a nerve in my neck.

I knew it was much more than that when I watched him read the MRI films. It was the only time I saw his face betray him. He sat me down and sat down with me and said, "Regina, I am so sorry."

I was pretty sorry myself. The only other time I'd heard about the disease was when I arrested an old lady at Lincolnwood Town Center. She was a purse-snatcher; I caught her sitting on a wheelchair full of stolen bags. I thought she was using the chair as a prop and I asked her to get up; she told me she couldn't because she had MS. I said I was sorry, but a disease was no reason to steal. She said the real reason she was stealing was because she was going broke paying for medication that didn't work, and that she just wanted to buy herself a goddamned drink.

The day I was diagnosed, I walked out of Metzler's office and into a bar.

A blur of gin and tonics later, when I was good and numb, I called work to tell them I'd come down with something—something viral, I said. Contagious. Then I drove to the store and absentmindedly bought groceries. At home, I made myself breakfast—wheat toast with margarine, nonfat yogurt, and a banana—the usual. But when I sat down to eat, the first bite of toast made me as sick as I'd felt in years. I'd fixed that food-pyramid-perfect plate for as long as I could remember—mostly to have at least one healthy meal a day, as it was impossible at work and unappealing afterward—but apparently it hadn't made a shit of difference. This disease, which I did nothing to cause and could do nothing to cure, was going to cheat me out of the best years of my life. The balance I thought I had struck was upended.

I threw breakfast away and vowed I'd never take another bland bite of anything. I was twenty-seven, and in no time at all, I'd be an old lady in some home where they'd serve me that same damn toast until I croaked.

I'd probably have done some real damage to myself that day if the spinal tap headache hadn't arrived when it did. I was getting dressed to go back to the bar when it hit me. For three days, I couldn't stand up. I couldn't sit up. I couldn't do anything. I thought I was going to die.

For a while there, I wished it.

But on day four, when I wasn't dead, I knew: I had been diagnosed with a disease that jumped time, and if I was going to have any kind of life, I had to jump with it, and roll through.

So I got up. I got dressed. I took a cab to the hospital for a blood patch. And as soon as I could see straight again, I figured out how I was going to live.

My research about the disease proved that without recommended drugs and a careful, gentle lifestyle, women like me are prone to various recurring problems. Spasticity, weakness, dizziness. Gait issues, vision loss, fatigue. Research also shows that taking the drugs and living the prescribed lifestyle doesn't necessarily work. Some women succumb no matter what.

I was barely a woman, and already screwed.

Still, if I was well enough to feel sorry for myself, I was ready to roll.

I started by going back to work. No one seemed suspicious about my made-up lingering cough. No one minded that I took overtime. And after a week, most guys stopped asking if I wanted to grab lunch. I said I wasn't hungry; I wasn't lying. Nothing tasted good anymore.

When I felt like I had a decent handle on things at work, I filled Metzler's prescription. Before I took my first shot, I prescribed myself a drink. I had to be tough, after all. And while MS might not be genetic, self-medicating runs strong in my bloodline.

The so-called flu-like side effects were more like a once-a-week bout with malaria, but my excuses held steady, disappearing from my so-called personal life for work and vice versa. It was easy, that part. Dating Tom made excusing myself even easier as he didn't want to chase me away, and everyone else assumed he'd caught me.

Things were going smooth along the surface until a few months into our relationship, when I woke up in the back of the Cloverleaf. I'd had too much to drink. It wasn't the first time, but it was the first time I woke up and heard them talking about me.

It was Tom and his bartender, Jeremy.

She's a piece, Jeremy said. *That sassy little mouth, sucking down gin all night.*

You like that? Tom sounded like he did.

She's too skinny for me, Sheridan. And too smart for you. What's she got her eye on besides your ugly face? Money?

I don't care about money. It'll never be alimony.

You don't want to take her out of circulation?

Shit, Tom said, *I don't want to take myself out.*

So, what happened is what happened in most doomed relationships: I wasn't thinking about commitment until I figured out Tom didn't want it. And then I was terrified. I didn't want to be alone. I didn't have a shared history to be fond about or a promising future to anticipate. I had now. And so I latched on to him. And I got him to commit to me. Or at least the mortgage.

Yes, it was stupid. Pathetic, even. But if I wasn't going to be a wife and a mother, I wasn't going to give up on my first shot at settling. I wasn't going to fail.

Then came Isabel.

When we arrive downtown, Isabel is excited: she loves the peg-lit skyscrapers, the midnight twinkle of Michigan Avenue's trees, the fog reaching in from the lake.

She does not understand where we are going.

At Lurie Children's, I valet and we take the elevator up to the emergency care center. I let her push the button. She tries counting the numbers. The doors open to a wall of pastel-painted balloons and no one in the room seems worried; no one is ruffled.

Isabel must think it's some kind of dream.

The intake nurse believes my story, whatever it is I tell her. Maybe because I'm still dressed, my star.

The nurse who does the second interview is extra thorough. Maybe because my narrative is spotty, nonlinear. Maybe because Isabel is not my daughter.

While I fill out paperwork, Isabel sits with Meatball and watches a cartoon about pirates. Her curiosity defies the late hour, and her condition.

Once we're in a room, the doctor comes. I don't know his name. He may have said. His skin is washed out from too many overnight shifts. His smile is the kind I want to believe.

Isabel hides behind my legs. He asks her about her bear, and her favorite TV show, but she sees the scope he's taken from his pocket. She begins to cry. She begins to understand.

He tries out the scope on Meatball; Isabel cries. He passes the bear to me and uses the scope on Isabel. She screams and cries. He passes Isabel to me, and tells me he wants to run some more tests. He speaks as though no one is upset. He says he just wants to be sure.

Isabel starts to kick.

The doctor says he will give her a sedative.

I want to cry.

He prepares the needle. I tell her it'll be just a prick. She can't hear me.

He gives her the shot and she stops kicking, and stops crying, and looks up at me, and gasps: I have betrayed her.

When the doctor leaves, I hold her and I rock her in a chair that does not rock. I tell her I love her. I promise I will not leave her side.

She is still awake when the nurses come and take her for an MRI. They let me hold her hand on the way down to the machine, but they won't let me join her in the room. They make a liar out of me.

They say the test will take a while. And then X-rays. They suggest I wait in her room.

As I wait, I get numb. Not the impermeable unfeeling I remember from the day I was diagnosed; this is more like the soul-flushed, heart-trashed emptiness I felt the day my father died.

It was an accident. He broke his neck. I was the first one to the hospital, and when I saw him, I knew he wouldn't make it. But in the moment—that moment I saw him on the bed, a halo brace—I couldn't believe it. I couldn't feel it. It seemed impossible.

My brother showed up. He saw Dad, talked to the girlfriend. Her story was that my father slept on the couch after a fight. And so he woke up in the wrong place, stumbled to the bathroom, maybe. And on the way, he slipped. After, he managed to crawl into bed. To sleep, the brain swell unrestricted. A matter of time.

In the morning, the girlfriend meant to apologize. Tried. Couldn't wake him. Called an ambulance.

Sitting in that room, waiting for those doctors, I kept thinking about a saying I heard in the academy: *Witnesses' stories tell their own innocence.* And then I started thinking I didn't have the full story.

Then, he died. Whatever the story was didn't matter. It was over.

Sitting here, I just keep telling myself that the story doesn't matter. And that this can't be over.

Sometime later, they bring Isabel back. She is asleep.

Sometime after that, the nurse comes in and finds me on the bed with Isabel. The machines and monitors are towering giants, impassive guards around the high, tiny bed.

"If you'd like to get some rest, in the sleep room . . ." the nurse says, her whispered voice an intrusion, an alarm.

I think I say, "No."

Or else she knows my answer, because she pushes the not-rocking chair next to the hospital bed, reclines the chair, and gives me a pillow. "You'll both be more comfortable," she says, and helps me from the bed to the chair without disrupting any of the cords or cables they've patched on or taped to Isabel.

I think I say, "Thank you."

Eventually, she leaves.

I watch the sun come up from this hospital room's window. I know being numb is selfish. Isabel needs me, and that should feel like something. Even if it hurts. Even if it's fucking terrifying. And even if she will never remember any of this.

Because this isn't over. It can't be.

"Mama?" I hear Isabel say, her voice droopy, deep.

I sit up and reach over the bed rail for her. "I'm right here." My mouth is dry as old cake and my neck feels like it's been fixed with pins; I must've dozed off.

"Mama," she says, trying to reach for me, too, but she's tethered by the cords.

I get up and move the chair and climb back on the bed with her. "It's okay, Spaghet." I stretch over her to press the nurse's call button. "Just stay right there."

As I stroke her hair, I pretend I don't see the knot on her forehead, so bruised it's black now. I smell her and I kiss her cheek and I whisper, "I think I slept a little. Did you have a good sleep?" I hope familiar banter will help her adjust to the unfamiliar environment. I say, "I had a dream about the moon. It was a strange, spongy place. Everything was blue. Kind of like this room. And there were cupcakes. Do you think they have cupcakes here?"

She says, "Juice."

"Juice, of course—they must have juice here."

"Good morning," a new nurse says, smiling her way into the room. She looks like a teenager, her freckles, her cinched ponytail. Her scrubs are owl-themed.

"Good morning, Cassie," I say, off her tag. I slip off the bed but I keep a hand on Isabel. "I think she's ready for some juice."

"Ooh," Cassie says, like I've just presented the best idea in the world. "We love juice!"

Naturally I'm annoyed when she says *we*. None of this happened to us.

Cassie rounds the bed to check the monitors. "Isabel, what's your favorite kind of juice?"

Isabel hides behind Meatball.

"I like moon juice the best," Cassie says, winking at me as she punches keys that make one of the machines beep and spit paper tape.

Isabel peeks at me like we're onto something.

"Moon juice," I confirm, though it feels awkward, having a stranger join our game.

"I'll page Dr. Davidson and he'll come in and go over everything," Cassie says, her voice making it sound fun, like we'll be bouncing beach balls.

I say, "I'd like to speak with him as soon as possible."

"You got it." She leans over to tell Isabel: "I'll go find some moon juice."

Isabel is thrilled.

I am not. I hate waiting.

I think Isabel is feeling better because she rejects the moon juice and throws a little tantrum about breakfast. I can't blame her; both arrive covered in Saran Wrap, the moon juice is definitely orange-flavored, and the scrambled eggs on the doctor-recommended soft-food plate may have come from another planet.

If we weren't in the hospital, I would argue that she needs to eat real food. I'd peel the foil tops from the yogurt and the applesauce; I would tell her to eat what's on her plate.

Instead, I wipe her tears, put the tray aside, and tell her, "I'll be back before you can spell milkshake."

"I not," she says, but she knows the key word. It lights her up.

I take the elevator up to the eleventh floor and step off into an indoor garden where bamboo trees grow in modern, bright-colored stands that border the path to the Sky Café. Behind the trees, floor-to-way-high-ceiling windows offer a mid-level view of the cityscape, a bland backdrop.

At the café they make me a vanilla shake with bananas even though it's not on the menu.

When I deliver the shake to Isabel, a cherry on top, her wide-eyed delight makes me feel proud, and then stupid. Who would ever brag about anything in a hospital?

Still, I'm glad to see her enjoy the shake and I'm also glad to finish her breakfast—the eggs in three bites.

When the doctor comes by, Isabel ditches the shake and climbs onto my lap to hide.

"Good morning," Dr. Davidson says. He is the same doctor who examined her when we arrived. This time, he's with a dark-skinned woman who has light green eyes and a head of wild, curly black hair. Her smile is perfect and her teeth are so white they're blue. She is gorgeous, the type who'd make a man attempt to write poetry.

In the daylight, Davidson looks more tired and less happy, but after he checks Isabel's head right where she hides, he is happy to tell me, "I've read the radiology report, and I believe the hematoma—the big bump on her head—is merely a cosmetic issue."

I could fall off the bed. "Thank you." I close my eyes and hug Isabel. The relief is overwhelming. And fleeting. Because it will never trump the guilt.

Davidson stands aside. "This is Dr. Chavda, one of our pediatric dentists." He turns to her. "I'll order the discharge paperwork, if you'll take it from here?"

"Thank you, yes." Dr. Chavda lifts the surgical mask from around her neck to cover her eyes. "Isabel," she says, and peeks. "Boo."

Isabel peeks back, reticent.

Dr. Chavda fashions the mask into a hair tie that makes her

wild curls look like a bouquet on top of her head and says, "Whatever you do, Isabel, don't smile."

The smile is imminent. And crooked, now.

"And please, no giggling. I can't have you giggling."

Cue giggling.

"Isabel! My goodness, you're listening backwards." She works a surgical glove over her hand and sits on the bed with us. "Now please listen, because there's one thing I don't want you to ever, ever do, and that's to bite this weird rubbery glove. Don't do it, okay? Please?"

Isabel bites.

As I watch Chavda do her exam, I'm amazed by her bedside manner. Everyone in this place has been so patient, and so kind. It gets me thinking: Why aren't all sick people treated with similar regard? Why is it cute when Isabel is scared, but a problem when someone like Kay St. Claire feels the same way? And outside this place, why are so many of us soft with children, and hard on our elders? It's amusing when a child can't remember a word; it's pitiful when an old person forgets.

"Looks good," Chavda says, snapping off the glove. "The X-ray shows a crown root fracture, but there doesn't appear to be any pulp involvement, and it isn't bothering her on palpitation. That means that so long as what's left of the tooth is stable, and without infection, it can stay. Since it's a front tooth, the concern, just like with the hematoma, is ninety-nine percent aesthetic. If you're worried about her smile—"

"I don't care what she looks like. What's the other one percent?"

"Well, some parents worry about compromised front teeth causing problems with language development. But I think her tongue will get used to her mouth this way, and pretty soon, she'll be telling you exactly what she thinks. She won't be misunderstood; of that I'm a hundred percent certain."

Isabel looks worried, and it's because she's taking cues from me, so

I put on a smile. "You're going to be fine," I tell her. When she smiles back—gashed and gap-toothed—I think I could kill my brother.

"Just to be safe," Chavda says, "I'd like to see her next week. In the meantime, I'll write a prescription for the antibiotic we've started her on here—five milliliters twice a day until it's gone. And Dr. Davidson has her on a steady dose of ibuprofen—for the inflammation, but also in case she has any pain. Keep her on the scheduled doses— whatever the bottles say—for forty-eight hours, and then see how she does." She takes out a scrip pad. "I'll write this down for you."

I guess I must look confused, or overwhelmed, or both, because her parting shot is to take my hand and say, "She *will* be fine."

Checkout takes forever, and I spend the entire time avoiding eye contact with other adults who catch sight of Isabel—a happy, healthy kid butterflying around the common area—nothing apparently wrong. Nothing, certainly, compared to the hundred-plus really sick kids and twice as many real parents here who are negotiating, or praying. And not for a baby tooth. For a day.

I have never been religious. Yes, I recognize a need for rules, but I've seen too much terrible shit to believe some One made them up. Now, though, I can't get a grip on this good fortune; the science of it doesn't come up even. There are Isabel's natural parents: one who never wanted her and another who still doesn't know what he wants. And then there's me, her stand-in nurturer, the one who can't stand steady.

And then there's Isabel. The reason to believe in something.

Just after two P.M. and sixteen hours after Isabel was admitted to Lurie Children's, we turn onto our street. In the hospital, time seemed abridged. Now that we're approaching home, it feels like we've been gone for a week.

"Isabel," I say softly, when I park. "We're home." I get out and unbuckle her and wrap her in the blanket she kicked off during the ride. It's cloudy, and cooler than it has been in a while; probably not blanket weather, but once she's in my arms, she takes to it like she used to when she was a baby-baby. I carry her in a ball, the rest of our stuff hanging in bags from hooked fingers.

"I tried calling," George says. He's sitting on the steps.

"A little help, here?" I ask, since he's just sitting on the steps.

He doesn't get up. His eyes are slits when he smiles. He wipes the white corners of his mouth. "I left messages." He is calm; he is controlled. He is high.

"My phone died in the middle of the night," I say. "As you can see, Isabel did not."

"Of course not. Not with you there."

"I can't believe you." I'm talking about the high.

"You were mad already."

My front door opens, and there's Soleil. She is dressed in ankle boots, high-waisted short shorts, and a ropy mesh army-green shirt that advertises her bralette. Her hair hangs over her shoulders in two loose bow-tied ponytails and her big, beautiful wide-set eyes are hidden behind oversize sunglasses—an essential accessory since the hardest thing for a girl like Soleil to cover up is the fact she doesn't give a shit.

Most women would look ridiculous dressed as she is, even if they could claim fashion. Soleil wears whatever she wants and it's like skin. It's not the fit so much as fitting the part. She could be a model. Except that she's really just a skinny, strung-out fuckup.

She comes down the steps, a red satchel sliding to the crook of her arm. She says, "We are leaving."

I see seven of the 101 Dalmatians on the satchel and then I know what she means by *we*.

I take a step back. "What the fuck?"

"Nice," Soleil says. "In front of the kid."

George says, "I got real upset, Gina, when I couldn't reach you? I felt so bad, about what happened. It was an accident. But I knew you'd blame me. I knew you'd want me to leave."

"So he called me," Soleil says. "He feels better now."

I cradle Isabel's head and cover her ears. "Did you take pills, George? Or did she crush them up for you, help you get there quicker?"

Soleil says, "I told him to use one of your syringes—"

"Just a minute." George holds up a hand. "I am high, Gina. Pretty fucking high. But at least I'm not going to lie about it. I'm not a liar. Not like you."

I want to ask him what he's talking about, but we all know. When he called Soleil to get high, she was happy to oblige, since her best high comes from getting control of people. And once she got him high, she went looking for a way to get control of me.

She went through my home. Looking for pills. For money. For leverage.

She found the syringes. The Avonex.

"I'm not a liar," I say. Not a good one, anyway.

George stands up. "I always told you the truth, Gina. No matter if I knew you'd think I was wrong, or stupid, or pathetic. It wasn't easy, you know? When I was a kid, or when—even when my ideas were good—like last year, when I told you I was going to go to church. You said I was avoiding my problems."

"You said you were going there to pray for a job."

"So what? People pray for all sorts of things. And I know you don't believe it, but asking for help is not actually a sign of weakness."

He's got me there.

"The church—they have confession there. I have to say it's a lot easier than telling you about stuff. Because there, when you tell the truth, you clear your conscious. You don't get a big bong hit of guilt with it."

I resist telling him the word is *conscience* but I do have to ask: "Did God ever get you that job?"

"I know you think faith is some big joke. But the priest—when I told him how I hurt my back, and how I got high all the time, and that I needed help? He told me that when the righteous cry for help, the Lord hears and delivers them out of all their troubles. I was confused, you know? When he said that? Because I always thought you were the righteous one. Then I realized he was telling me I needed to be righteous. So I've been trying—I really have."

"I know you have," I say, "though prescription drug abuse doesn't really fit that scenario—"

"Don't talk down to me," he says. "I'm up here."

"I'm sorry, George, I just don't understand what this has to do with Isabel's well-being."

"I don't want her brought up by a liar."

"I'm not a liar," I say again, though I'm not sure I even convince myself.

"You are sick, and you are lying about it. You are single and you lie about it. You have a dangerous job; you lie about it. You only tell the truth when it makes you look good, Gina. You are not righteous; you just want to be right."

"I only want to keep Isabel safe."

George gets up, comes down the steps. "I'm taking her."

"George, please," I say, clutching her in the blanket. "You aren't seeing reality, here. You can take her—sure—she's your daughter. But don't do it now. Not while you're high."

Soleil comes down, stands with George. "I'm sober, and I can see reality just fine. You know what I see? I see that you don't want

George to get what he wants. Ever. And now that he's standing up for himself, and he's making a choice, you're trying to act like an authority. You're pretending to be his mom, just like you are with the kid."

"Maybe that's how it looks through Percocet-colored glasses."

"Gina," George says. "Give her to me."

I don't. I back away. "I'm sorry for the way I've acted. You're right, I need help. But so do you. Don't take her now. You're unfit."

Soleil finds her phone. "You want me to call DCFS?"

"You wouldn't do that," I say to George, because fuck Soleil.

"Sure I would," Soleil says. "I'll tell them everything I know, and then we'll see which one of you is unfit."

"You'd break our family apart," I say. "They'd take her to foster care—"

"I would never let that happen," George says, fighting both of us, now. He reaches for Isabel, takes her from me. I can't stop him.

"Mama?" Isabel asks, roused by his clumsy handling.

She sees she's no longer with me and starts to struggle, her whole little body lurching, reaching for me; I open my arms, I'll take her— "Spaghetti—"

"Aww, listen to that," Soleil says, swinging Isabel's satchel over her shoulder. "So cute. So motherly."

"Mama?" She's stressing now, resisting, but she's trapped in the blanket—

"Please," I say to George. "She's all I've got."

"No," George says, "she's not." He holds her tight and carries her off.

"Mama!"

I try to follow, but Soleil cuts in front of me. She takes off her glasses, proving she is sober. Which makes this just a little better, and so much worse.

"Isabel's medication—" I say, finding the bottles in my bag. "Will you take it? I don't mean take it. I mean give it to her—"

She takes the bottles, reads the labels.

"An antibiotic and an anti-inflammatory," I say. "They can't get you high."

"Mama!" Isabel wails, now, which only makes George more determined as he stalks toward Soleil's car.

Soleil tucks the bottles into the satchel, looks over her shoulder at them. "I know DCFS isn't much of a threat, being who you are. Plus, there's lag time with that group. Just ask my foster mom; I told them she beat the shit out of me and she's still got a nine-year-old living with her." She puts her glasses back on. "I do have another call I can make. Our mutual friend, Ray? We've been talking lately. I don't bring it up in front of George—kind of a sore spot—but you know how it is. Anyway. I'm pretty sure Ray would love to hear the truth about your little situation. I'll bet *that's* a threat. Being who you are."

"Just go."

"Been trying," she says, and saunters off, one boot crossing in front of the other.

I grab on to the fence and find the ground beneath my feet and I can't fucking believe what's happening. I can't do anything. Legally, I can't do anything. This informal arrangement worked perfectly when George wanted it to.

As I watch Soleil's crappy Buick drive off, I realize the world I've created for Isabel is nothing more than an elaborate game of pretend.

But with good reason. Because this world—the real one? It fucking sucks.

15

About twenty seconds goes by before I'm headed to Soleil's. Fuck her, and fuck Weiss. Fuck DCFS; fuck MS. Nobody sane could look at this situation and think George should be Isabel's caretaker. I mean, he's got a disease, too, and he isn't seeking treatment—he's abusing it. And while neither of us has been forthcoming about our health, I don't actively attempt to destroy myself. Or drag around baggage like that manipulative bitch.

Before I leave I do a sweep of the house—mostly to see what I'll have to take back from them besides Isabel—but they didn't pack one thing for her. Not diapers, not wipes; not pacifiers, not pajamas. Not snacks, not a single fucking toy. What the hell did Soleil put in the satchel?

I never figure out what the hell, because I'm back out the door when I realize they drove off without a car seat.

It should take me fifteen minutes to get there; Friday afternoon traffic makes it forty-five. I try George's phone on the way. I get his voice mail. "This is George Simonetti." His voice sounds fake, trying for official. "Please leave a message."

I should apologize. I should explain. But when I hear the beep, all I say is, "George. It's Regina. Please call."

I park on Elston around the corner from Soleil's. She lives on an angled block in Avondale in one of the only houses that doesn't display a union support sign. She's got what's nicely referred to as a garden apartment—a basement unit with a view of the upstairs neighbors' hanging plants. Her entrance is off an alley that's shared with the parking lot of an auto repair shop. Avondale is pretty nice these days; her place is not.

Soleil's ground-level windows are open, though the cheap aluminum miniblinds are pulled closed. Her tabby cat, Boudelaire— yes, I looked up the name and no, there's no way Soleil has a clue about French poetry—has spent enough time sleeping against one of the screens to bow it outward, a little hole worn through. Enough time spent right there, I think, to make it feasible that it could rip, and someone could get inside.

It's also feasible, if no one answers, that someone will be me.

I go down the steps, knock on the screen door. Out here it smells like a wet ashtray because of the butt-stuffed beer bottle left sitting on the ledge. It also smells like vomit, but thankfully, that's from the neighbor's gingko tree that hangs over the fence.

I don't know why I'm thankful about that. I doubt it's much better inside.

I knock again, screen rattling. "George? Soleil?"

Nada.

I open the screen door and knock on the door. I try the handle. I wonder if they can hear me trying the handle.

"George," I say, "I brought some things Isabel needs." By *things* I mean my car and me, so we can go back home.

Nobody responds.

"George," I yell, letting the screen slam shut.

I go back up the steps and crouch down by the window to see if

I can hear them, but what I hear is the air-conditioning unit click on for the upstairs unit. Traffic chasing through a green light over on Elston. An airplane curling toward its flight path to O'Hare.

Maybe for a layover on its way to Atlanta. Or California. Or anywhere Isabel could dream of going. I wish I could take her. I wish we were gone.

I look over at the window just as Boudelaire noses out through the blinds and sits there, watching me with zero interest.

"Are they in there?" I ask. I don't expect an answer from the cat, but I'd like to establish some rapport before I let myself in. I don't need my eyes scratched out twice.

I stick my finger through the hole and pull. The screen pops out, and I slide in, feet-first.

And then, all I smell is filth. It's the filth that creeps onto everything when the only thing in sharp focus is the flame that lights the pipe, or the bottle that holds the high. It's spoiled food, cigarette smoke, cat shit, garbage. Moldy towels, spilled beer, dirty clothes. It's burned-out candles, a backed-up sink. It's junkie squalor, post-party, when nobody gets sober.

It isn't messy, though; it isn't unlivable. The cat has food and water and there are flowers, still alive, in a vase on the table. But I know it's all here.

I open the fridge; there's white bread, generic peanut butter, and the honey that comes in the bear-shaped container. Also orange juice, and beer. All George's staples.

I'm sure Soleil doesn't stay here. Probably hasn't come back since the party that started this mess. Probably, she's been shacking up with whoever caught her eye that night. And George is the idiot who stayed, who cleaned up. Tucked away all their secrets. Made it look like everything is okay.

Soleil probably did come back once, to feed the cat, maybe. She'd have been high, and upon discovering George was there—and sober—she'd have gone mad. Hard mad. She'd have called George pathetic for thinking he could stay clean. Put his stuff out, told him to try it without her. Stone-cold wished him well. She'd have closed the door and waited for him to leave before she left herself. And she'd have kept control simply by pretending she didn't want it.

I know this because she got control in the first place by relieving George's pain. And by that route, she also very easily showed him just how bad he could hurt.

I know I showed him some hurt, too. And maybe I steered him back in her direction. But I hope that when George held Isabel in his arms today, he saw through his hurt, and remembered he had dreams of his own once. Dreams that are so much better than this.

I pet Boudelaire though neither of us cares for it and then I let myself out. As much as I hoped to find Isabel, I'm glad they didn't come here. The question is: where the fuck else would they go?

16

I put my hair up. Eye shadow. I wear a blue slip dress, short but tasteful, the back cut out. I wear perfume. And heels.

I walk to a dark, trendy bar on Western Avenue. Sportsman's. I order gin. I choose the booth in the middle, the darkest. I sit there and drink until it's just as dark outside. I think about the difference between looking for someone who doesn't want to be found and someone who doesn't want *you* looking. I order more gin.

When I leave, I don't bother trying George again. Instead, I call Calvin.

He assumes I'm calling about St. Claire. He says, "I'm not working."

I say, "Neither am I."

"Do you party?"

"I'm looking to."

We agree to meet. He says where.

I take a cab to a not-so-dark, not-so-trendy bar. This one on Fullerton. Pool tables and televisions and pitchers of beer. Called the Two Way. I don't know which way I'm going.

Dressed in plain clothes, there's nothing plain about Calvin. He sits at the bar watching baseball, tattoos on his arms following lines of muscle all the way down to his hands, poised around a pint glass. His jawline, defined by a recent shave, makes me nuts.

"Hi."

He turns on his stool, opens his legs. "Hi."

The neon that runs around the street-side windows bounces off the bar mirrors, doubled, and I feel dizzy.

I like having a reason to feel dizzy.

"You want something to drink?" Calvin puts a hand up for the bartender.

"I want something." I want to lean into him. I want him to hold me up. To hold me. "I've already had a drink."

He quits trying for the bartender. I can't tell if that cancels other offers.

"I had a rough day," I clarify.

He reaches into his shirt pocket and gives me a peek at the mini plastic zip bag. "Want to have a rough morning?" The tabs are white, a V stamped on each one. I know what they are. Not because I'm a cop. Because I'm George's sister.

He opens the pack. "I promise you'll have fun between now and then."

I just saw what this shit does to a person; just took a self-guided tour through addict-rubble. And before that, I'd built my life around protecting Isabel from it. But it was always right there, wasn't it? Just one bad decision away. Of course, I always thought George would be the one to make it.

I take the Oxy. Pinch it in my fingers. I say, "Nice not knowing you." I put it on my tongue.

The tab sits there for approximately two seconds before I feel it dissolving and I panic—I've never taken this drug, and I don't know what it'll do with alcohol and steroids and whatever else is left in my system, too—so I say, "This isn't my scene. I'll be across the street." I use Calvin's solid arm to help myself off the stool and I brush against him on the way out.

I spit the pill into my hand as I'm crossing Milwaukee Avenue and toss it into some bushes and lick the chalky residue from my fingers before I duck into the Whistler.

On the red-lit stage, the DJ spins something more upbeat than I'd like; it's that time of night when most people are just starting to party. I feel like I'm just about done. Then again, I'm usually in pajamas by now reading books with more pictures than words or telling made-up stories in a made-up nest in a made-up life.

I take the corner seat at the bar. I can't see the stage, and I don't care. I ask for water and scan the cocktail list. When the bartender returns I order a Bitter Buddha—a cocktail made from gin, sloe gin, Campari, and absinthe bitters. This way, if Calvin doesn't show up, I'll kiss myself good night.

He shows up. Behind me. My ear. "This better?"

I turn to him, my legs open this time. "Too many people," I say, even though it's only starting to get crowded.

"You want to go somewhere else?"

"I just ordered a drink."

"You don't have to drink it."

"You don't have to stay while I do."

He looks up, catches the bartender, signals for one of what I'm having. Then he pulls out his wallet. There's cash. Too much of it.

"What: you robbed a bank?"

"Wouldn't that be a story. Cop falls in love with a wanted criminal."

"That would be something." If I fell in love.

"The hospital doesn't pay the bills," Calvin says. "I sell a little on the side."

I cross my legs. "A little what?"

"Relief."

"Twenty-two," the bartender says, setting the drinks. I let Calvin pay and take a sip. It tastes like stepping off a cliff.

I spin around on my stool and my head spins twice. "I'll be back."

The bathroom is a gender-neutral single toilet, same candlelight as the bar. I drop the seat and when I sit down to pee I feel so fucking good: I've had enough alcohol for my brain to float in my head just so, just so I can't worry about anything but peeing, and that's really nothing to worry about.

Thank God, I think.

Which makes me think of George again.

Then I have to puke.

I flush and I'm washing out my mouth when someone knocks on the door.

"Just a second," I say, and dry my face and hands and find lipstick and hand sanitizer and gum and I'm opening the door thinking how I hate those girls who take for fucking ever, and I'm ready to say sorry, but then there's Calvin.

He pushes me back inside and closes the door and locks it.

He doesn't say anything, just takes my face in his hands. I wrap my arms around him and we kiss. I taste gin and I don't know if he can taste bile but if he does it doesn't faze him. Pretty soon he's got his arms around me and he lifts me up and sits me on the sink. I'm straddling him and I'm wearing this dress—it could be easy; I could be easy.

I want to be.

I reach down between his legs and let him know it.

Then he pulls me back by my hair to kiss my neck.

I've never really been into that.

Also, I can feel water from the sink soaking through the back of my dress.

And I don't like that my feet aren't touching the floor. And I hate that I can't feel my feet.

And now I'm thinking too much.

"Wait." I slide off the sink, pushing him away as I do. When I have my feet firmly planted I say, "Let's go." I open the door and lead the way, though I avoid eye contact with anybody who might notice us both exiting. Or my wet dress.

Calvin follows me outside. "Where are we going?"

"I don't know."

"We could hop the L, head downtown, find a club."

"I'm not feeling that bitchy."

"We could stay local, find a dive, play the juke."

"I'm not feeling that friendly."

"Where, then?" He puts his arm around me.

"Where's your place?"

"You want to go to my place?"

"You have something to hide?"

"No. But I live in Forest Park."

I duck out from under his arm to look at him. "You live in the suburbs?" I sound shocked, which I then find really funny. I'm fairly certain it has to do with the gin and maybe the Oxy, even though I spit it out. It also has to do with the fact that I feel like I'm losing control and the damn funny joke is that I ever thought I had any control in the first place. When I can manage, I ask, "Why do you live in the suburbs?"

"I live in *a* suburb and I don't care if you laugh. I don't know why everybody thinks this city is so great. My place is affordable and it isn't shitty and I don't have to be a security guard when I get home."

"Have you washed your sheets lately?"

"What? Yes, I have."

"Okay, then." I flag a cab.

We head south. The driver is Pakistani, according to his plac-ard. He has all the windows rolled down; still, the cab smells like old sweat. He smokes while he listens to an AM station where the talk-show host is ranting about national health care. I snuggle up to Calvin, partly so I won't catch any ash in my hair or eyes and mostly because *he* smells real good.

Calvin is less receptive since we caught the cab; I can't blame him. The ambiance is tough. Still, if he's feeling half as good as I do, he should be interested.

He looks out the window, a sudden heaviness to him that makes me wonder if this whole thing is on the downturn.

I try to think of something to say. I don't come up with anything. I'm here because I didn't want to talk, and I'm cuddled up to a man I don't know at all.

Then I look out the window, and I see his view: we are approach-ing Sacred Heart.

"You must be sick of sick people," I say, and then I think about what I said and I sit back, because I don't see him knowing me at all. Knowing me, diseased.

He watches the place go by. "The doctors are the ones who make me sick. They don't care about the patients."

"That can't be true."

"It's true. All the bullshit they order? And patients don't know any better. You go in, you think you're dying, of course you're going to agree to tests. 'Diagnostic certainty' is what they call it. You prob-ably don't need half the workup, but you'll never know the differ-ence. Nine times out of ten you're okay, and ten out of ten, your insurance pays the bill."

"What about the uninsurable?" I say, but I think that's exactly what the guy on the radio just said. I feel a distinct surge of en-ergy. The cab windows look like they're bending; the back of the front seat seems five feet away from me. I reach for it, but I can't reach it.

"It's a conspiracy," Calvin says, "when the only way to get by is to close your eyes."

"To get by what?" I ask. I close my eyes.

"Making a living, I'm talking about."

"I honestly don't know what you're talking about." I'm really tripping.

"I sell scrips, Gina. And I tell myself I'm helping people. Helping them feel better."

"I feel better." I don't, actually. "I don't, actually. I feel . . . unusual."

"That's the cotton. You know what the docs call it, when they snow you? Deagitation. They act like it's all part of treatment."

I ask, "What cotton? What snow?"

The car speeds up, and when I open my eyes the driver has merged onto 290 and joined the race west. He turns up the radio, probably so he doesn't have to listen to us.

The radio host says, *"Even our insured are in trouble. Because we are so deeply corrupted, so cash strapped, that our doctors cannot afford to treat our sick, and our sick cannot afford to survive. Here's just one more example: the new drug for Hepatitis C. The patients awaiting the drug all have health insurance. Their doctors are licensed physicians. There is no shortage of the drug— and it's a cure, I repeat—it is a cure for Hep C. Still, patients cannot get this treatment. Why? Because our state can't afford it. Did you hear that? We know our legislators are thieves, but did you know they are also murderers?"*

I look over at Calvin, who's winding a pink rubber bracelet around his wrist. I hadn't noticed it before. I think it symbolizes breast cancer awareness. I wonder who has cancer. I wonder what color the Hep C folks wear.

I wonder if Calvin would ever wear an orange bracelet. If he'd care to be MS-aware.

The driver swerves around a dust-caked semi truck and the interior of the cab seems to bend more, like taffy. I go with it while I think about everything else I can think of—except I try not to think about Isabel, or George, or what the fuck I'm going to do to get her back with me. I don't have any idea—that's why I'm here. No idea.

When we exit the expressway, the cabbie is smoking again. And Calvin is looking at his phone. I'm losing him. Or I'm just lost.

"Forest Park is fucking far," I say, to myself I think, except then Calvin looks at me, streetlights winking in his blazed eyes.

He pockets his phone and reaches for me. "We're almost there."

Then, I'm on top of him. His lips are soft; his hands are too soft. I want to think he's holding back. I want him to not be able to stop.

Then the cab stops. The dome light comes on. The driver kills the radio. He says, "Thirty-three dollars."

I slide off Calvin and wipe my mouth and get out. I assume he'll pay the fare.

While I stand there and assume, I look up and realize I'm outside Doc Ryan's, an Irish pub. I know the place is Irish because on the sign, a smirky leprechaun winks at me with a mug of beer in his hand. He looks exactly like the guy painted on the Cloverleaf's men's room door.

When the cab drives off I ask, "What are we doing?"

"I thought we could get another drink."

"We could have done that thirty-three dollars ago."

Calvin looks up the street, somewhere real far away. "I don't think you know what you're doing. I feel like I'm taking advantage of you."

He's right: I don't know what I'm doing. But, "There's no advantage."

"When we first met," he says, "you didn't seem like trust came easily."

"I don't trust anybody. Trust has nothing to do with this."

An old bearded man stumbles out from the bar doors. He knows where he's going; it's his feet that aren't caught up with the plan.

I know how he feels.

I take Calvin's hand. "I don't want another drink."

He says, "I live around the corner."

Calvin lives on the second floor of a two-flat. I follow him up-stairs and into the kitchen. He snaps on a harsh overhead light. I don't want to be a cop—I don't want to investigate the place—so I look at his shoes while he gets us water. He wears Pumas.

He gets four bottles. I take one, he downs another. Then he leads me to the front room. He lets the streetlights be the lights. Heavy, humid air sits inside the open windows. It feels raw. How I want it.

He says "Have a seat" about the only couch. He messes with his tech for some music.

I don't feel like sitting, so I go to the windows instead. Outside are trees and between them, snips of light from the houses across the street. I focus on the trees. I try to see the dark.

Calvin plays a popular song I know but can't place, giving me a few years on him. The melody is electric, the base a thrumming heartbeat.

I twist the cap on my water bottle. It isn't carbonated, obvi-ously, but the bottle constricted in the fridge and now it spills down my dress, a cold shock. I take a sip that tastes like nothing and everything and I swear I can feel it when it gets to my stomach, the cold, and pretty soon I'm thinking of ice caps and water shortages and that I'm made of water, mostly. And I'm so, so thirsty.

As I finish the bottle, I feel Calvin behind me. His hands again, around me; one of them holding his own cold-sweat bottle against my dress. His touch is more confident, now. What I wanted.

I slip out of my heels. My whole body shifts, a relief. My right toes tingle on the hardwood. My breath catches.

Calvin moves side to side and I think he's trying to get me to dance but then I realize he's following me: I'm already dancing. Slow. Hips leading.

We move like that until I can't tell if I'm moving at all anymore.

Then I turn around. I take Calvin's water. I drink the rest.

And then he takes me.

"Shit. Shit!"

I open my eyes to near-blinding sun through unfamiliar windows.

"What?" I say, while I'm remembering who.

"I thought I set the alarm," Calvin says, out of bed, pulling on pants.

I sit up. I'm still in my underwear, or back in it. Oh, boy.

"I should go," I say, beating him to asking.

"It's just, Sabrina," he says, buttoning his shirt. Like I know who that is.

"I'll go." I get up and look around for my clothes and find just my heels sitting next to two bright pink frames on top of the nightstand. The same little girl smiling Calvin's smile in both.

I cringe. Not because I have no idea what happened in this room last night, or because Calvin's apparently got a kid, but because I should be waking up in my own room, with my own kid. I get back into bed and pull the sheet over myself.

"I'm sorry," he says, "I don't mean to rush out on you. It's just, Sabrina's mother won't wait. If I'm late, I miss my time. And, like I told you, I don't get much."

"Sabrina," I say, about the pictures.

"You get it, right? I mean, I guess you get her side of it. You want what's best for Isabel, and your brother ain't it. But I'm not like that. I pay up, I show up."

"I'm sorry," I say, "I don't remember talking about this last night."

"Last night? No, girl, we didn't talk last night. It was in the hospital, when you told me about Isabel, and everything you're going through—"

I do not remember talking to him in the hospital, either. "What is it you think I'm going through?"

Calvin stands up. "I'm not—I mean, I don't know exactly. And you were pretty snowed, then. But you said, you said you didn't want to do it alone. And I get that. And this—what's happening here?—I think this could be something good."

"I do not know what you are talking about." Snowed? What the fuck?

"I thought we connected." He sounds disappointed. "Whatever. I should go." He pockets his wallet.

"Do you know where I left my clothes?"

"In the bathroom."

"The bathroom?" Jesus, I don't even know where it is.

He leads me in through the kitchen and now that we're sober, and I'm holding up his day, I don't look around at his stuff because I'm embarrassed. I go inside and close the door.

My bag is on the floor. I get dressed and eat gum and use one of Isabel's wipes under my armpits, one of her bands to tie my hair. I can't bring myself to look in the mirror. I can't bring myself to look at myself. I think of Andy. I understand why he hasn't replaced his mirror. You lose who you love, your face is just a reminder of how amazing it was that someone used to love you back.

I'm about to toss the wipe when I notice pill blister packs in the trash. A lot of them. I take one out: the pills are gone, but between the foil I can make out it's Klonopin. There is a sticker mostly torn off the back that declares the sample destined for someone whose last name is *Adkins*.

I take another. It's ripped in half. I find the other half and work out it's something called zolpidem.

The third is Oxycodone. There is no foil, or sticker. I recognize it just by the package.

I pick out a second pack of Klonopin. This one, too, has a partial sticker *for the offices of Dr Lawr——kins*.

What the fuck? A *doctor*?

As I rifle through the rest, different drugs and presumably different doctors, pieces of last night—those fearless moments in the bar bathroom, and the cab, and at the window; Calvin's hands, and his mouth, and his need for me—they all fall away as I remember the Oxy, the triple-gin drink, and Calvin's side job: selling scrips.

Yes, last night, I wanted relief. Yes, I was reckless. And yes, this morning, Calvin is nothing but a fucking pill pusher with a crappy apartment in the burbs and joint custody of a kid.

I may as well have just shacked up with my brother.

I put the bottles back in the trash and open the door. Calvin is waiting for me. He's finishing a bottle of water, and I think he just swallowed something.

He asks, "You want one?"

I assume he's talking about the water but I say, "I'm good."

He's lucky I remember where the front door is, because I'm thinking fight or flight, and seeing him self-medicate before he picks up his daughter almost makes me want to stay and knock him one.

At the door I say, "Bye," without the *good*. I curse myself all the way down the steps, even as I hear him behind me—

"Hey—Gina—wait—just so you know? Nothing happened last night." The way he says it doesn't sound like disappointment; it sounds like he'd like another shot.

"Okay, Curtis," I say, making it clear that I don't care.

17

The cab is a remorse ride. In the heat and sunshine, I think I might die. I ask the white-haired white-burb driver to turn down the radio and to turn up the air. The yellow Vanillaroma car freshener hanging from the never-used ashtray makes me want to throw up, but I've got nothing in my stomach. I lean my head against the window and try not to think. Again.

The thing is, all I can think about is Isabel.

I call Walter.

"Is this a pocket dial?" he asks when he answers.

"No. Are you at work?"

"Not corporeally."

"I need help."

"I don't do tech support over the phone. Meet me."

"Say where."

A half hour later I'm salivating over the menu at a taqueria on Eighteenth Street. I could try to grease my hangover, chorizo

and eggs, but I decide not to add heartburn to heartache and order a tamarind drink instead. Plus, Walter doesn't need to see me
chew.

I get the drink and join him at a table for four—the only one
open. He's eating bacon and scrambled eggs. White toast.

"That's authentic," I say.

"I hate spicy food."

"Why come here, then?"

"I live around the corner and I've got, like, twenty minutes before I've got to get back to what I was doing when you called."

"I assume I shouldn't ask what."

"I assume you wouldn't be interested."

"Try me."

"I'm alpha-testing a software program I wrote that lets users alert
emergencies to police."

"Isn't that called 911?"

"It's more of a panic button. You use it if you believe you're in
danger, and we know who you are and where you are."

"What about false alarms?"

"Working on that."

"What about misdials?"

"Working on it."

"What about—"

"Working. On. All. Of. It."

I watch him stuff a half slice of toast into his mouth. I think about
taking the other half.

"I'm sorry," he says, "but this is starting to feel like a false alarm.
How about you tell me why we're here?"

"I need you to find someone else."

"Let me guess: you figured out Marble was the wrong guy and
now you want the right one?"

"You knew he was the wrong guy? Why didn't you tell me?"

He shrugs. "Didn't seem like it mattered."

"Well this—this is different. This is personal."

"I don't know, Gina. I shouldn't make a habit of exploiting work resources, even if it's for a good cause. I'm there for the paycheck. I don't want trouble."

"This isn't part of a case. This is my brother."

Walter takes a bite of eggs. Thinks for a minute. Swallows, says, "Give me his name and number."

I get my book, tear out a page, and write down George's information. "He's an addict," I say. "He got angry with me, and he got high, and he took his daughter."

Walter looks at the paper. "Who's the provider?"

"Well, I am. She's been with me almost a year—"

"I mean the service provider. For his phone."

"Oh. I don't know."

Walter uses his own phone to dial George's number. He picks at his food while he waits on the line, then hangs up. "Nobody's home."

"He doesn't have a home."

"Is the phone in service?"

"It was last night. Knowing George, though, he let the battery go dead."

Walter shrugs. "If you had someone at the FBI, they could track the phone, power it up, give him a call—shit, they could use it as a mic to spy on him. Me? I can't do anything. Not unless he uses it."

"But if he uses it?"

"I can get you the cell tower."

"That's closer than nowhere." I take a sip of tamarind. It tastes like a smoothie made with steak sauce. Naturally, I think of Andy. I say, sadly, "I don't have anyone else I can count on. You're onto something, that panic button. I wish I had one."

Walter puts down his fork. "Consider it pushed."

I get home just before one. I charge the cab fare to my Visa and practically crawl into the house. Calvin was right about a rough morning; when I see that the place is obviously empty, I know I'm also in for a rough afternoon. Especially because all I can do now is wait.

Inside, it's so fucking quiet and so fucking empty that I have an impulse to take a whole bottle of Tylenol. I'm not suicidal, though; I'm gin sick. I take two pills and make some eggs.

My phone rings. It's Andy calling. I don't answer. No way I could fake normal.

I try to eat the eggs. Nope. I make a cup of coffee. Nope. I check the phone, even though it didn't ring.

Andy didn't leave a message, so I text him:

All fine.

He may not believe it, but at least he knows I'm alive.

He may not believe this, either, but when I find Isabel, I'll make changes. Big ones. I'll quit the force. I'll get a civ job working security—I'll patrol a mall if I have to. Or I'll just work at a mall. I'll sell dishes at a department store. Or necklaces. Whatever. Just so I simply work to live. To create a safe place. I'll sell my half of the house to Tom and move to an on-the-cheap apartment in the suburbs. A suburb.

I'll do whatever I have to so long as Isabel is raised to know that real strength and real love come when you stop putting yourself first.

I am crying the next time my phone rings. Because it's Andy calling again. Not Walter, not George. It's Andy, who won't help me—can't—and now I think I finally understand why.

I don't answer.

He sends a text:

U = full of shit.

He's right. I don't reply.

I fall asleep some time in between worrying about Isabel and feeling sorry for myself. I wake up just after seven o'clock. I drink all the juice I can find. I take a shower. The bottom of the tub is waxy from Isabel's crayons. Her bath toys are at my feet. I get clean and get out, in case the phone rings.

I brush my teeth. I put on a robe. I take a prednisone. And then I steel myself to take Avonex.

I sit on the toilet, open my robe, expose my left quad. The stiff one. The gimp. I rub an alcohol pad on a spot high up, where I don't think anyone will be able to see it. I wait for it to dry. I take a breath. I stretch the skin. I try to pop the intramuscular needle in; it doesn't go all the way. I take it out and try again. Same result. The third time, I press. It fucking hurts and layers of tissue crackle as they're punctured, a horrible sound. When the needle is in to the hilt, I depress the plunger. When I take the needle out, it draws blood.

I press a gauze pad to the site and sit for a moment. I fucked it up; it'll bruise. I am sweating, and my hands are shaking, but really, it wasn't as bad as I remember.

I clean up the bathroom and go back to bed before the fever comes and the rest is just as bad as I remember.

"Gina?"

I open my eyes. I'm shaking again; my whole body this time. I'm in my bathtub; the water feels cold. It probably isn't. A warm bath is what always gets me through these nights. I'm near certain I ran it.

I have no idea why Ray Weiss is the one who helps me out of it.

18

I wake up from a nightmare, the covers wrestled off. I don't remember much about the dream except that it was dark, or dark blue, and that I was trying to find my way through a series of rooms with plateaued floors. I kept having to get down on my knees to feel for the wet, slippery edges, which was infuriating—because for once I could actually feel my fingers, but not the edges. I wanted to stop, but I couldn't. And I was so afraid I would fall. It was hard to breathe; I felt like I couldn't, or maybe I shouldn't.

If dreams are the brain's way of solving wake-time problems, I'm obviously fucked.

Still, good news: as in the dream, I can feel my fingers—no shit!—all except the last two on the right. My head hurts, but not terribly; the ache is peripheral, in the brain-shell. And, hell yes: my claw foot is gone.

My fever broke in a major sweat some time ago, my hair and tank and underwear now cold soaked. I am nauseous, but also hungry. I am sick from Avonex, and getting well from the prednisone. I feel like shit, but so much better than yesterday.

I swear I smell coffee, though I certainly don't crave it. I need bland. I need fizz. I need the food form of Alka-Seltzer.

First, though, I need my phone. I'm disappointed to find no missed calls, but I'm glad I didn't miss Walter.

I sit up, and I'm sure I can make it to the kitchen for a box of saltines and a juice box.

I sit right back down when I see the sliding glass door to the back deck standing open.

I didn't set the alarm last night. I didn't even lock the doors. In case, well—in case George came around.

I look over at the door. Did I open it? There's a tiny, rational part of my brain that thinks so. Yes, rational; yes, the tiniest part.

I drop and army-crawl to the closet. I get my Ruger. I make sure it'll fire.

Adrenaline is a painkiller and I clear the place room by room, quickly, my gun ready as I buttonhook each doorway, my moves textbook tactical. I keep my back to the wall and I close each door behind me when I exit. I don't find anybody in Isabel's room or the bathroom.

"George?" I call out, though there's nobody in the living room, and he wouldn't be the one to run the TV news on mute.

"George?" I call out again, in the kitchen. There's hot coffee in the pot. Not my brother's morning M.O. either.

"George?" I call once more down the hall, the question as logical as the possibility.

The front door is locked. I'm the only one here.

So yes, I may have slept, and yes, I must have gone sleepwalking.

I angle back toward my bedroom and I think I must be nuts, my overblown emotions driving a tac operation just because I'm home alone.

Then I get back to my room, and I have a clear view out to the deck, and in the early-Sunday sun, I see Ray Weiss sitting in the dove's nest. He's got his head back, eyes closed. His hands around a mug of coffee.

What the fuck?

I get back, out of sight. My focus switches from situation-aware to self-aware and here I am, a white tank and bikini underwear—now sweat through. I have no idea what happened to my robe.

I crawl back to the closet and pull on a T-shirt. I find a pair of jeans. Then I remember, just a glimpse: last night. The bathtub.

Then I don't know what to do. Be mad? Thankful? Play it true? Cool? I don't know what he's doing here, but now he knows. He must know.

I button my jeans. I leave my gun and cock my attitude.

I slide the door open some more.

"Good morning." I say this with no surprise, no resentment, no warmth.

"Morning," Weiss says, trying to make a sudden and fluid exit from the nest, which I know is impossible. I make it more awkward by watching him without saying anything.

When he gets his feet on deck and the coffee mug level he asks, "How are you feeling?"

It's a valid question. But. "I'm fine." Of course.

"That's good to hear. I—when I got here last night? I wasn't so sure."

I don't remember letting him in. "I don't remember," I say, crossing my arms, "inviting you."

"Your front door was open. I called for you. I heard the water running. And you, well, you were, I heard you moaning—"

"And you came in? What if I'd had company?"

"It wasn't that kind of moaning."

"What, you're a moaning expert?"

He looks down at my feet. "I know addicts."

"This is just a hangover."

"It's not my business." He takes a last sip of coffee, says, "I'll go now, since you're obviously okay."

I block the door. "Why did you stay?"

He looks at me and he's too close; I back off.

"Because you asked me to."

I don't remember that, either.

He brushes by me, barely, the hair on his arm. He says, "I hope you don't mind, about the coffee. I made a pot, in case you wanted some—"

"I think all I want right now is for you to leave."

He looks down at his empty mug and he looks so sorry. Or bummed.

I'm not sure which pisses me off more. I take the mug.

"Why did you come here in the first place?"

He stops, his back to the mirror that hangs over my dresser. From where I stand, I can see him, 360, and I can see myself.

He starts to say something, but then I see myself scowl, and I have another flash from last night, or else from my dream: my fingers slipping. My breath caught. The water; he must think he saved me.

I put the mug on the dresser. "I'm sorry—what did you say?"

"I thought you were mad."

I cross my arms. "Why are you concerned about me at all?"

"Honestly? I wasn't concerned about you until I got here. The reason I came was to talk about Johnny Marble."

I see myself smirk. "I'm sorry you couldn't find him yourself."

"I'm sorry I didn't tell you not to." Weiss shifts on his feet, tucks his hands in his back pockets. There's something stuffed into one of them. A hat. Black.

He says, "You know now that Marble couldn't have hurt his mother. And that he probably wasn't hard to find. So I thought—I don't know, professional courtesy?—I thought you should also know I was trying to figure out who did. Before I turned him in."

"How considerate." I cross my arms again, the other way. "Except that professional courtesy would have been to tell me this from the beginning." I'm trying to be a bitch because I feel exposed. And I feel like he knows that, and he's getting leverage by going along with the act.

When he takes the hat from his pocket, I realize George wasn't the one Maricarmen saw casing my house while I was in the hospital.

I also realize Weiss has got a nice couple of back pockets.

"Jesus Christ," I say, because I can't believe myself. I am nuts.

"I'm sorry," Weiss says. "You should be mad. But I didn't tell you because I thought you were trying to jam me up."

Then, I can't believe him. "How, pray tell, could I possibly do that?"

"By acting like you couldn't possibly." He looks at me. "You're good at that."

I don't argue. I probably am.

"I get it, Gina," he says. "You aren't the only cop who'd like to throw my star in the river. With me wearing it. And I'll admit: it's hard to like me. I don't work by the book because the book doesn't work. I don't play fair because fair doesn't get us anywhere. And I guess, also, I can be kind of intense. But I'm not going to find the guy everybody wants just to put him through a meat grinder with a couple pieces of evidence and turn out a nice sausage case for the state. And I'm not going to send one guy up the creek when he couldn't have done it without help. Life is messy. People are fuck-ups. And sometimes, those fuckups are cops."

"Me. You mean me."

"I thought I did." He curls the hat bill in both hands. "When you started looking for Marble—against Iverson's orders? It made me wonder who was really turning the crank. Was this supposed to be a case against Marble, or a way to save you?"

"Save me? From what?" I know I sound defensive. I am.

"I found Marble about five minutes after I got the assignment. Five seconds after that, I knew he didn't hurt St. Claire. Anybody who's ever met him knows that. You had to know that. I mean, the dude is a giant child. He lives in an apartment run by parakeets."

"Some people would say that qualifies him as a psycho."

"Some people would say it makes you a candidate for use of excessive force."

What? "That's ridiculous. I was the one who wound up in the hospital. He was the one who took off with my gun."

"Yeah, well, how things turned out that way isn't exactly clear when you know Marble's got the mental capacity of a kakapo."

"So what? You don't need much of an IQ to be mad."

"When I found him, he was terrified. He said he had a deal with the cops. That if he stayed away from his mother, she would be safe—"

"He told me the same thing when we arrested him. He kept saying, 'Stay away and mama is okay.' He kept saying my name, too, like it was on mental repeat." I mimic: "Gina Simonetti," my voice low, loud and flat. "So he heard me identify myself. And he obviously understands I'm a cop. But me, the one cutting him a deal? How does that even make sense?"

"I thought you were afraid he'd say something that'd get you in trouble—"

"So you thought I fucked up, and I wanted to cover my ass?"

"Something like that."

I won't admit it was almost exactly like that. I will say, "I need to sit down."

"I'll go."

I don't sit. He doesn't go.

I can't believe I'm accused of being too tough when the truth is, I wasn't tough enough. I get out of the way of the mirror because I don't think I look so good. When I get enough nerve to look at Weiss, I do and I say, "I didn't use excessive force."

"I know that, now." He looks down at his hat; it's got a Pittsburgh Steelers logo. Reminds me of that conversation we had so long ago, drunk at the bar, when he thought injured players should pay for their mistakes.

He must be here because he thinks I ought to pay for mine.

"What would you have done," I ask, "if you found out I *was* covering my ass? Would you have turned me in?"

"It wasn't about you. I just like to get to the truth." He smiles, and I see something different in it. Something knowing.

I remember Andy's warning, about Weiss charming me to get what he wants.

Then I think about Soleil, and what she'd do to get what she wants.

"This isn't professional," I say. "Or courteous. In fact, I'm starting to think this is all pretty personal. Coming here uninvited. Asking Andy about me. Following me. You want to get to the truth? How about we get to Soleil?"

"Soleil?" The dismissive way he says her name makes the notion sound as preposterous as it is entirely possible.

"Go ahead, tell me again: you can't stop her from doing what she wants. But you can't stop wanting her, either, so you'll let her ruin my brother's life, and mine, too—"

"I should go." Weiss pulls on his hat, the bill low, a disguise for his eyes. His mouth hangs open, like he's got something more to say, but he clears his throat instead. Then he heads for the front door.

I follow him. "Do you have any idea what I lost while I was trying to find Marble?"

"I guess I don't." He opens the door and steps outside.

"Let me rephrase, then, before you go. Do you have any idea what I lost while *you* were protecting him?"

He turns around and looks at me from under his hat. "Will you accept my apology?"

I close the door.

19

I take Tylenol, and I try sleeping, but I'd call my headache more clusterfuck than cluster, and it's a bright and beautiful Sunday. Plus I can't stop fiddling with my phone, contemplating calls I should make while worrying I missed Walter, and trying George again, and again, and again.

I can't keep this up, being alone. I need a friend. I drink two cans of 7Up, get dressed, and go.

I take the Kennedy and get off at Harlem. I stop at the golden arches drive-thru for a couple strawberry-banana smoothies and a large order of fries.

The fries are gone by the time I pull up to Andy's.

I double-fist the smoothies and elbow-knock the door. I'm gambling since it's his day off, but I didn't want to say sorry over the phone. I hate apologies; I suck at them. Especially in person. But sucking, right now, is kind of the point.

"Kanellis?" The blinds in the front window are open but it's so bright, the sun directly overhead, that I can only see an inch past the window. I hear music playing somewhere inside, an eighties metal song I recognize that causes every man I know to pump his fist, but it could be Andy's poor man's security system—all the lights on, noise going.

Since Loni hasn't come around, her usual bark and scratch, I think maybe they're both gone. I have a funny vision of them at the dog beach. I see Andy throwing a ball. I see her looking up at him like he's an asshole. I see him going to fetch the ball himself.

I ring the bell. I get nothing. I try one of the smoothies. I should've ordered myself a milkshake.

I knock again, and try the lock, and then I start to think this is a dumb idea. It is Sunday. A real day off. And a perfect day to go to the park, or the zoo, or the playground.

Of course I wonder what Isabel is doing.

I'm about to give up when a bird flies into the window. From the inside. It hits the glass and bounces, flutters, and disappears.

"What the?" is all I say before Loni shows up in the driveway and starts barking her head off.

"Hey, Bologna."

She bristles. Growls. Shakes me off, and goes back the way she came.

I wonder about the bird. I follow the dog.

She trots toward the garage, snippy glances over her shoulder, tail high, like she's always been right about me.

"I'm not arguing."

She darts left, into the backyard.

When I get there, she's climbed up onto the hot-tub deck, where steam seems redundant, this heat. She sits at attention, top of the steps, a guard over her master, who is currently alone but immersed to his neck, the only parts of him above water his head and the hand that's keeping track of his icy drink.

"Hot," I say.

"Hey, baby!" Andy says. The exclamation proves there's booze on that ice. He sits up and raises his sunglasses. "You look like shit."

"George took Isabel."

"Jesus, G," he says, like someone died. "I'm sorry."

"Yeah." I climb two steps and lean in to hand him his smoothie. Loni growls at me. "Relax," I say. "It's a peace offering."

Andy picks up Loni and deposits her on the other side of the tub. "I'm already at peace," he says to me, and sucks down a few gulps of the smoothie. "Why don't you come in? The water is perfect. Hundred and two. And you look like you're the one who needs to relax."

"Didn't bring my suit."

"You could use Amanda's."

"Yeah, no." I'm not supposed to sit in water that's warmer than body temperature—heat equals inflammation equals numbness— but Andy doesn't know any better. He probably thinks I'm worried about fitting into his girlfriend's extra-small bottoms and extra-large top.

Andy grins, a real shit-eater. "You could not wear a suit."

He's fucking with me. I love him for it.

I climb the other two steps and lose my shoes. "How about my feet."

"Suit yourself," he says, and laughs at his own lame joke. He seems happy, somehow. Alone like this. It's not the booze. I wish I knew what it was.

The music he's got going inside, a Bob Seger song now, pipes out from the open sliding-glass door.

He sings along, "She was a black-haired beauty with big dark eyes . . ."

"What's with the bird?" I interrupt.

"You saw—wait. Out of the cage?"

"Flew into the window."

"That son of a bitch. I know which one it is. He—or she, I don't know, how can you tell?—he seems like a he. He knows how to pick the cage lock—"

"There's more than one?"

"I didn't tell you?"

"Maybe you did. Seems like people have been telling me a lot of things I don't remember."

Andy finds his Marlboros. "Marble's place was a petting zoo. Birds. Cats. A couple Chihuahua mixes. The furry ones went to the shelter, but nobody knew what to do with the birds. You know me. I can't let anything go. I thought I'd give one to my niece, maybe. Get the rest adopted. But my sister said no and the place I was going to take them, this bird club in Villa Park? Seventy bucks per, just to give them away. Tests for bird flu or whatever. Did I say how many birds?"

"You did not."

"Sixteen. That's over a thousand dollars. If I had that money to spend, I'd build a big gold cage and keep them myself."

"What are you going to do?"

"No idea." He starts to laugh. "It's funny, really. Amanda won't come over. The fucking peeping."

"Is that why you're playing the music? So you can't hear them?"

"I'm playing the music because I like it. And so do they." He smiles. "I know Donna is laughing her ass off." He lights a cigarette. "I'm glad you're here. I thought you were miffed because I wouldn't come on for the Marble thing."

"There is no more Marble thing."

He takes a drag. "We don't have to talk about it. I sure as hell don't want to talk about it. But what the fuck."

"What the fuck" is right.

"Iverson had me in for a powwow. Said St. Claire's tox report was presumptive positive for morphine and Thorazine and that Pearson said the old lady doesn't have a prescription for either. Yet, St. Claire is still resisting the rape kit—"

"So we are talking about this?"

"Nah."

I find a jet in the tub. Let it carry my feet to the surface, one, then the other.

Andy sits there, smoking and soaking and singing along, "Workin' on mysteries without any clues."

I think about St. Claire. I hope she has a scrip for morphine now, her broken ankle. But, I can't remember, "What's Thorazine for?"

"It's an antipsychotic."

"Could it have been Marble's?"

"I don't know, Gina. Are we talking about this?"

"St. Claire has an irreversible neurological disease. She is vulnerable, and her health is deteriorating, and nobody cares. I wanted to protect her. I was trying to build a case."

Andy reaches for his real drink. "St. Claire doesn't want your help, G. In fact, her daughter went on the warpath when she found out we put Marble in the clink. Called Iverson to say she's hiring an attorney."

"I don't understand. She wants someone to represent her brother on a charge her mother brought against him? How is anybody taking that seriously?"

"Because she's looking to sue the department. Coercion of a witness. Wrongful arrest." He hands me his drink.

"That means they'll dig up reports, take depositions . . ." Shit. I take a long sip.

"I wouldn't worry. Any smart defense attorney is going to prove St. Claire can't be coerced. Even if she wanted to, she can't tell the same story twice."

"But we'll have to." I take another drink. There's nothing much left in the glass but ice. I chew it. I taste rum. I want more. I could sit and soak and drink and do whatever else it takes to forget.

But I remember what Christina Hardy said, her ready response about how she'd never ask her mother for a dime. And now she's stepping in to be the advocate? "She's doing it for the money," I say. "The daughter."

"That's what a lawsuit is, baby. Financial justice."

"I wonder what else she's doing. She has the guts to press us, there's no doubt she's squeezing her mom." I pull my feet out of the water. "I'm going to talk to Kay."

"Gina, no. Your bleeding heart? It's going to bleed out."

"May as well."

Andy gets up, sits on the tub ledge. "You remember last year, I chased that junkie who swallowed the bullet of heroin? It was fifty-fifty, whether he'd die—and my career, too, same breath. And then it wasn't about what the junkie did, why he ran from me. It was about me—my behavior. Was contact warranted? Was pursuit reasonable? Did I make any mistakes? I sat there watching the medics work on the guy and I questioned myself when *he* was the bad guy. I quit trying to be a hero then and there. And you know what? The Job is much easier now that I've stopped giving a shit."

"That's what I should do? Stop giving a shit?"

"Yep."

"Like you."

"Like me."

"What about the birds, then?"

"Those birds are sixteen examples of what happens with the best intentions and no backup plan."

"You say I've got a bleeding heart."

"Mine's not bleeding. It's broken." He still smiles when he says this.

"I'm sorry," I say, and get up. "I still give a shit. I'm out."

"Disappointing, baby." Andy extinguishes his cigarette in a puddle on the deck and gets out of the tub to hug me. All wet. I feel his belly and his strong arms and his smoky breath and his fingers, on one hand, curling up my hair. He loves me, too.

I say, "I wish you were my brother."

"I wish you were ten years younger. And stupid."

I lean back. He finds his rum smile. "Just saying. Young and stupid *and* hot? We'd be perfect for each other."

We are perfect for each other. We are true friends.

Which is why I'm not mad when he proceeds to throw me in the hot tub, all dressed.

20

I stop at home to change clothes—back to black slacks, white button-down. Back to work.

I shove the receipt from yesterday's Blue Cab ride into my lanyard, hit the pantry for a bag of pretzels, and take off. I don't set the alarm. Just in case. There's really nothing anybody can take that I'll miss now, anyway.

I park on Division and walk so there'll be no question about my filthy not-blue not-cab. It's just past five and the sun angles through a haze in the western sky that will hang there until at least eight.

On the way to Haddon Street I smell barbecue. I salivate. When I get around the corner, I find smoke rising from an unmanned grill in the church parking lot. The church's loudspeakers play the kind of R & B music I'll bet Jesus would dance to. There's one guy taping plastic tablecloths to folding tables. Another one comes out the church's back door carrying a heavy aluminum-covered metal pan.

Ahead of me, dressed-up ladies get out of an SUV to right the hems of their summer-night dresses. They look a bit too breezy for church, but maybe not the church parking lot. I wonder if today is a religious holiday. I wonder, too, if they'd let me join the party; I could be saved, with the right rib sauce.

Outside St. Claire's, I buzz the gate.

"Yes?" I think it's Robin Leone.

"Hi, this is Gina—I was Kay's driver last week? I'm here to collect the fare."

I get no response.

"Listen," I say, "when I brought her back, I got the address mixed up. We were running behind, and I was afraid I'd lose my next job. It was my fault I didn't collect."

More silence.

"I have the receipt," I say, and then I'm afraid I sound too reasonable, like a cop, so I say, really pissy, "I don't expect a tip."

The gate buzzes. I go inside.

When Robin opens the front door, her smile is shrewd. "You didn't mix up the address."

I don't know if she's accusing me of lying or of conspiring with Kay, but I'm pretty sure a real driver would say, "I still need to get paid."

"Come in." She steps aside to let me through. She is taller in bare feet than I am in my boots. She wears cutoff denim shorts with her scrub top, which makes her look more like a doctor's girlfriend than a nurse. A Complete Care LLC logo is stitched on her shirt pocket. It's hard to believe she and Lidia are from the same service; the company must have a contract with Sacred Heart.

When I get inside I'm struck by how much the place smells like mine: its dichotomy of old wood floors and fresh paint, baby powder and wet diapers. I hadn't realized how distinctly new-life's odors mirror those of old people. Must be their proximity on the circle of life. Or else the constant use of liquid soap.

There is a marked difference in appearance here, however: there is no clutter. No toys, no newspapers, nothing waiting to return to its cabinet or drawer or closet. In fact, this place is in such order that everything has, in its right top corner, a perfect inch-thick capital-lettered label.

The TELEVISION is off; a cuckoo CLOCK keeps time. Robin switches on a LAMP using the LIGHTSWITCH and says, "You can wait here," about an easy CHAIR.

"Okay," I say, but I don't sit.

"How much is the bill? We like to keep questions to a minimum, to avoid stress."

"Twenty-three." That's what the receipt says. I show her.

"I'll be right back."

I wait around. I look around. Family photos stand in wood frames over the FIREPLACE. It's too bad the photos aren't labeled, too: who and where and when. I recognize the triplets, younger and pudgier than they are. And I recognize Christina, much thinner than she is now, pictured in a cheerleading uniform. I don't see the resemblance to me, even back then, though her young smile was dispirited. To that, I relate.

She wears the same smile in her wedding photo, next to her husband, who looks eternally grateful. Next to that is a pregnancy photo where the two stand facing each other, bellies exposed, near-equal bulges.

The most recent photo shows Christina and her husband at their heaviest, both sadness and gravity winning. The three boys really are identical, though I recognize Sammy, the sick one: he is the only one in the family whose smile is hopeful, rather than a result of *cheese*.

Down the line, past a fashion-dated dinner-party shot of Kay and somebody who looks like her brother, Johnny Marble sits for his studio graduation photo, class of 1977. His mortarboard is tipped right; he's looking off to the left.

He isn't looking at the camera in the next photo, either, because he's smiling up at the dark-skinned black man who has him by the arm. The man, who must be his father, looks at the camera, no smile. He looks tired, eyes sunken, skeletal. He wears a worn white wife beater, the wire-tight muscles in his arms flexed as he holds on to Johnny, who must've been a handful.

Robin comes back and says, "Mrs. Kay wants to see you. She's very particular about money, I'm sorry."

"Don't be sorry."

I follow Robin down the hall. Along the way, three old portraits hang in ornate oval frames. The first is black-and-white and shows a man and woman, each of them holding an infant. The next shows the same couple a decade later, a single child between them, a bow on top of her head. In the third, the woman is missing. It is color-touched, though the man is graying. The girl, older still, holds an infant. The blanket is blue. The baby is black.

It must be Kay and Johnny, as well as an illustrated version of why Kay's father moved her out of the city in 1959. She was a baby. She had a baby. In 1959, Kay was in big trouble.

In the KITCHEN, Kay is seated at the table flanked by a pill dispenser and a stack of mail on one side and some type of hospital-grade monitor on the other. The adjacent chair is pushed out, supporting her legs, the one still in a cast. She has a teacup in front of her, and she's staring at it like it fell from the sky.

"This is Gina," Robin says. "Your driver from last week."

"Hello, Kay." My smile is careful; I'm not sure what she'll remember about me.

She looks at me and says, "It's cold."

Robin takes her teacup. "It isn't cold. I told you: you've burned your tongue."

"I'd like milk."

"We need to write Gina a check."

We. Again, I don't get it. Someone suggests we write a check, I hope it's not my money.

"I can do it," Kay says. "Hand me a pen."

"How about I write it and you sign it? We don't want to get confused."

"I can do it. Just tell me how much."

"I told you. Twenty-five dollars."

Wow. Some tip.

"Please, CeCe," Kay says to me, "I'll give you the money, but I want to talk to you. Sit down."

"She is Gina," Robin says, "and she doesn't have time."

"I have a few minutes." I pull out an empty chair and move it close, and then I sit and place a delicate hand on Kay's knee, above the cast. "What happened?"

She looks at her leg, the cast registering. "Oh, I'll be fine."

"That's not what you said two minutes ago." Robin puts the teacup in the microwave.

"I think I said I was feeling sick," Kay says to her. "Sick is not the same." She puts her hand on mine. "I'm glad you came back. I hate to see you so mad."

"I'm not mad."

"You and daddy—"

"She thinks you're her daughter," Robin interrupts.

"Christina," I say, validating the fact Kay has a daughter with that name—and also, if Kay thinks I'm her now, I'm not invalidating the idea—

"Bad subject," Robin says, calling me off in either case.

But there's one other case. "What about Johnny?" I ask. "How is he doing?"

Robin's glare doubles for *Shut the fuck up*. "The worst subject."

"I'm sorry," I say to Kay, like I don't get it. "During the ride, you spoke so fondly of him—"

"They put him in jail," Kay says, and slaps the vinyl tablecloth with both hands, the stack of mail listing, an envelope sliding off the table. "They put my husband in jail."

What?

"Her son," Robin clarifies.

"In jail," Kay repeats.

I don't know what to say. I pick up the mail from the floor and stare at the return address from Bridgeview Bank.

"They're both called Johnny," Robin tells me. "Her ex and her son. She gets mixed up. Her son is in jail."

"If you'd just let him stay, he wouldn't be in trouble—"

"You're right," Robin says, and then, under her breath, "and you'd be dead."

Kay looks at me. "CeCe, tell her Johnny would be better off here."

Robin steps between us. "Christina isn't here."

Kay's eyes clear, and her lips curl. "Stop interrupting, you bitch."

Robin looks away, Kay's words hitting a few bumps as they roll off. "Let's calm down now, Mrs. Kay. I know you're upset about Johnny, and Christina, too, but let's not take it out on Gina."

"Who's Gina?"

I reset the stack of mail. I feel guilty. I don't know what I was thinking, coming here to ask about Christina's lawsuit—no matter who Kay thinks I am. "I'm sorry." I mean it when I say it this time, but neither woman acknowledges me.

Robin takes the tea out of the microwave without ever pressing START. It's a funny way to heat something.

Funny, too, that the microwave is labeled the SINK.

And the sink is called the STOVE.

The stove is the REFRIGERATOR.

The fridge: the MICROWAVE.

A mess, indeed.

I shouldn't judge—it's easy to understand how things could get confused here. It could have been a grandkid who switched the labels—one of the triplets who, like Isabel, has to get her hands on everything. Could have been a cleaning lady who was in a hurry, or who doesn't speak English. Or it very well could have been Kay.

Or it was Robin. Losing ground. Losing patience. Losing her mind, too.

Robin puts Kay's cup on the table. "It's warm now."

"Would you like some tea?" Kay asks me, her eyes cloudy again, anger lost somewhere behind them.

"No thank you."

Robin shows Kay her checkbook. "Are you going to pay her, or am I?"

Kay looks at the book, doesn't recognize it, says, "Get my checkbook from the vanity."

Robin shoots me a look, asks, "Who does this go to, Gina?"

"Blue Cab Company."

Kay says, "I like blue."

"I know you do." Robin writes the check and then, like a grade school teacher, stands over Kay's shoulder to help guide her hand so she can sign her name.

I push my chair back and look at my feet. I can't fathom what it must be like to care for someone who will never get better. To help someone who will not learn what you teach. To watch a person forget you.

I check my phone. There are no calls. I pray Isabel is okay.

As they're dotting the *i*, the pill dispenser chimes. Robin depresses a button, and then another, both to unfavorable result.

"This thing is useless." She picks it up and shakes it. "It does everything except give pills." Shaking it doesn't work.

"You broke it," Kay says.

"I did not," Robin says.

I wonder who did.

"I'll get them from the bathroom," Robin says. "Right back."

Kay watches Robin go, then looks down at the check she wrote. "I don't know what this says." She looks up at me. "Is this yours?"

"It's yours, mom," I say, figuring this is the time to take the chance.

Kay's eyes refocus. "Oh, CeCe, I'm sorry. You have to believe me when I say I can't afford to help anymore. And I'm so embarrassed to say that."

Christina must have asked Kay to fund the lawsuit. If she asked for money, it doesn't make sense she'd also be taking it. So, "I don't understand what happened to your money."

"I know you're upset. I know you wanted it for your boys. But honey, they'll grow up to take care of themselves. Johnny never will."

"You gave money to Johnny?"

Kay glances in Robin's direction. "Please, be quiet. You know how she is."

"And you know how I am." I lean in, look at her. "Please, Mom. Let *me* help you." I reach for the checkbook. Underneath the check they wrote to Blue Cab, carbon copies show Robin's handwriting and Kay's signature, all following similar grooves. Not much variety in the amounts or the recipient, either: I can make out a hundred dollars for Robin pressed through again and again.

So Christina isn't writing herself checks. But Robin is.

I ask, "Why doesn't Robin want Johnny here?"

"She doesn't understand about Johnny, honey. She's never loved anybody. Been in love, maybe, but that's not the same thing."

"No it isn't." Don't I know it.

"Johnny and me, we tried. And it was more than love. The years, you know, the years, and the struggles, they bind you. I don't say that to upset you. We're family, too, and we've had our struggles."

"I guess we have."

"I feel so helpless, CeCe. I'll admit I can't remember when to take what pill or what time it is, for that matter, but I still know how to love. Nobody will let me do that. My Johnny . . ." she says, and trails off.

I still don't know which Johnny she's talking about, but her inability to distinguish the two might not be dementia so much as it is the graying of her memory against her love for her family, still all wild red and deep blue.

I get it, though—the way love can make you exploitable. Boy, I get it. That's why I pick up the letter atop the mail from Bridgeview Bank that says *Statement Enclosed,* fold it in half, and put it in my pocket.

"What are you doing?" Kay asks.

"Just taking the check you wrote to me." I tear the check out of the book to prove it. I show her: "Blue Cab."

"You aren't Christina," she says.

"No, I'm not," I say. "But I am going to help you."

"You—you—" is all she can manage.

"Gina Simonetti," I say. "That's who I am."

"Mrs. Kay, what's wrong?" Robin comes in, high alert.

"She's a police officer," Kay says, her eyes on me: she knows.

"She's confused," I say to Robin. "She kept calling me CeCe. She accused me of stealing. Then she threatened to call the cops, and now, apparently, I am the cops—"

"She's lying—" Kay leans back and swings her legs off the chair. She means to come after me.

Robin lunges, pills skittering on the floor as she catches Kay's feet before they hit the hardwood. She looks up at me. "You should go."

Kay looks up at me, too, like I've betrayed her.

I put the check for Blue Cab on the table. I say, "You're crazy." And then I go.

"Gina," Robin calls as I'm opening the front gate. She comes down the steps, the check scissored in her fingers. "Please take this. And don't feel bad. She'll have forgotten the whole thing by dinnertime."

"Maybe, but I won't."

"Listen. Mrs. Kay is paranoid. She thinks the police are extorting money from her to keep her son out of jail. She thinks the doctors are trying to kill her—or that the medication they've prescribed is killing her. And don't feel special: she thinks everyone is stealing from her. She doesn't understand how the world works anymore, let alone how expensive it is to be old and sick."

I try real hard to sound compassionate when I say, "I'm sure it's no cakewalk for you."

"Well, I understand she isn't herself. Who she was yesterday, even, is gone. Some people resent that. Her daughter. But Mrs. Kay hired me to deal with who she is, day by day. Whoever she is. It changes. By the moment, these days."

"You couldn't pay me enough to do what you do."

She shrugs. "I'd say the same thing to you. But we don't get to pick who needs us, do we?"

She hands me the check and I take it, to keep her talking. I say, "My job involves spending an hour with someone I'll never see again."

"So does mine." Her smile fades. "Sometimes, honestly, I'm glad she's gone."

I can't believe she could say that about someone she is supposed to care for. But, while she's being so candid, I may as well dig a little: "Is it her son or her husband, who hurt her?"

"Her son. Her ex-husband lives in Los Angeles. She hasn't spoken to him in years, probably twenty years, I'd guess."

"She still loves them both."

"Yeah, well, as far as Mrs. Kay knows, it is twenty years ago. That's the excuse I make for her, anyway. Because if she had a single rational thought in her head, she would be glad they aren't here now. Her ex was a deadbeat and her son is no different. Johnny Junior is mentally ill, though, so her guilt about that gives him a pass. Still, he has done physical and emotional damage. And I know, given the chance, he would kill her."

"Jesus," I say, because I want to believe her. Shit, I'd be convinced if I didn't know the truth about Johnny—that he wasn't here when she said he was. That he didn't do what she says he did. "I guess you're the one who takes the blame for keeping her safe."

"Part of the job."

My phone buzzes and I check the message, a text from H964212:

Dialup here. Calling from a disposable in five.

"I've got to run," I say. "A fare."

"Duty calls."

"Sorry, again, if I made things difficult in there."

Robin smiles. "That wasn't so difficult."

21

I hustle back to my car and I've got it in DRIVE when Walter calls.

Please, oh please: "You found my brother."

"Maybe. Someone used his phone. Pinged a tower up off West Peterson in Sauganash—"

"It's him." Because it's Sauganash, on the far north side of the city, where we lived in high school, when we lived with the Metzler's.

"Did you get an address?"

"Just an area. He made a call, but only talked for a minute be-fore powering off again, so I couldn't use his GPS. I tried refresh-ing, but all I could get was the tower."

"Where's the tower?"

"The north side of Sauganash Park."

Sauganash Park, where we played long before we lived with the Metzler's. When we would visit for dinner. Before we had any idea about divorce.

"When did he make the call?"

"About fifteen minutes ago."

"Do you know who he called?"

"I have the number." Walter gives it to me. It's Metzler's.

"I'll call you back," I say, and I am crying by the time I hang up. Sobbing, really. Because there's no way Soleil would have agreed to let sane grown-ups into her world. That means high or not, George put his best two brain cells together and did something good for Isabel.

I'm crying, too, because I know Rick and Janine, Isabel's god-grandparents, will take them both in, and offer George the goodwill I can't.

And yes, I'm crying because now, I'm going to be alone.

I pull myself together and ride the Kennedy up to the Edens. Traffic is light, and fast. I exit Peterson and cut into the neighbor-hood where trees canopy the streets and yards are delineated by flower beds instead of fences.

I turn onto Thorndale, a real memory lane. The Metzlers live two blocks up. As I approach, I get nervous: What if they don't want me to see Isabel just now? What if they want to let her acclimate with-out confusion? I imagine their house, a combination of how it used to be and how I hope to see it: a Christmas-in-July—well, June—storybook scene in the front window, Metzler reading an actual storybook to Isabel while Janine is on her way into the room with a plate of sugar cookies.

Let there be no confusion: I want that for Isabel. But I want to be there, too.

Though the place is dark and there's no scene at all in the win-dow, I park curbside, get up the nerve, and go up to knock. No one answers, but since I got up the nerve, I may as well wait.

I take the footpath that runs between two homes that've stood here since I was Isabel's age, likely longer. When I get to the play-ground, I'm the only one; it is after six o'clock, though, and I'm in a place where supper is a certain time, and kids scramble home for it. Up the way, little leaguers play on the ball fields, their fans around the fences. When George was a kid, we'd watch those games. He never did want to play.

I pick the swing at the end of the row. The equipment looks new and reminds me of Humboldt, its climbing arches and curvy slides. I know Isabel will love it here. It used to be my favorite spot, even when we were too old to play. It's much different now, but enough the same. Kind of like me, I guess. George, too—though we never could have predicted the way we turned out. George was the one who wanted to be a cop. Military, like dad. But, like mom, he had a flat foot. When the recruiter said they wouldn't take him, George picked a fight—a federal offense. Luckily, I guess, that the recruiter turned out to be a hotheaded asshole who deftly fought back with the butt of his service weapon. So George didn't do time, but he sure shot himself in the flat foot.

As for me, I just wanted to be in love. Married. Not like either of my parents at all.

As it turns out, I also have a knack for self-sabotage.

I lean back and kick my legs out to get the swing going. I get up there toward the treetops and I'm planning to swing well past suppertime when Kay's mail slips out of my shirt pocket.

Speaking of federal offense.

I ease back down, swipe the envelope, and tear it open.

The statement is from Kay's checking account. It shows a balance of over $80,000—serious cash for a fluid account. I keep about two grand in mine, enough to cover monthly bills plus a small cushion. Either Kay's got stiff bills, or a real fluffy cushion—she ain't broke.

Page one of the statement reports last month's activity: everything in and out during May. There are two deposits. One, a social security payment for nearly $3,000; the other, a direct deposit from Champion Mortgage for $99,400.

There are dozens of deductions: monthly debits are taken by

Liberty Mutual Insurance, Blue Cross Blue Shield, and Complete Care, LLC—they took a flat $4,000. Individual charges include Sacred Heart Hospital four times, the amounts which total, on quick math, about $3,500. There are five debits for a hundred dollars each time listed as ATM POS; I assume that's machine cash. And there is one big charge billed by the Cook County Treasurer for $7,927—most likely a property tax payment.

I flip to the next page and find check photocopies. Every single hundred is made out to R. Leone, confirming what I saw on the carbon copies in the book. A check for $2,200 is also made out to cash; the other big one for $4,500 goes to someone named Christopher Heltman, Esq.

All said, she spent over twenty-five grand; a lot of money for one old woman in a month's time. Robin is right—it's damn expensive to be old and sick.

It must also be pretty lucrative for Robin, with nobody to stop her from snaking a hundred dollars here and there. Last month, here and there netted twelve hundred bucks.

I look over the statement once more. What's missing here isn't money. It's Johnny. Again.

I snap phone photos of the statement, and I call Walter's burner.

"How'd the reunion go?"

"Still pending."

"Sorry, Gina. I can't do anything until he turns on the phone again—"

"It's okay. I think he's okay."

"What about you? Are you okay?"

"I'm preoccupied. Do you remember that case you and Delgado told me about? The hinky handyman?"

"Sure."

"I think Kay St. Claire's caregiver is working a similar scam."

"Wait. We're back to work now?"

"Crooks don't work business hours."

"So what, St. Claire has a broken window?"

"More like a broken memory. Currently, she thinks she gave all her money to her son."

"The schizo?"

"Yes."

"And she wants it back?"

"She doesn't know what she wants, Walter. She's got Alzheimer's."

"Where does the caregiver come in?"

"She's skimming hundreds from St. Claire's savings. Apart from that, I can't figure what money is missing. I have her bank statement. You think you could take a look?"

"Wait. Did St. Claire *give* you her bank statement?"

"Doesn't matter," I say. "It isn't evidence. It's information."

He sighs, the only counter to his own earlier argument. "I'll look, but I won't touch. We should meet."

"Where?"

"You pick. I'll be there." He hangs up before I can name a place.

It's nearly dark when I go back to my car. I'm disappointed, because Metzler's house is still empty. It's Isabel's bedtime; I wonder where they are.

I take surface streets and wind up in Wicker Park. It's eight o'clock on a summer Sunday, and on a popular street: perfect for one last weekend cocktail on the patio, as evidenced by the hordes of twenty-somethings knocking back drinks outside a string of old bars I recognize with new names I don't. It's been a while.

I park on Division near St. Claire's; I must have been mentally steering in her direction. It's got to be odd, being old and living so close to the hipster world of Jager bombs and mini sliders, craft beers and locavore menus. Even I feel out of touch here.

There is a bar that still sits around the corner on Damen, though, still and always. It's been serving PBR since it fell in and out and in and out and now, cheaply, in favor again. No patio. No bombs. No food.

I go.

I order a gin and tonic. I hadn't planned on drinking but I can't think of a reason not to, which depresses me enough to drink it quickly.

I call Walter; he doesn't answer. I order another drink and get a booth. The place is dark and near empty but the bartender is playing James Brown and so it seems like there's more going on.

I'm just starting to feel the gin when Walter sits down across from me, his own drink.

I sit back. "I'm impressed. Even though it's creepy, just showing up—"

"You shouldn't be impressed. You should update your phone's privacy settings." He smiles. "You have the statement?"

I get it from my bag and hand it to him.

After he gives it a once-over he asks, "Did she refi?"

I make an I-don't-know face. "Why?"

He turns the statement around, shows me, "This is a lot of money to get in cash at once. She either got a home equity loan, or took out a reverse mortgage."

"I've heard of that: you sell your house back to the bank and use the cash?"

"You buy back your equity with the property, basically. If you're a senior and you need cash, and you've paid off the bulk of the loan, it makes sense. Assuming your heirs aren't expecting to inherit the place."

"It's through the government, though, isn't it? So it has to be aboveboard."

"Unless it's a jumbo loan. Private companies are starting those up again now that the economy is better."

"Either way, it doesn't seem right for Kay. She does have bills—serious medical bills—but it's clear, here, that she isn't strapped for cash. If she doesn't need the money, what's the benefit?"

"I don't accept the premise of that question. Money is the benefit." He looks at the numbers upside-down, points to the Champion Mortgage line. "There's another thing: even if she got a loan? She took a lump sum."

"So what?"

"The majority of people take monthly payments or incremental amounts for specific needs. There's less tax that way. Better return. And seniors who do this often use the money to get by—to pay bills, like you said."

"What's the minority use the money for?"

"Investing. Buying a second property. Or home renovation, maybe."

"Kay's got Alzheimer's. I think she would very much prefer everything stay exactly as-is."

Walter sits back. "This has got to be on the up-and-up, then. For one thing, the money is there. For two, it's froth."

"A hundred thousand dollars is froth?"

"Nobody steals kind-of-a-lot anymore. Especially through a bank. The reward's got to be worth the risk."

"What if the caregiver plans to siphon it, a hundred at a time?"

"We're talking about the woman who, like, helps St. Claire in the tub, and on the toilet?"

"Yes."

"And she's also the one who called the cops on Marble?"

"Yes."

"And she gets, what, thirty-six divided by fifty-two minus the company's take so maybe five hundred a week? To clean up all that mess?"

"Maybe why she's stealing."

"Still. That's a lot of care for a slow little payoff."

I sip my drink. "You're right." I look at the statement again. "I don't get it, though: Kay says she's broke and this doesn't show it. And when you have a disease like hers, and you believe bad things are happening, people don't listen when you cry theft, or fraud, or abuse. They just call you paranoid."

"One question," Walter says, and carefully. "Is it possible she *is* paranoid?"

I think about Johnny, and Christina, and Robin. I know I misread one of them. But then I remember the mixed-up labels in Kay's kitchen, and I have to say, "No."

"I'll do some digging." Walter picks up his sweating, untouched drink, tips it to mine, and takes it back in one easy swallow. "If I find anything, I'll let you know." He gets up and goes.

I finish my drink and drive home on a buzz, arriving with a hunger that's only satiated with an entire frozen pizza covered in string cheese.

After I eat I get into jammies, hit the couch, and put in one of Isabel's movies. While the good guys win, I go over the bank statement again.

First, I question the big cash—the hundred-grand payout. I find Champion Mortgage Company's website and wind up lost in the complicated world of reverse mortgages. I'm virtually cornered in a theoretical refinance when I decide I should quit the money and start on the people.

First person in question: Robin Leone. I Google. I get nothing. I put her name in quotes. I add *caregiver* and *Complete Care LLC* and I get a hit for the company on a website called Manta, a small business directory. The listing describes it as *a privately held company located in Chicago, IL, categorized under Home Health Care Services. Records show it was established in 2012 and incorporated in Wyoming. Current estimates show an annual revenue of $500,000 to $1 million employing a staff of approximately 10 to 19.* The address is on the north side, Albany Park.

I'm looking for the company's official website when my phone rings.

It's Walter. I'm hopeful. I answer, "Is it George?"

"It's St. Claire. You were right: she's broke."

"What do you mean? The bank statement—"

"Was from last month. Ninety-nine percent of that money was transferred out on the first of this month. It's now in a private trust."

"Send me the new bank statement."

"I did. Look for the important message in your spam folder from Maria regarding your eligibility at Florida Tech. Drag the file to your desktop and delete the e-mail."

"Okay. What about the trust? Isn't that something Kay would have to set up?"

"She would. With an attorney."

"The attorney," I say, finding his name on the paper statement— Christopher Heltman, Esq. "He cashed a check for forty-five hundred last month." I highlight the search bar on my browser and plug in his name.

"That was probably his service fee. It's smart, really, to set up a trust for someone like St. Claire. So she knows her money is safe, and will be distributed how she wants it when the time comes."

The top hit in my search is a *Chicago Tribune* link to a *Candid Candace* event page. A society page seems irrelevant, and I wouldn't click through, except the article's headline grabs me: *A Hospital Fundraiser Full of Heart.* Underneath, search tags show up for

Leone and *caregiver* and *Heltman,* and I realize I didn't delete my previous search—I added to it.

"I don't know, Simonetti, I think it's legit—"

"Wait," I say. I click the link and find a photo spread for last year's Sacred Heart benefit. I scan the faces. Four photos down, I recognize Robin Leone. She wears a black sleeveless dress and a smile that dies in her eyes. And her arm is linked around James Novak, Sacred Heart's CEO.

"I think it's bullshit," I say. "Let me call you back."

I hang up and check the photo tags and confirm I'm looking at Robyn Leone and James Novak. So she spells her name with a *y.* Still, I think: *Can't mislabel this, bitch.*

I check the other tags for Christopher Heltman and find "Chris" at the bottom of the page, far left of a group of five men. The photo shows he's nothing much to look at—a thin-haired white guy wearing a neckerchief and a tight smile, an aging version of the three men to his right—but together, the four stand in stark contrast to Dr. Kitasaki, posed on the other end.

What. The.

The accompanying article is fluff, a piece with plenty of wordplay on *care* and *giving,* not much detail about the well-to-dos who were there. Novak gets quoted, canned as ham: "Though we, as caregivers, invest our hearts, health care is not free, and so we are grateful to those donors who afford us the ability to continue saving lives." Apparently, the gushing paid off: the event raised nearly a half million dollars.

I look over the photos again. Most of the attendees wear buoyant picture smiles, riding the philanthropy buzz, there for a good cause.

But Robyn. What's her cause?

And Heltman. What the fuck is he doing there?

Well, okay, yes, he could be an ambulance chaser, which makes a hospital fundraiser more like a job fair. And yes, there were hundreds of people in attendance. And yes. There were three other men in the photo between Heltman and Kitasaki.

And yes—yes, yes god dammit, I'm looking for a connection.

But there is one. Got to be.

For now, the attorney is mine.

I go back to my browser and search for Christopher Heltman, Esq. I follow a link for a local lawyer directory and get a listing for the Offices of C. P. Heltman, Attorney and Counselor at Law. There's a phone number and a business address on West Chicago Avenue, a few blocks from Kay's.

See? Connection. I'll call first thing in the morning. But not on behalf of Kay. Not as police. No, I think I'm going to seek him out for legal advice—

A knock at the front door makes my not-so-charitable heart race from possibility to probability and back. It has to be George; who else would show up after ten?

Who else knocks again.

At the door I hesitate; I'm wearing pajamas and I've probably got old gin on my breath. I'm practically undressed, not to mention unarmed.

But it has to be George. I open the door.

It's Maricarmen. She looks like she's been crying. She says, "I came as soon as I could."

"What? What's happened?"

"The other night, I'm talking about. When Isabel got hurt."

"Oh, Mari." I try to get her to come inside with me, but she won't.

She takes my hands and puts hers against it, prayerlike. She looks at me through tears. Says, "Mama. I am sorry. I can no longer care for Isabel." Then she lets go, lowers her head, and turns to leave.

"What? Mari, please don't go—I'm the one who should apologize. I should have talked to you days ago. I was out of my head when

Isabel got hurt. I know it was an accident—I shouldn't have blamed you—you of all people, and now George has taken her, and, and—" And I'm following her down the street now, ready to tell her the whole thing, but she slows to a stop, and there's Geraldo.

He looks at her. "*¿Qué le dijiste?*"

She turns to me, but doesn't look up. She says, "They say I have diabetes. It has gone in my eyes. The sugar causes problems. The Pepsi, the sweets. I thought I would get new glasses. I was going to make an appointment. But that day, when Isabel fell, it was bad. I couldn't wait. And that's where I was, when you needed me. At the doctor. Even though I know in my soul that only God can save me."

I hear myself say, "They have medication," and then I feel like an asshole because she isn't asking for advice and she isn't talking about diabetes. She knows there is medicine. She is talking about fear.

I put my arms around her and I hug her and I say, "I'm with you," because it's all I know to say; it's as personal as I know how to get.

Maricarmen steps back. Looks up, finally. Says, "I thought it was George, outside your house. I wanted to believe that. And when you said everything was fine? I wanted to believe that too. That's why I didn't tell you when I saw the man come back."

"When?"

"A few days ago. And again last night."

That doesn't rattle me because, "I know who it was."

"You do?"

"Yes." Weiss. "It's okay."

She looks relieved, but also sad. "I couldn't see. And now, I can barely see you. I can barely see you to know it is you to tell you I am sick, and I am no longer able to care for Isabel."

"I can't care for her either. I may as well be blind. It's, it's . . ."

it's then, right there in the street, right in front of Geraldo, that I do tell Mari the whole thing, entirely.

When it's done, and we've both come clean, I watch Geraldo guide Maricarmen home. I'm glad he's there, as her loyal cousin or whoever she needs him to be. I didn't pursue the truth there. I'm glad she isn't alone.

I'm also glad Mari and I will stay friends. It's kind of funny, really, that we'd been lying to each other for the same perfectly good two-year-old reason. We both projected such strength. Now, our weaknesses are our bond.

I climb the steps, go inside, and lock the door. I'm headed back to my laptop when the lights go out. "What the fuck?" I turn around, the red READY TO ARM display blinking on the security keypad, letting me know I can arm the place, just key the code.

It also lets me know a fuse didn't blow just now. Because it would code yellow.

And it also lets me know I shouldn't set the alarm, because I'd be doing it with someone inside.

In the TV room, faint blue light shows me where my computer monitor is, still illuminated, running on its battery.

And then I see a flash of steel at the same time I realize that someone has tried to strike me in the head with a knife. I don't feel anything, and I don't think I'm hit, until blood runs into my eyes.

I crouch low and lunge, pushing off the wall. I put my shoulder into a man's knee. I know he's a man because I get a feel for his build when I knock him back—blunt steroid strength. I topple forward with him, my knees nowhere near as hard as the hardwood. My blood blinds me.

"What the fuck?" I ask again, in complete disbelief.

He says nothing, though I can tell by the adduction of his leg muscles that he's about to swing the knife again.

I jump back and hear the blade swipe air. I try to grab his arm but I miss and fall forward, on top of him, his knife-arm above us. I spit; I spit my blood at him. He doesn't react; doesn't make a sound. Instead he comes at me, so I lean into him to block his chance to strike me again. When he tries to push me away I go with momentum to get distance. Then I feel the wall at my back and get against it and push myself up to standing. I wipe my face but I can't see anything. My blood is everywhere.

Then I feel the blade slice my leg, my quad. It seems the pain comes on a delay. Before my leg cramps and puts me on my knees, I lean against the wall and turn and kick, a heel strike in his direction. I don't get him straight on, but my forefoot catches him in the head.

He still doesn't make a sound.

I collapse, my leg useless now. And I can't see him, but I know he's getting up.

I push myself up, hands and knees, and then on my good leg, all my weight, all my strength. And as he comes at me again, I take a chance: instead of raising my arms in defense, I turn and move left, back to him, putting myself in striking distance as I reach for the security pad. I can barely feel my fingers but I don't need to feel them to push the buttons. *PANIC.* It's there somewhere.

And then I feel the knife strike, and tear down my back.

As I fall, the alarm blares.

"Two minutes, motherfucker," I yell, looking up, seeing black. "They'll be here."

I sense him coming at me again, over me. I grab at his legs. He shakes me off, steps back, and kicks me in the stomach. And then he steps over me, opens the door, and goes.

I curl up. I cover my head and my face and I'm afraid he'll come back and I think I'm going to die.

And then, an operator says, "Emergency services have been dispatched."

I manage to say, "I've been attacked."

"Are you able to verify your identity with your security password?"

I say, "Isabel."

22

And then I'm in the hospital. Again.

I don't recall triage or transport. I went into shock and it was all bright lights, big trouble.

Once my vitals were stable, things came into soft focus. The emergency room team disbanded and a lone nurse completed my intake forms. She didn't care what happened; she just wanted to know who was going to be responsible for paying to fix it. I signed on a dotted line, and the exams got under way.

The resident ER doctor was dispatched to examine my back.

He didn't like what he found.

He did some diagnostic tests.

He didn't like the results.

Then came a steady stream of visits by medical professionals, this nurse and that doctor and some specialist who concurred my text-book neuropathy was worrisome but weren't sure what to do, each one unable to gauge just how close the third knife strike came to my spinal cord. Eventually a neurosurgeon showed up. I remember his title because I sure as hell hoped he wasn't planning on surgery.

After he performed the same exam all the others did, he called his nurse, who put in an order for an MRI.

Yes, another MRI. I didn't argue. I didn't say anything at all, because I was fucking scared.

I waited. I slept. And I woke—just now—to hear a dick from Fourteen arguing with the primary nurse. He isn't getting anywhere.

"I don't care who she is," the nurse says. "In here, she's a patient. And in here, officer, you're in my jurisdiction. If you aren't next of kin, you aren't talking to her."

"I'll wait."

"Not right here you won't."

I assume she shows him the waiting room door. Makes me wonder if Fourteen has been able to notify Iverson, or Delgado. For once I wish the news would spread.

After what seems like three tomorrows an orderly comes to take me to the tube. As he wheels me down a sun-drenched hallway—it's tomorrow, at least, by now—I lie there and study his undersides. I think I see him clearly, though so much seems off: his chinstrap beard doesn't follow the round shape of his face, his Adam's apple shifts diagonally when he swallows. When someone passes by, his thin nostrils flare unevenly, part of his smile.

I think back to the ER, the neurosurgeon. I don't know when the pain stopped, but without it, this has all become so dreamy, so increasingly surreal, that I start to feel like a corpse.

This guy ignoring me doesn't help.

I raise my arm, kind of, and try to wave. "I'm still alive, right?"

He doesn't look at me. Says, down his long nose, "Right through here."

Like I know where *here* is; like I'm following instead of being pushed. I try to think of something funny to say, to show I'm okay; I wonder if I can't think of anything because I'm not.

He takes me through a double set of double doors into the

radiology department. No windows in here, either, and fluorescents stand in for sunshine. He hands my paperwork to a nurse and rolls me past her desk and the control room straight into the imaging room.

"The technologist is on his way." He's gone before I can manage a thank-you.

I close my eyes and wait.

Other than the steady drone of the machine's cooling system, the room is quiet.

The quiet is unnerving.

I open my eyes and wait.

The imaging room is a replica of the one Metzler sends me to on North Avenue. The questions the neurosurgeon's nurse asked when she prepped me were the same, too: *Have you ever had surgery? Been shot? Have any metal implants, devices, or dental work? Are you or could you be pregnant? Claustrophobic?*

My answers were all *no*, same as always. Sad, though, that I seem to have a higher chance of taking a bullet than I do of getting knocked up.

Hey, that was kind of funny. Maybe I'm not going to die.

"Hello, Ms. Simonetti," the radiology tech says, a bald man with a blond nurse in tow—a blond nurse so perfect I'm certain she has to say *yes* when asked about surgery, implants, and dental work.

The tech, on the other hand, looks like he may say *yes* to bullet shrapnel—his rough face, a pugilist's ears. Sharp-edged black tattoos fork up from the collar of his lab coat.

He rolls foam earplugs between his fingers as he comes around one side of the gurney, the nurse around the other. "We're going to get a look at your spine today," he says. "If you experience any further discomfort, let me assure you it's because you're flat on your back in a cold metal tube. Just try and stay still, and we'll get you in and out of there, fast as we can."

The nurse lays a blanket over my torso and they both look down at me, easy smiles as the tech fits the plugs in my ears.

I say, "Thank you." My voice sounds syrupy, drugged.

They move the bed in line with the machine. It clicks into place, raises, and starts into the tube.

"Here we go" is what I read from the tech's lips.

I close my eyes. The entrance is the worst part.

Inside, the familiar tinny voice comes over the transom: "This first test will take about thirty seconds."

I start to count, not seconds, but knocks: *one, two, three, four . . . one-two-three.* I try to let my mind wander. I imagine a woodpecker, his beak ricocheting off the metal. I think of Woody Woodpecker, his maniacal laugh. And that song—for kids, really?—*It's nothing to him, on the tiniest whim, to peck a few holes in your head . . .*

The knocking stops.

"Ms. Simonetti," the tin voice says. "Can you hear me?"

"Yes."

"Good. Now, it's time you listen. You're lucky to be alive."

"What?"

"I said you're lucky. To be alive."

"Who is this?"

"I am anybody. And I can get to you anywhere. To you, or to Isabel."

"What? What the fuck? Let me out of here—" I try to bang on the wall, but the space is too small. I can't move my hands or my arms or anything else. I am trapped.

"Ms. Simonetti. Can you still hear me?"

I look in the mirror above my head—the one that gives a glimpse of the way out. I see my feet, splayed and barefoot. I am defenseless.

"What the fuck do you want?"

"This is about what *you* want. If you want to live. If you want Isabel to live."

"Jesus Christ—this is insane—"

"If you want those things, quit the case."

The case? The fucking case? "Where is Isabel?"

"You don't know? Isn't your duty to serve and protect her?"

"Who the fuck are you?" I scream, the earplugs amplifying all the noise in my head. I thrash around the tube. I try to push myself out. I try to inch myself toward the opening. I try every possible way to get out, and I exhaust myself so much that by the time I finally speak again I just say, "What do you want." I say, "What."

"I said, this first test will take approximately four minutes. Hold still . . ."

Then the knocking begins again.

I scream until it stops.

When I'm rolled out of the tube, the radiology tech and his nurse are there, flanking the gurney, same easy smiles.

"Ms. Simonetti," the tech says. "Did you forget to tell us you're claustrophobic?"

"What? No." I try to get up off the bed. "What the fuck just happened?"

They look at each other, hold the smiles. Take my arms. Hold me. "Careful," the tech says.

"How long was I in there?"

"Not very—"

"The voice. Who was that? Who was talking to me?"

"On the intercom? That was me, communicating the procedure—"

"Where's Isabel?"

Again he exchanges a look with the nurse; this time to confirm a red flag. The nurse nods, checks my pulse.

"Ms. Simonetti, you're exhibiting signs of a panic attack—"

"Damn right I'm panicked—"

The nurse takes that as her cue, pivots, and goes.

"Where is she going? Who's in charge, here?"

The tech consults the chart chained to my bed. "Dr. Tacker. The attending. I'll page him. In the meantime, we'll give you something to calm you down—"

"I don't want to calm down—"

"It's very important that we do this test."

"No. I'm not going back in there."

"Okay, tests aside, for your safety, you need to calm down—"

The nurse returns with a syringe. She isn't smiling anymore.

"No! I don't want to fucking calm down! I want to see the doctor. I want to see the cop who was waiting for me in the ER—"

I try to fight the tech as he pulls a strap across my chest and fastens it, a belt over my arms. I kick my legs; he pulls straps tight over my knees.

"Ms. Simonetti," he says again, his fighter's face unmerciful.

"Okay. Okay: I hear you loud and clear. I'll quit the case."

They both look at me like I'm insane.

The tech says, "We cannot let you harm yourself in here." He gives the nurse the go-ahead with the needle.

"No—" I say to her. "Wait."

She doesn't.

In another thirty seconds, I'm out.

23

Now, I hear people talking. Men, talking—
She must have surprised a thief.
It looked like a smash and grab.
Witness said it was a black guy.
The neighborhood, you know—still rough.
That stretch is disputed MLD territory . . .

I don't recognize the voices, but they are casual as much as they are informed, proving they must be police. I count three. From Fourteen, probably—caught this case on account of time and place, just like I did St. Claire's. And, just like me, they're starting without any real fucking clue.

Soon, talk turns into debate about details of the attack. The kind of knife. Where it came from. Where the attacker came from. If he knew I was police; if he knew me. If he held a grudge.

They believe the suspect must be injured. They know I fought.

I want to speak up. To tell them the fight isn't over. To tell them what happened in the tube.

But. *I am anyone.*

He could be here right now. A cop, a doctor. A cockroach.

That possibility is why I will let them believe I am asleep. That possibility is why I will say nothing if they rouse me.

When the cops run out of things to speculate, they begin retelling their own war stories, spit-shined and ballsy.

I tune out and try to get my bearings.

In the room, central air hums beneath the ticks and tones of a pair of monitors. To my right, I hear the indirect echo of street noise—a garbage truck idling, a siren swirling. I must be a few floors up; I probably have a window on the alley with a view of the building next door. To my left, I hear doctors being paged and patients being impatient, call buttons like part of a techno soundtrack, giving rhythm to the business of a hospital.

I don't know which hospital.

I do know I am not in pain. I am gummy. I am connected to machines. And I am trapped. Again.

And, when I tune back in, I am stuck listening to this:

"Fucking bone was sticking out of his arm and he was still trying to swing at me."

"They should have a special code for guys in the ozone like that. Ten-fifty plus ten-ninety-one-V, what's that come to—?"

"Suspect under the influence of a vicious animal?"

"No, I'm trying to add the codes together . . ."

"It's twenty-one-forty-one-V."

"That sounds right. A vicious animal under the influence—"

"You can't add twenties. Twenty oh-one, forty—"

"Gentlemen," a new voice says. A woman. Not a gentle one. "Since you're bending your brains, try this one: how many police does Fourteen have to put on a case so none of them can figure out they can't interview an unconscious victim?"

None of them answer. I wouldn't, either, because it's Iverson doing the asking.

"What about the door?" she asks. "How many does it take to man the door?"

Still nothing.

"Okay. Do any one of you know where the doctor is?"

Someone comes over, presses the call button alongside my bed.

"There you go. Now, please. Go wait in the hall. And make yourselves useful: talk to the floor nurse when she arrives—she's the blonde in the blue-striped scrubs, name's Sandra?—ask her to page the attending physician."

I hear the shuffle of feet, the room going quiet.

"She's very attractive," Iverson calls out. "Try not to trip over each other." Then she takes my hand—but only so she can move it in order to get to the TV remote.

She switches on the TV. "Mind if I hide with you, Simonetti?"

She skips over the noon news channels and tunes into a cooking show, some Italian chef whose English is staccato, syllable-timed: *let me share with you what are my favorite wines to go with these shellfish . . .*

"Mediterranean mussels?" Iverson asks. "Who the fuck wants to cook that?"

She watches anyway.

I wonder if this might be a good time to regain consciousness. We're alone; I'd have the chance to tell her what happened. I'd have the chance to appeal to her on a personal level.

The problem is, what I currently know about her personally is that she probably would not enjoy cooking mussels. I'm actually not sure what appeals to her—except *useful* information. Information that fits into a promising story she can present to the bosses.

I don't have much information and I definitely don't have the makings of a promising story. To Iverson, now, I'm the flower that got ripped off the vine. She's not going to want to know about this unless I bring her the whole thing in a big, nasty bouquet, indisputable and prosecutable.

On TV, the chef is showing the host how to debeard a mussel. I think I hear Iverson gagging.

I guess I could go the other way: wake up, remember nothing, quit the case.

But. *I can get to you anywhere. To you, or to Isabel.*

With that threat, where could we ever feel safe?

I'm about to wake up and get Iverson to put out an APB when I hear another someone come into the room.

"Hello, I'm Dr. Tacker. You are?"

"Her supervisor," Iverson says. "But I'm here as a friend. A good friend. Can you tell me what happened?"

"I'm sorry. I can only share medical information with her next of kin, or with the investigators handling her case."

"Those idiots outside?"

Tacker doesn't answer. Probably wise.

Iverson clicks off the TV. "I couldn't stand them in here, their thoughtless talk. Gina needs rest. She needs support." I feel her hand on my arm. I try not to flinch.

"Well, I'm glad to know she has someone." The way Tacker says *someone* makes me think he thinks Iverson is my partner the same significant way Kitasaki thought Andy was my partner. It's certainly something she can clarify.

She doesn't. She says, "I'm just really worried."

"Well," Tacker says, "I can tell you that she looks worse than she is. She did lose a lot of blood, but she was struck in the head, which is very vascular. The knife wounds themselves, though? They are completely—amazingly—superficial. There is no arterial injury, or sign of complication in the leg—"

"What about her back?"

"Well, we were worried about that. Multiple muscles were involved. But the MRI shows no injury to the spinal cord. She is lucky."

Lucky. Just like *he* said.

"And her face?" Then Iverson actually touches my face. Either she's putting on quite a show, or I really look like shit. Or both.

"She'll have a scar," Tacker says, "but it will fade. Probably sooner than the residual trauma."

"Are you kidding?" That's Andy asking, from where I think the door is. At first I assume the question is for Iverson—caught pretending to care—but then he says, "Gina's not going to be traumatized. She's going to be pissed."

"Dr. Tacker," Iverson says, "this is Gina's partner. Officer Kanellis."

"Hello," they both say.

Thank Christ! is what I wish I could say.

Andy asks, "What's the prognosis?"

"Positive," Tacker says. "She'll be immobile for a bit, and she'll need physical therapy, mostly for her leg—"

"How come she's asleep?"

"Everyone reacts differently to anesthesia. She should be coming around soon."

"She's going to be pissed." I can hear Andy's smile.

I bet Iverson is glaring at him.

Tacker says, "This will be easier for everyone once she's coherent and we can speak with her directly. Right now, though, I'll put the wheels in motion for recovery. I'll get her file over to our rehab center—"

"Can they rehab her attitude?"

"You're beating it dead, Kanellis." Iverson leans against the bed. "Doctor, will she have to stay here, for rehab?"

"We do have a number of excellent programs. We're also contracted with independent clinics, as well as in-home services. She'll have a liaison to help her make those arrangements."

My stomach drops. *Immobile. Long-term. In-home.* I can't believe he's talking about me.

A pager buzzes and Tacker says, "If you'll excuse me?"

"Of course," Iverson says. "Thank you."

I'm not sure Tacker has both feet out the door before Iverson shifts gears, back to low and grinding: "Kanellis. This place is a shit-hole. How did she end up here?"

"I don't know. It's close to her house?"

"That doctor was all right, but seriously? I asked one of the nurses a question and she acted like I was holding a gun to her head. I have to pee and I'm holding it, because in the bathroom, I was sure I'd contract something. And Jesus, the smell. It's everywhere—like someone mopped with a week-old chicken carcass—"

"Nice hospitals are just nicer places to die."

"Aren't you a big bright shiny light. Did you get anything from the idiots out in the hall?"

"No. But I just got off the phone with Cam Janssen—he's the lead. He thinks the perp is the same one they've been looking at for a string of thefts in the area, a guy with a pattern of hitting gentrified homes."

"Simonetti lives in a nice house?"

The silence tells me Andy's letting the joke die. "Janssen talked to Gina's neighbor, who was talking with her on the street right before the attack. So it could be Gina didn't have the alarm system armed, and she went in and surprised the guy. That fits with the perp's M.O.—he hadn't had any contact with his victims until now. It also fits with what the doc told Janssen about the knife— he said it was short and thin bladed—a lock or a sheaf of some kind—a tool more than a weapon. That makes the attack seem unplanned."

No, I think. This was planned.

"What about prints?" Iverson asks. "DNA?"

"They found a partial shoeprint and a couple latent handprints. A lot of blood—likely all Gina's. The scene is a mess, though. I guess the medics were more concerned with saving her life than they were preserving evidence."

"So they don't know what they have."

"They can probably figure the brand of shoe, the type of glove."

"What about the suspect? They have a description, at least?"

"Black, six foot, one-eighty, wears a hood. Janssen says they're trying to pull an image from a surveillance tape outside the last hit, a few weeks back, a few blocks over."

No, no, no, I think. That can't be *him.*

Iverson says, "Sounds like a matter of time."

Until they find the wrong guy?

I want to object, to wake up and tell them what's what, but finding the wrong guy is exactly what has to happen if I want the right one to think he's immune.

"You okay?" Andy asks Iverson.

After a moment, she says, "I hate that one of ours gets hurt and I'm stuck on the sidelines. I hate that my job is not to do police work, but to justify it. I can't justify this."

"You shouldn't have to."

"Yet my instinct is to downplay. Honestly, I don't know how I went from catching cases to squashing them. To checking the most benign boxes so the bosses won't get anxious. Pandering to civilians so they won't police us. Pretending I don't give a shit—"

"You're really good at that."

"Funny. Do you know I had to release Gina from the Marble case because she was actually doing the job?"

"Aren't you glad there are still police like her? Police who want to know who did what, instead of who wants what?"

The silence is long enough for me to want to peek.

Then she says, "I'm jealous."

"Why not say fuck it, then? Go back to the street?"

"Because I have two kids and I want them to be better than me."

So her heart does beat for more than the blue. I hope they don't catch me smiling.

Andy says, "I'm not solving anything standing around here. I should get back—"

No.

"No," Iverson echoes. "I want someone here when she wakes up."

"You got three uniforms outside."

"I mean a friendly face."

"What about you?"

"I said friendly."

"C'mon, Sarge. I still got two cases pending—"

"They can wait. Marble's forty-eight is coming up and Pearson's got nothing. I need to find a mental-health facility other than the jail."

"Hey: that's giving a shit."

"No, that's the superintendent up my ass about the sister's lawsuit."

"Okay," Andy says, "I'll stay."

"Good. Call me when she wakes up."

I wait until it's quiet a moment and then I open my eyes to slits to get a bead on Andy, who's by the door, thumbs going, a text.

When he's through, I open my eyes all the way and I say, "Kanellis."

Right away, he looks suspicious.

That means I must look guilty.

"Listen," I say. "I'm not going to tell you what happened because you'll either feel obligated to help me, or guilty for refusing. And I'm not going to lie, because you'll know if I do, and then you'll be worried. So I'm just not going to tell you anything. And I need you to trust me. And, I need your phone."

He comes toward me. "Can I say something?"

"Yes."

"Everything's going to be okay."

"You're right," I say, because arguing that point would require details I can't give him.

"Can I call the doctor?"

For all I know, the doctor could be the threat. But I can't let on. "Yes. First, please, I need to make one call."

Andy goes over to the window where someone left a white plastic bag labeled *Patient's Belongings* and roots through it. "The medics brought some things from your place. Maybe your phone is"—he finds it—"here."

"Thank you." I missed a call from *Dialup* this morning. Seeing the nickname—Walter's tease—is no joke: I'd be a fool to use my unprotected phone, especially for this call. I switch it off.

"It's dead," I say, stuffing it into where my bed inclines. "What if I use yours while you go find the doctor?"

He doesn't want to.

"Just one call."

"I guess you got thick skin and a hard head." He hands me his phone. "I'll be right back."

Before he goes I say—"Kanellis? Where am I?"

"The hospital."

"I got that, thank you. Which one?"

"St. Elizabeth."

"The patron saint of bakers."

"Yep: a hard, real weird head, baby."

When he's gone I scroll through his contacts. I'm looking for the one guy I never thought I'd talk to again. The one guy I need now. I find him and call and when he answers I say—

"Weiss. It's Simonetti. I'm at St. Elizabeth Hospital. I'm in deep shit. I need your help."

24

I'm polishing off the fries Andy picked up from Sam's Red Hots—another errand I sent him on after he couldn't find Dr. Tacker or drinkable coffee—when Weiss shows up.

"Wow" is what he says.

"Are you talking about my appetite or my face?" They'd used glue on my forehead instead of stitches, and when the nurse showed me a hand mirror, it looked like they'd given me a second mouth up top, the lips pinched shut.

Weiss says, "I like an appetite. What's the doctor say?"

"Haven't seen him yet. Apparently the attending left for the day, and I'm still waiting for the new one."

"You feel okay, though?"

"I'm in my right mind, if that's what you're getting at."

"I heard you rallied the guys from Fourteen."

"I gave them the information they wanted." When Detective Janssen and his team came in to inquire about my attacker—or rather, to confirm their theory about the local thief—I fed them the description I heard Andy tell Iverson, thereby giving them the go-ahead to find the man they wanted to find in the first place. I wanted them to leave here—all of them—with no blanks to fill, and no one concerned for my safety.

Weiss glances over his shoulder at the door. "What about Andy?"

"I didn't tell him anything. Except that I was starving." I take the last handful of fries. I eat them all at once.

"He's got to know something's up. You called me from his phone—"

"And then I deleted the call." I put the greasy bag aside and say, "I can't fuck around. Someone has me cornered here, and he threatened to hurt Isabel. I don't know who he is, but he is not a six-foot-one black man in a hoodie. He is not a smash-and-grab thief. And he is not after my television. He wants me off St. Claire's case." I put the bag aside and say, "He is who you were looking for when you found me."

Weiss comes over to the bed. "So you trust me, now?"

"I don't have a choice. You're the only person who . . . knows."

Weiss goes around to the daybed. He sits facing the door, leans forward, and says, "How about you tell me what else it is I need to know?"

I guess I don't have a choice there, either. "Johnny Marble didn't attack me. I chased him and I fell. I fell on top of him and he fought me off, and then he took my gun and ran. I didn't know he was mentally ill, but I lied about what happened to protect my job, and to protect Isabel. And to protect myself. I'm not an addict. But I am sick. And the lie . . . I'm afraid it's made things much worse than the truth ever could have."

Weiss looks relieved. "The truth isn't for everybody." Could be, I told him or, more likely, he's relieved I told him what he knew.

I do wonder if it was Soleil who told him.

He says, "The last undercover case I worked? I wound up busting unfortunates like Marble. Addicts. Lowlifes. And a poor-schmuck cop whose work-related injury got him caught up in a Ponzi scheme for painkillers that parlayed into a big-time hard-drug trafficking operation. That case, I worked from the bottom up—"

"Is that where you picked up Soleil? From the bottom?"

"I was in that world a long time. I felt something for her. I don't now. But I also don't want her blood on my hands, okay?"

"She's not a victim."

He sits back and looks out the window, somewhere way off. "She doesn't have to be a victim to destroy herself."

I feel like he's talking about someone else. I wonder if it's me.

"When I got the assignment, to find Marble, it was clear pretty quick that St. Claire was one of the unfortunates. And you—well, you know what I thought about you. So I had to see where Rosalind Sanchez fit in."

"You found her?"

"I caught up with her at her boyfriend's place. A penthouse in the West Loop. The guy's older—older than she is, anyway. And real pretentious. Pictures of himself all over. The kind who wears linen pants and sandals to the office. I felt like he was waiting for me to ask about his sailboat."

"A sugar daddy?"

"I guess, except he wasn't very sweet with her."

"What did Sanchez say? About Marble?"

"Not much. Captain Yacht Club did most of the talking. He wanted me to know that he was half out the door to find the motherfucker when Rosie, he called her, wouldn't let him. When I tried asking her what happened, he commandeered the conversation. Said Rosie didn't actually know who attacked her. That she was too embarrassed to admit she was walking down the street Facebooking when she got smashed in the face."

"That falls in line with what her boss said about her—she's tripped over her technology before."

"Yeah, well, she's twenty. What tripped me up was the way she looked at the captain when I asked her if she could have misidentified Marble. She admitted as much, but when most people fess up, they don't look so anxious. I got the idea she was protecting *him*."

"You think he beat her up?"

"Maybe. But he wasn't the one who did St. Claire or you, either. I thought there'd be a connection among the three of you. The only connection I could figure *was* you."

"Because I stuck to my story."

"And because you were adamant you'd testify."

"You thought I was covering my ass."

"It did stand to reason."

"Until I found him."

"No. Until I found you." Weiss sits forward again, hands between his legs. "When I figured out what was going on with you, I took a step back. I took a wide view. And I realized it wasn't you—or St. Claire, or Sanchez, for that matter—who wanted to crucify Marble. It's the people around you who made you do it—who made your lives hinge on your secrets. St. Claire's daughter. Sanchez's boyfriend. Your brother—"

"My brother never made me do anything. I chose to help him."

"That doesn't seem to be working out very well for you."

He's not wrong. But. "What about St. Claire? You think she gets to choose anything, anymore?"

"No—and that's what's got her daughter up in arms. Up until recently, Christina Hardy thought her inheritance was accruing profit in a trust fund to be given to her in full when St. Claire dies."

"How do you know that?"

"Because that day we went to Berwyn? I *did* pay a visit to her husband afterward, out at that motel in Elgin. Matt Hardy. Nice guy. Not at first. Not until I showed him how a shower cap can be a weapon, and promised I'd sooner handicap him than put his mentally handicapped brother-in-law away. He got straight with me after that."

"Why'd you go see him if you already had Marble?"

"You said you thought Christina was hiding something. I guess I . . . wanted to believe you. So I wouldn't have to suspect you."

"What did the husband tell you?"

"He said Christina had been executor of the trust, but in one of St. Claire's recent realities, she thought Johnny should get a say. She opted to open a new trust. Christina threw a fit; she said her mother didn't have the capacity to make decisions, and Marble didn't have the capacity to handle money. That her family was about to blow her millions on soda pop."

"Christina told me that money had been her dad's. I'll bet she didn't expect she'd have to split it with her half brother."

"Matt said it's not the money. She just thinks she deserves the control."

"Makes her would-be lawsuit look like an attempt to make up with Kay, and get control."

"Or, you know, getting Johnny jail time would make her the only one who *can* take control."

"That means the caregiver is in on it. It fits—she's the one who called us on Johnny. And she's been skimming cash from Kay, which Christina tried blaming on Johnny."

"Poor old Johnny," Weiss says.

"Unless," I say. I sit up. "Someone's been standing in for Johnny."

"Who could pull that off?"

"Listen. The man who did this to me? He made it clear that unless I quit this case, he can get to me again. To me, or to Isabel. And I believe him, because he got to me here. In the hospital. During my MRI—"

Weiss double-takes. Twice. "What the fuck are you talking about?"

"The man spoke to me. Over the intercom. When I was in the tube—"

"How is that possible?"

"I think he either bypassed the intercom system or bribed the radiologist."

"There's no way. Either way."

"Oh, come on: think about the liberties we take on the Job. The favors we call in, the things we let each other get away with—"

"But we deal with bad guys."

"Who is it you think I'm dealing with?"

Weiss sits back. "This is crazier than Johnny fucking Marble."

"He told me he could be anywhere. Said he could be anybody. He's got to be connected. He's got to have some control. When I started screaming, the radiologist acted like I had a panic attack. They sedated me. Does that sound like normal procedure for claustrophobia? For someone who isn't claustrophobic?"

"It sounds crazy."

"Exactly how it's supposed to sound. I'm crazy: sedate me, shut me up—"

Weiss eyes the door. "Does that mean you're in danger here?"

"No—not here. This is right where he wants me. That's why I called you."

Weiss looks at me. Considers. Maybe considers me crazy. But asks, "What do you want me to do?"

I want him to find Isabel. I want him to get the fugitives team together, blaze a trail, find her—and George—get them some place safe.

But if I send someone, *he* will know. He'll know I'm still in the fight, and then what? I've got no leverage. Unless . . .

"I want you to go to my place," I say. "Make like you're from Fourteen. Pretend you're poking around. Get my laptop. Find St. Claire's bank statements—they're hidden in my spam from someone named Maria in Florida. Then see if you can get to somebody at the bank, or the mortgage company, or the attorney's office. Someone who might be able to point to Christina for this."

"I will," Weiss says, "but I can't leave you alone." He reaches around the back of his waistband and pulls out a .40 S&W.

My service weapon.

"You? How?"

"Marble gave it to me when I found him."

"And you just kept it?"

"I didn't know if you were trouble, or in trouble, remember?"

He tucks it under the daybed's seat cushion; I guess he finally trusts me, too.

He says, "Now you're not alone." He gets up.

"Thank you, Weiss," I say, thinking I should've called him Ray.

Just before he's out the door he says, "Don't go anywhere."

Who, me?

25

I'm still waiting for the attending when Metzler shows up. I assume Andy called him; I also assume I'm going to have to explain why I'm in the hospital again.

"Regina," he says, a rare tinge of worry in his voice.

"George has Isabel." I say *has* instead of *took* and I try not to sound desperate about it.

"Yes," Metzler says, without indication that he has any feelings one way or the other. He comes over and takes my hand. "How are you?"

"I'm alive."

He looks down, my legs. "And kicking?"

"More like limping." I know this from a failed trip to the bathroom, when putting weight on my right leg was about like getting stabbed again. "I'm a little sore."

He goes to the nurses' computer, clicks around.

"What are you doing?"

"Trying to determine which medication has made you so forthcoming."

I try to laugh because he's trying to be funny.

When he's through he comes back and checks my vitals. "I see you've eaten," he says, to the empty Sam's Red Hots bag on the empty dinner tray.

"I didn't get stuck in the gut."

He takes my wrist, a gentle hold. "You're tough, like your mother."

"What—" *the fuck does she have to do with anything?* I wonder if he feels my pulse spike. I clear my throat. "I'm sorry, I didn't expect a lecture."

"Yes you did. You just expected that it'd be about *your* behavior. Your obstinance."

I can't argue. He's right.

"Your mother was tough; you know she was, even in her last breath."

"Well, I heard."

"I wish you could let go of the guilt you feel for not being there." He steps back, puts his hands in his pockets. "You don't know this but you were there, the first time. When she had cancer. You wouldn't remember. You were so young. And, well, she didn't tell you—"

"How young?"

"You'd just started grade school, I think—"

"I remember." I remember prancing into my parents' bedroom one afternoon, my dad wrapping a bandage around her recent mastectomy. "Breast cancer." I didn't know what it was called at the time, but I was never so light on my feet after that moment.

"She didn't want you to be afraid."

I remember the constant strain in their voices. How I'd perform for them—literally a whole song and dance; how I'd try to make them laugh. How I'd ask to pour the wine at dinner, filling their glasses, sensing the way the stuff eased the mood. How I'd play second mom to George. I was good at scolding.

And I remember how I'd sneak into the hall after bedtime to listen to them, barely able to hear the words, praying for laughter.

Yes, praying. And to God, who I pictured as a backlit man with feathered hair, a dimpled chin, and a mug-shot appearance. He wore a black suit with a T-shirt, a toothy smile and horn-rimmed glasses. He was one part David Bowie from the cover of *All Saints*, another part John Travolta, and also our elderly neighbor Mr. Zins, all men my mother seemed to favor.

He rarely answered my prayers.

I say, "I was afraid anyway."

Metzler says, "So was she."

He goes to the daybed and sits right on top of the gun. He crosses his legs. I try not to look concerned but I must, because he elaborates: "She thought she could protect you from the cruelty of the world. She went to great lengths—do you remember your folks' trip to Puerto Vallarta? It was over Thanksgiving—you and George stayed with us."

"It was third grade," I remember.

"It was actually her surgery. She billed the so-called souvenir she brought you as the little Mexican mermaid, even though it was just a Disney doll from the hospital gift shop. You were so pleased you didn't question the gift, though you did wonder why they didn't have suntans. Rain, she said. And when you asked about vacation pictures, she told you—"

"Dad tried to take the camera scuba diving."

"You do remember."

"So?" I try to shrug, but it hurts. "The turkey was always overcooked anyway."

Metzler looks at me. No judgment. Which makes me feel like a jerk. After all these years, who hangs on to a detail like dry turkey?

Still. "Now you're going to feed me her line," I say. "She was only doing what she thought was best."

"No. Now I'm going to tell you you're doing the same exact thing."

"I thought you said this wasn't about me."

"To be sure, it's about much more. I see you being tough. I see you doing what you think best. And I see you going to great lengths to protect the people you care about. But *you* don't see how your decisions affect those people. You don't see that trying to protect Isabel from the fear and insecurity you felt when you were a child is going to cause her to develop the same negative attitude you had—still have—toward your mother. And, Regina, I'm afraid you don't see that at the breakneck rate you're going, Isabel may never know you at all."

That last bit makes my face hot. Son of a bitch: he's absolutely right. But. "You think George is doing any better than I am? I'm sure he didn't tell you he was popped when he and Soleil showed up to take Isabel. Or that he's still shacking at her place—or should I say her help-yourself pharmacy—"

"Stop, Regina." Metzler gets up. "I've never asked you or George to tell me each other's problems, or secrets. Come to think of it, I've never asked either of you for anything." He comes around, bedside, hands on the rail. "Now, though? I'm asking you both to stop this—this emotional-distance competition. You need to be together—to band together—for Isabel. You need to quit taking risks and quit making excuses." His expression remains even, though his fingers are curled tight around the rail. "You need to straighten up and sober up and god damn it, grow up."

"You're right," I say, out loud this time. "Did George agree, too?"

"I haven't spoken to him."

"What?" My blood goes cold. "You haven't seen him? Or Isabel?"

"No."

"But he called you, yesterday."

"We were at the theater."

I raise the bed up as high as it'll go. "May I use your phone?"

Metzler reaches into his pocket, pauses. "Why?" He's got the phone in his hand, anticipating my answer, but then a new nurse shows up, over his shoulder—

"Ms. Simonetti? I'm Cerita, I'll be taking over for Jemelle."

"Hi," I say, though I don't remember Jemelle, or the nurses who came before her.

"I'll just be a minute," she says to Metzler, who steps out of the way. She puts a plastic shot-glass-size cup of pills on my tray and pulls a set of rubber gloves from the receptacle on the wall. "Can you tell me your level of pain?" she asks, checking the monitors, going through the protocol that seems perfunctory with a seasoned doctor twiddling mental thumbs behind her.

"Two," I say, and then I remember what Metzler just said. "Plus three. So five."

"Okay," she says, adding that number to the equation that includes whatever the monitors tell her. She unwraps a set of plastic-wrapped tools and sets them on my bedside tray. "I'm going to need you to sit up." She helps me.

She removes the dressing, examines the wound on my back. While she's at it I look over at the tools and I notice the scalpels and I remember: the detective told Andy the knife the attacker used was short and thin bladed—a lock or a sheaf—a tool more than a weapon. A tool. A surgical tool.

Andy also said there were latent handprints at my place. That happens with gloves. That could happen with surgical gloves.

I'm sure my face plainly registers the wild realization, though I hope the timing coincides with what would be an uncomfortable move, my spine bearing weight. I play it that way. "Sonofa," I say to Cerita, "make that a seven."

"I'll speak to the doctor," she says. "He may want to adjust your medication. It's a little tricky, with you just coming off prednisone—"

"Please do speak to him," I agree. I don't want to wind up taking something that's going to prevent me from getting the fuck out of here.

Cerita passes me the cup of pills. "This should help in the meantime." She pours water and stands over me while I take the pills and I swear Metzler watches to make sure I swallow.

"Thanks," I say, and as she retreats to log my latest particulars into the computer, I smile at Metzler. I hope it doesn't look as put on as it feels. "As I was saying, I'd like to call my brother."

"That's great, Regina." Metzler hands me his phone. I don't think he suspects a thing, though it's not George I'm calling now. I mean, what the fuck. I've got visions of a hostage situation, and I'm in no position to negotiate.

"Will you give me a minute?"

"Of course." As soon as Metzler clears the door I get my own phone, still wedged in the incline of my bed. I look up the number for Walter's burner and dial it from Metzler's.

Walter doesn't answer, probably because he doesn't recognize the number.

I leave a message: "Dialup. I'm in the hospital. St. Elizabeth's. I need you to come. And bring an extra phone. And if anyone asks, you're not you and you're here to see your sister who is not me." I'm looking at Cerita because I know she'll sneak a glance at me for that one—when she does I say, to both of them, "Actually, it's nobody's business why you're here. Tell them to blow." Cerita looks back at her screen.

I hang up, delete the call in the phone's log, and think about calling Weiss to tell him about the knife, and the gloves; I should trust him.

But this is Isabel. I won't risk her life on *should*.

I dial George: straight to voice mail. My knee-jerk is to hang up, but that's because I don't know if George has turned away from me, or been turned.

So after the beep I simply say, to whoever might get the message, "George. I'm trying you from Rick's phone. I just want you to know that I'd never do anything to put you or Isabel in danger. Please believe that, and please, come home and let me prove she is my only priority. I love you, and I love your little girl. Will you tell her so? Because really, that's all that matters."

Then I hang up and begin to plan my escape.

26

It's after dinner by the time Walter shows up and I'm starving because I didn't eat dinner, because they brought chicken, and I couldn't get the picture of Iverson's carcass mop out of my head. Even the fruit cup, foil-sealed and syrup-soaked, was unappealing.

Walter pulls off his beanie and says, "Hey, sis." He doesn't look at all shocked by my appearance so I figure word spread through the ranks, or else he used his tech savvy and currently knows more about what happened to me than the misguided mooyacks at Fourteen, who have probably put the finishing touches on their all-points bulletin and gone home to watch Monday night baseball. Not a criticism; I gave them the go-ahead *and* the go home. Because the less they work, the longer I've got.

I say, "Walter: I'm closing in on the bad guy."

"Not the guy who's got Fourteen all aflutter."

"No. And I'm not talking about a thief after froth, either. This is somebody connected to St. Claire. Somebody who knew how to find me at my home, and in this hospital, and who has enough pull to trap me here by threatening me, and Isabel—"

"Wait. Who's Isabel?"

I shut up. I never told Walter about her. I also never told anyone at Sacred Heart about her. And she's a child, and she's not mine, so how could anyone know?

Lidia, that's how. Lidia, Robyn Leone's Complete Care coworker. Lidia has been in my home. She was there, in fact, when Isabel got hurt. There to help.

Just like Robyn, there to help.

"Gina? Are you okay?"

"I've got to get out of here. I need you to spring me."

Walter laughs. Then he stops. Because, "You're serious."

"I also need to make it look like I'm still here."

"How am I supposed to do that?"

"I don't know, you're the tech guy. Can't you loop my heartbeat? Dispense the IV bag into a bucket? Hook this pulse thing to some program on my phone?"

"You have no idea what you're talking about. You think I can fake a human being?"

"If my human-beingness is being monitored by devices, yes."

"What about the nurses?"

"There was a shift change at seven. The new nurse said they'd give me meds again at nine and then I'm not scheduled for anything else until six A.M. "

"But they'll check on you, won't they? Don't they?"

I point to the monitors. "These machines are part of the hospital's network. They can read them from the nurse's station, and if everything's fine, there's no need to come in here—" I stop talking, because he's looking at me like I'm speaking in a code he doesn't understand. "I'm surprised I have to explain this to you."

"I understand the hardware, Simonetti. It's faking *you* that I don't think I can do." He opens the standing closet next to the window and sticks his head inside. It's empty, except for three hangers. "Somebody is going to come in. And if you aren't in bed—"

"Then I'm in the bathroom," I say. "Please. I just need tonight. I'll be back before sunrise."

He closes the closet door, tries the cabinet above the computer monitors. "I wonder if there isn't a better plan."

"The best plan would have been doing this on my own. But I can't. I need you. Your brain."

"Brain," he says, "huh."

"Huh?"

He smiles, closes the cabinet, gets a phone from his pocket, and hands it to me. "As requested," he says. "I'll be back at nine-oh-five. Use TextSecure if you need to reach me. I'm the only contact there, and the only one you can message safely. I mean, you can use this phone, but the less, the better."

"Okay."

"See you in a bit."

I try to wait patiently for nine-oh-five.

At eight fifty-five I dial Weiss. I tell myself I'm simply calling so I can truthfully say I'm at the hospital, and also make sure he's not coming back to visit, but when it rings on the other end, I anticipate hearing his voice.

"This is Weiss."

"It's Gina. I'm on a friend's phone."

"I was just on my way to you. I—"

"No," I say, same as *fuck*. "I mean, you can't. Visiting hours are over in about five minutes and I still don't know who's watching me. You showing up here might trip a wire—"

"Gina. Not for nothing, but I spent a good deal of time under-cover. I had a plan. I didn't know you had a phone."

"What was the plan?"

"It doesn't matter, now. Now I can just tell you—I mean, can I tell you? What I found?"

"Yes."

"Or is the phone on its way out with your friend?"

I think he thinks I'm full of shit. "You can tell me."

"Maybe you already know. I mean, it was on your computer."

"The bank statement?"

"No. The picture—"

"What picture?"

"From the *Sun-Times*. Sacred Heart? It's Captain Yacht Club."

"What? He's in the photos?"

"He is Chris Heltman."

"Sanchez's boyfriend—"

"Yes—"

"—is the attorney."

"Yes. You know, I'm terrible with names, but I could pick that guy out just by his sailor scarf, the mope—"

"Kay St. Claire paid that mope nearly five thousand dollars last month."

"I saw that. And first I thought maybe it was a payoff, to get Sanchez to drop the charges on Johnny. But the check is dated before Sanchez called the cops, which means the money came before the attack."

"She paid Heltman to set up a trust." I sit up. "You know, when I saw him in the fundraiser photo, I pegged him as an ambulance chaser. But now I'm thinking he chases patients home from the hospital. Patients who may or may not be coherent enough to seek legal services to, say, apply for a reverse mortgage, or to set up a trust fund."

"You think Heltman struck up business with St. Claire before Marble supposedly assaulted her? So he knew about her condition, or at least her situation—"

"And her money. Maybe Christina Hardy has nothing to do with this."

"But Sanchez—what does she have to do with it? Why come down on Johnny after the fact, I mean?"

"It's like that old handyman scam. A guy comes by to fix your broken window and says you've got water damage inside the frame. He offers to take on that job, too—bad flashing, or something—and you figure he's doing you a favor—"

"And pretty soon you're forking over dough for shit that isn't wrong."

"If this is the estate-planning version of that, Johnny is Kay's leaky roof."

"Who started by assaulting Sanchez."

"And Heltman is the handyman."

Weiss says, "I'm going by his office."

"Now?"

"Talking to the Captain isn't going to get me anything but a boat ride. Finding out how he pays for that boat—that's something I'm going to have to dig for. When no one is looking."

"Get going, then," I say. "And call me on this line—my friend is leaving his phone."

"That's a good friend."

I consider the curious inflection in the statement. I let it ride. I say goodbye.

We hang up and I look at the clock and I wonder if Walter is waiting impatiently like I am, so I press the nurse's call button.

When she shows up at the door, a young Hispanic girl with gel-wet hair, I decide to be rude, to preempt the chit-chat: "I am so fucking tired. Cerita said I could take my meds at nine and be left alone until morning."

"We will certainly try to let you get some sleep after your MRI—"

"What? That's not right. I already had an MRI."

"I'll check your file when we're through here," she says. "Here is your medication."

The cup barely hits my tray before I take it and toss the pills back like chewable candy. I thought about faking and pocketing them so I'd have all my wits about me but I am in pain, and I don't need wits so much as I need to be able to walk.

I ask, "What's your name?"

"I'm Monica."

"Monica, I swear I'll walk the fuck out of here before I let anybody trap me in that tube again. You check the file."

I slug water from the plastic pitcher Cerita left bedside while Monica gets the hint and goes over to the computer. The second hand ticks around the clock once, twice.

"Yes," she finally says, "the order is here. Someone should be here to get you momentarily."

"I need you to page the doctor."

Just then, someone pushes a gurney through the door.

"Hi," Monica says.

"No," I say.

"How ya doing?" the man says, all cheerful, like he's here to take me to get ice cream.

"I want to talk to the doctor," I say again.

The man comes in, turning the gurney to line up with the bed. He's wearing scrubs, a mask. He's got a clipboard under his arm. "Is this Gina Simonetti?"

"There must be some mistake," I say.

He takes down his mask.

He's fucking Walter.

"Hi, Gina Simonetti," he says, smile big as shit. "You mind if we borrow your brain?"

"She's nervous," the nurse says.

"Agh, don't worry. I know how to drive this thing." He turns to the nurse. "Monica, is it?"

"It is."

"Will you help me get her unhooked?"

"Sure thing." Monica peels the electrodes off my chest, takes the thing pinching my finger, undoes the tangled cords. She frees me from the machines.

"I already had an MRI," I say to Walter, because I shouldn't quit protesting now.

"Yep, for your spine. This time, we need your brain." He winks; he's pretty proud of himself.

I try not to smile.

He looks over me, at Monica. "It's pretty backed up down there. They say they're on schedule, but I think they mean yesterday's."

"They're always behind," Monica says.

"Do we have disconnect?" Walter asks.

"We do."

"What about the IV?"

"She can transport with it. Just have them switch bags downstairs."

"Help me move her?"

"I can move," I say. I climb onto the gurney. The pain is about as amazing as the fact that I'm actually getting out of here.

Monica leads the way, Walter pushing me. He says, "I'll have her back by breakfast."

"I'll tell the charge nurse."

He turns the gurney around again so he meets Monica, pulls a Dum Dums lollipop from his scrubs pocket, and twists it around like a flower. "You have yourself a sacchariferous night."

She takes the Dum Dums, gives him the sweetest smile.

When we're a good distance down the hall in the opposite direction, I say, "My gun."

He slows down. "Is where?"

"Back in the room. The daybed."

He stops. "That would have been good information to have earlier—"

"And I need to bandage my leg. And I left the burner—"

"I have another one of those for you."

Not with Weiss's number programmed. "We have to go back."

"Shit." Walter puts the brakes on. "I'll go. Just lie here and, I don't know—act sedated or something."

I close my eyes and listen to his shoes squeak down the hall. Then, after a few minutes, I hear his shoes squeak back, accompanied.

He says, "I don't know, Monica, I'd probably want my phone on me at all times if I had your number."

She says, "You're such a flirt."

"You're the one who offered to buy coffee." Cue a sacchariferous silence. Then Walter says, "I think this tape will do the trick."

"We use it to secure the carts, too, so it should be strong enough."

"It'll be fine until I can swap out the caster. Thanks."

"My break's at eleven. I'll see you down there?"

Walter unlocks the wheels. "You will."

We roll.

He whispers, "Don't say anything until I get you downstairs."

I keep quiet, though I think of about a million anythings.

We take the elevator to the second floor and as we head down another corridor he leans over, says, "Okay. I'm taking you to the bathroom up here on the left. There's a backpack in the last stall. I brought some clothes; my girlfriend is about your size. The rest of what's in there is always in there—my GTFO bag—but you should know I'm not much of a survivalist, so if I ever do have to get the fuck out, I might wind up just going bird-watching or something. Anyway. When you're dressed, take the stairs across the hall—I disarmed the alarm there and that exit spits you out in the alley. There's a blue Honda parked around the corner on Le Moyne. Keys are in the front pocket of the pack."

"What are you going to do?"

"Apparently, I'm going to have coffee with Monica." He stops outside the women's bathroom. "Okay: on three, I'm going to help you sit up. Act like it hurts. And like you have to pee. And take the plastic-belongings bag I hung on the rail, there. It's your stuff—probably stuff I should carry if I actually want to survive."

"Okay," I say. "I'm getting the fuck out."

"One," he says. "Two—"

"Wait. How am I getting the fuck back in?"

"I'm working on that."

"Okay," I say. "Thank you, Walter."

Walter says, "Three."

In the bathroom I sit on the toilet and remove the IV line. I put tape over the catheter and then I tape my leg. I start from just above the knee and wrap it tight all the way up to the stitches.

When I'm done I pull on a pair of leggings that are as tight as the cloth tape and a shirt that falls off one shoulder, not because it's too big, but because it's the style. The shoes are stretchy ballet flats, thank the lord Jesus. They are too big, but they stay on over the thick hospital socks.

I put the .40 S&W in my very snug waistband and the burner in my back pocket. I take Walter's beanie out of his pack and pull it over my forehead. And when I emerge from the bathroom, I feel about as confident as anyone would who's sneaking out of a hospital to stalk a nurse.

But I make it out. On an adrenaline crutch and a stony high, I fucking make it out.

27

I find Walter's car and zip down to Kay's, which is only six blocks away. I spend more time looking for parking than I did driving here and I wind up double parking, hazards, outside the church. If there is a God, I hope he'll forgive this trespass.

Kay's front windows are dark and the gate is locked. The fence is a decorative cast-iron job, and not even shoulder high, but I'm in no state to climb.

And, anyway, I should see who's inside before I make a move to go in.

I strap on Walter's bag and cut through the church's lot to the alley. Wood fencing borders Kay's backyard, flush with the garage. I slip between a pair of garbage cans and check the back gate, which is locked, but the height of the fence dips at the gate's hinges so if I stand on tiptoes, I can see the back of the house pretty easily, about twenty feet away.

I can't stand on tiptoes.

Then I remember: bird-watching.

I go across the alley, lean against someone else's fence, find Walter's binoculars, and dial in.

A half-level up, Kay's kitchen windows are lit, and Robyn is sitting at the table refilling the pill dispenser while talking on her cell. She's got six bottles lined up and the nocs are good enough to read the medication labels: Aricept, Risperdal, zolpidem, trazedone, Zofran, Hydrocodone.

I can't believe a single person could take all those, in a day or in a lifetime.

I zoom out a click and look at Robyn, who's concentrating on her conversation while rolling a white trapezoid-shaped pill between her fingers. She's wearing dark eye makeup that matches her eyebrows and the roots beneath her white-blond hair. Her lipstick shimmers when she speaks. No hint of warmth otherwise.

After an obvious disagreement with whoever's on the line, Robyn takes the pill, washing it down with a short glass of red wine. Then she pushes back from the table and takes the glass to the sink—which is labeled SINK, now. The stove is also the STOVE, and the fridge the REFRIDGERATOR.

Looks like somebody straightened up.

Robyn attempts the same with her dress, but it's cut so deep on top and hemmed so high below it's impossible to cover everything at once. Her bra is trimmed with lace and her legs are perfectly trim. Whoever gets the pleasure of her company tonight will be distracted one way or the other.

Dressed to kill. Heh.

When she hangs up the phone and disappears from view, I go back across the alley between the garbage cans to sit down for a minute. I have to. I'm light-headed, and I know I'm in real pain, but it only comes through as unrelated discomforts—dry mouth, sour stomach. It's like some metamorphosis gone wrong, my old self hanging on, my wings still tucked along my spine, throbbing, unable to spread. This is what painkillers do.

Painkillers also make me ponder shit like metamorphosis instead of what the hell I plan to do now that I'm here and Robyn is inside, just as I'd hoped.

I open Walter's bag to see what else he's got for dire straits. I find a cheap pocketknife, a penlight, three flash drives, an oversize energy drink, a two-pack of Tylenol, and a tin of curiously strong mints. I suck down the drink and hope Walter never actually needs to get the fuck anywhere.

I walk the alley to find something I can use with the knife to jimmy the gate's lock. I pry a nail from a shingle somebody didn't successfully tack to the roof of the rehab two doors down. Then I'm back at the gate, on my knees, holding the penlight between my teeth.

I've maneuvered both stand-in pins in the lock when Kay's back porch light comes on—apparently on a motion sensor. I peek through the wood slats: the sensor is sensing motion, all right—Robyn has exited the back door, and she's heading my way.

I fall back, breaking the knife blade off in the lock. I turn and catch myself. The penlight clanks to the pavement and rolls in an arc, its light swallowed by the yellow alley lamps. I steady myself on one hand, go for my gun with the other.

Then I get up on my knees again. A matter of seconds. Not even. But when I look back, Kay's yard is dark. The motion light is out. The kitchen light is out. And I'm not hiding at all in the alley, one of the most well-lit places in the city.

Kay's garage door crawls up on rusty hinges. A car door slams. An engine starts and purrs and ticks.

A black Benz backs out of the garage. I know it's a Benz because the emblem on the back end stops two feet from my face. I wonder if the car has a rearview camera; if Robyn sees me on my knees, sees my gun.

"Hello," I say, just in case, and I stay put, aimed at where I think the camera would be. I get the plate number, and I say it over and over as Robyn shifts into DRIVE, the tires kicking gravel back at me. I shield my face; I cough at the exhaust fumes. Then I watch the brake lights wink before she turns out of the alley and heads north.

Pretty nice car for a woman who doesn't drive.

I get my ass back to Walter's car to follow her.

The street is a one-way, and that means Robyn will either have to drive past me or continue north to reach a main drag. I figure I'm at least a minute behind her, and since I don't see oncoming headlights, I go against the one-way and shoot up to Division.

At the intersection, I take a guess based solely on her outfit that she's headed east. River North. Or near there. A club with a cover.

And it's a good guess: once I muscle through the intersection at Damen and Division, I see the Benz a half-block ahead.

I follow her on Division through Goose Island and past the big-box store that stands where Cabrini Green used to, the brutal lore of public housing replaced by the promise to *expect more, pay less.*

A few blocks later, the last car between us peels off at LaSalle. I back off as we approach the Gold Coast.

She turns south and snakes her way to a stop in front of the valet booth outside a popular steakhouse. By popular, I mean tourists go, but frequenting the joint means you're either pushing sixty and making so much money that quality yet gimmicky dishes at inflated prices are worth the see-and-be-seen, or you're pushing legal age and using your cleavage as leverage for a free, three-bill dinner. I bet the number of hot young women who actually buy martinis is around zero.

Robyn keeps my estimate low when she smooches hello with a gray-haired gentleman and he holds the door.

I back Walter's car around the corner and leave it in a loading zone. Parking is impossible in this neighborhood, and double-parking ill-advised, but I feel so gray from the brain down I'll take my chances on a ticket over collapsing on the sidewalk. I don't have to exaggerate the limp as I make my way inside.

I do have to exaggerate my smile once I'm in front of the hostess, who looks barely old enough to work there but puts on a fully developed bitch face as she looks down on me from the podium.

"Do you have a reservation?" she asks, like I'll say no and go away.

"I'm meeting someone," I say. "Last name Weiss."

"For how many people?"

"Two."

While she clicks around her screen looking for what's not there, I peek around the podium to get a look at the reservations.

"There's no reservation under that name."

But there is one, VIP-starred, for a *Dr. Larry Adkins.* I know that name. How do I know that name?

She angles the screen away from me. "I'm sorry. Are you sure you're in the right place?"

"Oh, I'm sure. Any chance he's already here?" I use the question to get a look in the dining room, where I see Robyn seated at a window table with her date.

"I'd have the name on my list."

Just then, a younger guy in a dressed-up button-down comes around the curtain from the bar that borders the dining room, a pager in one hand, his date's elbow in the other, like he steered her in from Schaumburg. "It's about time," he says.

The hostess takes the pager. "I'm sorry. Even customers with reservations have to wait tonight."

"For an hour?"

"Thank you for your patience."

I wonder how come Robyn didn't do any waiting.

"Follow me," the hostess says to him.

They head for the dining room and I follow like it's a party of three. I split off for the bar and pick a spot in between occupied stools where backs are turned so I can get a good, long, unnoticed look at Robyn and her date.

Dr. Larry Adkins, I think, and I'm looking at his slender face—deep-set eyes, deeper lines—but I can't place him. I didn't see him at Sacred Heart, or St. Elizabeth, or in the newspaper's photo spread.

As he looks over the wine list, the waiter summons the sommelier. Adkins makes a selection and then the two servers take turns agreeing about it. When they leave the table, the cheeky looks they exchange suggest they just sold Adkins an expensive bottle, or they just shared a view of Robyn's cleavage, or—

"Excuse me, ma'am?"

I feel shoulders part so I turn around—apparently, I'm ma'am, and the bow-tied bartender has found me—the only woman without a drink.

I take off the beanie so he'll see my forehead. As I'm doing it I think I'll get some sympathy, but he does a real good job pretending I'm as fine as anybody.

"What are you drinking?" is what he wants to know. Not even *if* I am.

"I'm okay," I say, because I didn't bring Walter's bag inside and even if I had, I forgot my wallet at the hospital. "I'm just waiting on someone."

"The same someone who's about to share oysters with the spiky blonde?"

Now I'm getting some sympathy.

"He's very familiar," I say.

The bartender stirs whatever's in his shaker, tips some out into a shot glass, and passes it to me. "That's not cool," he says. "Consider this your parting shot."

So it wasn't sympathy. It was this guy thinking I'm the problem.

I decline the shot, salute him, and make my exit before he blows my thin cover.

Back in the car, I drive around the block and park where I can see the restaurant's entrance. I don't really want to wait for Robyn and the doctor, but I don't have a better plan.

I dump Walter's bag on the passenger seat in search of the burner. I might as well call Weiss, see if he turned up anything I can use when Robyn does finally leave. Also, I remember the mints.

Among Walter's things, I see the Tylenol two-pack.

And then I remember Dr. Larry Adkins.

I get the phone and get online. I search "Irish pub" and "Forest Park." I find six Irish places on the main street, and then the one with a leprechaun on the bar sign, and then I ditch the surveillance idea and head toward Doc Ryan's—yes, the bar in front of Calvin's—most likely before Robyn and her medico-beau have decided on surf or turf.

I shoot out on the Ike and I'm exiting at Harlem when Weiss calls. I roll up the windows and try to sound sleepy. "Hello?"

"How you feeling?"

"Like somebody wants me dead."

"Well, Gina, I'm not sure Heltman's the one. I just cased his office and I think about the only thing that could get him into trouble is the set of pictures he's got tucked in his desk of a young brunette on his boat posing with her boob job."

"What about St. Claire?"

"No bikini shots."

"You know what I mean."

"I made a copy of her file. I'm looking at it now. And obviously, I'm no attorney, but everything seems aboveboard."

"I want to see it," I say and then I regret saying it because I don't want to sound like I'm inviting him to swing by the hospital. "Better yet, will you read me the details? Give me something to Google?"

"Okay, well, you were right: Heltman drew up the trust. His invoice is here. Then there's the trust itself, and paperwork from the funds—one from Champion mortgage and one, a life insurance policy that's worth over three-fifty—"

"What I want to know is who gets the money."

"Says here the beneficiary is Johnny."

"Just Johnny?"

"He's the only one listed."

"And Christina, is she the trustee?"

"No. The trustee is a company called Legacy Investment and Management, LLC."

"I thought a trustee had to be a person."

"It's probably assigned to someone within the company. Somewhere in here Legacy is described as a third-party servicer. That means—well, let me read it to you . . . I think it's here . . . here: 'neither principal nor income of any trust nor any beneficiary's interest therein, while undistributed in fact, shall be subject to alienation, assignment, encumbrance,' etcetera, blah blah blah— never mind, that's the spendthrift clause—let's see. Payment to beneficiary. Here: 'the trustee'—that's Legacy—'may make any payments of income or principal directed to be made to any beneficiary under any provision of this Agreement, including any distribution on termination'—shit. That's not it, either. But basically, what this says, wherever it says it, is that Legacy will be paid a portion of the principal in exchange for distributing the funds to Johnny. People usually hire companies like this when the beneficiary doesn't know how to handle money. For tax purposes, protection from creditors, all that. Sometimes protection from the beneficiary's spending habits. That way, they can avoid family disputes—"

"How come you know so much about this?"

"I had a friend who . . . died. He'd wanted to leave everything to his wife, but there were some legal issues. Because some of the money was stolen. Different sad story. Anyway: this isn't so bad. This will probably set Johnny up for life."

"I can't believe Christina was completely boxed out."

"Well, I'm sure there's still a will. And she'll get dibs on whatever's outside the trust via probate. The house, all the stuff. Maybe St. Claire figured it'd even out."

"How much money did you say Johnny gets?"

"About a half-million dollars. Minus the service fees—I don't know what the going rate is for a hired trustee. Could be pretty significant."

"That still doesn't seem fair."

"You think Johnny's ever had it fair? And he's what, in his fifties? That means he's still got twenty more years of medical expenses, minimum. This way, St. Claire knows he's got someone looking out for him. And she knows he isn't spending it all on soda pop."

"You seem sure about this."

"The only thing I'm sure of is that Heltman runs a tight ship. If there's a scam here, it's not on paper. I'm going to have to go talk to him direct. See about that boat ride."

"I'm sure he'll be impressed by all your absurd nautical references."

"Don't you think?"

"No. But I do admire your ability to amuse yourself at a time like this."

"Someone has to."

"Call me after Heltman throws you overboard." I'm smiling when I hang up.

Calvin's place looks just like I remember it—what I remember of it, anyway: a white-sided two-flat that's seen more renters than repairmen. The lights in his front windows flick blue and white, the television going. It's nearly eleven, so I'm hoping he's in there, alone, and sticking to his mental guns about not needing any kind of security.

I leave my actual gun under the driver's seat and use the rear-view to see what Calvin's going to see. It ain't pretty. But this visit isn't going to start a romance anyway, so I smile at myself and go.

When Calvin opens the door he is pleasantly surprised and then not surprised and then not at all pleasant. "What," he whispers, "you just show up to re-up?"

"No," I say, "I am here to give you one chance to tell me what the fuck is going on at Sacred Heart."

"Or what?"

"I'll have you arrested for selling illegal prescriptions."

"You're going to do me like that? After the other night?"

I get a foot in the door, let that be my answer.

"Shh," he says, "Sabrina's asleep."

"Then tell me quietly."

He steps back, letting me in, conceding.

We pass the front room where we'd been all over each other three nights ago and I see a little girl curled up on the couch. The apartment is hot, and she's naked except for pink underpants, her sweet face undisturbed despite the harsh soundtrack from the grown-up show playing on TV. When she stirs, I imagine her sugarplum dreams are fevered, typical on nights at Daddy's.

Calvin leads me into the bedroom and pulls a sheet across a curtain rod over the doorway for privacy. I hadn't noticed it before. I'm sure that's not the only thing.

He lights the lamp next to the bed and sits down, same side he slept on. Then he looks up at me and says, "I'll tell you what I know, but please, you of all people: you've got to understand that everything I do is for my baby girl."

"I can promise you. I understand."

"I swear: I'm not in on what they do there. I just put my head down and do my job and that's how I keep my job."

I cross my arms. "What about all the prescription samples in your garbage can? What part of the job are those?"

"I sell scrips. You didn't seem to have a problem with it the other night."

"Where do you get them?"

"One of the docs."

"Are you talking about Dr. Larry Adkins? Because he's a known associate of the caregiver who's stealing money from Kay St. Claire—"

"That's him. He pharms, but I don't know anything about him otherwise. Everybody's real careful since the lawsuit."

"What lawsuit?"

"Last year. A group of patients sued for wrongful procedures. Tracheotomies, if you can believe that—"

"I saw a patient there with a trache tube. How does someone wind up with *that* when they don't need it?"

"Because Medicaid cuts a big check for that procedure."

"How many were in the lawsuit?"

"Only three—three who came forward anyway. The hospital wound up settling and the couple doctors who were named got fired. Things have been pretty straight on the topside since then. I mean, they'll still snow you and slip in an unneeded test or two—they stick by that policy—I told you, they call it 'diagnostic certainty.' And maybe there's a kickback—I mean a consulting fee—here and there. And I swear, some days they're *looking* to do traches, even just to prove themselves. But for anybody who's curious, Sacred Heart is clean. And clean broke, which is proof they're clean, isn't it? Plus they had those layoffs, and the state's intervention. I mean, they're actually being given money by the government to stay up and running."

"So what's on the underside?"

"More like the outside. Outside, all a doctor needs is one friend in Big Pharma. But that's not as profitable as it used to be, back when the docs would get paid to push drugs. Some of them even got straight-up sponsorships. Now a doc is more likely to take a meeting with a drug rep and come away with a free week in Bali or a five-star meal or a round of golf. It's the same result for Pharma: the docs still write scrips aplenty. But they aren't seeing cash anymore."

I think of Robyn and Dr. Adkins who are, at this moment, probably sharing a slice of comped black forest cake. "The money is safe, though," I say, "already spent."

"Yes. And there's some of that inside the Heart, too. All they need is one prime patient—someone who isn't going to get better. Then it's diagnostic tests, trial-and-error drugs, aftercare. I can't prove they keep people sick but, damn, I don't see many get cured—"

"By aftercare," I say, "do you mean home care?"

"You seeing that safe money now?"

Ding. Ding. Ding.

"It starts inside," Calvin says, "and it's safe, because the money doesn't go through the hospital."

"Does it go through Complete Care, LLC?"

"That's the one." Calvin looks up at me. "But hey, I don't know what happens once somebody's discharged. I only know they'll probably be back."

"Do you know which doctors are involved?"

He shrugs. "Any. All. You got an M.D. after your name? You're either smart enough not to get caught up in it, or else you think you're so smart that you won't get caught doing it."

I sit down next to him. "These people, they threatened my little girl."

"I'm sorry." Calvin puts his arm around me and I don't expect it at all but it doesn't seem wrong. In front of us, on the dresser, Sabrina smiles from the photographs I saw Saturday morning, the smiles he probably depends on most of the week.

"What would you do?" I ask. "If it was Sabrina?"

He takes his arm away, makes a fist. "I'd fucking kill them."

28

It's midnight when I get in the car and make my way back to the city. About two minutes into the trip, I realize I've still got Robyn's license plate on mental repeat, so I text it to Walter on the security app to see if he can ping her address.

I tell myself not to freak out when he doesn't respond right away; he did say he'd be getting coffee with Monica.

Then I freak out over every other possible reason for his silence, most of them based on Walter being discovered by hospital staff—corrupted or not.

Too late now.

When I get back to Kay's, it's been nearly three hours since I followed Robyn from here, but there are no signs she's returned. The front of the place is pitch-dark and I'm kind of surprised Kay would be here alone without so much as a night-light. What if she's thirsty? How can she read the signs that tell her where to get a drink?

Maybe she's so medicated she can't get up. Or maybe, who knows? Maybe Robyn tied her to the bed.

It doesn't matter. I'm going in.

I chew a bunch of mints—their strength much more straightforward than advertised—and then I open up Walter's glove box to see if he's got anything of use to someone who's about to break into a home. I find cords, chargers, plugs, and batteries. One city map and a hundred old parking receipts. And a Halloween-grade stash of Dum Dums. I take two.

I put my gun in the front pocket of Walter's bag and stuff everything that's left on the passenger seat back into the main compartment. Then I get out of the car, shoulder the bag, and jam the burner into my back pocket.

I chew the root beer lollipop off its stick and start on the other one. I can't tell what flavor it is. I go through the church lot to the alley again and look both ways before I tip one of the garbage cans, a step stool to get over St. Claire's fence.

Once inside the yard, I peek in the garage—no Benz. I creep along the fence to avoid the motion light and take the gangway to the front of the house.

I climb the front steps, and then I use the lollipop sticks to pick the lock.

Except I can't. In part because it's an old tumbler lock, maybe some rust inside, and also because the sticks are made of paper and they fray right away. And then there's that other part where I can't feel my fingers. I'm pretty sure I have a better chance of breaking in using my bad leg as a battering ram.

I sit against the siding below the bay windows and give myself a minute. My back is killing me. I'm losing strength. I should go back to the hospital. Get some sleep. Have Walter or Weiss help me in the morning. I'm fucking tired, and there's a part of me—I'd like to think the rational part—that wants to curl up and close my eyes. Just for tonight.

If I knew Isabel was safe, I would.

And all I need is confirmation: I need to know if it was Dr. Adkins who sent Kay home from Sacred Heart with Risperdal and all those other meds, too. If he's the one who prescribed her ruin.

I get up and try the lock again, a dumb idea to begin with. Dum Dum. Heh.

I can't. I quit. I lean back, paraspinal muscles aching, my reluctant wings. The drug-coated, sugar-spiked feeling I'd been riding is wearing off, and so is the confidence that came with it.

I close my eyes. I feel the breeze, and hear it move through the trees. I marvel at the quiet, the middle of this wild city. I take a slow, deep breath.

And then I wonder if I'm about to die, because I suddenly smell my house—old wood and dry powder and wet diapers—and if olfactory hallucinations can be a precursor to a stroke, here I go.

I get up on my feet and smile and raise my arms and say, "The sky is blue in Chicago," just to see if I can pass the FAST stroke test.

That's when I also see that Kay's bay window is cracked open, and the smell is her house, not mine.

That's right: old people, new people. Same life stink.

And, yes, that's right: it's pretty simple to get into an open window.

Inside, I take Walter's girlfriend's shoes off and leave them by the easy chair with the backpack. I tuck my gun and cross the room, the no-slip of my socks like suction on the hardwood, the tick-tock of the cuckoo clock timing my steps.

Kay's bedroom door is open and inside, there's a faint intermittent glow from a blinking Lifeline base station charging on the vanity. It gives off enough light to show me there is no one in the adjacent bed.

I make for the kitchen, the pills. That's when I notice two thin streams of light under the bathroom door at the end of the hall.

I train my gun and edge in as I get close to the door. I stop short. I focus on the shadows for movement. I wait and I wait and I know somebody's in there. But nobody moves.

"Kay St. Claire," I say, official, police.

No answer.

"Kay St. Claire," I say again, moving around the door to get on my dominant side.

And then I feel something soak through my no-slip socks.

I step back. I say, "God damn it," because the something is urine, seeping out from under the door, pooling where the floor is warped.

I reach across and try the handle. It turns. I push the door with my forearm. It's stuck. Something is blocking it.

I step forward and push harder and I feel like I could bleed out, the weight on my leg, but I get the door to give enough to see Kay's lower half, prone and contorted, one knee wedged beneath her, underpants pulled taut from her good ankle to the broken one, and shit everywhere in between.

I say, "God damn it," once more, because this can't be good for her, or for me.

I tuck my gun and turn and push, all my weight against the door. I angle in and pull her nightgown down from where it's bunched around her and I find her wrist and check for a pulse.

Her face is turned away and I don't need to see it to know she's gone but I step over her body anyway, and I look.

Blood-tinged fluid has run from her mouth. It must be vomit; she can't have been dead long enough for the body's natural death-purge. Maybe she choked. Or maybe she was on the toilet and started to cough, and then vomited, and then passed out and fell. Or maybe she passed out and fell and then vomited and then choked—

I feel like I'm going to pass out. Vomit. Choke.

I step out and use Walter's girlfriend's shirt to wipe the door handle and then I feel like a fool: Do I think I'm getting out of here undetected? If this gets considered a crime scene, I've been all over it.

I feel like my body could separate: my head, so light, could float away; my leg could fill with all my blood and coagulate and slow the rest of me to a stop.

Then I realize I can feel the urine through my socks. I can feel my feet. I can feel my fucking feet! I can't give up now.

I squish down the hall to her bedroom. I close the door and flip on the light. In here, the drawers are labeled, too—makes it easy to find the SOCKS. Apparently, Kay preferred thin knee-highs, the old-lady kind that are more like tights, not at all cushioned. I take off the no-slips and bag them in a pair of the thin ones, put on a pair and pull another over my left hand like a glove, which I use to wipe down the bureau handles.

In my periphery, the Lifeline base still blinks green. Green seems good; I assume it would make a noise or display a more ominous color if someone had been alerted.

I probably shouldn't assume. I probably should get the fuck out of here.

I'm about to cover my tracks, a pair of huge old-lady underwear from that drawer as my rag, when I see another drawer at the vanity labeled MONEY. It may as well be blinking green, too.

Inside, files are alphabetized: *Bridgeview, Champion, Complete Care, Legacy, Liberty Mutual, Sacred Heart*—a catalog of her financial players. I pull the one for Legacy. I find the trust.

It's just as Weiss described: Johnny is the beneficiary, Legacy Investment and Management is the trustee. What Weiss didn't mention was the fact that Legacy's address is in Wyoming. Which wouldn't be worth mentioning if he didn't know that Complete Care's address is in Wyoming. And also because we are nowhere near Wyoming.

And, if I put those companies side by side? The money circle that starts with Sacred Heart is complete.

I can't take the file; doing so would never provide evidence of anything except that *I'm* a thief. I do, however, want to provide Kay with the opportunity no one else would in her last days, and that was to make her own decisions.

I find a pen in the top drawer and make a few addendums to the trust. Then I tuck the file back in the drawer, wipe down the vanity, and backtrack.

At the door I hit the lights and wait a second so my eyes can adjust to the dark. What I don't adjust to is the fact that there's now light coming from the other side of the door.

I pull my gun. I open the door real slow, using it as a shield. When no one comes in I climb over the bed and make like I'm in a bunker. When no one comes in again I low-crawl, on elbows, to get a look, boot-level. There's nobody in the doorway.

And no sound, either.

I get up and go to the door. I clear it and then, gun trained, I step into the hall.

Robyn is outside the bathroom. She clearly doesn't register I'm there. She looks suspended, standing there, silk shawl caught at her elbows, one side hanging in the urine.

She looks out of breath. She looks ashamed.

I probably don't look so innocent.

Makes us a pair.

"Robyn," I say, "you're a little late."

She doesn't look at me. "I came as quickly as I could."

"In time to write yourself one last check?"

"I should call someone." I can barely hear her.

I see the phone in her hand and so on approach I make sure she sees the gun in mine. I point it at her face.

"Someone who will cover this up, is that what you mean? You killed her, didn't you?"

"I don't know what happened." When she does look at me, her eyes are vacant. She starts to shake.

I don't give a shit. I take her by the back of the neck. I say, "I'm guessing it was an overdose." And then I push the door open and make her look. "What's your guess?"

"Oh my god." Her knees buckle.

"Was it Dr. Adkins who supplied the juice? Or did you mix up her meds, so you can say she took the wrong dose again?"

She pushes back against me, trying to get out. She's not that strong but I'm pretty weak, so it's an even fight. She says, "She'd been complaining about stomach pain—"

"I don't know why you're acting so surprised." I hold her, I keep her there. "You basically admitted you'd be glad she was gone—"

"Her grandson is sick. A stomach virus. Her immune system was compromised—"

"You aren't going to blame a child for this—"

"She said she was feeling better when she went to bed—"

"This is not better. This is dead."

"I didn't do it," she says, pushing back with all her strength this time, and I can't hold her. We fall back and wind up on the floor, in the urine. We struggle to get away from each other but once we're apart, we don't get up. We just sit there, me with my gun, which I'm not going to fire; her with her phone, which she's not going to dial.

I want to cry my leg hurts so bad, like my heart is down there, throbbing, ready to explode.

Robyn cries instead, and they're real tears.

Still. I say, "Don't."

"I tried to make her life better."

"You were here for the money."

"I was paid to take care of her." She isn't argumentative. "I cared for her."

"You kept her sick."

"I tried to keep her comfortable. She was not going to get better. The disease was destroying her." Snot runs from her nose. She doesn't wipe it.

"She would have lived a lot longer without you in the picture."

"Who else would fight to get her to eat, or change clothes, or take her pills? Who else would try to protect her?"

"Oh, right, from big bad Johnny."

"She was a fighter. When she had to be subdued, I was told to report her son."

"So the black eye, the broken ankle—you did those things?"

"No. I never did anything to hurt her. Injury was not part of the plan."

I'd fall over if I hadn't already. Did she just admit to a plan? "I'm sorry, what plan is that?"

She looks down at the floor. "The care plan."

I make sure she sees my gun. "Keep talking."

"My job was to care for her until her death."

"Did that include writing yourself checks?"

She looks at me, cold. "We had a private arrangement."

"I guess you'll get away with that, too, since nobody believed her when she actually could cry for help."

Robyn looks back at the door. "I did not want her to die."

"Tell that to the jury," I say, "along with your story about the deadly three-year-old."

"Am I under arrest?"

"For what?"

She double takes; she thought I had her. She finally wipes her nose. "You don't know anything."

"Well, I think I know a little something. I think I know the care plan, as you call it, started with Kay's first trip to Sacred Heart. She was admitted, and once the doctors—maybe your boyfriend Larry?—realized she suffered from Alzheimer's, they privately diagnosed her with an inability to keep track of her big bank account. They gave her tests to confirm that profitable condition, and medications to keep her opinion irrelevant, and then they sent her home with *you*. It was your job to 'make her comfortable,' as you say, while they worked out how to strip her finances—and that's where Legacy came in. And Mr. Heltman. Of course, there were a few bumps along the way—Kay's family's protests, and her cries for help, but if things got too messy, well, you'd just send her back to Sacred Heart and the rest of us on the hunt for Johnny. The hospital would admit her and the doctors would order more tests and give her more drugs and they'd send her home again with more supposed reason to keep you around. Her family was pushed away, and there was nothing she could do—nothing she would do—because you convinced her you were her ally. And you were: I mean, like you said—who else would get her to eat? Get her to change clothes? Help her with her medication, and help her sign her name—to checks, and what else? Mortgage documents, medical forms, trust addendums . . . does any of that sound right to you?"

She doesn't answer, but I know some of it must sound exactly right because she's got both hands over her mouth. While I was talking, I watched shock turn to grief. Her cheeks flushed, and then drained, and now she's so pale I wonder if I should tell her to take a breath. But. Fuck it.

"I guess none of that matters anymore. The papers are signed and Kay is dead. Christina is totally fucked and you know she doesn't have the financial means to fight. Johnny's looking at maybe ten cents on the dollar after Legacy's trustee fees; sadly, he'll be none the wiser, because he *can't* be—"

At this, Robyn straightens up. "I am sorry for Kay, but I don't give a good god damn about her children. I wasn't lying when I said Johnny would kill her. He nearly killed me, when I tried to help him—"

"Help him? You just told me you sold him out."

"He came here, after you chased him from the hospital. He wanted to stay here, but I told him he had to leave for Mrs. Kay's safety. He refused. He held me here. And then he saw you bring Kay home."

"You knew I was police."

"*He* knew you were. You actually . . . saved me. You gave me a story."

"Stay away and mama is okay."

"Yes."

"What about Christina? What story did you tell her?"

"I didn't tell her anything. She'd have just as soon let her mother die. She wasn't kind to Kay a day in her life. She didn't care that Kay was sick; she never called to talk, or came by to help; the only thing she wanted was the money. When Kay believed you were CeCe, I almost didn't correct her, because I thought she could have at least one moment when she believed her daughter had been decent to her. I rescued Kay from those two. Johnny couldn't love her, and Christina simply didn't—"

"You think that earns you the money?"

"You're right about a lot of things, but you're wrong about me. When I started working for Complete Care, they took on clients who were dying. I was hired to care for people who had no one else—no family, no support. I had nothing to do with the financial arrangements, but after death I was paid—compensated, really—for my work. And I did earn that money."

"You may have earned it, but you can't be paid with stolen money."

"The money wasn't stolen. It was meaningfully invested."

"That's bullshit."

"The clients didn't think so. They found peace through the process."

"But *you* know it's bullshit."

"I thought it was fair. Why should the money be left to next of kin, a windfall for sharing a bloodline, when they shared nothing else in life?"

"Oh, I don't know, because it's the fucking *law*?"

"I find it hard to believe you would make the same argument with regard to child custody." The look on her face? Now she thinks *she's* got me.

Fuck. That.

I get up and use my gun to force her down, facedown. She tries to curl up in defense, but I press my knee into her back—my bad leg, which comes down like an anvil. Her legs splay and rip her dress since there wasn't much dress to begin with. I press down, into her spine, and she goes flat, more reflex than surrender.

I say, "If you want to find peace through *this* process, tell me where my little girl is."

"I don't know. I was only trying to make you understand that the law isn't always fair—"

"So you think you don't have to be fair, either. You manipulate clients *and* their families. You break them down and turn them against each other. You make sick people believe they have nobody else, and *you* make them crazy. That's what you did to Kay—"

"No. I took care of her—"

"Oh, please. You're nothing but a shill for Complete Care's long con."

"I loved her—" She sobs, so I put the gun to her cheek and I push until I feel bone. It shuts her up real quick.

"You tell me where to find Isabel, or I'm going to make sure *you* understand that I don't give a fuck about the law, or about your love, either."

She starts to shake. "Last I was told, your brother had her. He was supposed to start work today, but—"

"Working where?"

"A client owns a trucking company—"

"You set George up with a job?"

"You just said they manipulate clients *and* their families. When you started investigating Kay, they decided they needed leverage. Your brother was approached—"

"You conned my brother?"

"Not me. Lidia. She was assigned to you."

I lay off her and sit back, the realizations coming in, cracking: George defensive about finding a job. Lidia there. George scrambling to prove his innocence about Isabel's fall. Lidia there. And before that, when I was in the hospital. The tests they did with my supposedly signed consent. The snowing. And the home care, a seeming condition of my release. "I was conned, too."

She rolls to her side, touches her face. "They do it to everyone."

"I don't understand why you keep saying *they*. You're just as guilty—"

"They do it to everyone," she says again.

Just then, the burner buzzes in my back pocket. I reach for it and find a text from Walter:

Lawrence Adkins 1539 W Jackson Blvd

The Benz. It's registered to Dr. Adkins, who lives on a quiet tree-lined stretch of million-dollar homes in the way-west Loop.

I turn off the display. I'll play along. "What did they do to you?"

"When I was given the job, I didn't have my license. They said it was no problem, and that I could complete the certification—it was only eight hours of coursework—during my first assignment. They said I was a natural, and it seemed so—I had six clients back-to-back before I got around to starting the class."

She starts to push herself up, looks to me to see if I'll let her. I do.

"Right around that time," she says, "they started taking patients who were facing mental decline. My first one was a stroke victim. He was completely insane. I was with him less than a month when he attacked me. He tried to rape me. I was totally shook—I wanted to quit—quit the client, and the job also—but they just moved me. Here, in fact. I was a week in when I was informed the stroke victim's son was having me investigated for abusive sexual contact. I went from being a top employee to being an unlicensed caregiver accused of trying to engage my client in sex acts for money. Complete Care protected me: they got me a fake license, fake resume. They also made it clear that the truth was theirs to use against me if I ever left."

"About the license?"

"Yes. And, about my previous profession." She tries to pull her dress down, but it rips some more. "Before I started there, I was a call girl. I *did* engage clients in sex acts for money. They knew it. They used it. They got me."

I wake the burner's screen and look at Adkins's address. "If they've got you," I say, "why do you have Dr. Adkins's Benz?"

She looks down at her dress, and at herself, exposed. "I guess I'm still a call girl."

I get up. I put my gun away. I look down at her. I say, "The way it looks now, you're going to have a wrongful death charge to add to your resume. Unless you're willing to *really* screw your employer, and pin Adkins for this."

"I can't." She looks at the bathroom door. She says, "Lawrence isn't the one who brought Kay in." She looks at me. "It was Kuro Kitasaki."

29

Kitasaki's place is not a million-dollar home on a quiet tree-lined street. It's one in a bank of cheap apartments on Lake Street under the L tracks. Makes me think the address is just a shell, like Complete Care.

I've pulled into a parallel spot a half-block away when Weiss calls the burner. It's going on two A.M. and I'm not sure I should answer.

I can't help it.

"You're up," he says.

"I'm up."

"I thought you'd be interested to know what happened at Heltman's."

"I'm interested."

"I went in prepared to bullshit about a new lead in Sanchez's case—I figured I had to have something pressing for the Captain like that, to show up so late. But when I got there, Sanchez answered. In tears. Said Heltman was out on his boat. So I decided to make a case against him instead. I used the brunette and her boob job."

"Good call."

"It was the perfect call," Weiss says. "She told me everything. Said Heltman gave her the black eye. They fought about the brunette—literally—"

"Do you hear that?" I ask when I hear the not-so-far-off rumble of an L train—a train that will be passing directly overhead in about thirty seconds.

"Hear what?"

I think about telling him the nurse just came in, but I'm afraid she won't be a good enough reason to hang up so I say, "This phone keeps beeping. I think the battery is dying—"

"Well, let me tell you real quick, then: Heltman made up the lie. About Marble. He fed her the assault story—they both knew him from the hot-dog place—a real romantic place to pick up a date, right?—May I take your order? I'd like a sausage, would *you* like a sausage—"

"Heltman conned her," I say, hoping this story moves a little faster than the train.

"She agreed to lie because she didn't want to lose him. Or the nice view, maybe. I don't know if you call that a con—"

"So we've got Heltman on assault?" I ask, my finger over the END button. The track buzzes above me. I've got about ten seconds.

"More than that. Sanchez also pointed to Heltman for the St. Claire assault."

"Heltman was Johnny Marble?"

"Makes the term *trust* seem revocable, doesn't it?"

"Will Sanchez testify?"

"I don't know yet—"

"Oh," I say without the *kay* and I hang up. And then I switch off the phone so my battery story seems true; if he calls back, he'll think he's calling a dead line.

The L grinds along the track overhead and I toss the phone on the seat. Now I'm really going in without backup.

Still, I'm optimistic: if Weiss gets to Sanchez, we can get to Heltman—and that gets me one gimp step closer to tearing the whole thing down.

But, first.

I get my gun and then I shuffle toward Kitasaki's. Shuffle, yes, because I'm wearing Walter's girlfriend's shoes without socks, and also it hurts like a motherfucker to actually lift my leg. I look ridiculous, I'm sure, but I'm not exactly looking to make a good impression on the not-good-at-all doctor.

The gates that surround the patches of grass in front of the apartments are thigh-high, installed for aesthetics instead of actual use, which is funny since this part of Lake Street isn't all that nice and the lack of security may as well be a sign that says FREE STUFF! for anybody who comes poking around from the industrial corridor that lies north of here, or from the ghetto to the west.

When I get to Kitasaki's cute little gate I act like I know where I'm going and that I expect it to be open. It isn't, which is what I actually expected, so I hike my good leg over the fence and stifle the cry that accompanies drawing the other leg over.

Kitasaki's unit is ground floor with a green fiberglass front door. The two front windows beside the door are covered by miniblinds, so I can't tell if he's home or awake or what. I just hope he's alone.

I knock.

I knock again.

I start to get worried he isn't home, or he knows it's me and he's forming his own last-ditch plan about how this is going to go down.

But then he opens the door, and I'm there pointing my gun at his face.

He's surprised to see us both.

He starts to turn and slam the door but I angle in and stop it with my shoulder. It fucking hurts but it works, because he doesn't get the door shut before he runs off.

When I get in, my back to the door, I see him duck into another room on the right.

Fuck! That's what I was afraid of.

But I'm not afraid. I'm here for Isabel.

I do a visual sweep of the room: it's clean, clutterless. An empty couch sits before a flat screen, the centerpiece. Just inside the door, on the floor: two pairs of shoes. A backpack. And on the coat hook to my right, there's a black jacket and a black cadet hat. It's the delivery driver's cap Mari thought she saw. It has to be.

"Doctor," I say. "Come out or don't, I'll still shoot you dead." I train the gun on the door he disappeared through, surroundings falling out of focus as I approach.

Kitasaki doesn't say anything.

I don't give a shit. I feel nothing—no pain, no fear. I say, "You should know this gun is my service revolver. Which actually makes it the perfect weapon because as far as anyone knows, Johnny Marble has it. Makes sense that it'd be Johnny Marble who'd come in here and shoot you dead. Revenge for what you did to his mother."

Kitasaki still doesn't say anything.

I don't give a shit. I stop just outside the door and get my back against the wall; from here I can see a corner of white tile. It must be the bathroom.

I say, "I guess we put a lot on poor old Johnny Marble. Maybe we could let him off the hook for this. I mean, he could have sold the gun. Or ditched it somewhere. Or maybe he gave it to his sister, and *she* shot you dead."

Kitasaki says, "You're crazy."

"Well, doc, crazy works out pretty well for me. Crazy is what got me an extra night in the hospital, isn't it? In fact, I'm there right now. So it wasn't me who shot you."

"They'll know it was you."

"They—you mean the police? My police? That works out okay for me, too. Because I actually don't give a shit and they won't, either. You're the bad guy. Fuck you."

"I'm talking about Legacy—" he starts to say but I wasn't kidding, I don't give a shit, so I cut around the corner and enter the room, my gun at close guard. I find him standing there holding a toilet plunger like a bat, so I plow into him—shoulder leading—and I take him down.

Then I'm on top of him, and I've got my gun in his eye. He drops the plunger.

"Is this the part where you con me? Where you tell me this is bigger than you and you *had* to come after me, too?"

He looks at me, his one eye. "You kill me and that's as far as it goes. They've done this over and over—dozens of patients—but you'll never get them. They set it up that way—they set me up."

I move the gun to his chest. "What do they have on you?"

"A surgery that went bad," he says, raising his rashed hands in surrender.

"How bad?"

"It was for spinal stenosis. A fusion. I don't know how but the patient woke up paralyzed. He said he would sue. They protected me, but that meant I could no longer move, either."

"Why didn't you just quit?"

"And then what? My student loans were—are—in the hundreds of thousands. And my father, he would never understand. It's honorable, this work. I want to be a doctor—I'm a good doctor. I do the best I can. I think you, of all people, should understand that."

"You don't know me."

"I know more than you think."

I slide back at the same time I move the gun from his heart to his balls. "You know where to find my brother and his child."

Kitasaki squirms, though it's purely defensive because I'm shoving the gun hard into his testicles, and it's natural for him to want to go fetal. Or shit on the floor.

I say, "My brother. His child."

"I don't know," he manages, heaving. "George disappeared . . . after the drug test. Which was the . . . point—to get him out of pocket. Away from you."

I don't believe it. "What about his daughter? What about Isabel?"

"That was Lidia's idea."

"*You* threatened her life. When I was in the MRI tube."

"It was all supposed to be a threat to you."

"Tell me where she is."

"I don't know—I swear to God—" I'm losing him, so I let off a little. I give him a sec.

Then I jam the gun in his balls and I say, "I want you to know that I can also be anywhere, anytime. And if you're lying to me about my family, I will be back, and I will shoot you dead. If you're lying about Legacy, I will be back, and I will shoot you dead. And believe me when I say I am not afraid. I will kill you and I will go down for it before you ever practice medicine again. You're done, doctor. You can pack up your knives, snap off your gloves, and say goodbye to your stake in this game."

"I can't—" he starts.

Then I cock the gun. "It's your *duty* to do no harm," I say. "Not mine."

Kitasaki vomits.

I get off of him; he curls up, tries to breathe.

Before I go, I say, "Be well."

At the front door, I take the cadet hat. I pull it on, a survival souvenir.

30

I call Walter on my way back to the hospital.

"Use the main entrance on Claremont," he says. "I'll be by the security desk. Ask to use the public bathroom. I'll take it from there."

"Okay, but I'm kind of a mess."

"Are we talking hot mess, or burn-victim mess?"

"Closer to burn victim."

"Strike that plan, then. You can't get admitted twice. Go past the main entrance instead. You'll see a set of doors between there and the annex. I'll be there to let you in. But this way might be a little more . . . intimate than you'd like."

"I'll snuggle with you if it gets me back to my room. See you in ten."

When I get there Walter cracks the door and I slip inside what turns out to be a vestibule outside a bank of administrative offices, none of which appears occupied at this time of night, despite the hospital's perpetual daytime lighting.

The lighting must really show off my best features, because when Walter gets a look at me he looks like *he* could use medical attention.

I hand him his car keys and tell him, "I'm okay." I still feel no fear. Pain is making its way back, and big-time, but, "I'm good, actually."

"I've heard extreme blood loss can lead to feelings of euphoria."

"Maybe that's what it is. But I'm onto them, Walter. The lot of them."

"There's a lot of them?"

"A lot of people getting conned, yes."

"So, everything is going according to no plan."

"Looks that way."

"Well, I'm happy to look the other way."

"What's the plan here?" I ask about the vestibule.

"That's actually the plan," he says, holding up a hospital gown. "For me to look the other way."

"This what you meant by intimate?"

"Should I have said awkward?"

"It's okay, Walter. I *want* you to get me into bed."

He grins, and holds the gown up like a curtain.

I lose the shoes, peel off the jeans. When I take off the shirt, I can smell death.

"I hope your girlfriend doesn't want this stuff back."

"Bloodstains are easy. Meat tenderizer and toothpaste."

"Death is impossible. It doesn't wash out."

"Death," he repeats, but not like he wants to know the details.

I take the gown from him and slip it over my arms. "Snap me?"

When he's through he balls up his girlfriend's clothes, pitches them in a trashcan, and says, "Now that you think I'm a respectful gentleman . . ." Then he picks me up, a fireman's carry, and takes me through the second set of doors.

"I can walk."

"Let me be the hero for a minute, would you?"

He turns down what I think is an empty hallway; when I lift my head, I only get a broader view of the rubber sheet flooring—and a sharp reminder that the muscles along my spine are torn to shreds.

At the end of the hall he pushes open a door and we enter a stairwell.

"Three flights," he says. "Hang on."

I hang, mostly.

From this vantage point, my head closer to where my feet should be, I'm reminded of the last time I was in a hospital stairway.

Funny that I'd say things are looking up.

"Here we are," Walter says at the top of the landing. "Your chariot awaits."

He helps me down. It's a wheelchair, sitting there.

I climb in, no hesitation.

As he pushes me back to my room, I realize the reason I was so mad at Tom wasn't because of the wheelchair comment. It was because I was afraid I was weak.

I guess I got that out of my system.

When we get to my room Walter swivels the chair so we can see each other and asks, "Ready for bed?"

"God yes," I say. "I owe you, Walter."

"You? No. You've made my life considerably more interesting. I mean, there's no algorithm to the shit you're going through. It's intense."

"Hopefully it's nearly over."

"Well, I'm here to help, okay? Not here, actually—I don't think I can come back here. That nurse might devour me."

"Must have been some cup of coffee."

"What can I say? Turns out I'm very charming when I make it up as I go."

"Think you can charm her into coming here, before you go? I could use some health care."

He nods. "Then I'll try making *my* escape."

"Good luck."

When he starts off down the hall, I roll into the room. I find a towel and get into bed. I pull up my gown and undo the tape. Underneath, my leg doesn't look as bad as it feels, which is good news—yes, it fucking hurts, but hey, I can feel it.

I pull the sheets up when I hear Monica.

"How are you feeling?"

"Like I survived battle."

She comes to the bed, turns my arm over. "Where's the IV?"

Fuck: I forgot. After all this, I'm going to get busted for not taking medication. Same way this whole thing started.

"Let me guess," Monica says, "they used the port for contrast and just taped it up when they were done."

"I guess so?"

She undoes the tape, sets to work replacing the line. "I bet you're wondering how you're supposed to get well in a hospital," she says, "all the things we put you through."

I lie back and close my eyes. "The question has come to mind."

31

In the morning, Andy is at my bedside. He doesn't look happy about it.

"Two days in a row," I say. "Did you lose a bet?"

"I've got bad news. Kay St. Claire passed away last night."

It isn't hard for me to look unhappy. "What happened?"

"Complications stemming from Norovirus, is what they think."

"Her grandson was there." Robyn was right.

"No," Andy says, clueless. "She was alone. Died on the toilet. Caregiver found her."

"That's terrible."

"Terrible, but no surprise. She got sick, and she was already sick. Immunocompromised, they call it."

I know that's what they call it; that's what they called it with Donna.

I also know that's exactly what he's thinking.

He looks down at his hands. "I thought you'd want to know, since it was, you know, personal for you."

I raise the bed. "Andy."

"Well," he says, surprised. As close as we've been over the years, I may have called him by name twice. Once was on the day Donna died, but he's right back there anyway, so it's not like I can make it worse.

I reach for his hand.

"You were right," I say, "everything's going to be okay. But I'm going to need your help to make it that way. I need you to keep the case going."

"Come on, Gina. St. Claire is gone. Isn't it time to move on?"

"Says the man who can't update his bathroom for fear his dead wife will frown upon the new color scheme."

He pulls away; I can't blame him. "Fuck you."

Guess I was wrong—I'd call this worse.

"I'm sorry. But someone's got to say it to you. When Donna died, you quit. You couldn't be her hero, so you quit."

"I did not."

"You admit as much! You blame that heroin junkie. You push it off on the way you say the job has changed. You say 'why risk?' and you spout off warnings like justifications. You are a cop-out—and not just at work."

I hate that I'm still talking, because Andy is just sitting there and he looks very, very sad.

Still. "You're closer to your dog than you are to your girlfriend and you'd rather take care of abandoned birds than friends. You don't want to reach out because you're afraid to hold on."

I reach out again, for his hand. He ignores me.

"I get it," I say. "I wish some things stayed the same. Mostly the things that never will. I wish Isabel would stay little—and stay mine, too. I wish I had the guts to share my life with someone over the age of two. I also wish you were still the man you were when Donna was alive."

He softens at that. Blinks away the possibility of a tear.

"I know that can't happen, Kanellis. But I do know that you can still be a hero. And I'm asking you—begging you—to try."

"For you," he says, kind of like a question, and also an answer.

I reach out once more. He takes my hand, and I hold on.

"I know you kept telling me to quit the case because you wanted to protect me, and discouraging me was about as close as you could get. But I'm not the one who needs protection. St. Claire—she needed it. And I know, now, that there are dozens like her who need it, too—"

"Sick people die, Gina. You can't protect them from it."

I squeeze his hand, and then I let go. "I'm not talking about dying. I'm talking about living. Sick people, old people, crazy people—each of them living every day—however many they've got left—without getting fleeced by the doctors, the caregivers, the professionals they pay to care."

"I think that's pretty common. They call it health insurance."

"Actually, it's called Complete Care, LLC."

"The home-care company?"

"Yes. It's a fraud. Part of a financial racket that starts with a trip to Sacred Heart and ends with a dirt nap in a cardboard box because every last dime's been 'meaningfully invested' in a moneymaking scam."

"You know this?"

I sit up. "I can prove it. I've got names, and I know the game, and I've got enough evidence lined up to take these sons of bitches out at the knees. But I need you to be the lead. I need you to take what I've got and build a case, and then I need you to bring it to Iverson. I want the two of you to come crashing fucking down on them."

"Why don't you want to do it?"

I sit back. "I may have bent a few rules during my investigation."

He sits back, too, and shakes his head at me.

"I take your reaction as a positive indication that you're at least thinking about it."

"I'm thinking it'll be tough to find a sick person who wants to fight this fight."

"Well, I know where you can find a crazy one." I smile.

"You?"

"I didn't tell you. About Isabel—the reason George took her. She got hurt when I left to arrest Marble—I was tracking his Ventra card—but that's a different story. The point is, I left Isabel with George and *my* Complete Care nurse. When I got back, Isabel had fallen down the front steps. She had a hematoma, lost a tooth. George and the nurse, they blamed me. Said I left the door open. I, of course, blamed George. But now I know it was the nurse who did it. She was told to stop me from investigating St. Claire, and she used Isabel to do it."

"How do you know that?"

"That's about four other stories. I've got a bunch, Kanellis. Including one for the man who put me in here."

"You know who it was?"

"I know a lot of things. And I want to tell them all. To you. And, you know, to a judge, if I have to."

Andy looks at me. Sees I'm serious. "You *want* to testify?"

"I'm a victim of this scam, too. But I survived. And I want to give other Sacred Heart patients a reason to believe the world isn't all that shitty, before they go."

"That makes you the hero." He looks down at his hands again. I wonder if he held his wife as she died.

"Please, Kanellis," I say. "Donna was lucky. She had you. But she shouldn't get to be the only one. These people need you."

He's quiet for a minute. Then he gets up and I don't know what he's going to do but I definitely don't expect it when he hugs me.

And when he does, he says, "I think I'll paint it blue."

I'm picking at a dish of plasticky macaroni and cheese—I couldn't very well send Andy off with a handful of leads and a request for lunch, too—when Weiss shows up. With flowers.

"Hey," I say, mostly to the flowers, a pink bouquet of roses so huge I really should be dying.

"Delivery," he says, "for Gina Simonetti?"

I play along. "That's me."

"Great. Where would you like them?"

"How about there in the window. If they'll fit? They're so . . . there are so many. I can't imagine who sent them."

"There's a card," he says, detaching a small envelope from the vase.

I open it up. At the top it says *GET WELL* in pink, curly letters. Beneath, in tiny, perfectly formed black block letters, there is a message:

HELTMAN SETTLED A CLASS-ACTION SUIT FOR
SACRED HEART. HE WAS HIRED BY JAMES NOVAK,
THE HOSPITAL'S CEO. GUESS WHAT? THEY'RE OLD
COLLEGE PALS. AFTER THE SETTLEMENT, THE
BOYS WENT INTO BUSINESS TOGETHER, NOVAK A
SILENT PARTNER IN A COMPANY CALLED LEGACY
INVESTMENTS AND MANAGEMENT, LLC. YOU MAY
HAVE HEARD OF IT?

FEEL BETTER,
ROSALIND SANCHEZ

I put the card back in its envelope. "What a thoughtful girl."

Weiss hands me a clipboard. "I just need your signature here." It's a delivery confirmation from Linda's Flowers and Balloons.

I sign on the X. I can barely keep a straight face. "Your level of detail is impressive. Except that I should have mentioned that I hate flowers."

Weiss looks over his shoulder like I'm blowing his cover. "Are you serious?"

"I am. Flowers die. Kind of a depressing gift for a patient, if you think about it."

He looks like he may as well stand beside himself.

I give it up and smile. "I'm just giving you shit," I say. "It's a good disguise. But you don't need it anymore. I'm off the case."

"You were never *on* the case. You were never supposed to be, anyway." As soon as he says it, he gets it: "There is a case, though. You've got enough to pass it up the chain."

"I'm passing it over, really. To Kanellis."

"What about you—your safety?"

"St. Claire died last night. That means I've no longer got a case. Anyway, I figured out who attacked me, and I'm certain he won't try anything like that again."

"I can't believe it," Weiss says. "I just spent an hour trying to get FTD-chic." He sits on the daybed and inadvertently knocks into the roses, saving them just before they topple and meet an even earlier end. I've never seen him fumble.

"I appreciate the attempt," I say.

"That get-well note took me some time, too, playing mental tennis with Sanchez like some wannabe shrink."

I turn the card around in my hands. "It's fucking great. We—I mean, Kanellis—can definitely use it."

Weiss studies me sideways. "Are you faking me out?"

"No. I'm off the case."

He tilts his head the other way.

"Look at me," I say about my forehead.

"You don't look so bad."

For a moment, I wonder if those flowers are part of more than a disguise.

"Well," I say, "I'm still off the case."

"What are you going to do?"

"What everybody's been telling me to do. Take some time. You know. Stop and, ah, smell the roses."

Weiss stands up and carefully extracts a single rose from the stuffed-full vase. Then he turns, hands it to me, and says, "Let me be the first to say I think you're full of shit. It's cute, though."

I take the flower and I'm speechless as I watch him walk out of the room.

Of course I blame the medication for the rush of blood to my head.

Later, after Dr. Tacker comes by with plans to discharge me in the morning, I close my eyes, and for the first time in weeks I fall asleep without feeling like I'm actually falling from something. Of course, I do take the meds they give me, and I do stay in bed.

When I wake up in the morning, I find I slept through a bunch of calls. From Metzler. From Walter. From Maricarmen. And from an unknown number. I listen to the messages. I listen to this one twice:

"Gina, it's George. I just wanted to call and say . . . uh . . . I appreciate your apology. Saying it that way probably makes it pretty obvious that Rick put me up to this, but I guess he's right. We both need to come clean. Or, I don't know, we have to be better. But you don't have to be better than me. Anyway. Isabel, she misses you. I, uh, it isn't easy. But we're making our way. I guess that's all. Oh, and I'm sorry. Goodbye."

I call the number back and nobody answers but then a voice mail clicks on to say, "You've reached the Catholic Charities of the Archdiocese of Chicago. Our office is currently closed. . . ."

There is a God.

I hang up as yet another nurse appears with my six A.M. pills. She says, "This is your last dose before you're headed home. They'll probably get you out of here after breakfast. Is there anything I can do for you in the meantime?"

"No," I say. "I don't need anything else at all."

32

The first thing I do when I get home from the hospital is take a shower. The second thing I do is look for George.

I call the Catholic Charities number again, this time during business hours.

"I'm trying to locate my brother, George Simonetti."

"Is he an employee?" asks the woman on the other end.

"No. I think he's maybe staying there? With his child?"

"He's not staying here. This is the main intake facility. Spell the last name?"

I spell it. I wait.

"He's in the system," she says. "Try this number."

I try it.

"Foourrr-ty-five hundred," answers a man, like an auctioneer.

"I'm looking for my brother, George Simonetti."

"Hang on."

I do.

"He's out on the trucks. You want to leave a message?"

"No—I'm sorry—I was given this number by the Catholic Charities, I'm not sure what it is you do."

"We're the produce warehouse for the W-I-C."

I don't know what that means, entirely, but what I really want to know is, "Where, exactly, are you located?"

He tells me.

I go.

It's just before five when I park around the corner from a flat, unmarked building that runs the length of three city blocks. In the front, on the other side of a chain-link fence, a parking lot full of workers' cars runs up to a series of red garage doors that must be where the trucks load. All of the trucks are empty. All the doors are closed.

I walk along the fence until I come to a driveway; there, a sign reads CHICAGO CATHOLIC CHARITIES WIC WAREHOUSE.

Just like the man said.

I find the entrance.

Inside, there's a counter that fronts a half wall constructed to serve as a welcome desk. Or, judging by the surly foreman behind the counter, a bitching box.

He puts down the yellow slip of paper he'd been concerned with and raises his eyebrows up over his glasses. "What can I do for you?"

"I'm looking for my brother. George Simonetti."

"Just started, yeah?"

"I think so."

He rifles through a stack of other yellow slips and finds the one, apparently, that gives him the information he needs. He picks up a nearby headset and, without putting it on says, into its microphone, "One-five-nine. Front desk."

I'm reminded of the Wizard of Oz, the way his voice echoes

over the warehouse speakers. And then, of course, I'm reminded of Isabel. I'd hoped we'd watch the movie together someday; I know she'd love the big adventure anchored by the desire to return home. And also the Technicolor.

"You can wait there," the foreman says, about the folding chairs along the wall.

I sit.

While I wait, I hear the once-familiar end-of-shift geniality rising in the voices of the workmen over the wall. I'd forgotten that feeling—the satisfaction of a good day on the Job. I'd become too focused on trying to get going, too worried about running late, too driven by the toddler tears caused by my absence.

Then again, before Isabel *and* after, I was rarely satisfied. I should probably admit that might have something to do with me.

When George appears, he looks tired—good-tired. He rolls up the sleeves of his stained uniform and when he sees me, he tugs at his hair.

"Gina? How did you find me?"

I'm a cop, dummy, is what I think—but I also think of his last message, my constant need to be better than him. So I stand up and I feel like I'm sticking my neck out when I say, "I wanted to see you."

He offers a hand instead of a hug and sits me down again. He smells like motor oil and tomato juice. "How are you feeling?"

"Shitty," I say, because I'm not fine, and I'm done using that go-to.

"Rick said you got hurt pretty bad."

"I'd have been fine if I followed hospital protocol and stayed in bed for a week."

"Are you kidding? You couldn't stay put anywhere for a day, even. Your head would explode."

"Speaking of. You think we could take a walk?"

George gets up and holds the door.

"I start physical therapy on Friday," I say, once outside. "And medication."

He squints in the sun. "That's good to hear."

"What about you? I don't mean that—I mean, I'm not talking about medication—I mean, well—this job?" I'm trying to be casual. I'm terrible at it.

"It's good," he says. "I load food onto a truck, I take the truck out to a site and unload it again."

We turn the corner and walk up the street, away from the Chicago Avenue rush.

He says, "The food is for low-income women and children. So far, it feels good and bad, you know? To be there to help, but to be around people who need a hell of a lot more than a bag of apples."

"Sounds all too familiar."

"Yeah, yeah. Of course it does."

"I'm talking about *my* job, Georgie. I'm supposed to help solve problems most people don't want solved."

"You're talking about me, too. It's okay. I get your frustration." He looks down at his feet, scuffs along the sidewalk in front of us as we walk. "I'm sorry about that other job. I know you tried to get me set up, and I was grateful. But I just can't take any more handouts from you."

I play dumb. I want details. "What job?"

"The guy you got Lidia to introduce me to. The dump-truck guy. The thing is? I'd been clean for a while. I wasn't even worried about the drug test. I couldn't fucking believe it when they called me in about the results. I knew you were going to be mad. And I was mad. Because even before the stupid test—before the job—I didn't want your help. So I bailed."

I can't believe it: of all people, George was the one who didn't get conned. Still, "I didn't have anything to do with that job, George."

"Lidia said you'd say that." He stops. Stops me. Turns to me. "You know what happened from there. I was a fucking idiot, and I'm sorry. I let Soleil talk me into what I thought I deserved. It wasn't until we were all three together, Soleil and Bell and me, that I realized Soleil didn't want Bell, and she only wanted me because she didn't want you to have me and her ex, too. Anyway. I'm sorry for the way I handled it, you know, taking Bell when I was high. I was pissed at you, though, you know? For lying to me about something real serious. Something that could affect all of us."

"It was just a rough case."

"I'm talking about your disease, Gina."

"You do know the chances of me not walking tomorrow because of MS are equal to that of me not walking tomorrow because I get struck by lightning. Standing here. Right here. Right now." I start walking again.

He follows.

We walk for a while.

"I miss her," I say.

"I know you do. But I think you also miss having someone to worry about. So that you don't have to worry about yourself."

"I worry about both of you. I always will."

"We're doing good, Gina. I got her into this kids' development center? It's basically daycare, but through the archdiocese—and it's only been a few days, I know, but she really seems to like it." George checks his watch. Dad's watch. "Speaking of, I'd better get back. I've got to get the bus."

We turn and approach Chicago Avenue again. It's a beautiful afternoon; a perfect day for the playground.

"Where are you living, George?"

"Place called Madonna House. My priest gave me the referral; it's actually really nice. It's for families who, you know, need a home—"

"You have a home."

"It's only temporary, until I get some money saved—"

"You could stay at my place and save money. It's home to Isabel, right? And it'd be a favor to me, really . . ."

He doesn't answer. He won't say yes and he can't say no.

"I'm sorry," I say. "I just want to help you."

I follow him to the corner as the sixty-six eastbound approaches, a hot-road mirage glaring in its wake.

George takes a Ventra card from his wallet. He says, "Gina. You can't work out your own life if I dump mine on you. Like I said, we've both got to come clean."

As the bus slows to its stop, George starts across the street, then thinks again and comes back to give me a hug. I hold on to him.

He says, "We're going to be okay. Really. All of us."

He flags the bus and makes a run for it. Just before he boards, he stops to shout, "You're thanking God, G! I know it!"

I resist giving him the finger and instead wave goodbye; it's about time he had one up on me.

It's also about time I take his advice.

33

After several days of rain, the storms quit just before I reach Eden Cemetery in Schiller Park. The clouds sit low, now, blanketing the air traffic noise in and out of O'Hare. I drive past a sign that says I'm entering a place *Where Memories Rest with Dignity.*

I hope there'll be some dignity for Kay St. Claire.

I park behind a string of cars, get out, and button my pants. They were the most appropriate pair I could manage for the occasion— black and hemmed short enough to wear with flats. Yes, I've finally given in: fucking flats.

And good thing: had I worn heels I'd be poking holes in the wet grass all the way to the gravesite.

When I get there it seems I'm late. I got wind of the proceedings from Andy, who thought I might want to attend. He told me ten o'clock, but it's barely past ten, and save for two of Christina's boys who are chasing each other across the grounds, the group is already huddled around the plot.

I edge around a big old elm tree and stand beneath its branches next to three older women, two of them sharing a large black umbrella and the one closest to me protecting her beauty-shop blow-dry under a plastic scarf. In front of us, twenty or so other mourners stand in a circle, heads bowed, while a man, presumably whoever's running the religious portion of the show, reads from the Bible.

"I can't hear him, can you?" one of the women under the umbrella whispers.

"It's Corinthians," I tell them—though I'm totally guessing—I wouldn't know an old testament from a new one.

"*Oh, death, where is your sting?*" she says. "I'd say it's stinging Christina right about now, wouldn't you?"

"What do you mean?" asks the woman next to her. She doesn't whisper, and catches the ire-eye of the gentleman in front of her.

"I heard," the other whispers, "all Kay's bank accounts were frozen in the investigation."

Partially true, I want to tell them, but—

"I heard the money's gone," says the woman in the plastic headdress. "Christina had to pay for all this."

"All what?" says the woman on the right; she either doesn't see the gentleman's backward glance or doesn't give a shit. "No proper church service, one measly spray of flowers, a pine box—"

Now the man isn't the only one looking.

"Shhh," someone says.

I take a step to the left, but I keep listening.

"Kay never did know how to handle money," the woman in the middle whispers. "Chess always kept it out of her reach."

"She's right," the woman in the plastic headdress agrees, "and it wasn't just the money. Chess controlled a lot of things. He brainwashed Christina. And Kay and me? We hardly spoke when Chess was alive. He made her cut ties from so many of her friends, and her interests—You remember what a great singer she was?"

"I think," whispers the woman in the middle, "he was afraid she'd go back to Johnny Senior."

"Did anybody call Johnny Senior?" the woman on the end asks basically everybody.

At that, nearly all the folks in front of us bristle.

"Shhh!" more than one someone says.

I step left again.

The women go quiet; the preacher drones on.

After another minute the woman next to me whispers, "Kay did her best."

From the other side of the gravesite, a man begins to wail, and I can picture the scene: Johnny Junior rocking, crying, ears covered, fears again realized.

I step left again, and I turn to go.

Halfway to my car, partially hidden by the trunk of another big old elm tree, I see Robyn Leone. I go over.

"Paying your respects?" I ask. *Paying* is probably a touchy word, but I'm not here to sympathize with her.

"I am."

"It's a pretty no-frills deal. Rumor is, Christina had to foot the bill. I'm guessing that was a tough blow, seeing as how the money she was due may as well have been set on fire."

"I am cooperating with the authorities."

"I know you are, and I appreciate that. And I'm sure Detective Kanellis appreciates it." I round the other side of the tree trunk and look back on the funeral. "I understand Kanellis put together quite a case—Sergeant Iverson says there's enough to interest the Feds. It'll be big. Probably take down Complete Care, and Legacy, and Wyoming Corporate Services. Did you know they've got hundreds of shell LLCs tucked away in just one little residential house out there in Cheyenne? It's a place for fake companies to hide money and protect the people stealing the money, too. But, they bust that place open, and I bet Novak will see some time. And Dr. Adkins, and on down the line."

"And on down the line," she says, like she's already been sentenced.

"I feel bad for the family. I'm sure you know how stupid angling over money seems when it comes down to losing someone. I mean, once they get the original will sorted—did Kanellis tell you that Kay actually revoked the new trust? That she took a pen to the paperwork and voided the whole thing before she died?—anyway, they'll get some money. But I don't think you can pay down guilt. Do you?"

Robyn doesn't answer. She looks out at the gathering of friends and family one last time, and then turns to leave.

And, having inadvertently said my piece—I do the same.

34

George throws Isabel's birthday party in September—two weeks late, but his first chance since signing the lease on the apartment.

I buzz the door and climb the steps to the third floor. I'm pretty well healed, and the relapse is over, but I'm still out of breath by the time I reach the landing—my own fault; admittedly, I haven't spent these last months getting anything into shape besides my attitude.

I knock at the door though it's cracked open, Isabel presumably gated or otherwise occupied somewhere inside. I take off my shoes—still flats, thank you very much—and hang my coat on the door hook with a few others.

I straighten the bow on Isabel's present—lately, she's as interested in unwrapping things as she is in the things she's unwrapping—and linger in the hall for a moment, readying myself. Sometimes, these days, she is interested in me. Sometimes not.

"Hey, G," George says, coming around the corner from the kitchen. He's got tomato sauce on his shirt, a clue as to what we're having for the birthday dinner. He gives me a hug and then I'm sure I'm also wearing it.

"Hi, Georgie."

"How was it?"

He's talking about my first day back at the Job; I didn't spend these last months in a rush to return there, either. But, "It was good. Walter is ever patient in showing me the virtual ropes."

"I never thought you'd take a desk."

"We all have to settle down sometime, right?"

"Where you going to settle, anyway?"

"I don't know. Tom thinks the buyers are going to ask for a short escrow, so I've got to decide soon. Maricarmen says I can stay with her, but she's already got her grandson and his kids there. I don't know. I'll probably rent somewhere for a while. Maybe closer to the office."

"The office, huh?" He's not asking about the office.

"Yes, George. The office." I try not to smile while I straighten the gift's bow again. "Where's Isabel?"

"Rick and Janine have her out on the back porch. I'm grilling."

"You got a grill?"

"Just a little hibachi. But it's a nice night, you know? And I've got a back porch. And, I'm so fucking sick of eating noodles that I thought we'd celebrate her birthday, too, have some steaks."

"Sounds great."

He steers me past the kitchen and into the living room-slash-dining room. "I've just got to get the potatoes going and I'll be out."

I approach the sliding door, and my reflection—my smiling face.

Rick opens the screen and steps inside. "Regina," he says, like he hasn't seen me in a year. He opens his arms and takes me in. "Feeling good? Looking good."

"Yes," I say. "I am."

"Mama!" Isabel says, jumping up and down outside the door. She looks taller than she did last week.

"The birthday girl awaits," Rick says, stepping out of the way.

"Hi, Spaghetti!" I open the screen and she bum-rushes me, arms around my legs.

"Mama!"

"Look what I have," I say, about the gift, but she ignores it and raises her arms; she wants me to pick her up.

"Hi, Regina," Janine says, and takes the gift so I can take Isabel.

"Mama Gina," Isabel says, her little brain starting to connect the appropriate dots. She puts her arms around my neck and rests her head on my chest. I hug her some more, knowing it's only a matter of time before I'll just be Gina.

"Isabel's got a little something for you, too," Janine says, and takes my gift inside, giving us time.

"What do you have for me?" I ask her, "Kisses?" I start to give her a hundred of them.

Isabel shrieks with joy. "Nest!"

"Oh, Spaghet, there's no nest here."

"Nest," she insists, and points at the other side of the deck. There, crammed between railings, sits a dove's nest built from two lawn chairs and some pillows I gave to George along with Tom's old couch.

"You're right," I tell her, and I get choked up, because she's too little to have come up with the idea. That makes George a hero. Finally.

I climb in. It's not as big as mine—yes, I still have it and yes, I get in to it on my own once in a while—but this one will do. This one will do just fine.

Isabel climbs in and snuggles against me and I feel her little heart beating as we look up at the night sky, the city lights our ceiling. I wonder who she will ask when she wants to know about the stars.

"See an airpane?" she asks, her words both more and less understandable to me.

The apartment building isn't on a flight path, but there just happens to be a plane up there, lights winking as it leaves O'Hare.

"There's one!" I say. "Where's it headed? California? Atlanta?"

"Home," Isabel says.

"Home," I repeat. She's starting to understand the word; I wish I could explain how much more complicated the concept becomes with age.

"Jezebel goes home . . ." I start, and then from inside, I hear Rick and my brother saying hello to Ray.

Took him a while to find a parking spot.

"Where you go home?" Isabel asks, and I realize she isn't so interested in Jezebel. The memory of our time together is fading; soon I'll be the one described in stories.

"My home is not far from here," I say. "But you know, no matter where I am . . ." I put my face against hers and smell her hair and whisper in her ear, "I'm with you."

"I like purple," she says, trying to replicate the sentiment.

I think of Kay St. Claire, who liked blue. Whose mental capacity was reduced to a toddler's. Whose family broke apart, whose life was ruined. Who was probably lucky to forget.

But who still remembered love.

I hope it's love that remains, when life peels away. I hope that it's love.

I look over and I see Ray standing there, inside the sliding door. Looking at us. Smiling.

I smile back. I say to Isabel, "I like purple, too."